TO WIN A WICKED LORD

SOFIE DARLING

OLIVERHEBERBOOKS

This title was previously published.

0 9 8 7 6 5 4 3 2 1

 Created with Vellum

1

———

LONDON, 20 JUNE 1826

Lord Percival Bretagne stepped into a room alive with the vibrancy of a young night and grasped in an instant that he would be known.

This gaming hell was exclusive, a playground for the ultra-wealthy. Here, the son of a duke—even a younger one, like himself—would be hard-pressed to remain anonymous. Society circles ran small and tight in London. He should have stuck to the dicier hells. But in those places the stakes were too low, and he needed to strike his enemy where it hurt: deep in his banking account.

From finely woven Persian carpets to walls bedecked with gold-shot silk brocade up to the high ceiling lit with crystal candelabra, bright opulence winked optimistic light and beckoned Percy to follow its uncertain promise. Impassive male servants circulated through the crowd, champagne and spirits balanced on trays polished to high shine. Strumpets, clad in diaphanous fabrics that left naught to the imagination, tripped through the room on light feet, flirtatious laughter trailing in their wake, laughter that didn't quite reach their eyes.

Percy's gaze narrowed on Number 9's patrons,

seated at various gaming tables that offered any man with the right amount of wealth or family connections the opportunity to test his luck. To a one, they wore the specific look of the well-heeled and moneyed, an air of Eton and Harrow hanging about them, half an eye on the gaming, the other half on the female flesh.

Percy descended three quick steps and entered the fray. A few faintly curious eyes glanced up, only to return to their game the next moment.

"Champagne, milord?" inquired a plaintive cockney whine at his side. He was about to decline the offer when he found a pair of familiar eyes the hue of a turquoise stone staring up at him. "Follow me," she said, low, her voice again her own. She led him to an alcove hidden behind a large curtain that she must have already scouted. Hortense was ever prepared.

"Where did you procure *that*?" Percy indicated her costume of gossamer silk that left little to the imagination. He didn't like her wearing such revealing clothing.

"From the doorman. He knew Nick."

Hortense didn't need to elaborate further. During their years in France and the Continent, Lord Nicholas Asquith, their handler and friend, had been expert at securing favors here and there, names and places passed along on the breeze, this or that useful bit of intelligence in exchange for a scrap of coin or safe passage across the Channel. This French doorman must have been quite useful to Nick for him to be in London.

Serious blue eyes snapped at Percy. Hortense had the sort of gaze that could see past skin and muscle, down to the marrow of bone. "Are you certain about tonight, Bretagne? This Savior of St. Giles business has taken on a life of its own."

Percy snorted. "*The Savior of St. Giles?* What foolery. The gossip rags have outdone themselves with that one."

"You can't go around bankrupting gaming hells and not expect anyone to notice."

"There is only one man whose notice I care to attract."

"Well, you've single-handedly shut down two of his hells, so you can feel confident on that score. But the papers have noticed, too. You're becoming a bloody folk hero."

Percy waved off Hortense's concerns. "Is that all?"

She persisted. "You're open to exposure. It can be used against you."

Her jaw set in determination. Percy had come to know that look from years of working by her side on the Continent, cracking codes and gathering information for Crown and Country. She was like a terrier with a bone once she got something between her teeth, and she wasn't letting this go, which, of course, was why he'd involved her in the first place. In truth, she was the most perfect agent he'd ever known.

A few months ago, before he'd caught wind of his enemy's illicit activities, Percy might have paid her worries more attention. But, tonight, he would allow her qualms no air to breathe, not when he had the scents of peril and possibility in his nose. Since stepping foot on English soil, he'd been most alive on these nights when he actively worked toward the destruction of Lord Bertrand Montfort.

Somehow, somewhere along the way, Percy had lost the talent for the aristocratic London life he'd once been so exceptionally good at living. A life he'd shed a dozen years ago on a scarred Spanish mountain pass that had been blown to bits by Napoleon's army.

It was Montfort who had, at last, found Percy, his memory ripped to shreds.

And Montfort who had ensured it stayed that way,

as that version of Percy had perfectly suited Montfort's purposes.

With Percy returned to England, Montfort's account had come due.

"We shall have everything we need on Montfort tonight, if all goes to plan," Percy said. "Then you can return to spying on rich men's cheating wives."

"Don't forget rich ladies' cheating younger lovers." Hortense shrugged one shoulder. "It pays well. Still, it has felt good these last few months, getting back into the thick of an operation."

Percy loosened the constrictive silk cravat at his neck before adjusting one, then the other, of the cuff studs at his wrists. It had been some time since he'd dressed in evening blacks. "Do I look the part?"

"Of debauched, entitled lord determined to fritter his life away on a single roll of the dice?" Hortense's mouth twitched. "Aye, I'd say you're hitting that nail on the head."

Percy chucked her beneath the chin. "Cheeky."

The seriousness returned to Hortense's eyes. "I'll be waiting in a hackney cab behind the building until dawn."

Percy lifted an eyebrow. "I doubt—"

"I'll be there." Hortense deposited the serving tray onto the nearest table with a loud clank and disappeared into the crowd, this role complete.

Hortense's concerns vanished with her as Percy stepped from the alcove and considered the room. He was champing at the bit to dismantle this place by using its own vices against it.

"Why if it isn't Lord Percival Bretagne," came a public school drawl.

Percy stopped dead in his tracks and met the gaze of one booze-soaked Lord James Asquith, Earl of Pembroke, standing at a hazard table, one hand braced on green baize, the other idly curled around a crystal tumbler of brandy. The man was heir to the infamous Marquess of Clare and older brother to Nick. *Blast.* London could be small as a country village.

"Pembroke," Percy acknowledged. "Hazard's your game?"

Pembroke gave an indifferent shrug of the shoulder. "The game hardly makes a difference. In search of a little oblivion, like everyone else." He craned his head and fixed cold gray eyes on Percy. The same eyes as Nick's, but not the same at all. Pembroke's were dissolute, jaded, and utterly, utterly bored. "Seeking the same?"

Percy nodded. It was clear Pembroke hadn't a care, but the man was Nick's brother, and Percy couldn't just leave it. He angled his body so only Pembroke could hear his next words. "You need to clear out of here."

A sardonic eyebrow lifted. "Concern about my moral well-being? From *you*, of all people?"

"Hardly," Percy said, ignoring that last bit. His licentious reputation didn't bother him as much as Society would like. "This night will have consequences. You won't wish to become embroiled."

Pembroke shot Percy a glance, surprisingly penetrating and sober. Then he returned his attention to the table action for a few more tosses of the dice that lost him an additional fifty quid before draining his tumbler in two great swallows. He gathered up his remaining counters and, without another word to Percy, shambled his way through the room, nimbly avoiding every strumpet who threw herself into his path. Percy slid into Pembroke's vacated spot and set his ivory counters onto green baize. The night was set to begin.

Of a sudden, the hairs on the back of Percy's neck prickled, and he felt it, someone's gaze upon him. He followed the feeling around until he located the source on the far side of the room: a woman, veiled and dressed in all black. Number 9's madam, presumably.

Unease began a slow crawl through him. Most of the madams he'd encountered in his short tenure as the Savior of St. Giles possessed a certain bearing, a brazen flash of the eye, a daring pout of the lips, and a view toward the winning angle. None of them hid behind layers of black lace.

Yet he detected a litheness to her figure suggesting freshness and, confoundingly, *youth*. In his experience, madams were neither fresh nor young.

The prickling sensation spread. It could be interpreted as a physical response to intrigue, but, in truth, it felt not unlike the initial stir of desire. He instantly tamped it down and pursued the other interpretation. What was her game?

"Dingo?"

Dingo. His nickname from long past Eton days. *Blast.*

He half pivoted to find Chauncey Talbot-Spiffington, otherwise known as Runt, waiting with an expectant look on his face. When Percy glanced back, he found the woman gone.

A beat of silence went on a tick too long. Runt's bushy eyebrows drew together and released. The man's feet shuffled with unease. "Just arrived in Town, have you?"

"It's been a few months."

"And you didn't call on me?" Runt asked, hurt running through the question.

Percy barely contained a snort. He hadn't the time or inclination to soothe a grown man's wounded feelings.

"Your scar..." Runt began and blushed.

Percy felt himself go tight about the mouth.

Runt, ever the sensitive one of the old Etonian pack,

must have noticed, for he continued in an obsequious rush, "It's quite fashionable and...and da-dashing!"

Percy wouldn't touch his fingertips to the scar, its silvery length running along the ridge of his right cheekbone, put there by the single slash of a French saber, his last memory before a well-aimed—or poorly, depending on one's point of view—cannon shot blacked out his world.

"Of course, we've all heard tattle about your exploits, Dingo." Runt's expression turned commiserative. "Wouldn't have expected such behavior from Olivia, though."

Percy clenched his jaw. *Olivia.* The woman who had once been his wife. The wife he'd left on this side of the Channel for a dozen years, letting her—and the world—think him dead. Once she'd been alerted to his continued existence, she'd petitioned Parliament— with the assistance of his own father, the Duke of Arundel—to set the marriage aside and succeeded, rendering the daughter he'd never met, Lucy, a bastard.

Lucy.

The pang of guilt hit Percy with its familiar swift, sharp jab to the gut, as it always did when he thought of his daughter.

No, Percy wouldn't be discussing Olivia or any of his family with Runt. He would only have to defend them—for they were absolutely in the right. Runt was determined to revisit the past. So, let them, and be done with it. "Where is Chippers?" Percy asked. This was the nickname for Lord Phineas Featherstone.

"Checking the betting books," Runt supplied.

Percy plowed on with his line of questioning. "And Bongo?" *Lord Jarvis Smythe-Vane.*

"Oh, he didn't come out tonight. His gout, you know."

Percy hadn't, but no surprise there. "And Tuppy?" *Lord Harold Ponsonby.*

"Tupping a wench upstairs, what else?"

Right. "And Bumpy?" *Lord Basil Arbuthnot.*

Runt jutted his chin toward a point behind them. "Passed out in a chair."

Percy glanced back and spotted the unconscious man, a thread of drool hanging from his open mouth.

And that was the old Eton tribe accounted for.

To survive Eton, a boy needed a tribe, and they'd formed one based on their shared status as younger sons, spares to the heirs. With no expectations placed upon them, they'd been free to be useless to a one, and they'd run with it, Percy included. In fact, as the younger son of a powerful duke, he'd been their leader. And they were exactly who he would have become had he not sped off to the Continent and war on a wave of misguided foolhardiness. Reckless vainglory had its uses.

But Runt and his cohort weren't the worst part of his past. Not even close.

Across the hazard table, the croupier caught his eye. "Your toss, monsieur," the man called out in a light French accent.

Percy found a pair of dice in his hand and gave himself a mental shake. Tonight, he had an opportunity to send the worst part of his past to the devil. It was time to get on with it. "Stay if you like, Runt, but I have work to do."

"Work?" Runt asked, as if startled by the very concept. "This is pleasure, old man."

"For some."

ONE HOUR later

Oblong green baize stretched ahead of Percy, a pair of dice rattling in his hand. Gathered round this hazard table stood a moneyed, bleary-eyed crowd breathless in anticipation of his next cast.

"Dingo," whined Runt's voice beside him, "haven't you had enough?"

Percy smirked down at the man. When had Lord Percival Bretagne ever had enough of anything? Never once in his life had he been able to resist raising the stakes when the opportunity presented itself.

Again, he rattled the dice, this time for effect. Another thrill of anticipation shimmered through air dank with bodies long in need of a wash and a sleep. He opened his hand. "Blow on my dice for good luck."

The ever-faithful Runt heaved a resigned sigh before doing as his old leader commanded. "Aren't you happy with your winnings?"

"*Happy?*" Percy scoffed.

Happiness had become an abstract concept the day he'd engaged in his first battle on the Peninsula, acrid cannon smoke filling his lungs, rifle bullets whizzing past his ear, and the realization sunk deep into his bones that they weren't playing toy soldiers. The stakes were infinitely higher, of life and death, and Death wasn't playing around. In fact, judging by the broken, bloodied bodies strewn about the ground in twisted poses of which only contortionists and the dead were capable, it had become clear that Death was winning. Death always won. It was simply a matter of putting off the inevitable for as many seconds, minutes, hours, days, months, years as one could manage and somehow make a difference in lives in the meantime.

How was happiness possible after one had come face-to-face with this reality?

Percy didn't place much value in the concept of

happiness. It only mattered what he did, not how he felt. *Feeling* had only gotten him into trouble in the past.

But this...a wicked smile curled up one side of his mouth...

This was mindlessness—a state he could slip into only too readily.

How he'd missed it.

He let it take him into its embrace and suck him inside as he glanced down at his stacks of winnings. It did appear he might have enough to get management's attention—and, from there, Montfort's—yet...

Percy wanted more.

He pushed his winnings, every last farthing, forward, eliciting a chorus of startled gasps, raucous *yeahs!*, and whistles that split the fuggy air. The only way to have enough—to have *everything*—was to risk everything.

Percy met the croupier's gaze across the table. Even as the man appeared to blanch at Percy's stake, he nodded. The odds were no friend to the reckless aristocrat on this roll, and they both knew it.

The blood whissed through Percy as he stood on the precipice of the unknown. At this moment, his purpose wasn't solely to wreak revenge and justice upon Montfort. A wickedness flowed in his blood, one that he'd only ever been able to control when he starved it completely. Once fed, even a scrap, it took on a life of its own.

His hand began a slow, relentless shake. With every rattle, the volume of the crowd increased until it crescendoed into a loud roar. The night had been building up to this one fateful toss.

He'd neither nicked nor thrown out on his last roll. If he rolled the main, a seven, the house would win. Sevens were always the best odds.

If he rolled an eight, both the chance and the worst

odds in hazard, well, matters would take an interesting turn. He would most definitely gain Montfort's attention.

Percy flicked his hand open and let the dice fly. Across green baize they hopped, skipped, bounded, and rolled, a series of gasps following their every rotation as they bounced to a stop, their numbers staring up for the world to see.

Percy's heart galloped in his chest, and he felt as out of breath as if he'd just run a mile at full tilt. He lifted his gaze to meet that of the croupier across the table. A bead of sweat trickled down the side of the man's face, the smile on his lips turned rictus.

Percy almost felt badly for the croupier, for the man would have to answer to Montfort. Then Percy considered the lives this place had despoiled and destroyed, families ruined as men were reduced to paupers and women to prostitutes. This man was part of that life.

"I'll settle up now," Percy spoke through the charged silence.

The croupier's throat undulated with a hard swallow. He and Percy both knew that he didn't have the cash on hand to pay out. He would have to summon his superior. This was the exact series of events that Percy had hoped to set in motion when he'd walked through Number 9's front door tonight.

He was close, so close his fingers twitched with anticipation. So close was the proof he needed against Lord Bertrand Montfort, younger son of the Earl of Surrey and long-standing servant of Crown and Country. It had taken a few months of poking around to catch the whisper that Montfort had been silently investing in gaming hells and brothels around London. Once he'd held this dark, slippery bit of information, Percy understood that if he kept pursuing this path, he would eventually hold the key to Montfort's ruin. In their rarefied world of wealth, excess, and privilege, reputation was life, and Percy would see Montfort's destroyed. A little quid pro quo.

The croupier's gaze shifted and widened on a point beyond Percy's left shoulder. That was when Percy felt it: a change in the air, an electric current that rippled through the room as it passed from person to person, brightening eyes and heightening smiles. He pivoted and followed the general gaze until he found the veiled woman, her attention fixed on him.

The world stretched away, receding to a great distance. A path parted for her, she one magnet and he the other. Although he could see nothing of her features beneath the veil, her focus never wavered as she moved forward...

Toward *him*.

With only a few feet of Persian carpet separating them, she stopped, her lush figure—waist cinched tight, breasts pushed up—somehow on full display beneath all that black lace. Through dense air fogged by cigar smoke and brandy, he caught her scent. *Honeysuckle.* Another word came to mind. *Sunshine.* How was it possible a gaming hell madam smelled of summer at its sweetest?

At last, she opened her mouth to speak, only to hesitate at the last moment. No, not *hesitate*. Women like her didn't hesitate. She'd paused for effect. "Shall we play for higher stakes?"

Percy blinked. Her *voice*. It was husky, a lower register than he would have guessed. Further, it held a foreign accent. The night grew more interesting by the moment.

Montfort had sent her. Percy knew it in a flash.

What he didn't know was *why*.

Familiar anticipation charged through Percy, urging him on, toward the edge of the precipice that would drop him into the thick of whatever this night—and this woman—held for him. As a spy, he'd loved nothing better than a path that bent at sudden angles.

"Lead the way," he replied, only just containing a cynical snort. What did Montfort think sending him a strumpet would accomplish? If this was a stratagem to catch him unawares, it was for amateurs.

The crowd, which had quieted to take in the exchange, burst free and broke into rounds of leers, hoots, and rowdy whistles. The frisson of unease returned and snaked through Percy, as if an unconscious part of himself understood that within this woman lay something he shouldn't get tangled up in.

Except...when had he ever let such a feeling stop him?

When hadn't that feeling, instead, pushed him into the thick of it?

Whatever game Montfort had planned for Percy, he would play.

And he would win.

2

———————

Layered in thin black lace and thick red rouge, Isabel Galante looked her part.

Harlot.

Except, was it playing a part once one did the deed and accepted payment? Wouldn't it, in reality, make her one?

She wove across the main floor, through tight spaces packed with gaming tables, chaise longues, and sweaty bodies, expertly eluding the excited grasp of a hand or errant jab of an elbow, and questioned all the choices and bad luck that had led to this moment, with *that* man at her back.

Her instructions had included a short description— *tall, dark, aristocratic*—along with his precise location at the hazard table. And this tall, dark, aristocratic man had been standing in that very spot. She'd expected to find a thoroughly intoxicated, boorish lout bent on dice, women, and self-indulgence.

Instead, she had a wolf dogging her step, which was an altogether different proposition. In the general sense, louts were easier to tame than wolves. They didn't lie in wait to consume one whole for a late-night dinner.

Further, she hadn't expected him to be so…so *devastating*.

The way he moved suggested, utterly and completely, a body at ease with itself. In this place, the men put on a bold show of the confidence exclusive to the upper-classes, but the man at her back, unlike those others, inspired the belief that he could follow his supreme confidence with action.

A shiver of portent purled up Isabel's spine, and a snatch of the conversation that had brought her to this moment pushed forward.

"What shall I have to do?" she'd asked.

"Hand me the keys to a man's ruin."

"Does he deserve it?"

"Likely not, but it's for the good of England."

Tonight, at last, after an interminable fortnight of waiting, Isabel had received her directive. It was clear, concise, and utterly distasteful.

A voice of doubt plagued her. *And how do you expect to succeed where Eva failed?*

Because she must. Because there was a debt. And it was she who must pay it. All other options had been exhausted.

Then, once paid, she would never look back on the sordid night that had bought her family's hard-won safety.

Her step stuttered, and a firm hand—*his* hand—found the small of her back for no more than a pair of seconds, but long enough to make her body flash hot and cold and hot again. Dizzy nerves jangled through her body.

To steady herself, she called upon an image of Eva's tortured, clammy face. Isabel's jaw clenched with resolve. Her family's future lay in her hands. Nothing else mattered. Her purpose regained its footing.

She found the first step of the staircase and glanced

up to find a young—*too young*—strumpet named Tilly cascading toward her with girlish vitality, slowing long enough to whisper in Isabel's ear, "Lawks, snatched yerself a right good 'andful o' man there, didn't ye?" A twinkle in her eye, the girl continued past on a giggle and a wink.

Wolf at her back—Isabel didn't need to glance around to know he was there. He was the sort of man who made his presence felt—she hesitated at the top landing and considered the dim hallway and the door at its end. She must keep placing one step in front of the other. Now wasn't the time to lose her nerve. Down the corridor she trudged, the discordant sounds of downstairs revelry fading fast. *He* stepped with a lighter tread than she would have thought for such a sizeable man.

Sizeable? Rangy and lean, he possessed a mass larger than the sum of its parts.

At last—or *too soon?*—the bedroom door handle was in her hand, and she'd pushed it open. The door clicked shut behind her, and her fate was sealed.

She was alone with this wolf.

If he decided to devour her, no one would be coming to her rescue.

Above her head, delicate, painted angels frolicked on the high fresco. Beeswax candles burned bright and clean in their polished brass candlesticks and candelabra, unlike the tallow to which she'd become accustomed these last few years. The air smelled fresh, expensive. Lush alabaster velvets and silks covered every soft surface, inviting the brush of a palm, the press of a body...or two. What better way to convey sinful luxury than with white?

She made a direct line across dense Persian wool for the libation cart, relieved it was on the opposite side of the room. On her way, she passed gaming table, chaise longue, and bed, a huge, canopied monstrosity that she had yet to sleep upon, having chosen the chaise longue instead. In truth, she'd only looked at the bed from the corner of her eye, knowing what she would have to do there when the time came, a time which was nearly now.

Numb fingers wrapped around the neck of a crystal decanter. "Brandy, my lord?"

"None." His voice was masculine and controlled, as if he never raised it above its current volume. It was a voice that spoke of power, latent and confident.

She held the decanter suspended midair. "Something else?"

"Nothing." Annoyance ran through the word. "Shall we begin our game?"

Isabel set the decanter down on a splashy clatter. "Of course, my lord. Your pleasure is mine." She'd been told to speak those terrible words, and to smile while saying them.

Well, that last bit was too much.

The next phase of the night awaited her. Trembling fingers found the knot of her shawl and tugged it loose. It slipped off her shoulders in a soft shush. On a deep inhale, she pivoted to face him. His dark gaze narrowed and fixed on hers. There they remained, inscrutable, never once darting to catch a glimpse of her bare breasts pushed up by the short whalebone corset that Tilly had pulled so tight that Isabel could hardly draw breath. Her traitorous, bare nipples puckered and all but screamed for his attention.

Instead, he broke from her gaze and strode to the gaming table. He settled into a chair with indolent ease and crossed his legs at the knees, a pose that would be effeminate on any other man. Somehow, it only increased his sure masculinity. Patiently, his pose told her, he was waiting for her to join him.

Unexpected anger surged. She was standing here, naked nips to the breeze, and he was acting like this was a mundane occurrence that happened every night of the week. Mayhap it was, for him, but not for her. Oh, why wouldn't he put her out of her misery and just bloody well get on with what they both knew he was here for?

What a confounding world that had closed its dark and seedy doors behind her. The same world that had treated Eva like a dishrag to be used and discarded. Again, memory beckoned...

"You're very like your sister, except—"

Montfort hesitated there, not out of discretion or consideration, but to draw out the moment. To toy with her.

"—Not as high spirited, and—"

Another pause, another dramatic tick of the clock.

"—Not as prone to vice."

How Isabel's palm had itched to slap Montfort's condescending face in that moment, but, like the *not as high-spirited* sister she was, she'd kept it by her side. It wouldn't do to anger the man who held the key to her family's safety, even if he was the same one who had endangered it in the first place.

Family was everything.

Just now, she slid onto a white velvet chair opposite the too-handsome wolf and patted the deck of cards before her. She was dealer. "What is your game, my lord?"

His long fingers gave crimson baize an impatient tap. "French vingt-et-un."

"French?" Vingt-et-un was the sort of game that involved more luck than skill. And a French version? She had no idea.

He gave his head a subtle nod, the shadow of a smile a cold glint in his eyes. "French." He reached inside his coat pocket, pulled a small black enameled box from its depths, and set it on the table. "Do you have your counters?"

"Of course." Isabel pulled open a small drawer and removed the velvet-lined box containing a set of heart-shaped, mother-of-pearl counters.

The man uncrossed his legs and shifted forward to shrug off his evening coat. From there, he proceeded to remove his cuff studs and began rolling his shirt sleeves up to his elbows, one precise fold over another, before resting bare forearms on the table. They were lightly dusted with fine, dark hair and tensile and strong as tempered steel, like the rest of him, no doubt.

She used the opportunity to really take him in. Tall, dark, and aristocratic—yes—wolfish, too. But here, with nothing more than a few feet of card table between them, his stark, hard-edged beauty foregrounded itself. Impenetrable, deep brown eyes set beneath black slashes of eyebrows. A mop of loose black curls that would have made Lord Byron green with envy. Cheekbones, nose, chin, jaw chiseled from smooth marble. Silvery scar running along the edge of his sharp right cheekbone as if to illustrate its perfect line.

He was the most forbiddingly handsome man to ever walk the earth.

"You can cover yourself," he said, off-hand.

Isabel's hands froze mid-shuffle as sudden awareness ribboned through her. Somehow, she'd forgotten the fact that she sat opposite this wolf of a man with her breasts bared. "Is it *your* pleasure that I cover myself?"

"If you don't mind."

Her mouth nearly fell open. She recovered enough to say, "Your pleasure is mine," as she reached for the discarded shawl. She inhaled the scream of frustration clamoring for release. The trajectory of this night had been predictable and easy. *Dreadful*, but predictable and easy. This man wasn't playing his part.

"And you can stop with the *your pleasure is mine* nonsense."

She almost said it again to spite him. It was something the real Isabel would do. Instead, she nodded her assent. The very last person she should be tonight was herself.

"And remove the veil. It's a bit much."

Without another word, she unpinned and discarded the garment.

At his leisure, he took in her features, one by one, as if committing them to memory. Her hands clenched into fists at her sides.

"Rather young, aren't you?"

Somehow, she felt more exposed now than she had with her breasts bared. "This establishment houses younger."

The muscles of his jaw clenched and worked. She'd unsettled him, possibly angered him. *Good.* One should feel disturbed and angry in a place like this.

"Shall we get on with this?" he asked.

Isabel detected an impatience to the man that she didn't understand. He didn't seem especially interested in the card game. He'd certainly displayed no interest in her physical person. What precisely was it that he wanted to get on with?

Still, get on with it, she would. Except when she looked down at the cards in her hands, she didn't know what to do with them.

"You've never played French vingt-et-un, have you?"

"Um, no."

He held out a hand. "I shall deal."

"Whatever you wish," she said as a variation of *your pleasure is mine.*

But it was true. Whatever he wished would happen

in this room tonight. After all, wasn't its outcome certain? Did it matter if she won or lost? By losing, she would win. Then she would walk away from this night and never look back.

Long, masculine fingers strummed crimson baize in a lazy rhythm. "Shall we set the value of the counters at five?"

"Shillings?" What an awful lot of money to gamble on a hand of cards.

He shook his head, an amused light flickering in his dark eyes.

"*Pounds?*" she asked, aghast.

His fingers missed a beat. "Five *hundred*."

She went speechless.

"*Pounds*," he confirmed.

Then she remembered: this game wasn't real—not truly—and the value assigned to the counters didn't matter. This was all a silly prelude to what would happen at his—*for* his—pleasure.

"You know the rules of the game better than I," she said. "How can I trust you?"

The sudden coldness of his eyes shot ice through her veins. "I have any number of vices," he said, low, menacing, "but cheating at cards isn't one of them."

She didn't know this man's name or his favorite food, but, so help her, she believed him.

He claimed the deck and began expertly fuzzing. "The first round of the eight is the ordinary game."

Isabel staked one counter and experienced a startling exhilaration. Five *hundred* pounds. She wanted to give in to the urge to play to *win*, a feeling she'd never had much success in resisting. Competition had ever made her nervy.

But she wouldn't. She was here to lose. More than a card game, at that.

He dealt the first cards and asked if she would increase her bet. She shook her head. He dealt them each another card. He revealed a seven and a knave; she a two and nine.

He met her eye and held it. "Why didn't you take another card?" Before she could answer, he continued, "Are you even trying to win?"

Isabel's heart stuttered in her chest. "I, um, yes," she said, that *yes* emerging more question than declarative statement.

His eyebrows drew together, and he snorted. "In all honesty, I thought you would be more"—he paused for a well-timed beat—"*formidable.*"

Isabel's gaze fell toward the table. Wounded pride, shame, annoyance, even anger, were all emotions that rose and swirled inside her. It was the content of his words, yes, but more it was the way he spoke them, like an indulged lord viewing her, speaking to her, as if her only reason for existing on this earth was to provide him entertainment and pleasure, and she wasn't holding up her end.

Of a sudden, she wanted nothing more than to beat this man. The outcome of this night, of this war, was already determined. Even though once he'd had his fill, she would be little more than a nothing to be used and discarded, that didn't mean she couldn't win a few battles along the way.

"Deal," she replied, the single word imbued with tempered steel.

It must have shown in her eyes, too, for the side of his mouth curled up into the semblance of a smile that made her heart skip two beats. It wasn't a smile meant to convey joy or reassurance. It was the smile a wolf gave his prey the moment before he devoured it. This man was the physical manifestation of the word trouble.

He dealt two cards face up. "Imaginary tens. My two

and your nine are tens in this round. Then we play ordinary. Understand?"

"Of course," she snapped. The predacious curve of his mouth diminished not one iota.

He finished the deal and took the hand. Annoyance flared through Isabel. She increased her stake from one counter to three.

He took notice. "Why stop at three markers? Why not increase to five?"

She shrugged one shoulder and tossed two more onto her stack. Appreciation glimmered in his eyes, and her body responded with a light flip of her stomach. A part of her that she couldn't control responded to pleasing this man. Disconcerting, to say the least.

"You'll like the third round. It's played blind."

"How fortuitous that I increased my bet," she said drily. It was as if aristocrats sought out new ways to toss their money into the wind.

He dealt them each two cards face down. "Stand or take?"

She tapped the table.

His brow lifted, and he dealt the card. "Another?"

Reckless, she gave crimson baize two more taps. "Why not?" When another card landed facedown on her stack, she waved her hand to stay.

He settled back into his seat, indolent and sure. What supreme confidence this man radiated. "Ladies first."

One by one, she flipped her cards over. "*Queen...*"

Not a good start.

"*Five...*"

A better middle.

"*Three...*"

She braced herself for the loss and flipped the last card over. She blinked, her brain a beat behind the number that met her eyes. "*Three.*"

Her gaze lifted and found a surprise in his eyes that matched her own, which in itself felt like a small victory. She had a feeling nothing shocked the man. Her heart a racehorse in her chest, she spoke around her triumph. "*Twenty-one.*"

"Well played." He tapped his two cards. "Should I bother turning mine over?" He wasn't truly asking.

First, he flipped a knave. An interminable beat of time dragged on as a long, masculine finger toyed with the remaining unflipped card. Isabel could have crawled through her skin. "Well?"

"Patience isn't your best virtue, is it?"

"Never was."

He tipped the card over, and Isabel's stomach dropped to her knees. She blinked, then blinked again, but the card remained stubbornly the same.

Ace.

But…but she had twenty-one. Wasn't that a push?

He quickly disabused her of the notion. "A natural twenty-one beats yours every time."

"*¡Pero quémierda!*" she exclaimed.

"Language," he tsked, even as his head cocked to the side and his eyes went speculative. "I thought your accent was Spanish."

This whole time he'd been taking in the bits and pieces she revealed here and there. Now he knew something about her that was true.

Isabel nearly repeated the obscenity. She'd allowed her competitive streak to undermine her purpose. This man was her means to repay a family debt. Just as she was nothing more than a plaything to him, he was nothing more than a means to an end for her. She was here to lose, she reminded herself.

She counted her gaming markers. *Thirty.* In their pretend world where these stakes mattered, she had £15,000 at hand, enough to bankrupt all but the smallest percentage of the population. She staked ten of them and awaited his next deal. He matched her, his focus pulled taut, as if he'd been toying with her before and was now coming in for the kill. Dread coiled low in her belly.

"Round four is Sympathy and Antipathy," he said as cards landed with light slaps on crimson baize. "Your preference."

She looked him in the eye. "Antipathy."

"Sympathy," he countered.

He flipped the cards and won, and she hardly cared. She'd lost her appetite for the game. Why did he insist on playing? Why not take her to that ridiculous bed and get this night over with? He appeared too intelligent to be this interested in a game that held no real stakes for him.

She caught herself. She knew nothing about his man. He could be stupid as a hitching post. Unlikely, but possible.

They streaked through the next two hands. He won the Rouge-et-Noir round; she the Self and Company. Only two rounds remained. Ten markers remained in her stack. She pushed them forward.

"The next hand is Paying the Difference, so keep your markers for now. We each receive two cards faceup. Then I will pay or receive a stake for the difference in the number of pips between our respective hands. Understand?"

"Of course." Not really, but who gave a fig?

He dealt himself an eighteen, and her an eight. The difference was ten. She tried to steady herself as she pushed her remaining markers forward, but she detected a slight tremble in her hand.

His eyebrows drew together. "Have I taken all your markers?"

She nodded. The air in the room intensified. Fingernails dug crescent moons into sweat-slicked palms. The time had arrived.

"There's but one deal left. It would be a shame to forfeit it." How utterly privileged he sounded. "Whatever shall we wager?"

Was he toying with her? He knew bloody well what her wager was. He was here for it, after all. "Whatever you wish."

Abruptly, he sat forward in his chair. Reactively, Isabel startled back in hers. "Do you have permission?"

She nodded, albeit slowly. What an odd question. Why else would she be here?

"And it's yours to stake?"

It? She wasn't sure if she wanted to laugh or cry. "To whom else would *it* belong?"

He steepled his fingers before him. "I'll require a witness."

"*A witness?*" What fresh depravity would she be subjected to on this night?

"I don't want you reneging."

Isabel bristled. "I assure you I shall see this night through to your satisfaction."

A look of puzzlement clouded his face. "Odd way of putting it." He combined his and her markers into a tidy pile, around £30,000 in the world outside these four walls. "Shall we make this interesting?" He pushed the pile forward.

She shrugged. She'd reached the limit of her tolerance with this farce.

"The eighth deal is the Clack." He went on to explain how it worked: The first card he placed down would be "one." If that card was an ace, he won. If it wasn't, he dealt the next card, the "two." If that card was a two, he won. If not, he dealt on in that manner until he reached "thirteen," its corresponding card a king. If ever the number he called matched the number of the card, he took all. If not, she won. "Understood?"

She nodded.

"One," he called. A three appeared. "Two." A knave.

And so it went, number by number, Isabel's heart doubling its rate of beats with the appearance of each new card, even as another part of her separated from her body and watched from a distance. When this game ended, a new one—the real one—would begin.

She must lose, to *win*.

But she didn't want to lose. She simply couldn't imagine what it would be like to share a bed with this devastating man.

To have his touch on her body.

To feel the press of his weight.

Would he extinguish the candles?

He didn't seem the type.

He reached twelve, and still he hadn't won. It was time for the final card. He met her eye. "Thirteen."

He flipped the card.

King.

Every last molecule in the room froze. Isabel's moment of reckoning had arrived. A wicked smile curled about the wolf's lips, and he sat back in his chair. Her breath caught in her chest. *Devastating.*

"The keys," he said.

His words had Isabel flummoxed. *The keys?* Was that code for something? "*Keys?*"

"To this establishment."

"But—"

"*But?*"

"Don't you want—"

A single dark eyebrow lifted above his hooded gaze. "—*me?*"

His brow furrowed, and he shoved forward in his

chair, his ear cocked to the side as if he hadn't heard her properly. "*You?*"

The way that *you* emerged from his mouth, the utter disbelief behind it, sounded alarm bells inside Isabel. If not her, then *who?* Something had gone very, very, irreparably wrong. What on earth could—

It hit her. *Oh.*

The awful words streamed forth with a will of their own. "*You're the*—"

His mouth twisted in disgust. "Do not call me by that silly name."

"*—wrong man.*"

3

Percy's hackles stood on end. He knew two facts at once.

He'd been correct. This was a trap.

But not for him.

Blast.

He'd experienced a frisson of unease that all wasn't what it appeared with this place, and he'd ignored it. Because he'd wanted to. Because the feeling charging through his veins at the prospect of this night wouldn't let him.

Now he'd landed squarely in it. What game was Montfort playing?

No time for that now. He needed to get out of here, quick.

But there was the not insignificant matter of the woman opposite him. His initial view of her had been the accurate one, he simply hadn't been observing her from the correct angle. She was young, lush, and possessed of the sort of beauty one didn't soon forget. It wasn't just her remarkable green eyes or her full lips the hue of a ripe cherry or her luminous skin, olive and radiant. It was the expression within those eyes—*fear*—

and the way her teeth bit her bottom lip—*uncertainty*—and the blush that pinked her cheeks —*soul-deep shock*.

That she was no madam was obvious to anyone with eyes.

Bloody hell. He saw, too, that she was his only lead.

His hand shot out across the table and grabbed her wrist before pushing to a stand. "Put on some decent clothes." If that flimsy shawl slipped off, he lacked the fortitude to keep his eyes trained on hers a second time. The first had tested him to the limit.

She braced herself against the table and angled her body back, trying to wrest away from his grasp. "I"—she pulled, twisted, tugged, all to no avail. He wasn't letting her go—"I don't know where they are."

He hauled her to her feet. "You're coming with me." He strode toward the door, strumpet in tow, her steps scrambling to keep up behind him.

"Don't I have a say in the matter?"

"No."

"You can't just—" she protested at his back.

"Oh, but I can." Hand on the door handle, he stopped. He couldn't very well drag her through Number 9's front entrance. The doorman would have something to say about that. "What is the back way out of this place?"

"I haven't the faintest idea."

Percy bit back a curse. It wasn't unusual for brothels to hold their ladies of the night captive.

He tightened his hold on her wrist, jerked the door open, and ducked his head out. The corridor was empty. Instinctively, he chose the direction opposite of the way they'd arrived. Instinct paid off when he found a narrow servants' stairway at its end. They were halfway down the first flight when they encountered a teary, slightly disheveled strumpet stomping her way up.

"Tilly?" asked the woman at his back. This night just kept getting better. "What is it?"

The girl—for that she still was, even if she was a strumpet—peered up, twin rivers of kohl streaming down her cheeks. "Oh, Izzy, Sir Felix broke it off, 'e did. Said I wadn't fine"—*foine*—"enough fer 'im." The girl's eyes widened. "Oi, what's this?" She jerked her thumb toward Percy. "Izzy, is 'e takin' ye 'gainst yer will? Oi! Oi!" She began shouting the place down.

Before Percy could clamp a hand over the girl's mouth, the woman at his back—*Izzy*, the girl had called her—squeezed past him. "Tilly!" she said in a whispered shout. "Stop that this instant!"

Tilly's mouth snapped shut, even as her eyes grew wide. Percy might have had the same reaction, he couldn't be sure. *Izzy*—how could that be *this* woman's name?—held a quiet command he hadn't noticed until now.

She grabbed both of Tilly's hands. "Come with me," she urged.

"Wait a—" Percy began.

Izzy rounded on him. "This has naught to do with you." She returned her attention to Tilly. "Tell me. Is this the life you want?"

The girl swallowed and shook her head.

"Then come with me," Izzy implored.

"Where are we goin'?" A baleful eye darted toward Percy. "With 'im?"

"I haven't the faintest idea." Izzy stabbed Percy with a hard glare. "But you'll be with *me*."

Tilly nodded, and the clouds cleared from her face that instant. Oh, the resilience of youth. "May we continue onward?" Percy asked, sardonic.

They had nearly reached the bottom step of the final set of stairs when the French doorman stomped into view, his brawny body filling the narrow width.

Impassive eyes stared out from beneath a low brow, the man's bald head the exact width of his thick neck. "You are free to go." He jutted his chin at Izzy and Tilly. "But not them."

Percy's fists clenched at his sides. Still, he would try diplomacy first. "They could. Name your price."

The man shook his head and widened his stance, ready.

Percy was going to have to fight his way through this massive wall of man. So be it. He occupied the high ground, therefore the advantage.

Strumpets to his back, he barreled down the stairs, pushing off the bottom step, the doorman taking a direct hit to the sternum with Percy's left shoulder. The man whooshed out a great breath, but didn't topple to the ground as Percy had hoped. In fact, the man barely moved.

Percy shuffled backwards and crouched low, reassessing. The other man smiled and cracked a few knuckles. *Right.*

Percy reared back his fist, but instead of striking the man as expected, at the last moment he changed tack and took a meaty shoulder in each hand before headbutting him, delivering a solid crack to the man's nose, which had surely broken given the spray of blood that burst forth.

Percy felt not a whit of remorse. It couldn't have been the first time the man's nose had been broken. Or the last.

The doorman swiped at his face in an unsuccessful attempt to stem the flow. "If rough play is what you want." He shuffled forward, fury in his eyes. "'Tis what you'll get."

Percy dodged the first fist, but wasn't so lucky with the second, taking a blow to the left eye that was bound to leave a mark. He feinted right and dug into his bag of dirty fighting tricks. He'd landed on one—a footplant to the knee designed to dislocate it—when around him shoved Tilly on an animal roar. Before Percy knew what the minx was up to, she'd delivered the most solid kick to a man's bollocks Percy ever had the displeasure of witnessing.

Time seemed to stand still as the doorman crumpled to the ground by heavy increments, until he rested on his knees, hunched over, a defeated shell of the man he once was. Tilly stood over him, breath coming in heavy gulps, radiant with triumph.

Percy found Izzy watching the events with wide eyes, as shocked as he. He grabbed her hand, slender and warm, and picked a direction. Down a short, dark corridor, they fled, Izzy's other hand latched onto Tilly. He shouldered open a door and found himself outside in a narrow, abandoned alley, the rancid reek of London life and vice left with nowhere to go but up one's nostrils. Izzy and Tilly rushed out onto cobblestones a step behind, while he located a plank of wood to wedge beneath the door handle, which should give the doorman enough trouble to buy them crucial seconds.

Three sets of breath puffed ragged in the midnight air. Percy glanced about to gather his bearings and met wide green eyes. Izzy was shivering, not from cold, he suspected, but from shock. "We need to move. Any idea which way?"

Her eyebrows drew together. "Left?"

"It's as good a direction as any."

At the end of the alley, Percy scanned up and down the street. Then he heard it: the thud of heavy footsteps. He glanced back and spotted the doorman limping toward them, murder in his eyes. One had to admire the man's tenacity in the face of possible permanent injury.

The door of a parked carriage flew open, and a head popped out. "Bretagne!"

Hortense.

Already on the run, relief flooded Percy as he, once again, grabbed Izzy's hand. He couldn't have her getting ideas of flight. He needed her alive and talking.

Once they reached the hackney, Tilly gave a great leap and dove in, followed by Izzy who, when she reached the top step, tipped backward. Without a second thought, Percy gave her rather well-formed rump a shove, and in she gracelessly lurched. He shouted up to the driver, "*Go, go, go,*" before following suit and slamming the door shut behind them.

Inside, he claimed the leather bench beside Izzy—Hortense and Tilly seated opposite—as the hackney jolted into motion. He peered through the tiny window at his back and found the doorman slowing to a defeated stop. The man never had a chance. Percy turned and met Hortense's eye.

Unfazed by the events of the last thirty seconds, she asked, "Were these two your winnings?"

"The night got away from me." It wasn't untrue.

Hortense gave a slow nod and kept her thoughts to herself. Tilly exercised no such restraint. "Oh, we weren't won. Or were ye, Izzy? Zounds! It ain't me 'oo knows what's 'appenin'."

Percy kept his gaze fixed on Hortense. She was waiting. "The night was a trap."

"Of you?"

"No."

Hortense lifted a single inquiring eyebrow.

"I don't know who—" It hit him. He did know. But he wanted confirmation first. He turned to Izzy. "You said I was the wrong man."

Her jaw clenched, and she attempted to wrest her arm free. When had he grabbed it again? "Can I release you?" he asked. Her mouth pressed into a stubborn line. "Hortense, the door."

Hortense nodded and wrapped her hand around the latch. There would be no brash escape. Percy released Izzy's wrist. As she rubbed it, he asked, "Who did Montfort tell you was the *right* man?"

Surprise flashed in her eyes. "You know Montfort?" The question emerged in a voice the contralto of smoke. A seductive voice, if one was in such a mood. "I was never given the right man's name."

"Then how did you come to pick *me?*"

"I was told to approach the man gambling at the hazard table at the exact place you occupied."

"Were you given a description of the man?"

She shifted in discomfort. *"Tall, dark, aristocratic."*

There. Just as he'd suspected. "The Earl of Pembroke."

Hortense started in surprise. "You don't mean—"

"Nick's brother."

"He's the future Marquess of Clare."

"If he doesn't drink himself into an early grave," Percy said slowly. A bigger picture began opening before him. "Pembroke is a future Member of Parliament." He gave a humorless laugh. "Montfort isn't out of the game."

"And we thought he was simply padding his pockets with earnings from dens of iniquity."

"This is about influence. Setting up a future marquess is political."

Hortense shook her head and snorted in disbelief. "Leave it to you to stumble into this."

Percy sat forward. "And"—he pinned Izzy with a hard glare—*"you* are involved."

Tilly gasped, eyes wide above the hands covering her mouth.

"In your little game with Pembroke," Percy continued, refusing to release Izzy's gaze, "what was the prize to be?"

———

My maidenhead, Isabel didn't say.

She couldn't speak the awful truth aloud.

Are you a virgin? That had been the question that had truly sealed her fate and brought her to this night. She'd experienced a flush of heat at the blunt intimacy of the question. For a moment, she hadn't known the correct answer.

Then she had. Only a few types of women were deemed worth anything by a man like Montfort and a virgin was one of them.

Yes, she'd replied.

It had been the correct answer.

The right man—most definitely *not* the man at her side—was to be seduced. Her directive had been simple: collect intimate information about his person and allow him to relieve her of her virginity. Stained sheets were to be the proof.

Her father would have been rescued from prison, and her family made whole again.

And this wolfish, devastating man next to her—*Bretagne*, she'd heard him called—who smelled better than he had a right to—was that sandalwood?—had wrecked it all to bits.

Except…he hadn't done it alone.

It was she who was truly at fault for destroying her and her family's future.

"Perhaps," Bretagne began in that hard-edged, self-sure voice of his, "your friend can inform us of the details."

"Leave Tilly out of it," Isabel all but growled. "She

knows nothing. I demand you stop this carriage and let us leave."

He scoffed. "I can't imagine that's in your best interest."

"I can assure you," Isabel protested, "it is *absolutely* in my best interest that you let us go."

She had to find a way to fix this night. How had it gone so wrong, so quickly?

"Whatever it is you're not telling us," Percy stated, "Montfort knows you know it."

With those words, Isabel's night went from bad to worse. Her best hope lay in the possibility of salvaging this night, but was it possible? The odds were looking worse by the minute.

"The safe house in Seven Dials," supplied Hortense.

Bretagne shook his head. "Montfort could find her. We need to get her out of London."

Out of London? Isabel snapped to. "You can stop discussing me like I'm not here."

"I have a place I can take her," Bretagne continued, ignoring Isabel's protest. The statement emerged from his firm mouth so sure of itself, even Isabel almost thought the matter settled. *Almost.*

Hortense nodded and gave the ceiling two sharp raps. The driver called out a "Whoa!" and the hackney slowed to a stop. "I'll stay in London and work a few contacts. You know how to find me."

Hortense pushed the door open, hopped down, and disappeared into the night. Bretagne shut the door and gave the ceiling another two raps. The hackney jerked into motion.

"Tilly?" he asked.

The girl's gaze widened. "Milord?"

"Exchange seats with me."

Once they'd maneuvered around each other in the cramped space, Tilly's arm slid through Isabel's and squeezed. Isabel met *his* gaze, intense and direct. Distance made him no less devastating or dangerous.

"I won't take you by force," he said.

That provoked a sharp laugh from her. "Haven't you already?"

"You're going to have to trust me."

Another laugh emerged of its own will. "*Trust* you?"

"Your life will be safe with me." He pointed at Tilly. "Hers, too."

This time, the laugh died in Isabel's throat. It defied all logic, but she believed him.

And the powerful man whose scheme she'd botched tonight?

Her life mattered not a whit to Montfort. Neither did her family.

Her family…

The reality of the situation hit her like a blast.

"I'll go with you," she said.

"Smart woman."

"But, first, we must make a stop."

4

As the hackney slowed, the only sound was the fading *clip-clop* of the horses' hooves. For a long moment, all was quiet, even Tilly. Bretagne leaned forward, peered through the carriage window, and read aloud, "*Galante: Dressmakers Extraordinaire.*" He lifted a curious eyebrow.

Isabel kept her mouth shut. Did the man have to be so observant? How she wished he didn't know this about her, but there was no helping it. She wouldn't leave London without coming here first.

She squeezed Tilly's hand. "Stay here while I see to a few matters."

Tilly jutted her chin toward Bretagne. "With 'im?"

Isabel addressed her next words to *him*. "I have your word that she will be safe?"

"Of course," he retorted, his reply ripe with insult.

Isabel reached for the door handle, but his hand got there first. "You have five—"

"Ten," she inserted.

"*Five* minutes before I follow." His intense gaze probed hers for the space of three rapid heartbeats before he released the latch and pushed the door open.

Isabel's feet met clattering cobblestones on a short

hop. Before her stood the unassuming storefront that had grown so familiar over the last year and a half. She craned her neck and saw dim light shining orange through an upstairs curtain.

Keenly aware of that man's eyes upon her back and the rapid tick of the five minute clock, she cupped her hands and peered through the front window, hoping to find Nell. Suddenly conscious of her appearance, she shrugged her shawl tighter about her, but there wasn't any way of disguising the truth. She was dressed like a harlot. In that man's eyes, she was one.

She picked up a pebble off the sidewalk and tossed it, a single glassy tap against the upstairs window. The curtain moved, and a face appeared for the slip of a moment. In less than thirty seconds, a wisp of a girl was at the door, twisting the lock. "Miss Galante!" Nell exclaimed. "Oh, I been worried sick about you. Where'd you go?"

Isabel gave the girl a quick embrace, even as she evaded the question, her feet already navigating the large rectangular tables and bolts of fabric to the narrow corridor that led to the back of the shop. She breathed in the scent of fabric and dust, familiar and home. She wanted to sink into it and pretend these last months were nothing more than a bad dream, that she was safe here.

But this wasn't the time for fantasy. She had fewer than five minutes before the wolf came after her. She had not a second to waste.

"Nell, have you had any trouble minding the shop in addition to your other duties?" she asked over her shoulder.

"Not a lick of it."

"And Eva?" Isabel dreaded the answer. "Is she...is she well?"

Isabel sensed hesitation before the answer came.

Nell tended to give Eva a wide berth, and Isabel could hardly blame her. "Aye."

Isabel forced herself to ask the next question. "And the babe? Is he—"

The next answer came on a happy rush. "He's right as rain, he is. Sweetest little mite you ever laid eyes on."

They reached the top landing, Nell's room to the right, Isabel and Eva's rooms to the left. "Nell, I need you to pack a bag."

Instant tears welled in the girl's eyes. "You givin' me the sack? What I done?"

"We're leaving London for a few days. Unless you have somewhere else you can stay until we return?"

"I ain't got nowhere, miss."

Isabel wouldn't consider the added burden those words placed on her shoulders. "Then you're coming with us. Pack your things and meet us downstairs in three minutes."

Nell nodded and snapped to without protest or a lick of shock. Such midnight developments must not have been unusual in her past. It was a harsh world out there for a lone girl, as Isabel had learned in recent years.

No time to spare, she opened the door to her left and dashed across the bare floorboards of the small front room that served as both sitting room and makeshift kitchen. With no small amount of relief, she saw that it had been kept tidy and neat, which she surely owed to Nell. When she'd last seen Eva, well, Eva wasn't quite up to the task.

Speaking of Eva...

Her gaze stole toward the bedroom at the far side of the room. A thin strip of light peeked between the floor and the closed door. Isabel turned toward the closer room, hers. Without bothering to light a candle, Isabel worked in the light of a late-rising moon. Quickly, she shed her harlot's weeds and threw open the wardrobe door. Several dresses hung before her. She couldn't think why, but she chose the two finest. She donned one and shoved the other into a worn duck travel bag along with a few other sundries.

Next, she fell to her hands and knees and slid a small box from beneath her bed. She flipped open the lid and grabbed the only items of value, besides the shop, she had in the world. The money, she stuffed into the bag. Mama's necklace, she latched around her neck, its delicate hamsa pendant hanging low between her breasts, out of view.

Then she was on her feet and back in the sitting room, her gaze locked on the other bedroom's door. She could avoid it no longer. She must face what lay on the other side with tonight's failure. Her closed fist hesitated just before it delivered two light taps.

No answer came. Isabel pushed the door open anyway. Eva had stopped answering months ago. She'd expected to find Eva in bed, curled onto her side, facing away from both the door and the bassinet at the side of the bed. The bed, however, was empty.

Isabel's panicked eye swept the room and found Eva in her night-rail, seated beside the window, her hand on the babe's bassinet, rocking it gently. Emotion, equal parts grief and hope, if that was possible on this night, surged inside Isabel. It was the first time she'd seen Eva tend or even acknowledge the babe. Could it be that her sister was recovering? That she'd returned to her old self?

At last, Eva's dark brown eyes lifted to meet Isabel's. *No.* All she saw was the same bleak emptiness that had stared out at her the last time she was in this room a fortnight ago. None of the vivacity that had defined Eva as Eva all their lives, only blankness. Eva had sacrificed so much for the family; she'd sacrificed everything. And, still, it hadn't been enough.

Isabel's fists clenched. She would ensure Eva's sacrifice wasn't in vain.

She would fix her mistake.

"Have you saved England yet?" Eva asked. There was no mistaking the bitterness in her voice.

Isabel's fingernails dug into her palms. "The night didn't go to plan."

A shadow passed in Eva's eye. She parted the curtain a sliver. "Is that hackney waiting for you?"

"Yes."

Eva's cheeks went paler than usual, and she stiffened. "Is *he* inside?"

"It's not Montfort. But, Eva," Isabel continued, gaze darting about the room, feet itching to be on their way, "where is your travel bag?"

"I'm not exactly dressed for travel." Eva tugged at the soft material of her night-rail to illustrate her point.

No time to explain, Isabel rushed to the room's one wardrobe, opening and closing drawers and doors, grabbing clothes and sundries, stuffing them unceremoniously into the bag. "Where are the babe's clean nappies?"

Wary, Eva pointed to a small chest beside the bassinet. "Why are you packing us up?"

Isabel stopped and looked her sister dead in the eye. The truth could be avoided no longer. "I failed." Oh, that her voice didn't crack on that word. "And we *must...go...now.*"

Isabel stepped to the bassinet and stared down at her nephew. He was peaceful in his sleep, no longer the fractious infant he was for the first few months of his life when Isabel had had to spend most of their remaining savings on hiring Nell to wet-nurse the babe. The girl's own babe had been stillborn only days before. Oh, how thin and weak he'd been, squirming and crying the house down. Now his cheeks had plumped up, and he was able to rest peacefully.

She bent over and bussed a light kiss on his forehead, inhaling his warm, sweet scent. She straightened, and her hands tightened around the two bags. "Would you like to dress? Or will you wear your night-rail?"

Eva's eyebrows drew together and released. "Does it make a difference?"

"Not to me." It only mattered that Eva was safe with her.

Eva stood and turned to the small table at her side. She opened a drawer and removed a small object. When she faced Isabel again, she held a pistol.

"Where did you get *that*?" Isabel asked in a shocked whisper.

"Such items can be got. The point is we shall not be defenseless." Eva's eyes burned with emotion. "Never again."

Isabel understood her sister wasn't leaving without the gun. She nodded, and Eva dropped the offensive item into one of the bags. Isabel stared down at the babe. "Will you carry him? Or shall I call for Nell?"

Isabel's heart stuttered in her chest as she awaited Eva's reply. "I," Eva began and swallowed. "I can." She reached into the bassinet and lifted the sleeping infant into her embrace, gingerly. Too gingerly.

Isabel wouldn't ask if this was the first time Eva had held her child. In a strange way, it felt too intimate a question. Eva had so many demons to battle, Isabel wouldn't add to her sister's burden by placing judgment upon her shoulders, too. Instead, she asked, "Have you—" She hesitated, not wanting to ask the next question, fearing its answer. "Have you named him yet?"

Eva gazed down at the babe in her arms, a cloud of

emotion in her eyes. "*Ariel*," she said, almost as if surprised at hearing the name spoken aloud.

A knot twisted inside Isabel. "After Papa?"

"*Sí.*"

"Mama would have liked that."

She and Eva didn't often speak of Mama—she'd died of a lung infection when Isabel had been ten years of age and Eva nine—but she was never too far from their thoughts. Mama was feisty and brave, and Isabel longed to be more like her.

Mouth pressed into a firm line, Eva nodded once, as if she couldn't trust herself to speak. How Isabel wished Eva would speak, shout, scream, cry, rail in fury at the hand Fate had dealt her. But Eva refused, forgoing emotion in favor of flat stoicism.

"Follow me," Isabel said. It was time to move before that devastating man in the carriage hunted her down.

Across their small rooms, down the narrow staircase and corridor, through the maze of fabric bolts, they fled, meeting a wide-eyed Nell at the front door. "Nell, do you have the key?"

As Isabel twisted the key in the deadbolt, she experienced a pang in her gut. This was the shop, the life, she and Eva had begun. And now she was leaving it behind and shuttered for an uncertain future. But what choice had she? The business was nothing to those in her care. She would rebuild when—*if*—she returned.

Door locked behind them, they crossed the short distance to the carriage. The door flew open, and Bretagne's face appeared, ripe with disbelief. It would be comical, if the circumstances weren't so deadly serious. "Are you out of your deuced mind, woman?"

Isabel signaled to Eva and Nell to stop and drew herself up to her fullest height. She'd known this fight was coming. "If they don't go, I don't go. Tilly?"

Tilly's face popped into view. "Yes, miss?"

"Come out of there."

Bretagne's arm blocked the door opening. "Now, wait a minute."

This, too, Isabel had predicted. She strode forward, now separated from him by a few inches. If he thought she couldn't be as fierce as he, well, he would learn. Mayhap she did have a bit of Mama's spirit. "I shan't leave them in London to face the danger I'm escaping," she hissed in rising anger. "Don't you have a care for another single person in the world?"

He flinched, a flicker of movement, but she caught it. She'd scraped across a raw nerve. Ruthlessly, she pressed her advantage. "It's all or none."

A pair of riotous heartbeats galloped through her chest before he drew back and grandly waved their motley group inside. She sensed sarcasm in the gesture, but she cared not. She would take what victory she could manage.

"Miss?" Isabel heard at her back.

"Yes, Nell?"

Nell's eye darted nervously toward the man inside. "I'll be ridin' up top, if you don't mind."

"Not at all."

"If the babe needs a feed, just tap the roof."

Isabel nodded, and Nell scurried up to sit beside the driver, who gave her a surly grunt.

First, Eva and the babe, assisted by Tilly, piled inside, then Isabel. Half in, half out the doorway, she glanced from side to side, the man to her right, Eva and Tilly to her left. Any other time, she would take the seat with the most spaciousness, but this was no usual time. She went left and squeezed her rump between Eva and Tilly. The man gave a snort before he tapped the roof twice. The carriage jerked into motion, and they were on their way.

An excited light in her eyes, Tilly squeezed Isabel's hand. "Zounds! What adventures we be 'avin'."

Isabel met the hard, unflinching gaze of the man opposite her. A chill of portent jangled up her spine.

Eva leaned over without disturbing the babe in her arms and pressed her mouth to Isabel's ear. "I don't know him."

It hadn't occurred to Isabel that Eva would, but shouldn't it have, given Eva's past and where Isabel had met this man? An unaccountable thread of relief ribboned through her. She didn't know this man, not really, but she hadn't thought him evil. Annoying and forceful, yes, but not *evil*.

Not like Montfort.

It wasn't long before a heaviness began to pull at Isabel, and sand scratched at her eyes. She was tired, so very, very tired, and the jostle of the carriage so very, very restful. Each blink grew more weighty as she fell headlong into slumber beneath the watchful eye of a wolf.

5

Eyes trained on the four sleeping figures opposite him, Percy wondered, not for the first time, what the blast he'd stumbled into.

Izzy and Tilly had descended into slumber rather quickly, considering, but the woman with the sleeping babe had trained a baleful eye on him until it could no longer hold open. Although no introductions had been made, it was clear she was Izzy's sister as they shared the same sable hair and olive skin. Only their eyes differed, the sister's a deep, bottomless brown to Izzy's striking green. Never had he encountered eyes like Izzy's.

Dawn began brightening the sky outside the window coated with London filth, illuminating familiar surroundings Percy hadn't viewed in over a decade. Although his father owned any number of properties, Percy had always considered this one his true home. Sentiment tugged at him, and he tamped it down. He wouldn't be staying.

He finally had something concrete on Montfort, and he wasn't about to ease off the pressure. He was needed in London.

The carriage made a sharp right with less care than

the driver could have taken. The man had been miffed at Percy's request to drive them this far outside London, but, in the end, he'd been unable to refuse Percy's coin. Still, his pique let itself be known in the quality, or lack thereof, of his driving. Opposite, his passengers stirred—Tilly emitting a mildly offended, "Whut?"—before settling back into sleep.

Percy's eye fell on Izzy. She'd surprised him with the dressmaker's shop in Cheapside. The neighborhood wasn't Mayfair, but it was respectable.

Who was this woman, anyway?

He'd been readying himself to storm the shop when she'd emerged, wearing a modest dress, no sign of sheer black lace, and with three additional passengers in tow. The woman had a knack for collecting strays.

He couldn't help studying her in the newly emergent light of dawn. She was young, but not so young as others in Number 9, like Tilly. No, Izzy had a fresh, soft look about her in sleep. If he were being dead honest, she looked like the most delectable sweet treat to ever cross a pair of lips. When she'd removed her black lace shawl to reveal upturned breasts, dusky pink nipples at their tips, he'd used every last shred of will he possessed to *not* look or react physically. Years of measuring and parceling his reactions had paid out in that moment.

She couldn't have been at Number 9 for very long. She was *too* soft, *too* fresh. Further, in her manner and in her speech lay...*refinement*.

About her speech, there was the Spanish accent she and her sister shared. Every instinct told him it was a crucial point.

He took in the details of her dress. It was modest. It was respectable. It wasn't the dress of a strumpet. In fact, she didn't look like a strumpet at all. Rather, she looked closer to a dressmaker.

How did she come to be in Number 9? One and one didn't add up to two with this woman.

He only knew this with any certainty: no matter how seemingly soft, how seemingly fresh, how seemingly refined, the woman was Montfort's creature. Yet Percy wasn't convinced she knew the details of Montfort's plan. Likely not. Montfort tended to hold his cards close to his chest, buried deep beneath his hale and hearty exterior of bluff English gentleman. Bit players only knew enough to perform their roles.

Still, this woman had mucked up Montfort's scheme last night, an outcome that Montfort wouldn't let pass without consequences, which was why Percy needed her out of London.

The house rolled into view, its gray stone burnished amber gold with the morning light. *Gardencourt Manor.* Constructed of Portland stone imported from Dorset, it had mellowed from white to an aged gray. At first glance, it struck one as a formidable fortification, a remnant of England's medieval warlord past with its fantastical towers and crenellations. The house, however, had missed the illustrious past by a few hundred years, making it merely a palace constructed fifty years ago to resemble a castle.

How Percy's eight-year-old heart had broken into a million pieces when his older brother, Michael, had meanly imparted this information to him. Percy had been convinced that William the Conqueror himself had ruled from here. The sight of it, now, brought his thirty-four-year-old heart no small amount of joy.

To soften the forbidding exterior, his mother had the grounds designed so the grand house appeared to spring up directly from a wild English garden. Or at least that was what he'd been told as a child. He'd never known her. She'd died giving birth to him, here, at Gardencourt, as a matter of fact. The story went that he'd arrived early, feet first and face up, and there had been no time to return to London and the family physician. Just as it was for Percy, this had been her favorite of the family's houses.

The carriage swung around the long arc of the circular drive and was now drawing to a rough stop. All four sets of eyes across from Percy flew wide in varying degrees of startled wakefulness. Izzy's gaze landed on him. "Where are we?"

"The less you know, the better."

Her eyebrows drew together in consternation, and her mouth opened to surely protest his high-handedness.

"Wait here while I set matters in order," he said, cutting off her protest before it could gain momentum.

He pushed the carriage door open and landed on the crushed shell drive. The next moment, he was pressing payment into the driver's hand, giving him the exact agreed-upon amount and not a farthing more, even as the man left his palm open. Percy snorted. Gardencourt had a famously extensive stable. He didn't need this hackney to return to London.

A loud wail emerged from inside the carriage. "Oh!" exclaimed the girl who had ridden up top. "The little master will be wantin' his breakfast." On a nimble hop, she descended and disappeared inside, shutting the door behind her.

It was a woman's world inside that carriage, said the driver's expression. Percy tacitly agreed. "I expect you to wait here until they've finished whatever it is they're doing in there."

An avaricious smile curled about the driver's mouth as he waggled greedy fingers. Grudgingly, Percy dropped more coin onto the man's expectant palm. On a lilting whistle, the driver meandered toward his horses.

Percy took Gardencourt's wide and imposing flight of front steps two at time as his mind worked out the fiction that would explain to the year-round skeleton staff the continued presence of four women and a baby while he returned to London. It was the perfect out-of-the-way place to stash them until he found out what game Montfort was playing.

On a whim, he tested the door handle. Solid oak gave and swung open on silent hinges. Unexpected.

Caution in his step, Percy advanced into the receiving hall. The scents of his childhood hit him first. An ever-present underlying mustiness that came with age, humidity, and country air. A sweetness from the breads baked in the kitchen. The expensive perfumes of duchesses past and present. The faint earthiness of the famous conservatory. Scents that could carry him to a past that didn't yet have a care in the world, if he allowed them to sweep him up in their spell. He'd always been rather susceptible to magic.

Percy opened his eyes, not having realized he'd closed them, and took in his surroundings. Just as Gardencourt's scents hadn't changed, neither had its substance. Same coat of armor tucked beneath the grand staircase ahead. Same row of stately marble busts depicting the philosophers of ancient Greece. Same Persian carpets, their intricate designs rendered in ripe crimson, indigo, and saffron, leading awed footsteps through to the center of the house where one would await the pleasure of the lord. It was a house that could easily feel forbidding, but it didn't. Wood paneling of English oak and exotic mahogany provided a welcoming warmth that invited one inside on the promise of safety and comfort.

The deeper into the interior he walked, the less care he had for the rag-tag lot of trouble he'd left outside. Still, he hoped they hadn't bolted down the drive. He wasn't too keen on running them to the ground. It had been a long day, and the comfort of home—his true home—beckoned.

"So, you decided to join our little country house party, after all?"

A half-inhaled breath froze in Percy's lungs. *No, no, no, it can't be.* He squinted down a darkened corridor as a tall figure emerged, the man's signature shock of white hair catching the light. *It can, and it is.*

Father stopped before Percy, a welcoming smile on his lips. First thing every morning, he made his way to the butler's pantry to retrieve his morning paper, rather than having it delivered to him as surely every other duke in England did.

Last night's strange luck seemed to have followed Percy into the day. Only now did the duke's question catch up to him. "*Country house party?*"

"Lucy will be glad you came. She was convinced you wouldn't."

"Lucy's here?"

There it was, the thing inside Percy that broke whenever he heard his daughter's name. He doubted she would be glad to see him. They'd arrived at a détente where she accepted his presence on prescribed days, but that was the extent of their relationship.

A terrible possibility now occurred to him. "Olivia isn't here, is she?"

Although the relationship he'd forged with Olivia upon his return to England was an amicable one, to see her now, with a host of rouged-up, disheveled women in tow, would be too much.

The duke shook his head and harrumphed discreetly. "Lucy begged to come here with Miss Radclyffe for the summer solstice. A bunch of chatter about druids and such. And since Parliament won't reconvene until next month, why not? Never could refuse the chit anything." The duke's piercing blue gaze shifted to a point beyond Percy's shoulder. "And, who, may I inquire, have you brought with you?"

Ice shot through Percy's veins. Given the softening of the duke's tone, it was a woman. One of the women he'd brought here. Pray God, let it not be Tilly.

He pivoted and saw Izzy, moving forward on slow footsteps. Reality fell on Percy like a two-ton rhinoceros.

How utterly and completely he'd fallen into his old life without a thought for its impact on his family. *Again.*

It was simply that when he was in the thick of the life that strayed wide of narrow aristocratic bounds of propriety, when its dangerous vibrancy was charging through his veins, he never gave a thought to the life he should be living, the one whose concerns revolved around the quality of his fare and clubs.

However, when confronted with a moment like this, well, that other life came into clear focus—sordid...all-consuming...*wrong.*

Yet...how it made him feel...

Well, it made him *feel*—and he couldn't resist its siren song.

None of this could he say to his father.

"She's my, *erm*..."

Think.

Mistress?

No.

"*Erm*..."

He looked into her curious green eyes and uttered the only word that could make her presence in his father's house acceptable.

"*Bride.*"

Her gasp echoed off oak paneling all the way up to the high, coffered ceiling. Silence, monstrous and shocked to its bones, filled the cavernous room. He'd just told his father, the Duke of Arundel, that a strumpet—or...what precisely was she?—was his wife. Two sets of eyes burned into him.

The pendulum clock ticked off another minute of time before the duke crossed the distance and wrapped his arms around Percy, giving him two manful claps on the back. "Let me be the first to congratulate you."

Had Percy picked up a note in his father's voice on the word *congratulate*? Just a little note of disbelief? Of playing along? His father had always been good at that game when Percy was a child. Whatever pretend world Percy created, his father never missed a step entering it with him.

But his father's visage betrayed not a hint of irony. Percy almost wished it had, because now...

Now he had to follow through with the farce that he'd taken a woman he didn't know to wife.

What was her trade, anyway?

Trollop? dressmaker? both?

The duke stepped back, and his focus landed on Izzy. Percy's stomach lurched with nausea. "And does your bride have a name?"

Percy's mouth opened and shut. *Izzy*. Women called by the name *Izzy* didn't marry into the aristocracy, much less a duke's line. Surely, a codicil decreed it so.

Green eyes wide and unflinching, she stepped forward. She possessed the most direct gaze Percy had ever beheld. Whether they shone with competition, fear, or purpose, they didn't shy away. If he didn't know better, he'd think them the most honest eyes he'd ever encountered. But he did know better.

"My name is Isabel, my lor—"

"*Your Grace*," Percy provided. She needed to know that she was the pretend daughter by law to not just any lord, but a duke. What a night. Would there never be an end to it?

"Your Grace." She dipped in a curtsy, deep and graceful. Where had she learned that particular skill? Not at Number 9. Or the dressmaking shop. Then, where?

The duke took Isabel's hand and bussed a courtly kiss onto it. "Enchanted, my dear."

Enchanted? Panic streaked through Percy. What had he done? Would he never cease to be the family profligate? He found enough presence of mind to ask, "Is Rosebud Cottage available for our use?"

The duke smiled. "Lucretia instructed the beds be made up with fresh linens only yesterday. She hoped you would join us. Rosebud Cottage only ever awaits your arrival."

That last sentence sliced through Percy like a cut, jagged and deep, leaving behind the sharp-edged pain of guilt. Percy could only assume the invitation to join this house party lay buried in the stack of unopened social correspondence that he rarely bothered sorting through.

He'd been too long on his own, too long reliant on himself only, to slot back in to the niceties of Society. *Nay, not Society*, his conscience piped up. *Family.* The duke was family, and Percy could do better. Hadn't this been one of his vows upon his return to England? Yet his determination to exact revenge upon Montfort had taken precedence.

He must do better.

The duke tapped his morning paper against his leg. "I trust you haven't forgotten the way?"

Percy nodded, and the duke cast a parting smile toward Isabel, a name, Percy thought with no small amount of relief, which suited both the woman and the situation infinitely better than *Izzy*. "Welcome to the family, daughter."

Percy inhaled the groan that wanted release. He'd made a monumental mistake of epic proportions.

The duke disappeared down the corridor to his study, where he would read the *Morning Chronicle* from cover to cover and take his first pot of coffee alone before the rest of the house stirred.

The rustlings of early risers echoed from the servants' wing. "We need to go," Percy said to Isabel. He couldn't face anyone else yet, not until he'd evaluated this turn of events and what it changed.

Actually, the answer was obvious. It had changed everything.

"Follow me."

He strode to the front entrance, still open from their arrival, and paused beneath the wide, Grecian-columned portico. "Don't think about bolting," he said, low and hard, when Isabel stopped beside him. He wasn't in the mood for nonsense.

"And how do you reckon I do that with a new mother wearing her night-rail, a babe, his wet nurse, and Tilly?" she retorted before brushing around him and joining her rag-tag sisterhood below, a trace of honeysuckle and summer scenting the air behind her.

The consequence of his lie to his father hit Percy square in the jaw. He was stuck here, in the country, with his "bride," leaving Hortense to handle matters in London without him.

How had the night, now day, gotten away from him so entirely?

6

Isabel's eyes flew wide open, and she sat straight up in a high, four-poster bed, breath scraping the back of her lungs in ragged gasps.

Where in the blazes was she?

The previous night crashed over her in a single, powerful wave. She was in Rosebud Cottage, in the bedroom she'd chosen at the farthest end of the corridor, next to Eva and Ariel's room.

Tension released from her body by slow increments as she took in the coral and amber color palette encasing her in its warm, velvety glow. The furniture was rather ancient, but well-tended. This room looked, smelled, and felt exactly how she imagined the inside of a rosebud looked, smelled, and felt.

Across from her was a large three-paneled window composed of leaded diamond panes, a holdover from the era during which the cottage was built, likely hundreds of years ago. Beyond the window, the green canopy of the surrounding copse of oaks swayed gently in a light breeze, its only sounds a soft, leafy *shoosh* and the singing of birds. It was almost enough to seduce one into the fairy tale it presented, that the world outside was as inviting and lovely.

Almost.

Her eye fell on the chair she'd wedged beneath the door handle. Her reality was anything but idyllic.

The sequence of events that had landed her in this room ran through her mind. The card game. The wrong man. Her failure.

Now, she was wedded to that wrong man, who just so happened to be the son of a duke.

A *pretend* marriage, she corrected herself. But the duke and his son were not pretend at all. They were, in fact, very real. *Too* real.

She swung her legs off the bed, still fully clothed, prepared for another hasty flight. On light feet, so as not to alert anyone to her wakefulness, she made her way to the washbasin in the corner. What she wouldn't give for toothbrush and powder.

She found her reflection in the small mirror. *Dios mío.* She looked as bad as her mouth tasted. She splashed water onto her pale, drawn face and pulled the pins from her hair, which fell about her shoulders and down her back in a stringy mess.

A soft *tap-tap* sounded on the door. "*Izzy?*" came a hiss through solid wood. "Milady?"

Milady? "Oh," Isabel groaned aloud. She was "married" to a lord, which would make her a lady. If it were true.

"Just a moment," she called out. She shimmied the chair out from beneath the door handle, and in walked the girl, her face bright with her usual smile.

"Tilly," Isabel began on a stammer, "what are you wearing?"

"Ye like it?" The girl's chest puffed out with pride. "Lord Percival—"

"Lord Percival?"

"Yer 'usband." Tilly gave a broad wink.

"Oh."

"Well, 'e told me to wear *this*"—she swept her hands up and down her person, indicating the modest black dress with the high white collar—"and tell any'un 'oo asked that I'm yer lady's maid."

"Oh." It struck Isabel that Tilly's maid's uniform was constructed of finer wool than that of the dress she was currently wearing. As a matter of fact, this was one of her two best dresses. And still not as good as that of a duke's servant.

Tilly's gaze clouded over in the dreamy way specific to her. "Yer 'usband, 'e's a right 'andful o' man, ain't 'e?"

Although she agreed whole-heartedly that Lord Percival would be a *right 'andful* for any woman, Isabel couldn't allow Tilly to persist in her current fantasy. "Tilly, you know he's not my husband. And I'm not your mistress," she added for good measure.

Tilly gave an indifferent shrug. "Well, that's 'oo we are while we're 'ere. Anyway, I ain't told ye the best part." The girl ambled over to the vanity, picked up a brush, and waved Isabel over. "Yer 'air is a right rat's nest." Once Isabel settled onto a low stool, Tilly continued. "I was goin' to sleep in a servant's room by the kitchen downstairs, but ye know 'oo beat me there?"

"Who?" Isabel knew *who*, but had to ask.

"*'Im.*"

Tilly didn't need to clarify. *'Im* could only be one man.

"And ye know what 'e told me?"

"I can't imagine. Truly."

"'E told me to take me pick o' rooms up 'ere and sleep there."

This came as no surprise to Isabel as he'd said as much to her.

"And ye know what?" Tilly continued, conspiratorially. "I did. Me arse ne'er felt feathers so fine and fluffy. A gel can really get a dream in a bed like that." The brush began running through Isabel's hair with more ease. "Lawks be, Izzy, ye got the kinda 'air to strike envy in the best o' us, all long and sable and silk. It's a right good thing ye got out o' Number 9 before Nan got ahold o' it."

"Oh?" Isabel met Tilly's gaze in the mirror. "Was my hair in some sort of danger?"

Tilly's light brown eyes went wide with alarm. "All it would take to separate yer 'air from yer 'ead is a sharp pair o' scissors, and ye couldn't be puttin' that sort o' thin' past Nan. Ever since she lost that front tooth, she bin mean as a squirrel."

Two light knocks sounded on the door. As one, Isabel and Tilly craned their necks around as a chambermaid shuffled into the room with a friendly, "A good morning to you, milady."

"And to you," was Isabel's wobbly reply. How did English aristocrats address their servants?

"The Duchess sent this for you." The girl extended a pressed newspaper to Tilly, who passed it along to Isabel on a snort.

A well-worn efficiency in her step, the maid set about her business, refreshing the basin water, smoothing bed linens, fluffing pillows, and so she went.

"What's it say?" asked Tilly.

Isabel glanced at the paper in her hands. The *London Diary*. "It's a scandal sheet," she replied, dismissive.

"Zounds! I love me some gossip. 'Oo's it about?"

Isabel gave the front page a quick scan. "Some twaddle about a Savior of St. Giles."

"Ye 'aven't 'eard of the *Savior of St. Giles*?" Tilly exclaimed, eyes wide.

"Should I have?" What did this savior have to do with anything? He wasn't here, saving her or Tilly.

Tilly giggled and clasped her hands together, only just containing her glee to be the first to impart this delicious tattle. "Well, it started in April. A man—a nob every'un thinks—won Tiny Titus's 'ell from 'im, and every'un got ready fer a big change, but not really a change, ye ken?" Tilly winked. "There ain't really no way to change a 'ell. Fancy or foul, they be what they are beneath the surface and behind closed doors."

Isabel could only suppose that was the sordid truth of the matter.

"Anyway, ye know what 'e did?" Tilly paused half a heartbeat. "'E shut the place down. 'Ad all the tables, beds, and furniture 'auled off. Place is nuthin' but bare bones. Then, ye know what 'e did next?"

Isabel couldn't help it, she wanted to know. "What?"

"A fortnight later, 'e did it again with another 'ell."

"*Again?* How is that possible? Wasn't he recognized?"

"Not 'til it were too late, 'e wadn't. 'E's got people thinkin' 'e's a European lord, or sumpthin'."

"That seems a smidge far-fetched." Someone had to insert a bit of logic into this conversation.

Tilly had no use for Isabel's stab at reason. "'Cause 'e's bin real quiet the last month. People are thinkin' 'e went back to one of them countries o'er there." Tilly waved her arm in the general direction of nowhere. "I always did 'ope 'e would show up at Number 9 and sweep me off me feet one night. But 'e don't go fer them fancy 'ells, only the ones like where I got me start in St. Giles."

"*Got your start?*" Isabel asked, a mite breathless. Her gut seemed to have fallen to her feet.

"Oh, yeah, when I was fourteen."

Nausea stirred inside Isabel at the very idea.

A dreamy light entered Tilly's eye. "But could ye just imagine if 'e did? Rumor 'as it 'e's 'andsomer than the devil 'imself."

A throat cleared, and Isabel half turned to meet the

chambermaid's gaze, eyes wide as saucers. Her ears had picked up everything. *Dios mío.*

"Will that be all, milady?" the girl asked in a small voice.

Isabel nodded. The girl dipped in a shallow curtsy and began to leave when she stopped abruptly. "Lawks! I almost forgot. These are for you."

She dug two missives from her apron pockets and extended them toward Tilly, who took them with another amused snort. "Guess these toffs don't do nothin' fer themselves."

The maid curtsied again and rushed from the room.

"Tilly, if this is going to succeed," Isabel spoke in a low voice that wouldn't carry, "you'll need to mind your tongue."

Tilly's eyes rolled toward the ceiling. "If ye say so."

Isabel broke the seal on the first note and scanned its contents.

You have a terrible megrim. It will keep you confined to the quiet of Rosebud Cottage for the duration of your stay. I shall make your apologies for you.
—P

She should have expected this, yet it rubbed her fur the wrong direction. She'd never been treated as someone to be ashamed of.

"What's it say?" Tilly asked.

Isabel folded the note. "My head aches."

"Ye seem fine to me."

Isabel opened the second missive, and her heart did a little flip when she read the signature.

Our dear Isabel,
Do consider joining the family in the breakfast room as it would give us great pleasure to welcome you to the family.

—*Lucretia, Duchess of Arundel*
Postscript: It is my understanding that you have a megrim.
As a frequent sufferer of the condition myself, I've devised a
remedy that offers great relief. Cook will have a batch
awaiting your arrival.

Isabel's hands fell to her lap. The note fluttered to the floor, which Tilly immediately retrieved, squinting at contents she surely couldn't read. "What's this 'un say?"

"Her Grace has invited me to break my fast with the family."

"Lawks be, don't know 'bout that. Bet she got a good spread goin', though."

"I shall go," Isabel said in sudden decision.

Even as part of her quaked at the very thought of joining a duke's family for breakfast, another part of her rose to the idea of tweaking Lord Percival's nose out of joint, *if* such a devastating man's nose could, indeed, be tweaked askew.

"Well, if ye're insistin', then ye'll be wantin' to look yer tidy best fer Lady Exeter."

"*Lady Exeter?*"

"She would be yer sister by law, if ye were well an' truly 'itched to Lord Percival."

"Who told you this?"

"Well, the chambermaid 'oo was 'ere? 'Er name is Jane, and she let me in on the runnin's o' this place when she delivered some food to yer sister and 'er servant."

"Nell isn't our servant," Isabel said before adding, "Not exactly."

"Well, then what is she?"

"It's a complicated situation." Wasn't everything these days?

"About yer sister," Tilly began and shifted on her

feet. It was the first time Isabel had seen the girl discomfited. "She don't say much, does she?"

"No."

"Is it all right to say she scares me a mite?"

Isabel nodded, desperate to change the subject. "About Lady Exeter?"

"She's the 'oitiest an' toitiest of 'em all."

It occurred to Isabel that she'd jumped from the frying pan directly into the fire. "Then do your best, Tilly."

She wouldn't enter that breakfast room looking a fright. She did have her pride, even if it had suffered a bruising in recent months.

Tilly's nimble fingers plaited and coiled Isabel's hair into a simple chignon at the base of her neck, leaving a few artful tendrils to fall in loose waves about her face. The girl bent down to admire her handiwork in the mirror alongside Isabel. "They'll not find a 'air out 'o place."

"You're a magician, Tilly."

Tilly should have been a proper lady's maid, instead of—well, instead of what she'd become. How had the girl ended up in that life?

Oh, any number of ways, Isabel had recently learned.

Tilly found a small pot of rouge inside a drawer. She pried open its lid and dabbed her pinky inside. "Now fer a few touches o' color."

"No rouge," Isabel said, firm. She was to be a lady.

Tilly gave a little shrug and set the pot aside. "I ain't sure ye need it with yer pretty, dark complexion. What did ye call it the other day?"

"Olive."

"Kin I ask ye 'bout sumpthin' I noticed?"

"Ask away." Isabel couldn't help but warm to Tilly. The girl had a welcome honesty to her.

"What's yer accent? I ain't 'eard one like it in all me sixteen years."

Sixteen years? Oh, life wasn't fair, and that was a fact. With her pleasantly rounded figure and light brown hair streaked with the gold of girlhood not quite gone, Tilly was just the sort of girl places like Number 9 consumed whole on a nightly basis.

"Spanish," Isabel offered around the lump that had become a permanent fixture in her throat.

"Ye're from Spain?" Tilly's mouth had fallen open.

Isabel nodded.

"Lawks be, ye're an exotic one."

Exotic. Isabel nodded tightly. She didn't care to be described with that word. She could never be certain it was a compliment.

Isabel's mind ran through the events of past, present, and future, namely last night, this moment, and her impending introduction to Lord Percival's family. The part of her that trembled at the strange reality of this situation stilled. There was, in fact, a—*slightly*—reassuring angle from which to view this calamity. It was presently keeping her, Eva, Ariel, Tilly, and Nell *safe*. She would go to any lengths to ensure they stayed that way, even if it meant deceiving a family of 'oity-toity aristocrats.

She gave each cheek a pinch, and this time when she met her own gaze in the mirror, she detected steel. "I don't suppose the informative Jane gave you the direction to the breakfast room?"

ISABEL CRACKED THE HEAVY, oaken door wide enough for her to squeak through and found herself slipping into the spell cast by this magical house and garden, just as she had five hours ago when Lord Percival had rushed them through. How was it possible she'd arrived such a short time ago?

Seemed a lifetime.

With its steep-pitched, thatched roof and wattle-and-daub walls, Rosebud Cottage screamed its English charm louder than any house she'd ever encountered. If the manor house was the fairy-tale castle, this was its cottage counterpart.

When a decidedly taciturn Lord Percival had pushed open the front door and she'd crossed its threshold, bleary-eyed and weary to the bone, Isabel had half-expected to happen upon an evil witch waiting to bake them in her oven. Instead, she'd found a cozy fire burning tamely in the fireplace and no witch in sight. All the tension had fallen from her body in that instant. Here was a safe haven.

For the moment.

As she followed Jane's direction to the manor house, Isabel allowed the feeling of safety to prevail as the trees gently swayed above her head, the birds trilled their songs in happy competition, and verdant leaves soughed in the breeze, a few fluttering to the ground in lazy arabesques.

One didn't get a moment like this in London.

London was all hustle and bustle with the energy and cacophony of a million lives getting on with their days. A different energy called out to her here, an energy content with itself, yet another reminder of her homeland. Not the verdancy, for summer's effect on Spain was the opposite. Its interior was a hot, brown terrain and possessed of a different beauty, rugged and rough.

It was this gentle easing into a day that took Isabel to her homeland, a life lived at a slower, gentler pace. Sometimes she missed it so much it was a physical ache in her body. She shook the thought loose. She couldn't think about Spain and maintain the single-mindedness she needed to survive breakfast with Lord Percival's family.

She emerged from the magical woods into the wide, open expanse of a formal garden, the hedges and flowers low and orderly. It was lovely and tame and lacked the magic of the wooded copse. She would never understand mankind's desire to assert its calculated dominance over wild and free nature.

Of a sudden, a yelling, laughing, shouting horde of boys screamed in from her left. She barely had time to scramble out of their way as they barreled past, not giving her a second glance as they disappeared into the woods, jeers and taunts trailing in their wake.

Where on earth had they come from? How many of them had there been? Four? Five? And who was the recipient of their teasing?

That instant, the latter question was answered in the form of a boy with no more than five years on him, red-faced and howling hot tears as he struggled to catch up to the boys. Poor *niñito*. It was tough being the littlest brother.

Isabel stayed the path. With every step, Gardencourt's manor house asserted its dominance over the landscape, while her sense of unreality faded and her logical mind had trouble keeping pace with her increasingly jittery stomach. With its towers, turrets, and crenellations that called to mind the pompous castles of Spain, it was the sort of house that wouldn't be denied respect and obeisance. And this imposing structure was the minor house of a duke, one in a dozen, undoubtedly. That sentence made little sense to Isabel, but it was true.

She ascended wide stone steps set into the side of a short hill rise and found herself standing on a terrace that extended all the way to the house. Detecting a slight crack in the set of French doors, she pointed her feet in that direction. They went heavy with dread, even as her stomach implored her to hurry it up. The scent of breakfast meats and coffee wafted on a light wind gust, and her stomach growled its approval.

Then her ears caught it: the dueling clinks of cutlery against porcelain and the low murmuring of several conversations happening at once. The family were beyond those doors, breaking their fast together.

And she was to join them.

It was all she could do not to turn back, but her stomach refused to consider the possibility.

"And the other hell was called," came a drift of conversation, "*Pizzy's Pleasure Palace*," the voice finished on a girlish giggle.

"Lucy!"

"Who is this character?"

"They're calling him the Savior of St. Giles."

"Some exaggerated fiction, to be sure."

That last voice, Isabel knew. *Lord Percival.*

Of course, he would be here. This was his family, after all.

Isabel steeled her nerves and pushed the door open the thinnest sliver possible for her to slip through. She averted her eyes in the desperate hope that she could sneak in unnoticed. All hope was dashed the instant the room went silent.

By painful increments, her gaze lifted. A quick scan yielded eight—*eight!*—sets of eyes fixed on her with varying degrees of interest, or disinterest as it was in some cases. Her tongue tied into a knot in her mouth, and her stomach filled the otherwise silent void with a long grumble that contained the scope and sweep of a German opera. She could melt into the floor.

"The poor darling," said one lady of advanced years

as she fidgeted with a set of gold bangles. She could only be the duchess.

Another lady's platinum blonde eyebrows shot toward the ceiling, equal parts dismay and disdain shining in her glacial blue eyes. She could be none other than the *'oity toity* Lady Exeter.

The discreet clearing of a throat drew Isabel's eye. There sat her pretend husband, cup of black coffee before him, dressed in gentleman's day attire—forest green jacket, loosely tied cravat, presumably buff trousers beneath the table—and studying her as if ice wouldn't melt in his mouth.

Isabel clenched her hands into fists to stay their trembling. About her heart that threatened to hammer its way out of her chest? Well, she couldn't control that.

Tall, dark, aristocratic...handsome.

She'd left that last word out of her description last night.

Lord Percival already knew he was handsome. A man didn't stride through life with his assuredness without knowing it and using it to his advantage. The scar along his right cheekbone only enhanced his dangerous, male beauty.

Again, the word for him came to her—*devastating.*

Not a single remnant of the last twelve hours hung about him, except for the faint bruise below his left eye.

Well, that wasn't precisely true.

She was a remnant of the previous night still hanging about him.

"So," cut in a young voice, the same that had delighted in imparting tattle about the Savior of St. Giles to the room. Isabel met the gaze of a blonde-haired girl of middle teen years whose dark brown eyes were regarding her with equal parts curiosity and hostility. "You're my new step-mama?"

7

"Lucy," Percy heard himself say, a warning in his tone that both surprised and unnerved him.

Lucy's gaze flashed to meet his, rebellion glinting in her eyes. She'd heard *it*, too, a distinct *fatherliness*. And she wasn't having it.

Every Thursday at one o'clock sharp, Percy arrived at the Cleveland Row mansion where Lucy lived for the fifteen minute, weekly call to which she'd consented. A footman would escort him into a formal drawing room —the one used for guests, not family—where he would find Lucy curled up in a blue damask Queen Anne chair, face buried in a book. He would sit on the sofa opposite her and let her direct their conversation.

Well, *conversation* might be a stretch. Every visit she poured them each a cup of tea, opened her book to a dog-eared page, and proceeded to read for the re-maining fourteen minutes of his call.

He simply sat across from her and marveled at this girl of thirteen years who was his daughter.

Isabel cleared her throat. "Our, um, wedding hap-pened so suddenly—in an instant, really." Her eye met his in an anxious flash. "Your father has spoken so

highly of you that I look forward to furthering our acquaintance."

Rather well done of Isabel, Percy could admit. The
woman had nerve.

All eyes at the table swung back to Lucy, as if they
were observing a tennis match. On her end, Lucy was
giving Isabel a glare equal parts appraising and dismissive, as only a girl of teen years could. Percy knew the
look well for he'd been its recipient on every occasion
he'd met with her. She was a force, a fury, a wonder, his
daughter, and how he wanted to know her better.

From his place at the far end of the table, the duke
peered over his second newspaper. The man read three
a day. Besides Percy, he was the only one not staring at
Isabel like she was a circus curiosity. "My dear, serve
yourself from the buffet. Then we shall endeavor to put
on our best behavior and introduce ourselves." He directed a pointed gaze toward Lucy. "Like the *polite*
family we surely are."

Lucy stared down at her plate and stabbed a sausage
with a single, sharp thrust, twin patches of scarlet on
her cheeks. Percy, too, felt strangely chastened. His father had always been good at that, at being a father.
Percy, on the other hand, knew nothing about it. He felt
the compulsion, but not the right. He hadn't yet
earned it.

Isabel skirted the edge of the room as she made her
way toward the sideboard stocked with all manner of
breakfast foods. Percy took a moment to observe his
wife.

She wore the same plain blue dress from last night.
When one looked closely, however, one noticed its cut
was sharp and precise, its lines clean. This was no
slovenly homespun dress. It had a bit of dash, even if
the cloth was a wool on the cheaper end of the spec-
trum. That sturdy wool set her apart from the other

women at table, who were clad in delicate muslins and fine silks.

During his years on the Continent, Percy had been careful to remark these seemingly small details about a person for, in fact, they weren't small at all. They told a person's story without them having to open their mouth, which was useful in a line of work where people held their secrets close. What secrets did this woman hold?

Why had she been in Number 9 last night?

If she would just tell him, it would make his life a sight easier. Certainly, she had her reasons, but in the end, he would uncover them all.

It was what he did.

At last, she settled onto the chair to Percy's left, the one the duchess had insisted on saving for his bride, even after he had protested the necessity since his *bride* suffered from debilitating megrims on a daily basis and therefore wouldn't be joining them for meals.

The duke met his gaze and lifted a single eyebrow. The time had arrived for Percy to introduce the newest addition to the family. He cleared his throat, and all eyes landed on him. They had been waiting.

"It is my great pleasure to introduce—" The next words stuck in his throat. He cleared it again to allow them passage. "Lady Percival."

The duke nodded approvingly and smiled. A measure of the room's tension dissipated. As head of the family, the duke's approval meant everyone must welcome her. "Lucretia," he began, addressing his own recent bride, the former Dowager Duchess of Dalrymple, "is it too early for a celebratory round of champagne?"

"Is it ever?" replied the formidable woman. Percy had always rather liked her.

While the duchess made the necessary arrangements with the servants, everyone at the table returned to their own private conversations. Everyone, except Isabel, who had tucked into her breakfast, bite by relentless bite, with an unexpected gusto. She was eating like a woman famished. Percy experienced a twinge of guilt. He'd expected her to have partaken of the breakfast he'd arranged to have delivered to Rosebud Cottage.

The way each bite crossed her lips, as if appreciated, thoroughly, down to its last scrumptious molecule, produced a discomfort inside Percy. He wasn't sure he'd ever seen a woman enjoy food, or frankly anything, the way this woman was savoring that slice of venison. He glanced at his usual bowl of oat porridge and cup of black coffee, both half empty, and couldn't muster the same enthusiasm.

In truth, the way this woman ate was decidedly sensual. His mouth went dry, and an unbidden thought crept in. Was this how she enjoyed *everything*, unreservedly and with utter abandon?

A side of himself sparked to life at the question. It was a side that experienced pleasure without reserve. He and she were similar in this way, except she didn't try to control it, and, oh, how that attracted him more than even her matchless beauty. This insight that she, too, possessed a touch of wickedness had his body responding, if his half-full cock was any indicator.

Her mouth stopped moving, mid-chew, and she went utterly still. Slowly, her head turned until she faced him. "What?" she asked, the question muffled by the currant bun she'd just inserted into her mouth.

A laugh—his first genuine one in years, it felt like—startled from him, loud enough to draw a few eyes. Before he could reply, servants began setting flutes of champagne on the table, even in front of Lucy and Miss Radclyffe. Again, protective fatherly concern surged, which he instantly suppressed.

Actually, not everyone had champagne placed in front of them. Before Isabel sat a glass full to the brim with a dense brown liquid that surely should be bubbling and giving off a noxious plume of smoke.

"My dear," began the duchess, "I promised you Cook's special megrim cure, and here you have it. You must finish it entirely and not neglect the bits and pieces that tend to settle on the bottom."

All eyes—ranging from those of an indifferent Lady Exeter to a horror-struck Lucy—swung toward Isabel, who smiled bravely. Beneath the duchess's watchful eye, Isabel's fingers wrapped around the glass. As she brought the concoction to her mouth, she darted a fearful glance toward Percy. Guilt pinged through him since his lie was directly responsible for getting her into this situation. But there was no escape, not while the duchess watched.

Isabel squeezed her eyes shut and began to drink, suspense building as she took one resigned gulp after another until she'd drained the contents to the last drop. She set the glass down and swallowed back what was surely a roil of nausea. A beat later, the room's collective breath released. Percy caught wonder in more than one set of eyes.

Isabel's empty glass was replaced with one bubbly with champagne, rather than eye of newt or whatever substance that had been in that glass. One could only admire the woman's aplomb.

Discreetly, he pushed his water glass toward her. She shot him a grateful glance. Was it so surprising that he contained a morsel of decency?

The duke lifted his glass. "To the newest member of the family. To Isabel!"

In unison, a few *hear hear*'s scattered around the table, glasses raised, and contents tossed back. For all intents and purposes, Isabel, the Spanish dressmaker-cum-strumpet—or was it the other way around? Or something altogether different?—was a Bretagne. *Blast.*

By order of precedence, introductions went around the table.

"Enchanted," emerged from his older brother Michael, Marquess of Exeter and heir to the dukedom, who hadn't bothered glancing up from his newspaper. Michael always had been a pompous ass. Even though their relationship was a complete sham, Percy felt the sting of insult on behalf of Isabel, on principle.

Next came Susan, Lady Exeter. "How delightful to have a new sister." Her tone and countenance matched her husband's in aloofness. "And one with such a delightfully healthy appetite," she added, clearly not delighted at all.

"Charmed." This from Michael and Susan's eldest son Hugh, Earl of Avendon and second in line to the dukedom. In appearance, he was the perfect synthesis of his parents' features, with his mother's blonde coloring and his father's amber eyes. In personality, too, was he a chip off his parents' block, supercilious and self-sure to the point of insult.

"If I am to understand the timeline of courtship to marriage," Lucy began when it became her turn, "then I believe my step-mama and I are old acquaintances by now."

Impudent girl.

"I'm Miss Radclyffe and am most pleased to make your acquaintance," said Miss Radclyffe, Lucy's stepsister, bosom friend, and apparently possessor of the best etiquette in the room. Contrary to the message their refinement sent the masses, aristocrats weren't a particularly well-mannered lot.

Isabel's stomach emitted a monstrous grumble into the quiet that followed. Percy detected a brightening of her cheeks. "Eat," he murmured. The woman had an appetite.

She lifted a forkful of food to her mouth and took a bite. Her eyes closed in momentary bliss as she chewed and swallowed, her throat undulating gracefully with the act.

Yet again, his mouth went dry, and his cock stirred.

Her eyes opened and met his.

Percy reached for his coffee, tamping down a physical reaction both unexpected and disconcerting.

Surprisingly, it was Lady Exeter who spoke next. "And who are your family, Lady Percival?"

Isabel's mouth stopped. A beat of time passed, and she swallowed. "My sister and I operate a dressmaking shop in Cheapside."

Stunned silence filled the room. Lady Exeter's head canted to the side, and a mean, little smile tipped at the tight corners of her mouth. "But *who* are you?"

Isabel carefully placed her fork and knife down. She drew herself up, regally, fire in her eyes. "I am the Señorita Isabel Galante, daughter of Don Ariel Galante, *un hidalgo de privilegio*."

Blankness met her statement.

"Her father is a Spanish lord," Percy supplied.

A few *oh*'s sounded around the table, and Lady Exeter's concern dissipated into indifference in an instant. Percy, however, sat shocked to the soles of his feet. *Hidalgo de privilegio* was a title that only the king of Spain could confer onto one of his subjects. Percy considered the possibility that Isabel could be lying. But, no, he didn't think so.

In fact, it explained a few matters that hadn't added up. The refinement of her speech. The elegance of her comportment. The grace of the curtsy she'd given the duke.

Who was this woman, indeed?

"Now, Isabel," the duchess intoned from her end of the table, "since we're only family here, you simply must tell us the story of you and Percy."

Again, the room's ears perked up.

"Oh, yes, you simply *must*." Lucy sat with her chin propped on her hands, eyes wide and innocent and anything but.

"Oh, yes, of course," Isabel floundered. "It's, um, it's quite a lively tale."

Percy should cut in and help her concoct a story, one the people sitting at this table would believe—he really should—but he decided to wait. He wanted to see what stuff this woman was made of.

Lips trembly with a nervous smile, she delicately cleared her throat. She'd opened her mouth to begin the tale of their precipitous journey to true love and, instead, inhaled a shocked gasp, all the color draining from her face. Her mouth snapped shut, and her gaze fixed on a point in the distance.

Alarmed, Percy located the object of her distress. Every muscle in his body coiled with tension, and a thin sheen of cold sweat broke across his skin. There, strolling through the doorway and making their way toward the buffet, were Lord Bertrand Montfort and his wife, Lady Bertrand, the pair known affectionately by most as jolly Uncle Bertie, a man whose very presence took up all the space in a room, not due to the considerable height and girth of his body, but by dint of his forcible personality, and flighty Aunt Dot, with her signature puff of frizzy white hair vibrating about her head.

Percy's heart thundered in his chest, and raw anger churned in his gut, each reaction beyond his control. Years ago, he'd vowed never to share a room with Bertrand Montfort again, for he couldn't trust himself to hold his rage at bay and not do the man bodily harm.

Yet Percy understood how the man had come to be here, for Society connections and familial relations ran deep and wide in the *haut ton*. Not only was Montfort the uncle of Olivia, therefore great-uncle of Lucy, his wife, Lady Bertrand, was the bosom friend of the duchess.

How well-regarded was Montfort as he spoke his good-morning's to the table—Percy's father's table, the table of a good man. It sickened Percy to his bones. His hands curled into fists at his sides, the resolve to expose this man for the fraud he was and see him disgraced, redoubled.

Some knew of Montfort's diplomatic connections, others of his Whitehall network. But few knew him for the spider he was. It was only after one became en-snared in his web that one understood, and by then it was too late.

At Percy's side, Isabel had the look of a woman whose house had been shaken to its foundations as she tracked Montfort with her eyes. He settled into the seat directly opposite her. "Now, what is this I hear about a new addition to the family?"

The question emerged all hale and hearty, jolly old England. No one could out-charm Montfort when he set his mind to it, which was, of course, half the reason he'd been such an effective operator for Whitehall over the years. The other half being his utter, dogged ruth-lessness.

"You must meet my new step-mama, Aunt Dot," Lucy said.

"Oh, dear," Aunt Dot gasped, reaching for her silk fan. Known for her delicate constitution, the woman kept it on her person at all times.

"Oh, dear, indeed," Lucy continued. "She was just about to regale us with the tale of how she and Lord

Percival met, fell madly in love, and married in the same instant."

"Oh, dearest dear," Aunt Dot breathed. Her fan flapped open as Isabel's fork clattered to her plate.

Percy well understood the cause of Isabel's distress. She'd mucked up Montfort's plans for the Earl of Pembroke last night. Percy knew from experience that Montfort didn't suffer mistakes lightly. Isabel was in trouble. But was she in imminent danger?

A territorial instinct flared inside Percy. Isabel was under his protection. If Montfort thought to cause harm to Isabel here, he would have to go through Percy first.

Isabel's chair gave a sudden scrape as she pushed away from the table. She shot to a stand and seemed to waver, as if her knees were composed of jelly. "It was lovely to make the acquaintance of my, um, husband's family, but my megrim has returned, and I must lie down."

"Of course, my dear," said the duke, his keen eye surely taking in the events of the last few minutes and drawing his own conclusions. Father missed nothing.

The duchess's eyebrows drew together in consternation. "Cook's remedy always does the trick. Fear not, I shall blend a fresh batch myself, and add an extra clove of garlic." With that, she made her imperious way out of the room.

Percy wasn't sure if he felt more sympathy for Isabel, who might have to consume yet another round of the concoction, or for Cook, who was yet blissfully unaware of the storm heading her way.

For her part, Isabel had cleared half the room, evidently set on fleeing it altogether. Percy rose to follow. She wasn't getting away that easily. "If you'll pardon me, I'll see to my—" The next word caught in his mouth. *Wife.*

"Actually, Percy." The duke came to his feet. "If Isabel can spare you, would you mind making a short detour with me to the stables?" It wasn't a question. "A certain old girl could do with a moment of your time."

"Not Lady Daisy?" Percy asked. The mare had to be...four and twenty. Could that possibly be true? "It would be my pleasure, Father." A safe pleasure that could be permitted.

As he and the duke walked to the stable, Percy's mind couldn't help but wander. All morning, he'd been chafing at the fact that Hortense was in London, investigating and doing all the intricate, most times dirty, work that he found so invigorating. Then, in the wink of an eye, fortune had smiled upon him, and the dirty work had seated himself directly across the table.

London, it seemed, had found Percy.

8

Isabel wouldn't run.

She would, however, walk very, very swiftly. Mayhap she would be fast enough to outpace the panic dogging her every step.

Montfort was here...*here* at Gardencourt Manor.

How had he tracked her down so quickly?

Except...had he?

There had been a flicker in his eye the instant it fell on her. Could it have been surprise? After all, he'd entered the room with his wife. Was it possible he was a guest of the duke, and this was all bad luck, the only luck she'd known these last two years? Was it possible he hadn't known she was here?

Well, he did now.

And she'd thought herself safe.

It was only when she reached a solid wooden door at the end of a corridor—what long corridors dukes had—that she realized she'd fled the breakfast room through an exit different from the one she'd entered. She twisted its brass handle and pulled the door open, finding herself in unfamiliar surroundings, a tiny gem of a pond sitting complacently in the not-too-far distance.

Accompanied by her pounding heart and heaving breath, she dashed across springy, close-cropped turf toward the water. It occurred to her that she could hie herself to Rosebud Cottage, gather Eva, Ariel, Tilly, and Nell, and flee, yet again.

It wasn't too late…

Or was it?

She needed a moment, just one moment, to collect herself and a rational thought. This pond with its elegant willows draped over the water's edge and its quaint white pavilion on the far side was the perfect spot to amass enough rational thoughts to formulate a plan. A breeze lifted off the water, rippling the placid surface and permeating the wool of her dress. As the sheen of perspiration cooled across her skin, her eyes drifted shut with the pleasing sensation. At last, the space to think.

"Isabel Galante," she heard at her back.

Her fingernails dug into her palms. On the count of three, she pivoted and found Montfort approaching and wearing a smile, one that could be construed as paternal, if one didn't know better. Unfortunately, she did.

"Or should I call you Lady Percival and offer my congratulations?"

Isabel's mouth pressed into a firm line, and her jaw clenched. She was unable to trust herself to speak. Not that he expected her to. Not when he was toying with her.

"My dear, you do look peaked, but if ever a view could cure a megrim, it would be this one." He knew her excuse to leave the breakfast room had been a lie. "You know," he continued conversationally, "I doubt there's a single fish in there."

Dios mío. Her heart was thundering in her chest and her future flashing before her eyes, and he was talking about a pond? "Then what is its use?" she asked, irritation bleeding into her tone. She wished he'd get to it—whatever *it* he had planned.

"Funny you should ask," he replied. Somehow, she'd asked the exact question he wanted to answer. "You're rather like an ornamental pond."

Isabel blinked. How did one react to such an outlandish comparison? "Your logic may be too advanced for my feeble brain."

"Only that there is great value in pure ornamentation. Beauty can distract."

Was he saying she was of no more value than her face?

"With your beauty," Montfort went on, "you could have married some sort of landed gentry or a widowed lord. It's even possible a brash lordling would have overlooked your rather unfortunate lineage. After all, you don't look like one of them."

Isabel's stomach flipped, and annoyance shifted into a rising anger. "One of who?" She knew exactly *who*, but she wanted him to speak it plainly, so she could hate him more.

Montfort flicked a dismissive wrist. "Your people."

She resisted the impulse to touch Mama's pendant, the hamsa, a symbol of their people that was said to ward off the evil eye. If only it could work its power on one evil man.

"Your mother and father took their responsibility of protecting you from your heritage seriously. It was quite well done of them. I see no evidence that it infects your relationships out in the world. You don't speak the language, do you?"

Isabel wished she could throw offensive Hebrew syllables at this man. But their parents had refused to teach either her or Eva.

Montfort jutted his chin toward the manor house. "I

doubt anyone in that room suspects." His gaze narrowed, penetrating. "It won't serve you to take my words hard, Isabel. I'm simply stating the truth of the world in which we live. Eva understands it."

Anger turned to acid in Isabel's stomach. "Do not speak to me of Eva."

"Now, now, no need for all that." He'd become all paternal placation. "She came with me by choice, as did you."

"And the laudanum you gave her?" Isabel spat. The question had wrung her insides to rags for too many months.

"Provided by a most reputable physician—"

"A physician provided by whom?"

"—For her nerves."

"Nonsense," Isabel said, unable not to. She understood precisely why Montfort had encouraged Eva's dependence on laudanum. To ensure her compliancy. "Eva has nerves of steel." *Had*, Isabel silently amended. Eva had returned to her six months ago a shell of the woman she'd once been.

"It was her choice."

And what of her babe? Isabel didn't ask. She swung around, no longer able to lay eyes on Montfort. What choice had Ariel?

She shuddered at the memory of him as a newborn, struggling and shivering, squirming in pain that wouldn't resolve, causing him to cry when awake and be fitful when asleep. Its cause was the laudanum, the midwife had said. She'd seen it before.

"*Laudanum?*" Isabel had asked the woman, confused.

"Aye."

"But she needs it. She trembles without it."

"I'm tellin' ye what I've observed these last thirty years of midwifin'. And babes born to mums 'oo take it, come out like this, all shaky and mis'rable, poor mite.

Two more things I'll tell ye fer free: git ye a wet nurse and stop givin' yer sister that rubbish."

Montfort drew abreast with Isabel, and they stared out in parallel at the pond. "Speaking of dear Eva, where is she while you're off gallivanting about the countryside and marrying the younger sons of dukes?"

It hadn't occurred to Isabel that Montfort wouldn't know Eva was here. He seemed to know all. But not this. Well, she wouldn't be the one to tell him.

Neither would she tell Eva that Montfort was here. She didn't know how her sister might react, but no good could come from it, *that* she knew with certainty.

"She's with the babe." It was the truth, if only a fraction of it. Isabel had never developed the knack for telling a convincing lie.

When Eva had returned to the shop, ripe with child, Isabel hadn't been able to contain the first question out of her mouth. "Who is the father?"

"A lord."

The answer had only encouraged another question, one whose answer Isabel had anticipated with dread. "Not Montfort?"

"Not Montfort," Eva replied, flat and hollow. "Ariel's father is French."

Just now, Montfort held out his arm. "Will you join me for a turn about the grounds?"

Although the question was phrased like an invitation, it wasn't. It was a command, and Isabel must obey. She touched her sweat-sheened palm to the navy superfine of his morning jacket, no more than the lightest application of pressure. Still, revulsion seized her as she caught his sweetish, musky scent.

Once they'd settled into their stroll, he began, "Would it be too forward for me to ask just what the hellfire happened last night?" His visage had transformed from jolly avuncularity to dead seriousness.

"I—" Isabel wasn't sure she could speak around the knot in her throat. "I got the wrong man."

Montfort chuckled humorlessly. "You most certainly did."

"I followed the instructions to the letter." Isabel hated the defensive note in her voice. "But it was *he* who was at the table."

"Is that so?" Montfort's brow wrinkled. "And, pray tell, how did you discover your error?"

"When he won the last hand, he didn't ask to take me to—" Oh, what a thing to speak aloud. "*Bed.*"

"What did he ask for?"

"He asked…" Isabel wracked her brain for a morsel of information to feed this man who held the future of her family in the palm of his hand. "He asked for *the keys*," she finished as the memory came to her.

Montfort's eyes narrowed on her. Had he found significance in that last part? Isabel hadn't.

"What do you know about Lord Percival?"

"Nothing." Which wasn't precisely true. She knew he was inscrutable and ruthless and devastating and, oh yes, handsome.

"While he was away on the Peninsula—"

Isabel blinked. "The Peninsula? Spain?" That was how he'd known her accent. Most English, like Tilly, dismissed her as *exotic.*

Not Lord Percival.

Montfort's mouth widened into a smile that seemed to delight in her discomfort. "He was one of those lordlings who thought he would look Napoleon in the eye before putting a saber through his heart. You must remember the type during the war."

Isabel bit back a sneer of disdain. They'd all come to her country for a taste of war and adventure. She doubted they noticed the suffering around them. As far as those men were concerned, her country had been a stage set for the enactment of their glory.

And Lord Percival had been one of them.

Montfort continued smiling that spidery smile of his, and it occurred to Isabel that he could be playing her emotions and prejudices to his benefit. "Well done, Isabel."

"For what?" Was this a twisted joke? She'd done nothing but fail over the last twenty-four hours.

"You've hooked a bigger fish."

Isabel's heart thunked a hard beat in her chest. Those weren't the words she'd expected to hear. "Oh?"

"You don't know him?"

What was Montfort going on about? Somewhere along the way, this conversation had turned into a different one. "Only what I've told you."

Montfort gave her hand two firm pats. It was all she could do not to recoil. "New objective."

"What?" she asked, an expulsion of nerves in word form.

"You have stumbled into another chance at securing your dear Papa's freedom and paying your and Eva's debt to me."

From the moment Montfort had sauntered into the breakfast room, Isabel had prepared for the worst. He would explain that her failure meant that her family had used up its last chance. She, Eva, and Ariel would be transported back to Spain where they would face the consequences for the "crimes" of their father. They would lose the life of promise that they had been building with their dressmaking trade in London.

And Papa? He would continue to rot in a prison cell. How long could he survive it? He'd been there for nigh on two years.

But *new objective* meant there was...*hope*.

Even as Isabel tamped down that slippery emotion, she made a vow. She would do anything this man said.

Anything.

"Before we get carried away, a single question." Montfort spoke with the sort of indifference one had when discussing the weather. "Are you, by chance, still carrying around your maidenhead?"

All the breath left Isabel's lungs. Mortification streaked hot through her. How she wished she could slap his face. In a past life lived long ago, she would have been able to do so. But not in this life, the one she'd somehow become possessor of. In this life, she must endure such insulting questions.

"Or did your new *husband* divest you of it last night?"

"You know he's not my husband."

"But you still haven't answered my question."

Isabel's eye fixed, unseeing, on a distant building. "I am yet a virgin."

"Excellent." Satisfaction twisted off Montfort in waves. "Your directive from last night?"

Dread slithered through her. "Yes?"

Montfort chuckled. "Must I spell it out for you?"

Isabel remembered Lord Percival's hooded gaze that conveyed an impression of utter indifference to her physical person. "I'm not sure he's that sort of man."

Montfort's eyes narrowed on her. "You've noticed, have you?"

Isabel's eyebrows met. "Noticed what?"

"Lord Percival's proclivity toward self-denial."

Isabel opened her mouth and closed it. She had known the man for less than a day. How was that long enough to understand such a thing about another person?

Montfort continued on, indifferent to Isabel's lack of response. "The boy was always prone to extremes.

Mad as a march hare in his youth. Admittedly, a difficult man to get close to, but you, Isabel, might be the temptation that breaks through his resistance."

Isabel noticed the building they were walking toward. The stable. Into view cantered Lord Percival, exercising a horse in the paddock, all his attention focused on the animal below him. If he was devastating on two feet, he was gloriously so by horse. The way he sat his saddle was so natural, an at-oneness with the animal.

"I have no idea how to get close to such a man," she murmured.

Montfort snorted. "Oh, these things have a way of working themselves out."

Isabel simply couldn't imagine Montfort was correct. Still, if this was her chance, she would seize it and worry about the *how* later. "Tonight?"

"Eager, are we?" Montfort emitted another light chuckle that scraped Isabel's nerves raw. "Hold on to your maidenhead until I say. Understood?"

Isabel nodded, mortified. Her eye followed Lord Percival as he took the horse through its paces. She would seduce *that* man?

Incomprehensible.

If she'd ever encountered a man who was unseduceable, it was he. He was too hard, too calculating. She couldn't imagine anyone ever got anything over on Lord Percival.

But she would, she determined then and there.

She removed her hand from Montfort's arm and pivoted to face him. He would meet her eye when he answered her next question. "And then the debt will be paid? And Papa's freedom secured?"

"In truth," Montfort said, his cold eyes belying the warmth of his words, "that is all I've ever wanted from you and Eva."

Oh, how Isabel hated this man. How she wanted to snatch up Eva and Ariel and run. But she couldn't. For Eva, Ariel, and Papa, she would do whatever it took to secure their safety, even if the thought tugged a strange pang of guilt from her.

Whatever Montfort had planned for Lord Percival —beyond her role—she wasn't certain he deserved it.

She shook the thought loose and set it on the breeze. Lord Percival was nothing to her. *Nothing.*

Her family were *everything.* If she must be the key to a man's ruin to secure their safety and freedom, so be it. Besides, she wasn't convinced Lord Percival was all that good a man.

Across the fifty or so yards that separated them, Lord Percival's eye met hers for the flicker of a second. For that tick of time, everything froze inside Isabel. The intake of her breath. The beat of her heart. The functioning of her brain.

A figure leaning against the paddock fence pulled her attention. *The duke.* Clearly, it had been Montfort's intention to walk her to the stables, and to Lord Percival, all along. How very smooth he was at working situations to his advantage.

Before Isabel could reply or ask another question, the duke waved at them. Isabel gave a half-hearted wave back. Montfort called out, "She was absolutely bereft and missing her groom, so I've delivered her to you." He gave Isabel's hand a paternal pat, purely for show. "I am going up to Town and must bid you adieu for a few days, Arundel, but Lady Bertrand will stay to charm you in my absence." To Isabel, "I shall be interested to see what progress you've made when I return."

With that, Montfort pivoted neatly on one heel and strode away.

A chill traced through Isabel as she stood alone and observed the duke watching his son with pride. Oh, the way that man moved in the saddle with an ease so very opposite the tense Lord Percival she'd observed this past day. She suspected it was closer to the truth of the man than what he'd shown her. And it was—*oh*—so attractive.

How did she get close to this man?

A lightning bolt of inspiration hit her, and a feeling pooled deep in the pit of her belly, light and variable, anxious, too. This was the moment. She either tucked her tail between her legs and skulked away in defeat, or she stood her ground and began as she meant to go on. If she was to best this man, she must start now.

To the duke, she was his son's wife, *family*. She was Lady Percival, and Lord Percival would treat her as such, at least when they were in the company of others. She could use the duke's presence to her advantage.

"*Tender husband*," she called out. Oh, that was bold. "Could you teach me to ride?"

With every fiber of her being, she *anticipated* his riposte with hitched breath.

How much more alive the beat of her heart felt now than it had thirty seconds ago.

9

Percy had been trying to ignore Isabel's approach. He had several dozen questions to ask her—but not here.

Not in front of the duke.

However, her question made her impossible to ignore. "You don't ride?" He sounded like a popinjay who couldn't conceive of a world where people didn't know how to ride a horse.

Through the seriousness of her gaze glinted an amused light. Was she toying with him?

"Percy," began the duke, "you can't have a wife who doesn't ride. I hardly know how you would spend any time together." He turned to address Isabel. "You see, my dear, you won't find a better horseman in all of England. Percy was born to the saddle."

Isabel's lips tipped up ever so slightly. Ever so *wickedly*. "Lord Percival," she began, "is the sort of man who would be the best at *everything* he attempts."

"You couldn't put yourself in better hands," said the duke, ignoring the clear double entendre.

Isabel met Percy's eye. "I can't imagine anyone whose hands I'd rather put myself into."

Percy's eyebrows nearly lifted off his forehead, and the duke cleared his throat.

He couldn't say no—*that* Percy understood perfectly —not without alerting his father's suspicions.

And the woman with the knowing glint shining in her eyes and smirk pulling about her mouth knew it, too. She'd located the chink in his armor—that he didn't want his family to know he'd brought home a wife who wasn't really his wife—and decided to use it to her advantage. She'd changed the rules of the game. If he wasn't so annoyed, he might admire her for it.

He'd be damned if it didn't stir him.

"My hands are ever empty without you in them, *my love,*" he said, matching her sauciness note for note.

The spark of triumph in her eyes fizzled, and she shifted on her feet as if he'd thrown her physically off balance.

Again, the duke cleared his throat, this time pushing away from the paddock fence. "I shall leave you to your lesson." He took Isabel's hand and kissed it. "It's wonderful seeing you settle into the family." He directed one last parting reminder toward Percy. "Consider what we discussed. The time has arrived for us to make the transfer."

Percy watched his father stroll away with an added layer of guilt. Now that he was a settled married man, the duke wished to gift him Gardencourt Manor. Percy had always known it would be his. But that day had ever been somewhere in the hazy future, if he survived that long. Well, he'd managed to survive, and the day had arrived.

Last night was gaining a momentum of its own and barreling down his mountain of lies and sweeping everyone along with it. He met the eye of the woman who had somehow become his co-conspirator. He caught a flicker of nerves in there now that they were alone. *Good.*

"Lord Percival—" she began.

"We've shot past such formality, don't you think? Percy will do."

"*Percy*, if you would rather not—"

"Oh, you'll be learning to ride today. I don't welsh on my promises."

She'd lost her nerve and was offering him the opportunity to beg off. Why was he insisting on the lesson? Could it be because she now looked like she'd rather not?

Perhaps he would teach her to be careful what she asked for, she might get it.

"Meet me inside," he commanded as he gave a light squeeze of his knees. The gelding responded with a well-disciplined pivot and began trotting toward the interior of the stable. Immediately, Percy questioned his decision. He wasn't sure he could trust himself alone with Isabel. Something about her sparked parts of him alight that he'd rather starve in the cold dark.

He'd just dismounted and handed the reins over to a groom when he heard at his back, "This must be the most magnificent stable in the world."

Head tipped back, Isabel's eyes roved across the vaulted thirty-foot ceiling that hung high above their heads. "I don't think I could get my arms around those timbers," she said of the massive exposed support beams.

"They have a heavy slate roof to support," Percy supplied.

Her gaze met his. Emeralds had nothing on her eyes for jewel green. "Was this structure built at the same time as the manor house?"

Percy found himself warming to her interest. "The stables were built about a hundred years after Rosebud

Cottage when it was Gardencourt's main house. Horses began making their way to England from Marrakesh and Arabia, and a good many lords went horse mad with this new stock." He spread his arms wide. "And they had to build stables worthy of those splendid beasts."

"Was something wrong with English stock?"

"Not particularly, but if one wants to win a horse race, one's odds steeply improve if one's mount has Eastern blood."

"And Gardencourt owns such horses?"

Percy nodded. "When Oliver Cromwell was attempting to rid England of its aristocracy during the Great Rebellion, he and his Parliamentary soldiers sacked the royal studs at Eltham and Woodstock, but it was when he set his sights on Tutbury that the Council of State decided he'd gone too far."

"What was special about Tutbury?"

"It had assembled the best, and most important, stable of horses in England through breeding and acquisition. It would have decimated the future of English stock to break up. So it remained largely intact, save a handful that were shipped off to Ireland and another handful that landed in Sir Arthur Hazelrigg's stable, a man who just so happened to be good friends with a Duke of Arundel. On the sly, Gardencourt was gifted a Barb stallion named Paragon. That duke built a stable worthy of him and his issue, which is what you see around you."

"His issue?"

"Paragon lives on to this day in his successors, one of which you'll ride today."

Isabel's face lit up in genuine delight, and Percy's gut did a nifty, little flip. Upbraiding his traitorous insides, he pivoted on one heel. "Follow me," he tossed gruffly over his shoulder. Why had he given that woman a history of the Gardencourt stable?

He felt Isabel at his back as they made their way down the wide center aisle, stalls to either side, herringbone bricks below their boots, the hustle and bustle of a vibrant stable buzzing all around. A few of the bolder lads gave him deferential nods, while others kept their heads down, attentive to their work, as they took his measure from a distance.

"There are so many stalls and horses," she said to his back.

"Thirty stalls."

"And the horses, do you know them all?"

"I did." One couldn't miss the bitterness in his use of the past tense and all it implied. Soon, however, he would know every horse by name, lineage, and personality, just as he would the stable lads and grooms.

Gardencourt was where he belonged.

He took in a deep gulp of air, musky with the scents of earth, hay, and horse. All these years he hadn't allowed himself to consider, even once, how much he'd missed this place.

They reached the stall he sought. Isabel read the mare's name off a brass plaque. "Lady Daisy?"

"Father let me name her."

"*You* named her."

Percy couldn't help it. He smiled. "I was ten."

"That is quite simply"—her eyes glittered with surprise—"*sweet.*"

"I've known her since she was a newborn foal. I was a boy besotted." And she was the last of the stable he'd known before he'd sped off to the Continent on a wave of misguided glory-seeking. He would keep that last part to himself.

"How old is she?"

Percy's eyes screwed up to the ceiling. "Four and twenty."

Isabel's brow lifted. "My age."

Percy fell back to earth before he realized he'd left it. How easy it was to talk to this woman. *Too easy.* He'd just seen her strolling arm in arm with Montfort. It was time to swing this conversation in a more useful, less personal, direction. "Montfort is returning to London."

Lady Daisy extended her head over the gate, and Isabel stroked her velvety muzzle. "It seems so."

"Without *you.*"

Isabel darted him a quick glance, ripe with disbelief. "How would it look if Lord Bertrand Montfort absconded with your wife?"

She rather had a point. Percy tried a different tack. "You appeared to be having an amicable conversation."

"I can see how it would appear so."

He would do them both a favor and shoot straight to the point. "Does he know we are not married?"

"I wouldn't know."

A lie. Montfort *knew.*

It was time to address another matter. "Your father is a *hidalgo de privilegio.*"

Isabel nodded, her lips pressed tight together. Lady Daisy gave a soft whicker, sensing Isabel's distress.

"Correct me if I'm wrong, but isn't that a title that can only be given by the king?"

"It is."

"Would you care to elaborate?"

"Not particularly."

He decided now was the time to jolt the conversation with a quick left turn. "Is it that you and your family have fallen on hard times?" It happened to any number of women and girls, particularly immigrants.

Isabel's breath audibly caught in her throat. Tension twisted the air taut. Percy sensed an advantage and pressed it. "Montfort is holding something over you, isn't he?"

She flinched. He almost had her.

As the next question formed on his lips, a throat cleared behind him. "Lord Percival?"

Percy twisted around. It took a moment for his brain to register the man before him. "Stanhope?" Half a beat later, he was greeting the aged, but still spry, stable master and clapping his back.

"I'm just back from Tattersall's to get a look at that stallion everyone was goin' on about."

"Anything worthwhile?" Percy asked, marveling at how easily their conversation fell into place, as if they'd last spoken yesterday, instead of a decade ago.

Stanhope sucked his teeth. "Shoulda known better than to go to London for horseflesh." He gave Percy a quick onceover. "Turned yourself into a man while you were hieing about frog territory all those years. It's good to lay eyes on you, and that's no lie. Now, what are you and your lady needing?"

"A sidesaddle for Lady Daisy, unless she's already been exercised?"

"Ach, no, it would do the old girl some good. I'll saddle her myself."

Stanhope set to his task, and yet again Percy found himself alone with Isabel. Or as alone as one could be in the center of an active stable. He glanced up and found her watching him with interest.

"Stanhope was my childhood idol," Percy found himself explaining. "He'd ranked one slender notch below only the duke."

"Yours was a happy childhood."

Percy was rescued from having to address her observation when Stanhope called out, "She's ready, Lord Percival."

He only just restrained himself from telling Stanhope to address him as Percy. It didn't seem fitting for a good man such as Stanhope to defer to the likes of him as his superior. But Percy was soon to be the man's employer, and it wouldn't do. He was forever Lord Percival, as was right in the tiered world the English had constructed for themselves. "My thanks, Stanhope."

"Will that be all, sir?"

Percy nodded his dismissal, and Stanhope continued on with his day, calling out orders and instructions to his stable lads and grooms as he receded into the distance. Percy dug into his pocket and produced a handful of sugar cubes. Without thinking, he'd grabbed them on his way out of the breakfast room. He never entered a stable without a sweet for the horses.

He motioned for Isabel to come closer, deciding to let their interrupted conversation lie for now. It needed a little time to brew in his mind.

He held out his hand, palm up, sugar cubes glittering pure white. "Here, take a few. Let her get a sense of you."

Lady Daisy's head extended forward, eager for her sweet. Before Percy could tell her to hold the treat with a flat palm, Isabel had already done so with one hand. With the other, she was stroking Lady Daisy's velvety muzzle as she leaned in, uttering the soothing nonsense one spoke to one's horse. Except she wasn't muttering nonsense. She was speaking Spanish to Lady Daisy. *¿Cómoestás? Belleza. Dulce.*

Her fingers traced the star on Lady Daisy's forehead. "Is this how she came by her name?"

"I thought it looked exactly like a daisy."

"*Señora Margarita.*" Lady Daisy emitted a soft whicker at the Spanish version of her name.

Percy's suspicions were aroused. "For someone who hasn't spent any time with horses, you are quite at ease."

"Mm-hmm," was all Isabel gave him by way of reply.

The woman was beautiful and intelligent, but those traits weren't half as attractive as her natural communion with Lady Daisy. Horses understood people in a way people didn't, or couldn't, understand each other. And Lady Daisy understood, and liked, Isabel.

Percy snapped to. He shouldn't be thinking about this woman's attractiveness in any context. "Shall we conduct our lesson? I have a day to get on with," he added with an unnecessary churlishness.

After one last stroke of the snip on Lady Daisy's muzzle, Isabel stepped back. Percy led them to a large box stall where they would have ample room to practice mounting. While he moved to Lady Daisy's flank to check the girths and straps of the saddle, Isabel was again cooing in the horse's ear. He averted his gaze and kept to the task. He wouldn't dwell on how damned attractive it was. The woman was a temptation, and that was a fact.

There.

He'd identified a source of the tension between them. Now he should be able to control it. He only had to get through this mounting lesson.

Mounting lesson? Instantly, his mind conjured an image, one that didn't help his problem with temptation.

He cleared his throat with a gruff harrumph that startled both horse and woman. "When you are ready."

One parting stroke of Lady Daisy's mane, and Isabel met Percy at the horse's flank. He dove right into it. "I'll hold my hands out like so"—he laced his fingers together and extended them forward as he crouched to a squat—"and you step on and push off as I spring up, placing your right leg over the pommel and left foot on the footrest. Understand?"

"Like this?" She placed her boot in his hands and,

before he knew it, executed his instructions with a fluid grace that had him staring up at her, flabbergasted.

Either she was the most natural horsewoman the world had ever seen or…

His eyes narrowed. "No one gets it perfectly right their first time."

She stared down at him, enigmatic. "I would guess there is a first time for everything."

"And you've never mounted a horse before now?"

She shrugged, and he knew he'd been had. "Shall we go for a ride?"

The minx. What was her game? In answer to her question, he shook his head. "Not in the heat of the day. It might be too much for Lady. I thought we would be spending more time learning to mount, but it appears you're a prodigy." He grabbed a handful of oats to feed Lady Daisy when he heard the delicate clearing of a throat. Isabel stared down at him expectantly.

"Mayhap you could assist me in dismounting?"

Instant dread churned Percy's gut. "Of course."

He should have called for a groom. Or fetched the mounting block from the tack room. Instead, he found himself settling into position to help her down, arms extended up to receive her. The moment her hands pressed into his shoulders, and his fingers tightened about her waist, he knew he'd been wrong, wrong, wrong as the heat from her palm seeped through the thin layers of his linen shirt to find his skin, and he felt *it*, that spark of awareness, that flash of desire.

She tipped forward, trusting, as he steadied her down, her fingers clenching and digging into bunched muscle. Her toes touched the ground, and her body lightly brushed against his for what would have been a fleeting tick of time. Instead, he found his fingers clutching her tighter and pulling her into him. An action primal, instinctive, driven by his body's response to her.

She inhaled a gasp that held, and her eyes flew up to meet his. He read confusion there, but desire, too…The spark of awareness flared into a banked fire that only needed a whisper of oxygen to turn into white-hot flame.

Her responding desire was such oxygen.

Experience understood where this feeling would take him. It would consume him whole until nothing was left.

He'd spent years—*years*—erecting defenses against his natural tendency toward wickedness. He wouldn't allow it to win today.

His hands released their hold on her, and he took a step back. Her brow furrowed.

"I suggest you continue with the headache fiction to my family," he said, his voice nearly unrecognizable to his own ears. "It will make the next few days easier."

Isabel blinked, then squared her shoulders. The glint in her eye said she'd recovered herself. "And what sort of bride would that make me?"

"*Bride?*" Was the woman mad? "We're not married."

She jutted her thumb over her shoulder. "*They* don't know that."

Hot blood turned to ice in his veins. "Are you threatening me with exposure? I don't take well to threats."

Her mouth snapped shut and opened again. "No, I, um, simply meant that I might enjoy being a lady for a bit is all."

He searched her eyes and found no malevolence there. Could he trust her with his family? He could. He felt it. "Do as you like," he relented. "Now, if you will excuse me, *wife*, I have other matters to attend."

"How will you explain it to them?"

Instantly, he took her meaning. "When the time comes, say in a month or so, I shall tell them that in our rush to be wed we hadn't done the correct paperwork, and the marriage is invalid. You will have decided you were better rid of me and ran away with an Italian lord."

Her head canted to the side, assessing. "How easily the lie comes to you."

He felt himself flinch. "They expect no better of me. I'm the scapegrace of the family, haven't you heard?"

With that, he strode out of the stall and called for a groom to attend Lady Daisy. Clearly, Isabel could handle herself. His boots a sharp *click-clack* against her-ringbone bricks, he stalked to the opposite end of the stable and climbed up to the hay loft, his mind racing. He grabbed a pitchfork and began pitching hay in no particular direction. He needed the physical exertion.

It was that bloody mystifying woman.

When he'd first seen her strolling arm in arm with Montfort and noted their close proximity, it had been all he could do not to give in to the urge, protective and unexpected, to pull her bodily away from the man. It was those eyes of hers. They were clear and direct, yet within them Percy sensed a vulnerability that caught between the chinks of his armor.

A woman with that gaze shouldn't have dealings with Bertrand Montfort. First, he would exploit her. Then, he would crush her. And, lastly, he would discard her like rubbish once he'd finished with her.

Sometimes circumstance and bad luck bent people to its will and left them with no choice. Percy understood at a fundamental level how expert Montfort was at exploiting such circumstances to his benefit.

Coercion was at the root of Isabel's relationship with Montfort, Percy felt it in his bones. He needed to get close to her. He needed her to trust him.

There was but one problem: he wanted her.

He'd convinced himself that he could control and channel his true nature into an asset as the Savior of St. Giles. He'd been wrong.

Instead, it had gotten him last night and landed him Isabel. He should have known that his wickedness, once wakened, took on its own life. He should have known he couldn't control fire. And now he'd landed in it.

He tossed the pitchfork to the loft floorboards and made his way out of the stable. He needed to send a message to Hortense, informing her of his location and that plenty of intrigue was to be had here.

Then he would get himself down to the estate's beach for a dip in frigid water.

How many years had it been since he'd felt the intimate touch of a woman? He'd stopped counting. The Percy who would have pursued the promise of a woman's touch and acted on his desire had been locked up long ago, the key thrown away.

He wouldn't become that man again.

10

The library of Gardencourt Manor was a grand room.

Anchoring it was a single long wall lined from floor to ceiling with all manner of leather-bound books that swept down its entire length as myriad bibelots from around the world filled in the remaining space, including a standing globe and pianoforte near the exterior French doors.

But so, too, was the library a cozy room, a place where the family could enjoy a comfortable evening. If one sought conversation, a large central group of sofas and chairs invited convivial repartee beside the carved marble fireplace. If one sought solitude, a snug nook or two beckoned one to settle in and read silently in the far corners of the room. If music was what one was after, the pianoforte and the free-standing harp awaited one's musical fingers. If one wanted to sample the room's intellectual offerings, a long rectangular table with bench seating ran along the wall of books, encouraging one to spread out several volumes and dig into their contents.

It was the latter pursuit that was currently occupying the Misses Bretagne and Radclyffe. Instead of books, they appeared to be consulting no fewer than three maps in muted tones not meant for the rest of the library's occupants.

The duke, Lord Exeter, and Lord Avendon weren't quite so circumspect as they discussed politics in the warm tones that implied more disagreement than accord. In truth, Lord Avendon didn't appear fully committed to the conversation between his father and grandfather as he kept half an eye on the girls at the opposite end of the room.

It was clear the girls were devising a plan. Isabel had a feeling that Miss Bretagne—she didn't feel she had leave to call the girl Lucy—was ever in the midst of hatching a plan.

She called to mind the girl Eva had once been. An ache of guilt and grief passed through Isabel, as it always did when she thought about the Eva who had returned to her after her dealings with Montfort.

Miss Radclyffe, however, was an altogether different girl from Miss Bretagne, and it wasn't simply because of her good sense and interest in science. With her prominent cheekbones and pearl gray eyes that spoke of a mixed Asian ancestry, Miss Radclyffe was a girl most English would not merely call different, but would dismiss as *exotic*, that narrow sobriquet that so irked Isabel. She sensed a complex story behind Miss Radclyffe's parentage—after all, she was the daughter of a viscount —but it was one Isabel likely would never know.

So here Isabel sat quietly in the chair farthest from the fire Lady Bertrand had insisted upon this midsummer night. She did her stitchwork as the duchess and Lady Bertrand gossiped about this—*"That Lady Conyngham." A shake of the head. "Prinny is ever so dependent on her"*—and that scandal—*"Surely, you heard the name the gossip rags gave him?" A furtive left-to-right glance to ensure no youthful ears listened, then a whisper.* "Mr. Long Pole."

Lady Exeter had excused herself half an hour ago on the pretext of visiting her sons in the nursery.

It was with a mild sense of relief that Isabel worked the dusty old sampler that she'd discovered in her bedroom in Rosebud Cottage. The other women viewed her as quiet and retiring and, that word again, *exotic*, therefore slightly unknowable. As such, very little was required of her, so she was free to stitch and observe Lady Bertrand in her full flighty glory as she proceeded to expound on every topic that popped into her head. It must be exhausting, being the vessel of so many firm opinions and so much umbrage. Isabel understood why Lady Exeter had gone.

Still, one of their number had avoided the library entirely after the evening meal. *Lord Percival.* He was at the stables, she knew it, but she couldn't quite summon the nerve to seek him out.

Today's boldness seemed to have abandoned her after, well, *the moment.* A moment that refused to remain tethered to the far reaches of her mind.

And she knew why.

It was her lack of resistance.

When he'd tugged her forward, she'd melted into the movement.

Why?

She could make the argument that she'd only been pursuing her directive from Montfort, that her action had been calculated.

While a morsel of truth could be located in that idea, another truth couldn't be denied.

She'd swayed forward because she'd wanted to.

Because he was too magnetic to resist.

Because she knew the smell of him—crisp sandalwood—and now she wanted to know the taste of him, too.

Because his long fingers curling about her waist felt right, like they anchored her to something real and steady.

Because the intense light in his eyes burned for...

Her.

She had so many *becauses* to consider for *why* she'd swayed forward, and not a single one of them had anything to do with Lord Bertrand Montfort.

And when Lord Percival had stepped away and broken their contact, she'd wanted to cry out in frustration like a thwarted child. Then her logical side had come to her rescue and asked a necessary question.

What was she to him anyway?

A nothing. Well, a *something*. A pawn in a game.

She was failing at the second chance Montfort had given her, just as she'd failed at the first.

Tonight, at dinner, she had noticed one thing: Lord Percival ate like a Catholic monk. *Proclivity toward self-denial.* Those had been Montfort's words, and they appeared to be true.

The man ate vegetables, yes, but no sauce. No meat. No desserts. He didn't butter his roll. In fact, he didn't eat his roll. Never once had she observed him take a sip of his wine. Strangely, however, he gave the appearance of partaking. He stirred the creamy soups. He cut the slices of beef, even brought the rich fare to his mouth, but not *into* his mouth.

And no one noticed. Save her.

Lord Percival was a different sort of man, one who might be immune to all the pleasures in life. Except, today, when he'd tugged her forward, the look in his eye...

Well, *ravenous* might be the word for it.

And every time she thought it, an ache pooled deep

in her belly, and even lower, a feeling new and wondrous and frightening and *irresistible*.

A sharp gasp, followed by a startled *Oh!* pierced the air. Puffy halo of white hair quivering about her head in distress, Lady Bertrand sat staring wide-eyed at the far end of the room. Isabel followed her gaze and couldn't help gasping, too.

Framed by the open doorway stood Eva with a sleeping Ariel in her arms, clad in the simple black dress she wore when they worked in the shop. At least it wasn't her night-rail.

The Misses Bretagne and Radclyffe hardly lifted their eyes from their maps at the minor fuss, and the men extended little more than a cursory glance. Lord Michael gave Eva a second look—and a third. Eva tended to elicit that response from men with an eye for her fiery sort of beauty. Then he sank back into conversation with the duke and his son, clearly having decided the mysterious woman at the door was the province of the ladies.

The duchess must have had the same thought, for she stood. "Good evening, might I inquire who you are?"

Eva's eyes lit upon Isabel, and a smile transformed her face. "Sister!" She all but flew across the room and gathered Isabel into an effusive embrace. Or, at least, as much of an embrace as she could muster with one arm, the other cradling a sleeping Ariel.

Isabel was slow to respond to her sister's enthusiasm. They'd seen each other not three hours ago after having spent the afternoon together. What exactly was Eva playing at?

"There's a sister?" Lady Bertrand asked, breathless at a development that might hold a hint of scandal.

Eva took a step back and gave Isabel a reproving shake of her head. "You didn't tell them about me?"

"Well," Isabel began, thinking fast, "you were so"—*oh, what could she say?*—"sick"—*yes*—"with"—*with what?*—"influenza—"

"*Influenza?*" Lady Bertrand's white linen handkerchief flew to her nose and mouth. A muffled, "Oh, dear," emerged.

"I can assure you that I'm quite cured of what ailed me." Eva's tone was so persuasive that Isabel could almost believe her. "Tonight, however, I found myself in dire need of company. So, when I learned about all the guests in the manor house—you know how servants like to talk—I had to meet everyone for myself."

How exceptionally bright Eva's gaze was. Her eyes had always been a luminous brown, the defining feature of her face, but tonight they flashed and shone. She'd gone from being a shell of herself to too much herself in the span of a few hours. For a terrified instant, Isabel thought Eva had found laudanum. But, no, they had discarded it all months ago.

Isabel glanced around to find the duchess and Lady Bertrand staring at *her* expectantly. *Oh.* "Duchess, may I introduce my sister Miss Eva—"

The duchess's eyebrows drew together, and she stopped twirling the bangles on her wrist. "*Miss?*" She dropped a meaningful glance toward the baby in Eva's arms.

"Oh, dearest dear," Lady Bertrand whispered, the handkerchief falling from her face in light of this development. Isabel's mouth went dry.

"*Querida*," Eva began, her tone light and airy, "you never did accustom yourself to my marriage. But, really, how could you? It lasted but a pair of months, and the only remainder I have of the wonderful Captain Gardiner is our sweet babe." Her eyes welled with convincing tears.

"Oh, you poor gel, Mrs. Gardiner." The duchess

reached for the long strand of pearls that hung about her neck, which she began winding and twirling. "I, too, know what it is to wear widow's weeds. But at such a young age? And with a babe?"

Eva nodded as if too emotionally affected to speak. She might have missed out on her true calling of a career on the stage.

Isabel continued the introductions. "And, Lady Bertrand, may I present—"

Eva's eyes narrowed. "Lady Bertrand *Montfort?*"

Isabel understood in an instant what her sister had heard from the servants and why she was here.

"Who else would I be?" Lady Bertrand asked, outrage in her tone. The woman did possess an exceptional talent for finding offense in every little matter.

"Oh, it is truly a pleasure to make your acquaintance, Lady Bertrand," Eva gushed. "Isabel speaks of nothing but your incomparable intelligence that is surpassed only by your supreme wisdom."

The duchess's eyebrows lifted to the ceiling, even as Lady Bertrand visibly warmed to the flattery, the blush of a debutante pinking her sallow cheeks. She patted the cushion next to her on the yellow damask sofa. "You may sit beside me."

"Oh, thank you, ma'am." Eva crossed the short distance in a rush, all obsequious obeisance.

"Now, I haven't the faintest notion of how things are done where you come from—" Lady Bertrand stopped abruptly. She'd flummoxed herself. "And where is that precisely?"

"Madrid," Isabel answered for Eva. She didn't want her sister to lie on this point. She'd told so many already. Lady Bertrand as intelligent and wise? Two words which surely had never been applied to the lady once in her life. Until now. Until Eva.

"Well, *in England*, you must leave the babe in the nursery in the evening. Haven't you a nurse?"

"Yes, ma'am, but I can't bear to leave him." Eva swiped at her eyes with her free hand. "He is all that remains of Mr. Gardiner."

This seemed to mollify Lady Bertrand as she leaned in for a closer inspection of the babe. "And does this handsome boy have a name?"

"He is called Ariel."

"What an unusual name," said the duchess.

"He is named for my and Isabel's father."

Lady Bertrand tapped a considering finger to her lips. "I know I've heard that name somewhere. It sounds so, so, oh, what is the word I'm searching for?"

"*Jewish?*" Eva asked, cutting Isabel a quick glance. She detected mischief there. More of the old Eva. Too much.

Lady Bertrand startled back, and her face took on the cast of a woman who had just swallowed a pickle, whole. "Oh, dear."

"Ariel means lion in Hebrew," Eva continued, relentless, even as Lady Bertrand appeared on the precipice of apoplexy.

"What a strong name to give your son," the duchess said, smoothness in her tone, steel in her eyes. "Wonderful."

"But, but," Lady Bertrand sputtered, "that means you"—she pointed at Isabel—"are a, a, a *Jewess*."

The duchess's face went stony, and the steel in her eyes tempered. "Dot, it's best if you lower your finger."

Lady Bertrand's hand fell to her lap—one didn't disobey the directive of a duchess—only to return to her mouth in horror. "Don't you see? She is Lord Percival's bride. A *Jewess* is now in the family of a duke of the realm. And their future issue..." She appeared too overcome to finish the thought.

"Aunt Dot," Miss Bretagne called out, "you've learned maths!"

Isabel glanced about the room. It seemed the exchange had commanded every last eye.

"But the bloodline, Lucretia." Desperation persisted in every syllable Lady Bertrand spoke. "The family line will be taint—"

"As usual, Dot, you've struck the nail squarely on the head," said the duchess, cool and determined. All the breath left Isabel's body. "That is exactly who Isabel is, *family*. This isn't the first time a member of the Israelite tribe has married into the English aristocracy, and it won't be the last."

This proved too great a trial for Lady Bertrand, and she wilted back into the sofa cushions, all the bracing ire and outrage from moments ago having deserted her. Eva sat, not twelve inches from her, a tiny smile curling about her mouth, utterly unflustered. The duchess gave Isabel a warm wink, and she could breathe again as gratitude flooded her. This wasn't the first time she'd heard views such as Lady Bertrand's expressed.

A movement caught at the periphery of Isabel's vision. There, in the open doorway at the far end of the room, stood Lord Percival, his intense gaze trained upon her. The assessing cant of his head told her he'd witnessed the entire exchange.

The duchess called out, "Lord Percival, how charming of you to join our little gathering."

If the prospect of an evening spent pretending to be Lord Percival's enamored bride didn't scare Isabel so, she might experience a mean satisfaction as the look of a trapped wild animal hung about the man.

"I would be delighted, ma'am." He looked anything but.

"Join us over here, my boy," the duke called out.

"We're having a civil discussion about the government needing more parity between the parties, and I could use an ally."

Lord Percival's features softened, and his feet began moving. "I welcome any opportunity to set Michael straight on his bloody-minded views."

The family took his words in stride. They were spoken with a smile and received with one, even by the dour Lord Exeter, who scoffed. Isabel had never seen Lord Percival like this, *relaxed*. She hadn't thought him capable of it, yet here was proof.

Miss Bretagne shot to her feet. "Well, Mina and I shall be off." She began folding the maps strewn about the long rectangular table before her.

Lord Percival's ease vanished. "*Off?* Where?"

"On our hike." Miss Bretagne didn't bother to glance up. "Well, more of a scientific expedition."

"But, Lucinda," said the duchess, "it is *night*."

"That is rather the point," Miss Bretagne breezed, matter-of-fact.

Miss Radclyffe stood and joined the conversation. "You see there's a rather exciting confluence of events happening tonight that we would be remiss to ignore." She held up her hand and began ticking items off a list. "A clear night. A full moon. The summer solstice. And a druidic ruin."

"A druidic ruin?" asked the duchess.

"On Mercy Island," Lord Percival provided.

Miss Radclyffe beamed her approval. "You know of it, Lord Percival?"

"Quite well."

"Then you must appreciate our mission. We must be there before midnight, for that is when the event will take place. That is, if the correct stones are still standing."

Before Lord Percival could respond, the duchess cut

in. "Any number of brigands could be brandishing about, Miss Radclyffe."

"According to the map, we're only two miles from the coast, and we shan't be leaving the estate's lands."

"My dear, you'll be out all night. And if you happen upon a poacher? What then?"

A dark storm clouded Lord Percival's features. "I forbid it," he spoke low and clear.

The room went dead still.

The tempest clouding Miss Bretagne's face matched her father's. "You *forbid* it?" She emitted a humorless guffaw. "*You* forbid it?"

The way Miss Bretagne spoke that last *you* confirmed something for Isabel: the girl despised her father.

Lord Percival's jaw clenched, and he seemed to dig in. "Yes."

Lord Avendon unfolded his youthful, lanky form and rose to a stand. "Uncle, if I may be so bold, I believe I can provide a solution to the present difficulty."

Lord Percival dragged his thunderous gaze away from his daughter and pinned Lord Avendon with it. "Yes, Hugh?"

"I shall accompany and protect the girls." He drew himself up to his tallest, lankiest height. "With my life, if necessary." So self-serious. So earnest.

Lord Percival was having none of it. "Hugh, you're little more than a boy."

"With all due respect, Uncle, I was eighteen on my last name day. I shall start my first term at Cambridge this autumn."

Without acknowledging his nephew's words, Lord Percival addressed his father. "Were you allowing her to go with no chaperone?"

The duke shrugged. "The girl's mind is quite made up. I doubt there's any stopping her."

"True," Miss Bretagne piped up.

"But to answer your question, yes. I see no harm in it," the duke continued. "Now that you mention it, how fortuitous her father is here to tend the matter."

Lord Percival cut his gaze toward his daughter. "If you go, I go."

"That's hardly nec—"

Lord Percival held up his hand and silenced her mid-word. "*If you go, I go,*" he repeated on a note of forged steel that ran the length of his words. Only a fool wouldn't believe him.

It was obvious his daughter wanted to stomp in frustration. "Very well."

"We shall meet in the front hall ten minutes hence," he said in the manner of a man well-accustomed to taking control of a situation. "Fetch a light overcoat. A clear night means a chilly night, even in summer. And Lucy?"

"Yes?"

"Do not attempt to leave without me."

"We won't, Lord Percival," answered Miss Radclyffe. "And our sincere gratitude for your escort."

Miss Bretagne shot Miss Radclyffe a look equal parts sullen and wounded, but nodded her agreement nonetheless. It wasn't difficult to see that Miss Radclyffe was the voice of reason in their friendship.

The Misses Bretagne and Radclyffe gathered their maps in a neat stack and exited the room, taking with them a thin sheet of paper that would serve as the night hike's guide. Lord Avendon was no more than ten steps behind them, giving Lord Percival the sort of nod men gave one another as he passed. Lord Percival spoke his good-byes to the room and followed in the group's wake.

Isabel sat in her chair, needlework in hand, watching it all come to pass, forgotten. They were leaving, without her. No, not *they*. Lord Percival was leaving without her. *No, no, no.* This was her chance—her second chance—and it was walking out the door.

The heat of incipient action flared inside her, and she shot to her feet. Lady Bertrand gasped. Reactions were ever close to her surface. The duchess merely raised an eyebrow. And Eva regarded her as if from a great distance.

"Husband?" Isabel called out. How she hated the wobble in her voice.

Lord Percival stopped in his tracks, back to her. Tension radiated off him in waves. "Yes, wife?" he asked without turning.

"*I* fancy a nighttime stroll."

He met her gaze over his shoulder. She wouldn't waver beneath its challenge. He unclenched his jaw. "Do you?"

"Quite. I'm ever a creature of the night."

Knowledge flashed in his eyes. "And pray tell, *sweet wife*, have you the necessary clothing for such an adventure? You can't venture outside without a cloak to guard you against brisk night elements, and we did leave London in quite a wild rush of abandon."

"Oh, dear," whispered Lady Bertrand, both scandalized and riveted.

Isabel had to consider that he may have defeated her. She didn't have the clothes for a midnight jaunt across the countryside.

The duchess signaled a servant. "Dobbs, have my gray cashmere cloak fetched for Lady Percival and meet her in the front hall ten minutes hence." The servant sprang to his mistress's bidding as the duchess glanced down at Isabel's boots poking out from beneath her hemline. "It appears you have the sensible shoes bit covered."

It was all Isabel could do to not shuffle her feet out

of view. 'Twas true she was wearing boots, but they were functional and quite comfortable. In truth, they were the best boots she'd ever owned. She wouldn't feel ashamed of them, not even for a duchess.

Lord Percival's jaw resumed its clenched position, but he gave an assenting nod before striding out the room.

"Duchess, Lady Bertrand." Isabel scrambled to catch Lord Percival, hastily discarding her needlework onto her vacated seat. She'd taken no more than three steps when she remembered. *Eva.*

She half pivoted to meet her sister's eye. Her earlier assessment that the old Eva had returned to life didn't quite hit the mark. This Eva's blood didn't run hot and impetuous. This Eva took her time, assessed a situation in a cool, distant manner. This Eva filled Isabel with dread. Now, more than ever, she didn't want to leave her alone. "Sister, would you like to join our excursion?"

"I am quite content to sit by the warm fire and soak in the delightful conversation happening around me." Her eye roved over Lady Bertrand like the cat who ate the canary. "Lady Bertrand has such wisdom to impart. I wouldn't miss a bit of it for all the world. Enjoy your night adventure, *querida*. You can tell me all about it on the morrow."

Isabel knew for a fact that she shouldn't leave her sister. But…her second chance was stalking away. If she stayed, she would lose it.

And then what?

Her eye fell on little, sleeping Ariel, curled and snug in his mother's arms. She wouldn't fail him.

She spared one final glance for Eva before proceeding into the uncertain night.

11

"Lucy!" Percy called out for the dozenth time to his daughter, who continued dashing ahead with Hugh and Miss Radclyffe. "I should take the lead."

They either weren't hearing him or weren't heeding him. While he suspected the latter, he couldn't race to catch them and leave Isabel on her own. She trailed at his back some ten feet behind.

As long as he could keep his eyes on the group ahead and his ears attuned to the woman behind, he maintained a sliver of control should a situation, however unlikely, arise. In general, smugglers and their ilk knew to stay off a duke's lands. There were other stretches of coast better suited to their needs with less risk.

This area Percy knew like the back of his hand, having chased along its dirt twists and turns his entire childhood. The muted crunch of old autumn leaf mulch and detritus long fallen beneath his feet. The full moon high above, dappled light shining through summer's fat canopy of tree leaves. The sea a roar in the distance. It smelled of damp earth and salty surf and, most of all, home.

And it truly would be soon. Gardencourt, with its

glorious grounds and magnificent stables, was his birthright, an idea that made him simultaneously giddy and sick. The deception had grown layers, increasing in size and heft at every turn. At this rate, soon, it would be entirely out of his control. Or was that delusion? Like as not, it was already.

Behind him, he heard a sound—or rather its absence.

Isabel's footsteps…They'd gone silent.

He glanced over his shoulder, only to find an empty path. *Blast.* "Isabel," he called out.

A faint response came from around the bend at his back. Meanwhile, onward marched Lucy, Hugh, and Miss Radclyffe. "Lucy!" he shouted. No response. "Lucy!" They just kept going. He couldn't very well leave Isabel, who must have found trouble. The woman was damned accomplished at it.

His feet kicked up into a light jog. He located her attempting to wrest the duchess's too-large cloak from the clutches of a tenacious blackberry bush. They grew rampant in these parts. "Are you in need of assistance?" he asked. He wouldn't mind if she said no.

"I shall have it, if I can just…" She was turned around inside the cloak, like a badger inside its skin. The bush appeared to have launched a rear attack. Her fingers steadily picked at thread and thorn. They could be here all night, so great was her patience at her task. All the while, Lucy, Hugh, and Miss Radclyffe tramped on.

"Allow me," he said, stepping forward. "I insist."

Isabel's shoulder hunched around, denying him access. "I would prefer not to rip the fabric. It's such a fine garment."

Impatiently—he couldn't lose the group ahead to her stubbornness—Percy circled around and reached for the cloak before she had a chance to move away, and his fingers touched hers. A heartbeat of hesitation, the light touch of gloved fingers, nothing more. It wasn't skin touching skin. Still, his hand jerked back.

Somehow, he'd maneuvered into the very position he'd been avoiding since the stables: physical proximity to this woman. Her scent enveloped him in honeysuckle and summer. A scent he liked too much.

And there *it* was, again, the tension of desire pulling taut inside him.

He clenched his jaw and tugged. The sound of rending fabric tore through the air.

She flashed him an annoyed glare and heaved a sigh. "You've ripped it."

"A small tear," he replied, gruff. He dropped the garment and hied off at a brisk pace. "We must hurry if we're going to catch them," he called over his shoulder.

Within a few steps, she was at his heels. They arrived at a fork in the path. *Blast.* He'd forgotten this.

"Which is the way to Mercy Island?" Isabel asked at his back.

"The path makes a large loop, so either direction will take us there." He glanced up at the sky. "On such a bright night, there isn't much risk of smugglers. They like to do their work beneath a new moon."

"Shall we go right?" Isabel asked.

It was as good a route as the other, and, either way, they would eventually meet up with Lucy, Hugh, and Miss Radclyffe. As Isabel walked ahead, she kept worrying at the cloak. "The tear is no more than half an inch," he called out, intuiting her concern.

She twisted around, slowing her pace. "I may be able to fix it."

He caught up to her. "I take it you're skilled with needle and thread."

"What was your first clue? My dressmaking shop?"

"I suppose I deserved that."

"To answer you, yes, I am," she said without a hint of braggadocio, "but not like Eva or Papa."

Percy could let it lie, or pursue it. In truth, he had but the one choice. "How did your father come to be a *hidalgo de privilegio?*" He pitched his voice low and, he hoped, nonthreatening.

"With his needle," she replied, wistful. "He is...*was* tailor to King Ferdinand."

Now they were getting somewhere. "And your father came to England, too?"

Isabel bit her bottom lip and shook her head. "He remains in Madrid."

The admission emerged tight and unhappy. This was part of her, the real *her*, a *her* she didn't want him to know.

Well, too bad. "What brought you to England?"

"Great good luck, of course." She gave a hollow laugh that implied the opposite. "Who doesn't want to be English? Especially when one's country is torn up by war." Her words emerged bitter in both content and tone, but her face shone with the helpless anger he'd come to know all too well through years of war and its aftermath. "You were in Spain, Lord Percival."

"*Percy,*" he reminded her.

"What of your time there, *Percy?* Did you enjoy yourself?"

"*Enjoy?* It was war." He parceled out each word, syllable by slow syllable. What the blast was she on about?

"But you're the son of a duke," she pressed, her eyes bright. She had a statement to make. He would let her. "You were a young, handsome, moneyed aristocrat, your country's golden son. I can't imagine you were conscripted."

"I wasn't."

"How very noble of you." She flashed him a fiery glance. "And did you have the showiest horse?"

"Yes."

"And the shiniest sword?"

"Brighter than the sun."

"And the tallest feather in your cap?"

"Bushiest, too."

Ever more acid swirled into her words with each question asked. So, too, did her Spanish accent grow thicker. He knew what she was not-so-subtly hinting at, but he had no desire to defend himself or disabuse her of her implications. For she wasn't wrong.

The Lord Percival Bretagne who had sped off to war had been concerned about each and every point on her list of trifling matters.

"I know your kind."

"My kind?"

Why was he encouraging her? A part of him craved the tongue lashing she was offering, that was why. He wanted to be punished, deserved it, in fact.

"*Sí*, you're definitely of a kind."

"The vainglorious popinjay? Could you be referring to him?"

While he craved a verbal beating, another side of him had a different need. It longed to look directly into her clear green gaze and offer an addendum to the narrative she was spinning. Yes, he'd gone to war the swaggering boy she described, but he hadn't stayed that way for long. It wasn't that the man who had returned to England was a better man, but he was a different one.

And how would dredging up the past serve him? Once this matter with Montfort was concluded, he would never see this woman again.

His questions hung in the air, the answer too obvious and insulting to speak aloud, the sheepish expression on her face said as much. So, they walked in silence, side by side, not touching, until the path suddenly cleared and they found themselves at the cliff's edge.

Isabel gasped at the sight before them. "Oh."

High above, the full moon lit upon the outstretched sea all the way to the horizon, illuminating placid waves as they rippled toward the shore, inviting the eye to return to the land. One hundred feet below lay a small island connected to the mainland by a short, stone bridge.

"Is that Mercy Island?" she asked.

"Aye."

"Oh, look." Isabel pointed toward three distant figures crossing the bridge. "Shall we join them?"

She took a few steps toward the smaller path that branched off the main one and switched back and forth to the bridge below. Percy's hand shot out and grabbed her arm, pulling her to an abrupt stop. "No."

Wide, surprised eyes met his over her shoulder, then fell pointedly to his fingers still wrapped around her arm. His hand dropped that instant. "We can watch them from here. My presence would only spoil Lucy's adventure."

Why had he felt compelled to add that last bit?

"Your daughter, she..." Isabel was clearly uncertain how to speak the horrible, obvious truth aloud.

"Can hardly tolerate the sight of me." He spoke it for her. "Choices have consequences. I didn't understand how far reaching they would be when I sped off to war."

The way Isabel was now looking at him, with understanding, made Percy want to kick himself. He didn't want her pity. Yet that look had another effect upon him, too. It warmed a part of him that had been cold far too long.

He broke the contact, strode to the other side of a

boulder, and held his hand to his forehead on the pretext of looking out to sea for smugglers. Isabel's light step drew closer. Didn't she know better?

He gestured toward the boulder that could easily serve as a bench. "Sit."

The command sat on the air for a trio of seconds, then Isabel broke into a laugh that sparkled on the breeze. It was the sort of laugh that could pierce a soul, if one wasn't careful not to let it.

"You sound like a long ago ancestor who lived in a cave. *Sit*," she mimicked as she settled onto the boulder and gathered the duchess's voluminous cloak around her, her back to him.

His eye fell upon the exposed nape of her neck, her olive skin glowing ivory in the moonlight, delicate lines of tendon running below the surface up to the curved shell of her ear. His mouth went dry.

"I can't have you skulking behind me all night," she called over her shoulder without turning. "*Sit*."

Percy smiled—he couldn't help it—and against his better judgment, he sat.

Instantly, he knew it for the mistake it was. Sugary honeysuckle on a warm summer's day reached out with its sweetness.

"What a lovely night," she said. The group below began circling an area. They must have found the druidic stones they sought.

But Percy had little care for that scene, not when presented with the opportunity to study Isabel's profile. It was worthy of the descriptor *classical*, the sort one would find depicted on an ancient Greek coin. Long, patrician nose. Full, lush lips. Delicate, but firm chin. Hers wasn't the simple beauty exhorted in tame Mayfair drawing rooms, but rather the wild, untamed beauty of a poem by the late Byron.

What was it he'd written?

> *She walks in beauty, like the night.*
> *Of cloudless climes and starry skies.*

That was the one.

After all these years, it seemed Percy's poetic side hadn't been entirely suppressed.

"Exquisite," he found himself saying. He wasn't speaking of Byron's words.

It must have been the dark rasp in his voice that made her go still and then, very slowly, pivot to face him. Her eyes lifted to meet his and held, silently seeking, questioning. Movement at her lap drew his attention. She was removing her glove, methodically, finger by finger. Then her hand was reaching up and, before he took her intention, touching his right cheekbone, tracing along the scar gently as a feather.

"Was your war really such a lark?" Her melodious, low contralto rattled and warmed his insides.

"Was anyone's?" he returned, his voice gone to gravel in his throat.

Unresolved pain flickered in her eyes, and all he wanted to do was take it away.

Instinctively, he understood that none of his actions from here would be guided by choice or reason. He took her hand and brought it to his lips, inhaling her sweet honeysuckle warmth as he kissed her palm. The breath hitched in her chest, but she didn't pull away, instead swaying forward ever so slightly, enough for him to recognize surrender.

His lips trailed to the pulse point at her wrist, thin blue veins beating beneath his mouth. Unable to resist, he licked her, and she gasped.

"Shall I stop?" He didn't know how he could, but he would.

Her hand broke from his grasp, and his gut sank to his feet. Then her fingers returned, feathering along his jaw, sliding around his neck, twining through his hair. She tugged him forward. Her mouth an inch from his, she whispered across his lips, "I think I would die."

On a growl more animal than human, he took her face in both hands and claimed her mouth. Soft lips opened beneath his demand. She inhaled his breath on a quick gasp. That she'd taken any part of him inside her made his cock swell. He wanted all of him inside her.

One hand found the middle of her back to steady her as he pressed forward, his chest a hard contrast against the soft give of hers. His tongue began a slow, deliberate tangle with hers, and he slipped into carnality. She tasted of salt and sweet and woman.

A taste wasn't enough. He wanted to ravish and devour every last inch of her with his mouth, with his body. Never had he been so hungry, so *famished*, for a woman.

She moaned in the back of her throat, and a part of Percy's brain that kept an eye out for his best interest knew that if he didn't stop this kiss this instant, he might never be able to let this woman go. He would be irrevocably lost to his wickedness.

With great pain, he broke away from her, gasping for air. Her eyes flew open, alight with a confusion and a frustration that might match his own. "Lord Percival," she whispered.

"*Percy.*"

She touched fingertips to kiss-crushed lips. If he didn't know better, he might think this her first kiss given the fresh flush of her cheeks. But he did know better. Except...

Did he?

"You kiss like a..." He hesitated a heartbeat. "*Virgin.*"

Her gaze skittered away.

His heart beat a hard thud. "You're a virgin," dropped from his mouth, each syllable slow and stunned and absolutely certain.

Wide eyes met his. "How can you know that?"

"Are you telling me differently?"

She swallowed. Silence prevailed.

There.

As he suspected: she was a virgin.

Isabel gasped in horror.

He followed her gaze and found, one hundred feet below, Lucy, Hugh, and Miss Radclyffe staring up at them from Mercy Island. It was clear they'd witnessed the kiss, which must have been on a par with the astronomical event given the gapes of their mouths. Lucy was the first to gather her wits as she broke from the group and stomped toward the bridge. Miss Radclyffe gave a little wave, which Isabel returned.

Percy snatched up Isabel's fallen glove as he stood. "I believe you'll be needing this."

Her head tipped back, and his gaze fell to her swollen lips. How he wanted to suck that full bottom lip into his mouth and give it a testing nibble, one that would make her gasp and smile and beg for another.

A *virgin*, came the very next thought.

She swallowed. "Thank you, Lord—*Percy*."

He gestured that she take the lead. "After you."

At the head of the trail that splintered off toward the bridge below, he and Isabel waited with a silence that was the loudest, tetchiest silence he'd ever endured. He couldn't press her now for here was Lucy sweeping past him. She hooked a sharp right and marched ahead without a single glance his way.

Next came Miss Radclyffe. Isabel inquired about the ruins as she fell into step with the girl. Miss Radclyffe launched into a detailed explanation about tonight's unique confluence of astronomy and archeology, to which Isabel listened with an attentive ear and asked questions where appropriate. Percy was likely the only one who could see the tension radiating off her. The woman was damned accomplished at pulling her wits together.

Percy waited for Hugh, who arrived last. The boy maintained a persistent silence as they brought up the rear together. Brow furrowed with the variety of deep contemplation uniquely available to those of teen years, Hugh's eye never wavered once from the tall, elegant form of Miss Radclyffe. The lad's uncompanionable silence suited Percy fine.

Here were the facts as Percy knew them.

Isabel was a dressmaker.

She was the daughter of minor Spanish nobility.

She was a Jewess.

She was a virgin.

Which changed nothing, not truly, not when one considered her connection to Montfort.

Yet…a *virgin* involved in the Number 9 scheme with the Earl of Pembroke as the target?

Coercion was clear. Montfort was just such a man to compel a virgin into seducing a future Member of Parliament for political gain.

Percy needed to keep Isabel close. So, too, he needed to stay away from her.

For another man, the mad kiss of minutes ago would have already begun to fade into memory, suppressible and distant. Not so for Percy. The madness pulsed through his veins with every beat of his heart. Now that it had been awakened, it would lie in wait for its next opportunity. His wickedness was patient in that regard.

Really, what he wanted at his deepest, darkest core was to sink into the feeling and become addicted to that woman. It would be the easiest thing he'd ever done in his life.

And the worst.

12

"Should it be this hot in England?" Miss Bretagne asked, dramatically fanning herself as if on the verge of a swoon.

Even Lady Bertrand had foregone a fichu. "After all, it's only us ladies."

Although a torpor hung about the usually airy library, Isabel didn't find it particularly oppressive. Neither did Eva, given the quick *Can you believe these English?* glance she shot Isabel. When Lady Exeter excused herself for a "bracing lie down" before afternoon tea, Eva shot Isabel another such glance, and Isabel had to hide a smile as she continued mending the duchess's cloak.

Miss Bretagne dragged herself to the piano and lifted the fallboard, exposing black and white keys. "Mina, come and compose a song with me. This Bach concerto is in dire need of lyrics."

Miss Radclyffe checked her pocket watch. "I shall be reading for the next seventeen minutes."

Miss Bretagne gave a little pout, but said no more as she began picking at piano keys.

"Are preparations proceeding for your citrus breakfast, Duchess?" asked Lady Bertrand.

"Citrus breakfast?" Eva's needle suspended mid-air. "You have citrus groves on the estate?"

"We have a conservatory, Mrs. Gardiner," explained the duchess.

"And it's bursting at the seams with every manner of citrus fruit you can imagine," Lady Bertrand cut in.

"And you have a day for it?"

"Well," continued the duchess, "it's a rather impromptu thing. In a few days' time, the village will put on their summer musicale, which shall be—"

"Dreadful," Lady Bertrand interjected.

"*Delightful*," corrected the duchess. "I am quite looking forward to being treated to the local talent. I've always enjoyed that sort of thing. In return, we are inviting the village round for a breakfast the following day to partake in all the oranges, lemons, and limes we can't possibly consume ourselves alone. Citrus is the best fruit for summer."

"Oh, Lucretia, I still don't understand why you're offering this to the public. How can you tolerate such people in your home?" By *you*, it was clear Lady Bertrand meant *I*. "We would never have such a gathering at Little Spruisty Folly. Bertie wouldn't hear of it."

As if Lady Bertrand hadn't spoken, the duchess continued, "Then I thought, well, since we're having the village here for the day, why not set up a tent and extend the gathering into the evening for a country dance? Which, I must confess, is quite selfish of me. I do delight in lively fiddles and country reels. Mrs. Gardiner, you must consider shedding your widow's weeds for the occasion."

Miss Bretagne's fingers struck a discordant key on the piano. "A dance? You never mentioned a dance."

"I hardly needed to, Lulu." The duchess flicked a dismissive wrist at the girl. "You, my dear, are not yet out. And neither is Miss Radclyffe, for that matter."

"But 'tis a *country* dance," Miss Bretagne whined. "No one in London need ever know."

A naughty smile quirked about the duchess's mouth. "I must confess to having attended one or two country dances when I was your age, Lulu." A dreamy look entered her eye. "They are such jolly fun."

Lady Bertrand emitted one of her signature *oh, dear*'s, and Miss Bretagne squealed with the knowledge that she'd won the day.

The duchess settled her gaze onto Isabel. "Dearest, if the day is a success, this is just the sort of thing that could become a tradition for Gardencourt Manor. It's vital you put your stamp and establish traditions early on, don't you agree?"

Every eye—except Miss Radclyffe's—swung toward Isabel. "Why, yes, of course," she sputtered.

The duchess's head canted to the side, quizzical. "Hasn't Percy told you?"

"Told me?" Isabel remembered who she was. Well, who she was supposed to be. "Oh, yes, *that*. I am, um, so looking forward to it."

What didn't she know?

"Well, I suppose he will get to it in due time."

"But, Duchess," Miss Bretagne piped up from her side of the room, "I haven't brought a dress for the occasion."

"You shall manage, my dear. The young and determined always do."

Eva twisted in her chair. "Miss Bretagne, any dress can be made festive with a few touches here and there."

"Oh?"

Eva snapped her fingers. "There is nothing to it. You see this dress I'm wearing?" She stood and waved an arm as if to demonstrate its many fine qualities.

Miss Bretagne nodded slowly, eyes wide, reconsidering her new step-mama's sister.

"I have remade it three times." She pointed at Isabel. "And her dress? *Five* times."

"Are you so very poor?" inserted Lady Bertrand, but no one paid her any mind. Not while Eva held the floor.

Miss Bretagne exclaimed over Eva's fine needle-work, clearly having decided she liked this new aunt of hers. "You are quite the excellent seamstress."

Eva went stiff, and a dark look entered her eye. Before Eva's inevitable hot retort could blaze forth, Isabel shot to her feet. "Actually, Eva is a dressmaker."

Eva drew herself up to her fullest height. "*Not* a seamstress."

"Oh." Miss Bretagne appeared quite crestfallen.

"The difference is that Eva designs the dresses she constructs," continued Isabel.

"Mrs. Gardiner," Miss Bretagne began, contrite, "would you consent to applying your talents to re-working one of my dresses for the dance?"

Isabel kept a nervous eye on Eva. These last several months, the sister she'd once known better than herself had become inscrutable to her. This Eva was calculated and measured. Why was she inserting herself into this family? A game was afoot, and Isabel wished she knew what it was.

Eva's face broke into a sudden, delighted smile. "I shall."

"And, possibly," Miss Bretagne continued, "you would do one of Mina's dresses, too?"

Nose buried in her book, Miss Radclyffe called out, "Entirely unnecessary," without looking up.

Miss Bretagne's features went stormy as she released a blustery sigh, signaling her frustration. The girl had more of her father in her than she knew.

"It doesn't matter what dress I wear," Miss Radclyffe continued, "as long as I am warm on a cold day and cool on a warm day. Or on a sweltering day, as the case might be."

Eva smiled knowingly, and Isabel saw her true sister emerge. "Ah, but this is where you are wrong, Miss Radclyffe. The clothes we wear are so much more than *functional*." She all but spat the word. "They are your armor against the world, not just the elements. Your clothing conveys a message about who you are, and you want that message to be clear. There is very little we have actual control over in our lives, but in this we do. I advise you to use it to your advantage."

During Eva's speech, Isabel noticed movement at the door and glanced up. Her stomach gave a lurch. Before them stood Lord Bertrand Montfort, returned.

So soon. Too soon.

She'd made no headway with Lord Percival.

Well, that wasn't precisely true. But it was the wrong headway.

"You kiss like a virgin."

Butterflies fluttered through her stomach, and it was all she could do to keep her hands at her sides and not touch her lips.

She wouldn't be telling Montfort about her first kiss. She'd hardly even allowed herself to think on it, stuffing the memory into an unused portion of her brain and turning the key in the lock. Too bad for her the door had cracks that the kiss insisted on slipping through.

Following Montfort into the room was a barrel-chested, red-faced gentleman and a slight young woman whose sharp gray eyes cast about, never settling on a single object for long. Isabel knew the moment Eva spotted Montfort, for she stopped talking mid-word. Isabel reached for her sister's hand and squeezed tight, attempting to quell the tremor she detected there. It wasn't one of fright, but of an anger so deep and dark no one could touch it. Isabel had tried and failed.

"Oh, Bertie," exclaimed Lady Bertrand, fanning herself, "you've arrived with friends. Have you brought a cooling breeze with you as well?"

"If it isn't the Baron Cheswick!" exclaimed the duchess, rushing across the room to greet her newest guests. "And I see you've brought Miss Fox with you." The young lady gave a shallow curtsy. The duchess clasped her hands before her in delight. "Now our little party shall come alive. A party was never *not* made better by Cheswick. One bit of business first." She crooked her finger at Isabel, who released Eva's hand with great reluctance. Eva's eyes hadn't left Montfort.

"It isn't yet common knowledge," continued the duchess, "but our Percy has taken a bride. Lady Percival, may I introduce Lord Cheswick and his daughter, Miss Fox, to you?"

"I am delighted to make your acquaintance." Isabel felt very certain those were the correct words for English aristocratic introductions.

Cheswick bent low over her hand and pressed damp lips to the back. She remained very still and didn't snatch it away. On the rise, he winked. "Lord Percival always did have an eye for a fine filly."

This drew a delighted rebuke from the duchess. "Oh, Cheswick, you are incorrigible as ever."

A snort carried across the room, courtesy of Miss Bretagne, Isabel knew without looking. For her part, Miss Fox held Isabel's gaze as she dipped into a shallow curtsy. The watchfulness of Miss Fox's eye didn't allow one to relax.

Cheswick exhaled a blustery breath and gave his protuberant belly a few pats. "Duchess, I am not what I used to be. A short lie-down might be in order."

"Who amongst us is, Cheswick?" The duchess signaled a servant. "Show the baron to Cowslip."

"Cowslip?" asked the observant Miss Fox.

"The bedrooms are all named for flowers, my dear. We'll put you in Primrose." Miss Fox's lips might have twitched with amusement. "Might you be in need of rest, too?"

Miss Fox shook her head. "I already feel enlivened by the good company of this room."

"I believe I shall follow Cheswick's lead and seek a rest," added Montfort.

With the departure of Montfort, Isabel noted a release of tension from Eva's body. If he'd been surprised by the presence of Eva, he hadn't betrayed the emotion. A splinter of portent wedged itself inside Isabel's mind. Both of them on the estate, each knowing the other was here, was no good thing.

"Oh, I know what we can do to counter the boredom of this deadly dull day," called out Miss Bretagne. "Let's ride out to the eerie ruined monastery that the Vikings destroyed a thousand years ago. Mina, does that sound interesting enough for you?"

Miss Radclyffe rested her book on her lap. "Yes."

The duchess set her hands on her hips. "And who will be your chaperone? I must meet with Cook and Butler about preparations for our village breakfast and dance. I cannot think who would venture out with you in this oppressive heat."

Malicious glint in her eye, Miss Bretagne smiled. "My new step-mama, of course. What a wonderful opportunity to become properly acquainted with one another. Really, it would be a tragedy to allow the chance to slip away."

Isabel opened her mouth to make her excuses when Eva spoke. "Isabel would love nothing more."

A flummoxed beat passed. "And you, dear sister?"

Isabel asked, hoping to give Eva a taste of her own tonic. "Won't you join?"

Eva shook her head. "I shall stay here and draw inspiration from Lady Bertrand about what new designs I should create for the Misses Bretagne and Radclyffe's dresses." When Miss Bretagne's face twisted with doubt, Eva winked at the girl. "Inspiration comes from many sources, no?"

"Possibly," Miss Bretagne said slowly, her misgiving not the least assuaged. "So, what say you, dearest stepmama?"

Isabel commanded her mouth to curve into the impression of a smile. "I should like nothing more."

Miss Fox gave a delicate clearing of her throat. "Would you mind very much if I joined your little party? I do love a good ruin."

Miss Bretagne clapped her hands together. "It's settled. We meet in the stables fifteen minutes hence."

———

Isabel relaxed into the easy trot of her mount.

Ahead, the Misses Bretagne and Radclyffe, along with Lord Avendon, galloped across verdant fields, tall grass swaying in a breeze scented with salt from the nearby sea, its shimmer in the far distance. A thick blanket of clouds had rolled in and cooled the air, making it perfectly pleasant for a ride.

Isabel, meanwhile, kept pace with a silent Miss Fox as it was obvious Miss Bretagne had had no intention of becoming further acquainted with her new stepmama. Isabel almost felt insulted. Then she remembered who she was.

"What a dashing love match you and Lord Percival have made," Miss Fox observed out of the not-so-clear blue sky.

Isabel stared ahead and emitted a noncommittal, "Hmm."

"But true love is quite a force, no?"

"Hmm."

"Unstoppable."

"You speak as if from experience," Isabel replied, hoping to catch the woman on her left foot.

Miss Fox chuckled. If a laugh could be a shrug, hers was. "Never, Lady Percival. I believe myself uniquely immune to love's particular poison. But I, like many a spinster before me, am a keen observer of it. And you are positively glowing from its salubrious effects. Unless, of course, you've caught a summer fever."

"Didn't you just call love a poison?"

Another unruffled chuckle. "One woman's poison is another woman's cure."

Isabel glanced over and spied a rather vulpine smile curling about Miss Fox's mouth. The woman was impossible to catch out. "You have quite a lively mind, Miss Fox. How do you occupy it? I can't imagine you lolling about a drawing room all day."

"Your opinion of noble ladies is so high as that, my lady?" Miss Fox was most definitely toying with her. "If you must know, a few years ago my father won a small press in a card game. I've taken an interest in its various publications. Recently, we added a scientific journal to its number."

"You run the press yourself?"

"Can you imagine Cheswick taking an interest in the written word?"

"I've only just met him."

"You've learned everything you need to know about my father, you can take my word for it. Outré sense of humor. Life of every party. Beloved by all, with the exception of his creditors." She spoke that last horrible truth lightly, but it was a forced levity. "However, let us not stray from our original subject. I find it infinitely more interesting than needlework and endless rounds of social calls. You and I know what Society doesn't. A woman needs to keep herself industriously occupied, even gainfully, if possible."

The fine hairs on Isabel's neck lifted on end. "You *and I* know this?"

"I refer to your shop, of course. *Galante: Dressmakers Extraordinaire.* Quite a grand name, if I may say."

"My sister chose it."

"Well, you and your sister are building quite a reputation for quality, fashionable clothes for women of the middling classes."

"I wouldn't go that far. We've had our challenges this year." Challenges she wouldn't be sharing with this woman.

"No need to be so modest, Lady Percival, your renown is growing."

Miss Fox was most definitely hunting Isabel, for there was no possibility of her knowing this information without having sought it out prior to today. She sensed Montfort's hand in this.

"Of course," continued Miss Fox, "I can't imagine Lord Percival falling madly in love with just any filly enough to elope with her, no matter how fine."

That last bit was a joke, a riff on Cheswick's words, but Isabel couldn't quite summon a laugh. It was very possible that Miss Fox and her curious mind would reach the correct conclusion about Isabel and Lord Percival's ruse.

And then what?

It was too horrible to contemplate.

"No, Lord Percival wouldn't want a wife who depended on him solely for her happiness and fulfillment. I believe he's been down that road. Didn't suit him, or the wife, I dare say." Miss Fox flicked her wrist as if the conversation was of little consequence. "I digress. My theory is that your Spanish-ness is what tipped infatuation into madness." From Miss Fox's lips, it didn't sound like a compliment.

"You're referring to his time in Spain during the war, I suppose?"

"And the ten years after that."

Isabel's brow furrowed, and she glanced over to find Miss Fox studying her reaction.

"It hasn't been a year since Lord Percival returned to England. You didn't know?" Miss Fox asked.

"He was in Spain all that time?"

"I rather suspect he was all over the Continent."

Isabel exhaled a frustrated huff. Why wouldn't Miss Fox simply speak a straightforward answer? "Doing what?"

"Hasn't he told you? Oh, this is rich."

Miss Fox's mouth curled into the sort of smile that said it was about to divulge a delicious secret. Isabel braced herself.

"Why, being a spy, of course."

"A *spy*?"

"That is the rumor, anyway." Miss Fox pierced Isabel with her pointed eye. "Truly, you don't know the story?"

Isabel shook her head, unable to trust herself to speak. Last night, Lord Percival had let her believe his war was a lark as she'd lashed out at him, as she'd tried to make him a hair less devastating. But in her heart she'd known differently. It wasn't only the evidence running along his right cheekbone, but the evidence that lay within his eyes.

"He was thought dead for over ten years. Slain at the Battle of Maya. That was the story."

"*Slain?*" Lord Percival's history took one strange turn after another.

"While his wife remained in London as a widow and raised their daughter. Then, a few years back, he turned up alive in Paris. I've heard rumors of amnesia, but never confirmed. Anyway, his wife raised a big fuss when she petitioned Parliament to set the marriage aside. Within a year she was swept off her feet by the oh-so-dashing Viscount St. Alban, who is Miss Radclyffe's father as it so happens. The whole matter set the beau monde on its ear, I can assure you." Miss Fox paused long enough to draw breath. "Lady St. Alban was delivered of twin sons in February, an heir and a spare in one go. I always thought her a clever woman. Of course, she is a twin herself, so not such a great surprise."

What a story to keep straight, but one point of curiosity Isabel would have Miss Fox expand upon. "And Miss Bretagne? How did she fare through all this?"

Miss Fox gave an indifferent shrug. "She seems to have come through with her spirit intact. But, technically, the girl is a bastard, as is any child whose parents obtain a *divorce a vinculo matrimonii*. If Miss Bretagne had been a 'mister,' Parliament wouldn't have been so acquiescent, no matter how much arm twisting the Duke of Arundel did on behalf of his former daughter by law."

Matters between father and daughter became clearer to Isabel. "It's no wonder Miss Bretagne cannot stand the sight of her father."

"Perhaps, but it may not be the direct cause of the enmity. To my eye, her bastardy hasn't the least impact on her life as her status in the family doesn't appear to have changed. A rumor floated around that St. Alban offered to adopt her, but nothing came of it. I suspect the Duke of Arundel wouldn't hear of such an action, as it's obvious the chit is the apple of his eye. My feeling is the cause is rooted in the fact that Lord Percival *chose* to stay away."

"If he was a spy," Isabel returned, "perhaps it wasn't his choice. He could have endangered his family had he returned."

Why was she defending the man? She hadn't known him long enough to have the faintest clue who he really was. She could ignore the tiny voice that offered a counter-argument that she'd met the real him last night.

And possibly liked him.

"A girl of thirteen or fourteen years might not be able to see it from that point of view," Miss Fox continued. "An absent father can inflict a surprising bit of damage onto a daughter. She might forgive him in time. Such a thing cannot be rushed."

Isabel intuited that Miss Fox wasn't speaking only of Miss Bretagne. Miss Fox spoke with the voice of experience.

They topped a short rise and, as one, drew their horses to a halt. "Oh, would you look at that," Miss Fox uttered.

The ruin with the sea at its back was the stuff of Romantic artists like John Constable. Set on the edge of a cliff, it looked on the verge of collapsing into the sea, a decaying ode to a time long ago of Catholic monks and the Viking marauders who regularly plundered their riches, now ghosts haunting its crumbling walls.

When Isabel and Miss Fox reached the outer wall, they found a groom waiting to tether their horses along with the others. Isabel didn't think she could ever grow accustomed to the luxury aristocrats took for granted.

Her insatiable curiosity pulling her along, Miss Fox swept past Isabel, so that by the time Isabel entered the ruin, Miss Fox had disappeared on her own adventure.

In truth, Isabel was relieved to be on her own as she

began meandering, her feet free to wander at will. The open sky above, the maze of brown stone walls that in some places only reached her hip, the cool of the breeze, the roar of the sea, the muffled chatter of the young people two walls over. She passed them exploring one room, and, in another, Miss Fox down on her hands and knees, dusting off a patch of ground that appeared to be a grimy floor mosaic. On Isabel explored until it caught her ear: the low rumble of cultured male voices.

He was here.

She rounded a corner and a blast of salt air greeted her full in the face as the view opened. There, not twenty yards away, at the cliff's edge stood Lord Percival and his brother, Lord Exeter, their voices carrying in snatches on the changeable wind. How similar the brothers were in height and coloring, yet how different in personality.

Isabel sank into the ancient stones at her back, eyes only for the one brother.

Lord Percival—*Percy*, he'd insisted—stood a tall sentinel, tousled black hair blowing about a face that was all irresistible, brooding angles. How could she look away?

And the line of that long, lean body of his, with his hip cocked onto the wall at his side, it shouted aristocratic poise and confidence and coiled tension. He appeared at his ease, but he was ready for action, the pose said.

Another action came to her: the kiss. Even in memory, it stole her breath away.

What other sort of kiss would a man like him deliver? *Of course* his kiss would scorch the earth and leave devastation in its wake. The trembly shimmer in her veins was a testament to it.

But that kiss, as wondrous and startling as it was,

had left an ache in her body. It was an ache that no amount of more kissing could assuage. It was an animal demand that wanted, *needed*, more. Of that *more*, she had no experience, but that man did.

His kiss had sparked something new into life inside her.

There is one way you can convince him to show you his experience, a small voice niggled. *Seduce him. Isn't that what Montfort wants from you anyway?*

But she knew down to the marrow of her bones if—when—she carried out the seduction of Lord Percival Bretagne, it wouldn't be for Montfort.

13

I sabel wasn't hiding her presence, but neither did she announce it.

Still, she was far enough away that she couldn't hear the contents of his conversation with Michael, which suited Percy well. Part of him wished she would discreetly leave.

Another, possibly larger, part hoped she would stay.

"Razing it to the ground is your best option." This from Michael.

Percy's gaze swept over the jagged walls of the ruin, three quarters of which lacked a roof, then out to the sea, gray as the sky above. "I rather like it."

Michael scoffed. His brother scoffed at least three times a day. "Romantic ideals still intact, little brother?"

Percy tried not to grind his jaw, and failed. Michael had delivered a direct hit by alluding to the frivolous young buck Percy had once been. But he'd be damned if he gave Michael the satisfaction of acknowledging it. "This place has history," he said.

"A history best forgotten." Michael gave his thigh a light slap with his riding crop. "It's crumbling to bits. Better to get rid of it, but your choice." Another slap of the crop. "And your responsibility."

Percy held his brother's gaze. "I take my responsibilities seriously."

"See that you do. The old man can't take another of your japes." That bit of business concluded, half a smile twitched about Michael's mouth, which was as much of a smile as one was ever to see from the perpetually serious Exeter. He pointed toward Percy's left eye. "You might want to put a cut of beef on that."

Percy touched gingerly fingertips to the bruise beneath his left eye. It had already faded to a muted reddish brown. "I ran into a door."

Michael shook his head on a gusty chortle. "That must've been quite a massive door."

"He was," Percy replied, drawing another laugh from his brother.

Percy knew the instant Michael noticed Isabel. His smile fell and the humor in his eyes faded, replaced by a hardness. That hardness suggested Michael thought Isabel another of his brother's japes. That he wasn't wrong on that score sat at an uncomfortable angle inside Percy. Michael gave Percy a curt nod in parting as he strode from the area, dipping his head in passing acknowledgment as he swept past Isabel.

Percy and Isabel's eyes met and held across the distance. His heart gave a ragged thump, and air became difficult to inhale. Her tongue gave her lips a nervous lick. His eyes dropped to her mouth. They couldn't help themselves.

Into the hushed space entered last night.

His lips upon hers, insistent, demanding.

Her sway, her surrender.

"For my actions last night," he found himself beginning, unsure where he would end, "I offer my sincere" —that was a stretch—"apology. It was a moment of madness."

Isabel's eyes narrowed into green slits, and Percy

suddenly felt that he'd somehow stepped in quicksand. Once one set foot in it, one was sunk. A long moment drew out, her direct gaze never wavering. Percy shifted uncomfortably on his feet. At last, she spoke. "You speak of a one-sided desire. *Yours.*"

Soul-deep shock raced through Percy. Was she truly implying what he thought she was?

"But," she continued.

"*But?*"

"*But* what of my desire?"

She was.

Isabel pushed off the wall at her back and took a few steps forward. Percy's insides did a little flip. "You think you had the only say in the matter? And who is to say whose desire was greater? Mayhap I should be apologizing to you?"

Percy's breath refused to budge from his lungs as his wickedness surged, heady at the prospect of the myriad ways she could offer her apologies. But...

She was a virgin.

He couldn't recall ever having been spoken to thusly by a virgin.

"Have you considered the possibility," she continued, "that I wanted your kiss with every fiber of my being?"

"I," he began and stopped. The woman continued to stun him speechless. It was all he could do not to push her up against that wall and explore what more she might want with every fiber of her being. His swelling cock agreed with the idea with every fiber of its being.

Stop this, man. The conversation could proceed no further down this path. It was time to right it. *Now.* "I need to ask you a question."

"Yes?" she asked, her contralto voice not making matters any easier.

"Are you being coerced?"

"I am exactly where I want to be."

"By Montfort."

Desire vanished from her eyes in an instant. *Good.* Except, already he missed it.

"Why were you in Number 9?" he asked. "Women like you don't inhabit such places."

He could see by the rapid rise and fall of her chest that she'd become short of breath. He'd given up on an answer when, at last, she spoke. "There is a debt."

There. As he suspected. "What sort of debt?"

Doubt had her pressing her lips together. He could see she was already regretting her words.

"I can help you," he pressed.

"Why?" she shot back.

"*Why?*"

"Why would you help me? I'm naught more than a pawn in this game. So, why would *you*, Lord Percival, help *me*?"

How had this conversation gotten so twisted around? He would give her the truth. She wouldn't settle for less. "I need your help."

A cynical smile curved her mouth. A mouth he'd been on the verge of kissing not two minutes ago. How quickly life could happen in two minutes. "Quid pro quo?" she asked.

"It's how the world works."

She laughed without humor. "At least, you're honest."

"With those who deserve it."

Her gaze searched his. She wanted to believe, he could see. He was close, so close...

"Oh, there you are, Lady Percival!" pierced a sharp voice. A woman he vaguely recognized strode into view.

Frustration howled inside Percy as he questioned

Isabel with his gaze. She answered with a resigned inhalation.

"This place," the woman continued, "what a marvel! I mean, it's an utter wreck, but what a marvelous one. Oh, Lord Percival!" she exclaimed, having only now noticed him. She looked back and forth between him and Isabel. She lifted a single eyebrow and tipped up onto her toes, then back onto her heels a few times, waiting, patiently.

Isabel, at last, intuited the source of the woman's hesitation. "Miss Fox, may I introduce Lord Percival to you?"

Miss Fox extended a hand, and Percy very correctly bowed over it. Introduction complete, a silence that was beginning to grow roots dragged on, the only sound the wind whistling through the loose mortar binding the ruin's walls together. As host, it was Percy's lot to facilitate his guest's comfort, even if he didn't know her from Eve.

"Miss Fox," he began, "you don't think we should finish what the Vikings started and raze the structure to the ground?"

Her brow furrowed. "And build what in its place? An ornamental ruin of the sort being erected all across the countryside?" She gave her head a curt two shakes. Somehow, the gesture told the story of her personality. "No, my lord, when one is in possession of the real article, one should hold onto it with both hands and not let go for anything or anyone."

He might not know Miss Fox, but he thought he rather liked her. A quick glance confirmed Isabel shared his opinion of the woman. It shouldn't matter, but, strangely, it did.

Lucy, Hugh, and Miss Radclyffe trooped into the open area. "We've seen it all," Lucy said with the authority of confident youth.

Miss Radclyffe pointed toward the sea. "Oh, just look at that," she said to no one in particular.

"What is it?" Hugh asked, all attentiveness. The lad was especially alert to Miss Radclyffe, who didn't seem to notice him in the least.

"The clouds have cleared on the horizon, and one can just make out the moonrise."

As everyone squinted into the distance, Percy stole a glance at Isabel. He had a rather difficult time keeping his eyes off her. Her gaze lifted and met his. He saw there a mixture of emotions. Vulnerability, query, and the unexpected, too: hunger of the unrequited variety that he'd had ample experience suppressing. His blood had no choice but to rush faster in his veins.

He tore his eyes away because he must. "We need to return before the sun sets. No use risking the horses."

Sunset wasn't for another few hours, but he needed the excuse to put some distance between himself and this hunger. Using his suggestion as an excuse to break free of the adults, Lucy, Hugh, and Miss Radclyffe sped ahead. Isabel and Miss Fox paired up, and Percy trailed behind.

Unable to avert his gaze, Percy studied the movement of Isabel. Where Miss Fox strode with confidence in her every pithy observation, Isabel walked with a bearing understated and graceful, content to listen to her companion.

Miss Fox stopped and pointed toward a patch of tile work that signaled what was once an entrance. "I believe this mosaic to be Roman." She twisted around to address Percy. "You should have an expert inspect it."

Even with its faded reds and blacks, the mosaic was impressive. He should be grateful to Miss Fox for pointing out its importance. But, in truth, he didn't give a fig about it, not with Isabel so near. All he had to do was reach out to touch her, to *feel* her.

Cold, ancient stones couldn't compare to her warm, vibrant flesh.

She'd sparked him alight with her hot words.

Outside, they found Lucy, Hugh, and Miss Radclyffe already mounted and on their journey back to Gardencourt. Miss Fox glanced back and forth between Percy and Isabel and cleared her throat. "I shall accompany the youth as chaperone and leave you newlyweds to whatever it is newlyweds—" She stopped, looking as if she'd swallowed a toad. "Do," she finished on a croak. Her cheeks blushed bright pink.

Although he wasn't much of one, Percy was still too much of a gentleman to acknowledge Miss Fox's unintended double entendre, even as an amused snort begged for release.

"I shall just," Miss Fox began and rushed to her mare before she could finish. She was galloping off in a matter of seconds. Percy had never witnessed anyone mount a horse so fast.

Percy took the reins of the remaining two horses from the groom. "I have it from here, Watkins."

Watkins nodded. "Milord."

Now Percy was truly alone with Isabel. That his blood didn't sing through his veins at the prospect. Even to be near her was to feel alive in his body in a way he hadn't in years, if ever.

A question occurred to him. "You rode out here on your own mount?"

Her eyes shifted to her feet, as if she suddenly found her boots a source of fascination. "I, um, yes."

"What an equestrian marvel you are, Lady Percival." He couldn't resist the impulse to tease. The urge of a boy of ten years with the girl of his infatuation. "Only two days ago, you couldn't mount."

Now it was Isabel who was looking rather frog-like. "I can ride."

He smirked as he reached out to help her mount. It was only when his fingers squeezed her slender hand for support that it hit him: this was the hand he'd kissed last night. Not chastely on the back, but intimately on the *palm.*

She cleared her throat. "I believe you need to boost me into the saddle."

"Right."

With a greater reluctance than he would have preferred, he released her hand and laced his fingers together to assist her. Settled onto the saddle, she fiddled with her dress, bonnet, and gloves as he mounted his stallion, a glorious creature that couldn't be fewer than fifteen hands high.

Side by side, they rode toward Gardencourt, the muted thud of the horses' hooves eating away the distance with ease. In the periphery of his vision, he couldn't help noticing that her body had the instinctive understanding of not only how to sit a horse, but of how to take it in stride. "You ride quite naturally."

He was prying, and she shot him a glance that told him so. "In Madrid, we knew a stable lad who had a tendre for Eva." She smiled at the memory. "Then he was called off to—" *War*, she didn't finish. She recovered herself. "Riding is the only activity where I've been able to best Eva." A smile played about her mouth. "I beat her in every race."

Percy wanted to encourage that spring bud of a smile into full bloom. "So, I'm dealing with an undefeated rider?"

She flashed him a saucy smile. It was all the reward Percy needed. "No one has ever come close."

Competition sparked between them, and Percy's stomach fluttered with anticipation, the delicious feeling shimmering through his veins. Like the night she'd sat across from him at the card table, he detected a will to win.

She leaned over her mount's neck and whispered into the gelding's ear, then she gave her tongue a few clicks and flapped the reins. The horse needed no further encouragement to lengthen its stride into a gallop. Her *woot* of pleasure carried to Percy as her bonnet slid off her head, saved only by the ribbon at her throat, and the wind blew through her hair, long sable tendrils whipping in her wake.

Percy was left breathless in her dust with a decision to make: to pursue or not to pursue.

It had been so long since he'd experienced the freedom she was offering. That feeling of racing for the simple joy of it, no other motives. In truth, he'd never thought to experience it again. But here it was, beckoning, and he was powerless to resist its wild call. A squeeze of his knees was all it took for his stallion to jolt into a gallop.

The chase was on.

As he raced to catch her, he considered letting her win, just to see the triumph in her eyes. But she was a true competitor and wouldn't accept a false victory. She wanted the genuine article.

Let her take it.

Ahead, she must have heard the relentless pounding of his stallion's hooves closing the distance between them, for she encouraged her mount into a full gallop. Still, Percy gained on her. When he'd drawn level, he risked a quick glance to find her smiling, unreservedly. He couldn't help but respond in kind to such full-throated joy.

They topped a short hill, and the stables, with the manor house beyond, rose into view. He pulled ahead by half a stride, then a full stride, with ease. Still, Isabel dug in, like he knew she would, even though she surely knew the race was lost.

She was a fighter.

He liked that about her.

This heady joy, it was the first pure joy he'd experienced in years. He'd forgotten how good it felt in his body, all the way to the cockles of his soul.

The race won, he tugged on his stallion's reins. "Whoa," he commanded, slowing to a trot. Breath heaving and ragged, he circled to face her as she approached. Her smile hadn't abated a whit. Even with night encroaching on the day, the world felt bright within and without.

"Before you crow victory," she called out, "keep in mind that you, good sir, are riding astride. I, on the other hand, am riding sidesaddle. Hardly what I would call an irreproachable victory." An easy laugh escaped her. It flittered through and warmed him.

"There is no such thing as irreproachable victory where winners and losers are concerned," he retorted. "And you, my dear, are the loser in this scenario."

Laughter bubbled up and overflowed from her. He'd delighted her, and he wanted to do it again. He wanted to reach out and draw her to him and kiss her light laughter into something deeper.

Increment by increment, his smile fell away. And, increment by increment, the laughter drained from her in response. He'd forgotten who he was, who she was, and who they were in relation to each other.

He cleared his throat. "I must attend an estate matter. Watkins will see to you at the stable."

With that, Percy circled his mount and galloped away, leaving the confused furrow of Isabel's brow and the pleasure of her in the dust. Into its void expanded the familiar emptiness.

What choice had he? She was the means to an end, and that end was Montfort. In a few days' time, he would never see Isabel again.

He could ignore that the thought only compounded his emptiness.

14

———

Under the cover of darkness, Percy walked the grounds from the stables to Rosebud Cottage, and his stomach growled dissatisfaction at its state of emptiness.

Tonight, he'd declined dinner with the family, citing concerns about a mare that was ready to foal. The truth, but not the entirety of it. In all honesty, he didn't want to sit next to Isabel for the hour it would take to sup.

Didn't want?

Oh, he *wanted*.

The fact was that he didn't trust himself to sit next to Isabel. Somehow, the woman had snuck into his bloodstream.

He needed to speak with her in private, not in front of his family in his role as infatuated husband, a role that, in truth, he might find too easy to play.

In addition to all he'd learned about Isabel, he'd received confirmation: Montfort was, indeed, holding something over her. A debt, she'd said. And then she'd said naught more.

Blast.

Patience, he reminded himself.

Then he'd gone and botched the rest of the conversation. When she'd asked why he would help her, he'd responded with the truth—*quid pro quo*—but it wasn't the entire truth. Another truth lay deeper and closer to the heart of the matter. He didn't like seeing this woman shouldering the burden of handling Montfort, alone. She would do anything for her family, that was clear, but that she was doing it alone, sat wrongly inside him.

She didn't have to be alone.

That was what he should have told her this afternoon.

To his right appeared the conservatory. He stopped to take in its stone and glass magnificence illuminated from within like a water globe held to the light. Legend had it that his mother had personally overseen its construction, ensuring it attached to the south-facing wall of Gardencourt and was constructed of ground-to-roof glass with just enough stone and mortar to hold the panes in place.

Deeper inside, movement caught his eye. *Isabel*, lit like an actress on the stage, meandering and weaving through greenery and statuary. Her face wore an unguarded expression, as if she ambled through an enchanted forest and desired nothing more than to become lost in its mysteries.

She was transfixingly lovely, he could admit, but not in the way so many women wrapped themselves in the cold fortress of their beauty. This woman was *appealing*, a warm humanity radiating from her that was rare. He'd spent too many years around people who had either forgotten or purposely discarded their humanity, who regarded it as weakness. This woman used it as a strength, as a guiding compass.

With a will of their own, his feet began moving, not toward his stark room in Rosebud Cottage, which somehow retained a wintery chill in the heat of summer and where he should be heading, but toward the warmth and the light.

Toward *her.*

He pulled open the iron and glass door and was instantly greeted by a rush of humid air and the particular earthy aroma of the conservatory. The door clicked shut behind him, and he began wending through all manner of plants. Orchids and gardenias and even a spiky American aloe, but mostly well-pruned orange, lemon, and lime trees that had doubled in size since last he'd seen them. All these plants and trees dated back to his mother, who had chosen them with an eye toward both practicality and beauty.

Even as his mind pulled toward memories of playing all manner of childhood games here, so too, was he very much in the present, all too aware that he drew nearer to *her,* his heart inserting an extra beat into its rhythm with every step he took. By the time he was within sight of her, his heart raced in his chest.

Just beyond a rangy camellia shrub, she tested the weight of a low-hanging orange in her ungloved palm, her cheeks flushed with humidity. Her eyes drifted shut as she leaned in and sniffed the fruit.

"You can take it if you like," he found himself calling out.

Her eyes flew open, and she startled back, a sheepish smile on her lips, a laugh escaping her. Then her smile faltered, but not before it occurred to Percy that to smile had been her first instinct. She contained a light inside her that hadn't yet been extinguished by whatever life—and Montfort—had thrown at her.

Percy wanted some of her light for himself. He had for days. And that wanting, no matter how he tried to avoid and outwit it only increased with every moment spent with her. For herein lay the trouble:

He did nothing by half measures. If he took a taste of her light, he wouldn't be satisfied until he'd consumed it all.

"Are you sure?"

"You're Lady Percival," he replied, only half ironically. "Nothing at Gardencourt isn't yours."

Her head canted to the side, and a private, little smile curled about the corners of her mouth. She was considering his words, whether or not to enter the fiction with him. She plucked the fruit. "This place is bewitching."

Percy moved closer, he couldn't help himself. He twisted an orange off a branch. "For a child, it's the most magical place in the world. At least once a day, I would escape my governess, the mighty Frau Gerta, and hide in here for hours at a time."

"Were you a very naughty boy?"

Oh, how he liked the way she asked that question. "Frau Gerta certainly thought so. I could never make her understand that I was an explorer of the deepest, darkest jungles of Africa and Amazonia."

"Ah, a misunderstood boy. On the hunt for gold, I presume?"

"Silver would do in a pinch."

"Did you wrestle jaguars?"

"Pythons, too."

"Fight off blood-thirsty piranhas?"

"I can show you the bite marks on my legs."

This got a laugh from her, and Percy felt like the lad he once was, the one who would go to any lengths to pull a smile from a pretty girl.

"Intrepid boy," she said as her thumb dug into the navel of her orange. A spray of fresh citrus cut a light swath through the heavy scents of dank earth and steaming tropics.

"My mother was involved in every step of creating this conservatory. The design, the materials, the plants."

"And what did she think of your exploits? A knighthood for your brave service to the Crown?"

Percy hesitated. Isabel didn't know. Why would she? "My mother died giving birth to me."

"The duchess isn't your..." The shake of his head halted the rest of the sentence in her mouth. "*Oh.* I'm so very sorry."

Percy swallowed, a knot in his throat, the first time he'd felt it in decades. Many others had spoken such words to a motherless boy over the years, but from those mouths the words had been mere platitude. Isabel's words held her heart.

He held up his orange. "This is my favorite food."

"*You* have a favorite food, Lord Percival? I thought it possible that you lived on air," she said, lightly.

"Can you peel yours in one go?" he asked.

Her brow lifted, ripe with disbelief that he would dare pose such a question. "*Claro.* I would have to forfeit all claims to my Spanish heritage if I couldn't."

Her fingers began moving to make her point, and Percy's responded. In silence, they peeled their oranges in unspoken challenge, playfulness in the air.

He *liked* this woman.

When had that happened?

Finished, he held up one end of the rind and let the rest fall in a spiral.

"Impressive." She balanced her unfurled rind on her palm. "For an Englishman." When she let her rind fall, it had double the spirals of his. "At long last, Lord Percival, I have bested you."

He smiled, he couldn't help it. Laughed, too. He couldn't help that either.

How long had it been since he'd smiled and laughed with his whole body?

This afternoon, actually, when they had raced.

She halved her orange and peeled off a segment. Before Percy could anticipate her next move, she brought the fruit to her mouth and bit it in half. A thin stream of juice trickled down her chin. A quickening occurred inside his body, his lungs suspended mid-breath, and hot blood rushed through his veins. His gaze had no choice but to fix on her lips.

With a laugh, she made to swipe the juice away. As if released from a coil, Percy crossed the distance between them and caught her hand mid-swipe. "Allow me."

The moment transformed. She felt it, too. He saw it in the release of her smile, in the flare of her pupils that pushed her irises into thin green rings. He knew that flare. Responding desire.

His thumb traced the sticky trail of juice from the delicate indent at her collarbone, up the column of her neck, over her pert chin, until it stopped just below her full bottom lip. Their eyes held.

Her hand wrapped around his.

With a subtle tug, and before he knew what she was about, she pushed his thumb into her mouth. Her tongue flicked across slippery skin, and desire sparked into pure lust, raw and demanding.

Then she sucked, her gaze never wavering from his.

He could give in to it, the pull toward his innate wickedness—after all, he was only a man.

With a feat of strength of which he wouldn't have thought himself capable, he broke away.

Her eyes filled with confusion, her lush lips, red, shiny, and slippery, formed a perfect "O" that demanded to be kissed.

He couldn't look at those lips and say what he needed to say. Through heaving breath and a loss for words, he somehow uttered, "This can't be."

Then he pivoted and ran like his life depended on it.

It did.

Or, at least, the life he'd fashioned for himself did.

INCREDULOUS, Isabel stared at Lord Percival's retreating back. Her lungs refused to inhale or exhale or do anything useful.

What in the blazes had she just done?

He rounded a corner and strode out of sight. Indignation flared through her, and her feet scrambled into pursuit.

He wasn't getting away that easily.

They weren't finished.

Fleet feet dashed across green and pink checkered marble as she wove through clumps and clutches of tropical plants in pursuit. She caught sight of the blasted man stepping through the exterior doorway and increased her pace. "Lord Percival," she called, "we're not—"

The door slammed in her face. *Rude.* Her jaw clenched in resolution, she dug her shoulder into steel and pushed the door wide. Across the expanse of the moonlit terrace, she saw the top of his head just before it dipped out of sight as he descended steps. Those steps led to the path to Rosebud Cottage.

He was going to hide from her in his room. To brood, or whatever it was he did in there.

Not on this night.

Resolve redoubled, she scurried into motion, her feet trilling down the stairs in chase. She wasn't sure what she was going to say when she caught him, but she was absolutely finished with all their unfinished interactions. Tonight, they would see this through to its resolution, whatever *this* might be, a prospect that both thrilled and quaked her to her bones.

"Lord Percival," she cried out again as he disappeared into the copse of woods. "This is..." She searched for the correct word. "This is..." He'd reached Rosebud Cottage, his hand on the front door handle. "*Unworthy* of you...of a man of your rank!"

Again, a door slammed in her face, but not before her ear caught an unimpressed laugh.

The cheek!

She rushed into the cottage and stopped short of slamming the door. Tilly, Nell, Eva, and the baby were upstairs. She listened for Ariel's cry for three rushed heartbeats, but detected no sound. She exhaled a sigh of relief. She didn't want Eva sticking her nose in where it didn't belong. This, whatever *this* was, was between Isabel and Lord Percival, whose bedroom door she heard shut on a muted click.

She lightened her step to a quiet tiptoe through the dark house, only stumbling into two chairs and one sharp table edge along the way. At last, she reached his decidedly closed door and twisted the handle. It didn't budge. She pressed her ear to oak and listened. Not a peep.

Her mouth to the crack where door met frame, she hissed, "Open this door." If a whisper could be a shout, hers was. "We're *not* finished."

Her ear again pressed to the door, she waited...and waited...for a sound, a sign, an acknowledgment, *anything*. At last, she heard it: a muffled shift, a light creak, a shuffle across bare floorboards.

Relief was quickly replaced with distress when the door opened and she all but fell into the room. He took a seat in a small, wooden chair, the picture of his usual laconic and devastating self.

Isabel stopped in the middle of the room and took

in its furnishings: low, narrow bed with one worn blanket and one flat pillow; nightstand; dresser with three drawers; washstand in the corner; the chair he sat upon. None of it embellished or ornate. Simple. Spare. No excess. "Whose room is this?"

"It was the butler's quarters when Rosebud Cottage was the main house."

Proclivity toward self-denial.

Confirmation settled inside Isabel. "You're the son of a duke, and you live in a servant's room?"

He shrugged. "Your family are upstairs. This is simpler."

"*Simpler?*" Really, this man. "You could be living in the manor house. You have access to every finery known to mankind. Yet you live in a servant's room"—she shivered—"that doesn't seem to have a heat source." Though it was summer, the nights held a measure of winter never absent from this island.

He flicked an unconcerned wrist at the wall behind him. "Heat would have come from the kitchens, but since they are no longer in use, a bracing chill persists."

"A *bracing* chill?" she scoffed. "So, the son of a duke does without."

"I do wish you would stop calling me that."

"The son of a *duke*? Which you are?"

He winced.

"It is important."

"If you say."

"I do say."

"Is that all?"

"In fact, it isn't. You do without."

Another shrug. "'Tis nothing new to me."

"To deprive yourself of worldly comforts and—" She hesitated on the next word. "Pleasures?"

He shifted and drew a distressed creak from the flimsy chair supporting him. At last, she had found a weakness in his armor. "You don't wear the fine silk and linen of your rank. You don't eat meat. Or sugar. Or cream. Or hardly anything, for that matter. You deny yourself like a Papist monk. Are you wearing a hairshirt, too?"

"You've certainly been observing me."

"Oh, yes, *husband*, I have, and the way you live makes little sense to me."

Yet another shrug. "I've fallen out of the habit of living like a lord."

"When you were a spy for a decade?" Oh, why had she said such a thing, like she had the right?

The frigidity of the air had nothing on the coldness in his eye. "You shouldn't speak of matters of which you know nothing."

Isabel shook her head. He wasn't wrong. She must return to the main conversational thread. If not tended properly, she had a feeling it would unravel in her hand before she understood the substance of it.

"It's like you're—" Understanding broke upon her like sudden dawn. "It's like you're *addicted*."

Slowly, he uncrossed his legs and sat forward, elbows on his knees, his focus square on her. The very portrait of a wolf ready to spring into action. She swallowed. This hadn't been her best idea.

Still, she would see it through. "You're addicted to *privation*."

His brow knitted for an instant and released. Had she read confusion there? One second ticked by, then another, the room shrouded in a stillness that couldn't hold indefinitely.

"I'm not sure," he began, the words rough and low in his throat, "how you could be so right and yet so wrong at the same time."

"Pardon?"

"You are correct in one regard. I *am* addicted." He

shifted back in his chair, which moaned its displeasure, and placed his hands behind his head as if taking a stretch. She wasn't foolish enough to think he was relaxing.

"But I am most definitely *not* addicted to privation." He spoke his shocking words casually. They were anything but. "Do you not suspect the true source of my addiction?"

"Should I?" Oh, that she could control the quiver in her voice.

"I've observed you to be a logical woman."

"But what you're saying makes no logical sense," she countered. "A fact cannot be wrong and right at the same time."

He smiled across the ten feet that separated them. The smile of a wolf fixed on his prey, primed for the chase. A shiver ran through her. "Can it not? Just as a coin has two sides, so, too, is my addiction privation's opposite. You've simply been viewing it from the wrong angle."

Breath held, she waited.

"It's *pleasure* I'm addicted to."

15

Isabel's body went hot.

Here she stood, in the middle of this room, *exposed*, the sole focus of this man who was now looking at her like he could devour her whole.

Who needed an external heat source? Her internal one was up to the task.

"You should turn and run," he said. "Wouldn't that be the logical course?"

Yes, she should say *yes*, but the word stuck in her throat and her feet remained rooted to the floor.

"You see, Isabel, a shift occurs inside me when my control is broken and my addiction unleashed." He unfurled his long, lean body and rose. "I do nothing by half measures." He took a step forward, more of a prowl. Now nine feet separated them. "My appetite for privation is equal only to my appetite for pleasure." Another step. *Eight feet.* "A wickedness courses through my veins."

"*Oh*," Isabel breathed.

Why, oh, why wouldn't her legs move? As quick as she thought it, she knew the answer.

Because they didn't want to.

She trembled and quaked, oh, yes, but not from fear.

"I want..." *Seven...six...*"And I want..." *Five...four...* "And I want."

Two more steps, and he stopped a foot shy of her. He tucked his thumb beneath her chin and lifted. Her eyes had no choice but to meet his.

"That wanting had been under control until..."

"*Until?*"

A dark smile lit within his eyes, curled about his mouth. "Until *you.*"

"Are you trying to frighten me away?" It was possible.

"Not anymore."

His hand formed a light caress. She swayed forward, into his touch. Her eyes opened—when had they closed?—to find his steady upon her.

"Is that all you do?" she asked. For some reason, she wanted to push him.

He lifted an inquisitive eyebrow.

"Think of your own wants?" She threw the question at him like a challenge.

The air went electric. His eyes narrowed. She'd intrigued him. Head canted subtly to the side, he took her measure, deciding if she meant what she'd said.

Her every last cell pulsed with sincerity.

"The pleasure I give is equal to the pleasure I receive, I can assure you." He closed the remaining distance between them. The banked heat of his body reached out to her. "Shall I demonstrate?" he asked on a low rumble. "Would you *die* if I don't?"

He was tossing her words back at her. "I think I would."

Now, if only he would *demonstrate.*

He cupped the nape of her neck, his head angling as he drew into her. She closed her eyes in anticipation of the press of his mouth against hers. Instead, his lips touched her ear, raising goose bumps along her skin, tightening her nipples into hard buds.

"For example," came his hot whisper, "I take great pleasure from kissing *this* sensitive bit of skin." His lips touched her neck, and she gasped. She felt the scratchy brush of his smile. "I believe your pleasure to be commensurate with mine. Correct me if I'm wrong."

She grabbed his shoulders for support, tense muscles bunched beneath her fingers, and angled her head to allow him more access as he trailed kisses down its length.

She wouldn't be correcting him anytime soon.

"But it's not enough to touch you. I would taste you, too." His tongue flickered along her collarbone up her neck to her ear.

And she thought she would die if he *didn't* kiss her?

"Soon, I'll show you what more I take pleasure in tasting."

A shiver rippled down her spine, down to the core of her sex. She pressed into him, her body urgent with need, unable to take much more of his slow seduction. He took her cue and reached around to undo the buttons of her dress and the laces of her short corset in a few efficient motions, the garments falling to a hushed puddle at her feet.

He angled back to take in her breasts. "Magnificent," he said, a rough utterance. Long, masculine fingers caught the delicate gold chain hanging from her neck, lifting it to reveal Mama's hamsa pendant. Isabel met a question in his eyes, but her hand wrapped around his and he let it drop.

Before she knew what he was about, he cupped her bosom from beneath and took one nipple into his mouth, sucking through the thin white cotton chemise. Liquid heat pooled between her legs, and she clutched his forearms to brace herself, cords of steely muscle running beneath her fingertips. Unable not to, again she pressed into him, needing to feel all of him. *Oh.* The rigid length of his manhood strained against her belly.

Liquid heat turned to lava as she went ravenous for him.

A virgin, she was, but an innocent, she was not.

She understood the cliff they were careening toward, and she couldn't step off its edge fast enough. She wanted, *needed*, this man inside her.

She reached between their bodies, humid with lust and sweat, and feathered fingertips along the, *oh*, so long length of him through the wool of his trousers. Though it was the lightest of touches, it dragged a long animal groan from him that called to the beast within her. She stroked him again, this time slower and with more pressure, evoking an even more gratifyingly primal sound from him.

"What are you doing to me? Trying to finish me off before we've started?"

"This gives *me* great pleasure."

He caught her eye. "It will give you so much more."

Oh, his words. The way he spoke them. Playful. Serious. The delicious promise within them that she would see fulfilled. She pushed his hard, lean stomach —truly, it had no give—and his brow furrowed in confusion. "You are overdressed for the occasion."

He took her meaning and stepped back until he reached the bed. One more push, and he sat. Greedy, she pulled his shirt over his head and gasped, utterly unprepared for the sight of him.

The man was a glory, all lean, corded muscle on his chest and stomach, which was divided into segments that she desperately wanted to lick.

But it was his skin that held her back, or, more accurately, the scars that littered it. Some shallow, some deep; some long, narrow slashes, others round, deep pocks. A story hid behind each and every one. Wounds only healed in the flesh, not in the heart or soul. They represented hurt, she knew that much from having looked into his eyes.

She touched light fingertips to one. "Who hurt you?"

"Do you have all night?"

"What happened to you?" she whispered.

He reached up and caressed her cheek. "Not now."

His fingers curled around the back of her head and pulled her down. It was only when his lips touched hers that she realized they hadn't yet kissed. It started gently before transforming into something immediate and ferocious as he pulled her between his legs and the full length of her body pressed into him. Before she knew what he was about, he'd flipped her around so that she now lay on the bed and he hovered above, his gaze roving across her body, eating her up with his eyes. "I just might devour you in one bite."

She shivered, though she burned. Oh, she wanted to be devoured. By him.

"Let's see if you're ready." She wasn't sure of his meaning until she felt it: the slide of his finger along her wet slit. He smiled, wolfish. "I'd say so."

Primally, she arched her back. She needed more of his touch.

"What was that?" he whispered in her ear.

Had she spoken aloud? No matter. She would scream it from the rooftops, if it meant getting what she wanted, which was…"*More.*" The word emerged ragged, pulsing with desperation.

On a low chuckle, his mouth found hers, heightening the pleasure of his finger pressing into her quim. Her back arched into him, and she moaned into his mouth. The tangle of his tongue and the slide of his finger had taken the kindling that was her body and lit it into full-blown conflagration, desire licking at her with white-hot flames.

All the while, a tension began to coil inside her, making her pant with ache as she strained against his hand. Then his thumb brushed a particularly sensitive spot, and she gasped, inhaling his breath into her lungs. He rubbed it again, a feather touch was all it took to send flutters of pleasure through her, even as that coil in her sex tightened, building toward something. His finger became a rhythmic slide. "You like that, don't you?"

"Yes," she exhaled, breathless.

Oh, she liked.

Very much.

Then *it* was upon her, the *it* her body had been reaching for, and she suddenly understood what this act was about and why people risked all to experience it.

She fell over an edge and tumbled headlong into a cluster of bliss she'd had no notion of as her body clenched and held for both the longest and shortest moment in the history of time. Then her body released in quivers that tremored through her, shot lightning into her veins.

His finger slid from her, and she mewled a tiny cry of protest. His voice rough velvet, he said, "I think you're ready."

He unbuttoned his trousers, and his manhood pressed against her sex. She glanced at its rigid length, thick and ready, and experienced a wave of raw lust. She wanted him, every last inch of him, inside her, *now*. He pushed at the slit of her sex, and her hips lifted to receive him, guided by instinct.

"So wet," he whispered, the hot, dirty words only increasing her lust.

He was so…*big*. She gave a cry of frustration as her

hands found and clutched his tensed buttocks. She wanted him *now*, didn't he understand?

His smile said he knew, and he wasn't going to give her what she wanted.

He would give her what she *needed*.

His body angled forward, his delicious weight pressing into her, his cock hard and ready at the opening of her sex.

He'd only begun to enter when he went still as stone. Unsettled eyes met hers. "*Bloody hell.* We must stop. You're a—"

She pressed light fingertips to his mouth. "*Shh.*"

If he finished that sentence, *they* would be finished.

And she wasn't done. "Not for much longer."

Her body adjusting to the thick feel of him, she wrapped her legs around his waist. His body trembled.

A storm gathered in his eyes. "I can't think when you do that."

"When I do what?" She squeezed her thighs.

The storm in his eyes hadn't abated, but the hunger in them expanded.

He wanted her, and she would have him.

"We are here, now. I *need* you."

Unnamable emotion flickered in his gaze. One hand slid beneath her and cupped her bottom, in the process tilting her hips up. "Are you certain?"

She nodded, never more certain of anything in her life.

With a single, swift thrust, he entered her fully, and she cried out in a combination of pleasure and pain.

He'd pierced her maidenhead.

She gave her hips a shallow swivel as she adjusted to the feel of him. Already, the pleasure outweighed the pain.

He tucked his thumb beneath her chin, forcing her to meet his eyes. "We are going to slow down."

"But—"

He pressed his mouth to hers, inhaling her protest that she didn't want slow, and gave her what she needed with a deliberate thrust of his hips.

"*Oh*," she moaned. How had she doubted him?

In and out, he moved, unhurried, their breath, their sweat, mingling, the pain from her maidenhead becoming a distant memory as he dealt out pleasure, stroke by deliberate stroke. Propped on one elbow, he alternated between kissing and watching her as she began to fall apart beneath his watchful gaze. Her fingers dug into his back, afraid that if she let go, he might stop and then she didn't know what she would do.

His knee slid up to give him the leverage to plunge deeper at another angle. "Oh, yes," crawled from her throat as her body began to be carried away along the same wave from minutes ago.

"Come undone for me again, Isabel," he growled as he increased his rhythm and his lust-glazed eyes— surely a mirror of her own—held hers, increasing her desire as his thrusts became more focused, more demanding. Her sex wound tighter and tighter until, at last, her world cracked open and crumbled, reducing her to a being composed purely of sensation, its tight flickers of pulse and release devastating her from the core of her sex to the tips of her toes.

Above her, he tensed in that sweet moment before climax and broke on a shout, the sweat of exertion trickling in thin rivulets down his neck, dripping onto her in air-cooled drops. Stroke by stroke, he slowed and then stopped, the aftermath rippling through her as his enervated form collapsed. She embraced the heavy feel of him.

When he slid to the side to relieve her of his weight, she experienced a pang of loss, and the reality of their situation began to steal in. She done what she'd wanted to do—part of her even wanted to do again—but she'd also done what Montfort wanted her to do. The very idea of it made her gut clench with anxiety.

Satiety transformed into urgency. She must leave this room and this man, who was now lying on his side and watching her with those dark, inscrutable eyes, *now*.

The moment her toes touched bare floorboards, she heard behind her, "Leaving so soon? I thought we might discuss a few matters."

ISABEL SHOT to her feet and snatched up her dress. She wasn't in the mood for a talk.

Well, too bad.

Percy was.

"This blood on the sheets?" He pointed. She didn't look. Instead, she grabbed her discarded corset. "It was for the Earl of Pembroke, correct?"

She squeezed her eyes shut, as if she could change her circumstances by sheer dint of will.

"It doesn't work that way," he said.

Her eyes flew open. "What?"

"Reality. It stays itself no matter how you might hope to wish it into something more palatable. Believe me, I know."

She gave a frustrated cry and swung around, crossing the room, her fingers wrapped around the door handle in a matter of seconds.

"I can help you," Percy called out. She froze, the posture of her shoulders suggesting she was waiting for the catch. "But you must tell me everything."

She inhaled a heavy breath, her shoulders lifting and releasing with the burden of it. She shook her head. "You cannot help with this," she said, her voice cracking.

Within that fissure, she revealed fear and frustration, yes, but more, too: *longing*. Longing for what, he couldn't know. But he did know this: she longed for her situation to be other than what it was.

She pulled the door wide enough to slip through, and she was gone.

Percy fell onto his back with a frustrated groan directed at a ceiling that held no answers. She'd been a virgin, and, still, he'd seduced her. The worst of what was whispered about him was true. *Wild. Debauched. Libertine. Wicked.*

He'd denied it air for years. Denial was the only solution that worked, for one pleasure inevitably led to another. It was a slope he was all too prone to slip down.

He could marry her, in truth. It was the after-the-fact solution pursued by many a pair of too-ardent lovers. She was the daughter of the Spanish aristocracy, therefore a suitable match in the eyes of Society.

No. He stopped the sequence of thought dead in its tracks. *No.* She might be a suitable wife, but he wasn't a suitable husband. He'd proven that once before.

Isabel didn't need a useless husband. What she needed was help and, though she wouldn't admit it, protection, too, for she wasn't a willing participant in Montfort's games. Percy understood this last point with crystal clarity.

"You cannot help with this."

Oh, but he could, and he would.

That light he saw in her, the one life hadn't managed to extinguish, it needed protection. Isabel would not be alone. She had him.

So help him.

16

I sabel strolled arm-in-arm with Eva, the mellow dawn sun peering through an elegant willow ahead, and could hardly countenance how she'd arrived here.

One moment, she was struggling through a night's sleep that succeeded in being both sated and fitful. The next, Eva was shaking her awake and shushing away Isabel's concern that yet again life had gone horribly awry and they had to run. But, no, all Eva wanted was an early morning walk before the day's heat was upon them.

It hadn't been in Isabel to refuse, for she detected traces of the old Eva in the Eva standing before her. That Eva who was always on the lookout for a new adventure, the one from before Montfort had knocked on her family's door and kicked their world sideways.

Now, boots wet with dew, they strolled beside the pond, light mist floating above as sun rays peeked through and scattered muted light. Eva squeezed Isabel close. "What a magical place. 'Tis quite a splendid family you've married into, *querida*."

A note of discord disturbed Isabel's sense of rightness, reminding her that she and Eva weren't in the *before*. "You know that isn't the fact of the matter."

"Ah, but that's the fiction of it." A cold smile curved about Eva's mouth. "And your present reality."

Isabel couldn't deny that particular truth. But since Eva had opened the door, Isabel thought she may as well step through it, for she wished to discuss a related matter. "You seem to have taken a decided interest in my"—oh, what strange reality had her uttering the next word—"*husband's* family."

A degree of warmth entered Eva's smile. "The Misses Bretagne and Radclyffe are splendid girls. They are well on their way toward becoming diamonds of the first water, wouldn't you agree?"

Isabel nodded. She had no doubt of it.

"When we return to London, I would like to ask them to pose for sketches in a few of my original creations."

"They are the daughters of aristocrats," Isabel pointed out, gently. Eva's ambitions could get away from her at times. "I'm not sure that is done."

Eva flicked a stray stonefly off her sleeve. "Surely, my logical sister with a mind for trade can see how such exposure would benefit us."

"I doubt you would be able to sew fast enough to keep up with demand." It wasn't the youthful branch of the estate's guests that Isabel wanted to discuss, however. "And how about Lady Bertrand Montfort? You do seem to be devoting considerable attention to *her*."

What little warmth had entered Eva's smile, cooled in an instant. "Such a delightful woman," she all but spat.

"She's the wife of Montfort."

"Her name does make that fact rather obvious, *querida*. Your point?"

"Such a friendship," Isabel pressed, "isn't the wisest—"

"Speaking of wisdom!" Eva exclaimed. "Have you

heard the pearls that drip from Lady Bertrand's mouth? Sometimes, their effect is such that I just want to slap her face."

Isabel pulled Eva to a stop and met her sister dead in the eye. "That is something you simply can never do." This was the Eva, the one who had become wild and unknowable, who Isabel feared. "*Never.*"

A spark of rebellion flashed in Eva's eye and was gone in an instant, replaced by a careful flatness. "So serious, *querida*, I spoke figuratively, of course. Come and continue our little stroll." She pulled Isabel's arm, tugging her forward. "Enjoy the cool nip in the air before the heat presses down on us. Do you know I feel more myself with every minute I spend here? I sincerely thank you for bringing me along on your impromptu honeymoon. We all needed a little break from London. I mean, look at you."

"*Me?*"

"Oh, yes, the estate has certainly worked its magic on you."

"Oh?" A certainty entered Isabel's mind that she wouldn't like the direction Eva was leading their talk. While she'd experienced a momentary fear that Eva had again procured laudanum, this conversation put that anxiety to rest. Eva might be altered in many ways from the carefree person she'd once been, but her sense of mischief had returned. A good sign, even if Isabel was on the receiving end of it.

"This morning, you have a…a…" Eva's eyes screwed up to the sky, as if she were searching for the perfect word. "*Glow.* In truth, I've never seen you so radiant."

Isabel cut Eva a sharp glance and pressed her mouth into a firm line. For her part, Eva kept her gaze trained on the trail before them, the picture of innocence.

"That said," Eva continued, "I have detected but one

botheration with our paradise found." She leaned in conspiratorially. "Rosebud Cottage has a ghost."

"Eva, you don't believe in such gothic silliness," Isabel dismissed.

"'Tis true, I didn't." Eva allowed a dramatic tick of time to pass. "Until last night."

Sudden sweat slicked Isabel's palms. "Last night?"

"Oh, indeed, the cottage was simply alive with all manner of creaks, moans, and groans. I even thought I heard a shout."

Isabel couldn't seem to draw breath.

"The noises didn't wake you?" Eva asked.

Isabel gave her head a mute shake, sound unable to pass her lips.

"They didn't wake Ariel, either." Eva's face had *the* look, the one Isabel had known since girlhood. The one that said she was going to toy with you and there was nothing you could do about it. "I suppose I was the only witness to the haunting. It did go on for a while, I daresay." Was that a smile playing about Eva's mouth? "Rather impressive."

Isabel understood what Eva had done. She didn't want Isabel to press her about her intentions toward Montfort's wife, so she'd turned the conversation around on her. *Touché.* Isabel would let Eva's sleeping dogs lie, if she would only return the favor. For here was the thing: Isabel wouldn't discuss, or even think about, last night.

Her body, on the other hand, didn't seem to have much of a choice. It tingled and ached with a delicious lightness that hadn't stopped rushing through her since last night. *Alive*, that was how she felt. Her body had never been so aware of how very alive it was. No wonder she was glowing.

But it wasn't a feeling she could bask in and enjoy, no

matter how her body tried to convince her otherwise, for it further complicated matters that were already entirely too complicated. In doing a correct thing, the thing she was supposed to do—lose her maidenhead to Lord Percival—she'd done a very wrong thing—lost her maidenhead to Lord Percival without Montfort's permission.

How that sequence of thought disgusted her.

What should she do? Steal the sheets and present them to Montfort as a *fait accompli*? She recoiled from the idea, body, mind, and soul.

Yet she couldn't have it both ways. She couldn't save her family, or what was left of it, and keep her integrity intact. After all, she'd only done what she was supposed to have done that first night in Number 9 with another man. But...

It felt so very different to have done it with Lord Percival.

"I can help you."

How perilously close she'd come to accepting his offer. And the temptation of it still reached out to her, for she'd seen in his eyes that he'd meant every word.

But it was Montfort who held the keys to Papa's freedom.

She couldn't rely on the uncertain promises of Lord Percival. She must stay her course. Her first allegiance was to her family.

Now that Montfort was returned to Gardencourt, she had no excuse not to go to him and tell him all. But she simply couldn't. To reveal what happened last night in Lord Percival's bed to Montfort would feel like a betrayal of the lowest kind. This situation had formed into a Gordian knot that no amount of logic would untangle.

"*Querida*," Eva began as they ventured to an unfamiliar portion of the estate, "you are so very quiet of a sudden. Has this glorious morning stroll quite cleared your mind of conversation?"

Isabel struggled to find a subject other than the one that occupied nearly all the space in her brain. "I'm happy to hear you speaking of our shop again, Eva." A safe and reliable subject. "These last several months have been rather dull without your inspiration, and I believe our customers have noticed. Do you have plans to return to your duties?"

"Oh, I have plans."

On the surface, Eva's words might have allayed Isabel's fears, but a cryptic quality wove through them that incited no small amount of anxiety. Before Isabel could quiz Eva about her "plans," a series of muted, popping sounds carried toward them on a light breeze. The sisters' eyes met, brows raised. A booming bellow, followed by a long groan, rent the air.

"Is that an animal?" Isabel whispered.

They slowed their pace to a standstill, their ears attuned to further outcry. The muted, popping sounds had a rhythm, but the animal sounds were less predictable.

"If I am remembering my animal sounds correctly," Eva began, "I would say we are hearing a human male animal engaged in some manner of strenuous activity. Either that, or"—she cocked her head as if listening closely—"the ghost from Rosebud Cottage is haunting this part of the estate."

The certainty set in that Eva was most definitely toying with her, possibly punishing her for not confiding in her about last night. Isabel simply couldn't. She didn't understand it herself. Except that she'd *needed* to have Percy, and, in the light of day, her mind was having trouble reasoning through that need, its sheer, unquantifiable force. It defied all logic.

"Sister?" Eve was staring at her expectantly.

"Yes?"

"I asked if we should investigate."

"Oh, yes, of course."

Down this path which wound through all manner of shrubbery bursting with a dozen shades of summer green, Isabel and Eva followed the muted pops and animal groans that grew louder with each step. At last, they left the bushes behind and entered a clearing. The sight before them stopped their feet mid-step.

Eva flashed Isabel a curious look. "I certainly wasn't expecting *this*."

"Indeed," fell from Isabel's mouth.

Across the distance labored Percy and Lord Avendon, sweaty, grunting, swinging rackets, striking balls, deep in the throes of the most intense tennis match Isabel had ever laid eyes upon. She'd seen many a match played on the royal courts in Spain, but those were mostly royal ladies and courtiers engaged in little more than light volleying. Nothing serious. Nothing like the paces Percy and Lord Avendon were putting each other through.

Hair stuck to their faces, cheeks bright with exertion, they sprinted up and down, side to side, in dogged pursuit of the ball, while wearing lightweight wool trousers and white lawn shirts, sleeves rolled up to their elbows. Each man's features were set in the determination particular to any competitive endeavor to annihilate the other, stroke by stroke, neither giving up on a point, the resolve to win too strong to ever let up.

Still, even as the match stoked her competitive fire, Isabel found herself focusing not on the play, but rather on one player. Percy's long, lean body in motion possessed both a strength and grace that commanded the court. Sinewy and muscular, it was a body built for endurance.

She'd experienced every inch of that body last night.

She heated up by several degrees.

And it had naught to do with summer.

Now that she'd had him once, experienced what that magnificent body could do, she wanted it again. She was shaky with the feeling. He wasn't the only one who was addicted.

"Careful, *querida*," Eva said.

Isabel found Eva's devilish eyes studying her. "Of what?"

"To keep your drool in your mouth."

Cheeks hot, Isabel swung her gaze back to the court, focusing her attention on the match. Her fists clenched at her sides...Her jaw went tight...Her heart raced, as she was hopelessly drawn into the competition of these two well-matched adversaries, no question of which man she wanted to emerge the victor.

After a particularly long point of them trading stroke after punishing stroke from the baseline, Lord Avendon rushed to the net and took the point with a light volley. Eva clapped and shouted an unrefined, "That's the stuff!" If anyone was more competitive than Isabel, it was Eva.

Both men's heads whipped around. Lord Avendon gave them a small, surprised wave. "Mrs. Gardiner, my thanks."

Percy's attention immediately returned to the ball he was bouncing in tight sets of three. Even from the distance of fifty feet, Isabel sensed his annoyance.

"First set point," he called out, and Lord Avendon crouched into a ready position. Percy tossed the ball high into the air and slammed his racket into it so hard Isabel wouldn't have been shocked if it disintegrated upon impact. Anticlimactically, it dug deep into the net.

Again, Percy performed the ritual of bouncing the ball until he was ready to serve. "Second serve. Second set point."

His body stretched and arced on the toss, and his racket struck the ball harder this time, an unusual strategy for a second serve which was usually played at a safer pace. The ball whizzed across the net and struck the center line at such a high velocity that Lord Avendon hadn't the faintest chance of reaching it in time to return it.

Once again, Eva cheered her appreciation, but this time Lord Avendon's shoulders slumped in defeat. The next instant, he seemed to remember he was a future duke—and that ladies were present. "Well played, old man," he called out with the jolly vacuity particular to the upper-class English gentleman.

"Indeed," shouted Eva, "play another!"

Lord Avendon opened his mouth to reply when Percy beat him to it. "I'm needed in the stable." He hadn't yet met Isabel's eye, and she couldn't help feeling both relieved and slightly irritated.

Lord Avendon gave his uncle a quizzical glance. "Aren't we to play a tie-break set?" His eyes brightened with an idea. "How would you ladies like to play doubles?"

Isabel swooped in to reply before Eva. "Thank you for your kind offer, but my sister and I don't play."

"Oh, Isabel, how you loved watching the tennis matches on the royal courts." Eva's eyes widened in mock innocence. "Don't you remember?"

Percy's head whipped around. She had his full attention now. The man's curiosity never had its fill.

"An idea has occurred to me," Eva continued. "You could give Isabel a lesson, Lord Avendon, and that would free you, Lord Percival, to return to the stable, which seems to be your natural habitat."

Isabel cut in before either man could reply. "I'm not dressed for such sport."

Lord Avendon offered a shallow bow. "I would be honored, my lady."

Eva settled onto the damp ground, pulled a sampler from her reticule, and took up her needlework. "It's decided, *querida*."

Feet heavy as lead, Isabel made her way to the court, keenly conscious of Percy's awareness of her, even though he hadn't directly acknowledged her. They were well past that point. Their bodies simply *knew* their spatial relation to one another.

With the buoyancy of youth, Hugh bounced over to the net. "Uncle, do you mind if we use your racket?"

Percy handed the item over with a grunt that could only be described as surly.

As a very earnest Lord Avendon illustrated the technique of a proper forehand, Isabel could only half listen and go through the motions as the other half of her attention fixed on Percy. First, he retied the laces of one boot, then the other. Next, he knotted a tear in the net, after which he inspected its entire length. Then he picked up a small leather pouch and began walking the white lines of the court. When he came across a smudged edge, he would dip into the pouch and sprinkle chalk onto the offending section, smoothing out the line. It seemed Percy was doing everything *but* returning to the stable.

Intent on his self-appointed task of creating perfectly straight chalk lines, Percy crossed over to their side of the court. Every molecule in Isabel's body sprang into a higher state of alertness.

Until now, Lord Avendon had been standing before her, modeling how she should hold and swing the racket. The lad had been patient, but apparently his patience had its limits as she'd mirrored his motions with only half a heart. He abandoned his stance and came to stand behind her. Percy's head popped up.

"Here…"Lord Avendon reached around and covered her hand before pulling it back. Percy's eyebrows drew together. "When you swing your racket forward, you must flick your wrist like…*this*."

On the forward motion, Lord Avendon gave Isabel's wrist a quick twist that pulled a startled, "Ow!" from her.

Percy was on them in an instant. "What are you about, Hugh?" he snarled. "Trying to break her wrist?"

Lord Avendon sprang back, brow knit in confusion. "Of course not."

Instinctively, Isabel placed a staying hand on Percy's forearm, corded steel below her fingers. "Percy," she spoke low and steady, even through the riot of emotion that was galloping through her, "it was nothing."

At last, his eye met hers. What she saw there was a Percy unmasked.

Bad temper and annoyance shone in his eyes, yes, but more. Protectiveness and concern, too. Each one of these emotions was unexpected, but none of them unwelcome.

In truth, they rattled and warmed her and made her wonder if she had made the wrong decision in rejecting his offer of help last night.

Then she noticed his forearm was bare, as was her hand.

Skin touched skin, humid and hot.

Like that, last night charged into today.

17

Only with great strength of will and character, Percy pulled his arm back and broke contact with Isabel. Still, the imprint of her hand remained.

What was *that* reaction? He had been ready to tear Hugh limb from limb.

Gruff, he extended his hand. "Your racket."

Hugh gave it over, a cautious glint in his eye. Percy tried to keep his churlishness intact as he took Hugh's place behind Isabel, separated from her by six too few inches.

It was her scent that first assaulted his senses. His mouth watered. He couldn't draw breath, or release it. She glanced over her shoulder, her eyes meeting his and telling him to get on with this farce. *Right.*

"Give it a swing," he said, unable to keep a rasp out of his voice.

"Like this?" She went through the motion.

"Not quite," he said, helpless not to lean forward, his mouth close to her ear, so close his warm breath might be sending goose bumps down her spine, raising the fine hairs of her arms. His cock twitched, and he used every ounce of his legendary restraint to will it into submission. "As you move your arm forward, twist your wrist as the racket strikes the ball to give it enough lift to go over the net. Try it with a ball this time."

Isabel went through the motion, resulting in a ball that bounced off the net.

Percy saw that he had no choice. He must touch her. "Let's take it slowly."

His hand covered hers. His eye snagged on the throb of her pulse at the curve of her neck. The length of his body pressed against her, her sweet arse giving his restrained cock ideas. Together, he and she swung through the motion. At last, she understood it, but Percy couldn't care less.

The addiction that had been awakened demanded more than a single night. It demanded that he throw her over his shoulder and find the nearest bed. He reckoned upright against a tree would do in a pinch.

"Miss Radclyffe!" Hugh called out, breaking Percy free from thoughts that served no useful purpose.

Isabel pivoted to face Percy. Cheeks bright, she met his gaze. It wanted to skitter away, but Percy pinned it in place. He wanted her to see her effect on him. "That might be enough lessons for today," she said, a touch breathless.

"Is that so?" Percy hardly recognized his voice, so gravelly it had gone with desire. "But I have so much more to teach you."

Her pupils flared. *Desire.* It was all he could do not to take her right here on the tennis court. Society thought it had been scandalized by his exploits of yore? They hadn't seen anything.

Here it was, nearly a tangible thing and exactly what he'd expected: his wickedness unleashed. This morning, he'd awakened, craving her with every cell in his body—the scent of her, the feel of her, hot and humid and alive.

So, he'd sought out Hugh for a punishing match of tennis, hoping physical exhaustion would clear his mind. For a while, he'd convinced himself his remedy had worked, then she'd appeared and he knew the opposite to be true. He'd indulged once, and once was all it took to feed his addiction into full life. Knowing she wanted him, too, only emboldened it.

"Is Lulu with you?" Hugh asked Miss Radclyffe. His daughter's name pulled Percy's mind from its haze of iniquity.

Miss Radclyffe, who had appeared content to continue on her way, now pointed her feet in the direction of the tennis court. "Lucy was still abed when I left the house just before dawn." She smiled wryly. "'Tis my lot to be both a night and morning person."

Hugh's brow furrowed. "You were walking the grounds in the dark? Any number of calamities could befall a lone young lady."

Miss Radclyffe shrugged a shoulder, indifferent to Hugh's concern. "I recorded the sunrise from the widow's walk on the manor house roof, then decided to take a bracing stroll before breaking my fast. Now I've encountered all of you." She gestured toward their rather disjointed gathering. Mrs. Gardiner waved from her place on the other side of the court. "That is the totality of my morning activities, Lord Avendon. Would you like to see my log?" She held out a small notebook.

A sheepish look crossed Hugh's features. Anyone with eyes could see the lad was head-over-heels infatuated with the chit, a condition Percy understood well, having once been similarly afflicted. Hugh's saving grace might be that Miss Radclyffe didn't seem the least bit aware of the lad's interest or inclined to return it. Left without the sunlight of her encouragement, the feeling would likely wither on the vine.

"Would you care to join us in a doubles match?" Hugh asked. "All we need is a fourth."

"I don't think I'm properly attired for such activity," Miss Radclyffe demurred.

"You look dressed for the occasion to me," Hugh persisted. Percy almost felt badly for the lad. "And your movement shouldn't be inhibited as you don't wear a corset."

The unflappable Miss Radclyffe's eyes went wide, and her mouth gaped ever so slightly open. "How very observant of you, Lord Avendon," she said evenly, recovering her composure.

Hugh's skin went a pale shade of green.

"You have certainly made your case," Miss Radclyffe continued. "I shall be most pleased to make up the fourth."

Hugh brightened. "I shall just retrieve two more rackets from the shed." The lad was off like a shot and returned in fewer than thirty seconds, but enough time for Isabel to flash Percy a bewildered glance. *How has it come to this?* it seemed to say. He shrugged, unsure himself.

"Shall it be the ladies versus the lads?" Mrs. Gardiner called from her seat on the grass. Percy hadn't spent enough time with Isabel's sister to gain much of an understanding of the woman, but she seemed intelligent and...mischievous.

"I'm afraid I shall let my partner down," Miss Radclyffe said. "I've only hit back and forth with Lucy on a few occasions."

"That might be a disaster, considering how these two play." Isabel pointed from Percy to Hugh.

"Then it's settled," Hugh said. "Youth versus age. I shall provide cover for you, Miss Radclyffe," he finished with a gallantry that had begun to grate on Percy's nerves. Young men and their heroics.

The matter settled, play commenced. It started off friendly enough with laughter and smiles all around as they engaged in a bit of light volleying. Percy was careful to direct all his strokes toward Hugh, for Miss Radclyffe hadn't been exaggerating her lack of experience, and Hugh did the same. But Percy also kept half an eye out for what he knew was coming, as Isabel began to find her footing and test the limits of her forehand, which was gaining precision with every shot.

Then it happened: Isabel stopped laughing, and her smile tightened before falling altogether. She focused on Miss Radclyffe's weaker play and began directing her increasingly precise forehands toward the girl's side of the court to take easy points.

Isabel's competitive spirit had been awakened. She wanted to win, and blast it all if Percy didn't find it damned attractive.

For her part, Miss Radclyffe laughed it off, which only irritated Hugh, who tried coaching her on technique. "Lord Avendon," the girl said, "I'm afraid you'll find me frustratingly impervious to all instruction regarding sport."

Although Percy couldn't have predicted what would happen next, he couldn't help thinking he should have.

Isabel in the forecourt, Percy served the ball. Hugh zipped a deep groundstroke to Percy, who rallied it back. Isabel, clearly not to content to be a bystander while the men played, shifted cross-court into Hugh's return, racket extended wide, and drilled the ball hard into Miss Radclyffe's side. Not her side of the court, but into her body.

"Ouch," the girl yipped in shock.

"Lady Percival!" Hugh exclaimed. "That simply isn't done!"

Cheeks bright and chest heaving with competitive energy, Isabel shot back, "What isn't done? Strategy?"

"Not that sort," Hugh sputtered. "Not in a civilized society!"

Isabel stood her ground. "What sort of fool thinks there's anything civilized about a competition?"

"Lady Percival!" Hugh seemed to have run out of arguments.

"That's my Isabel!" exclaimed Mrs. Gardiner.

Percy held his tongue, but not the smile that pulled at the corners of his mouth.

Hugh drew himself up with indignation. He would make a formidable duke someday. "We do *not* batter one another. It's best we end the match here."

Miss Radclyffe stepped forward. "Oh, don't stop play on account of me. I am uninjured and rather enjoying myself."

"I do offer my apologies, Miss Radclyffe," Isabel said, battle-lust fading from her eyes. "I can get carried away in the heat of a moment."

Hugh looked at Percy meaningfully, as if telling him to keep his wife in line. Percy responded with an almost imperceptible shrug, but Hugh caught it, and his nostrils flared in frustration.

First, Isabel wasn't his wife to order about.

Second, even if she were, he wouldn't dream of it. He liked her like this.

He gave the ball three tight bounces and readied his serve. "Set point." He tossed the ball into the air, hoping to deliver an ace down the center line when a scrum of four wild-eyed boys blasted from the shrubberies, shouting and waving their arms in cacophonous battle cry as they ran circles around the court, taunting and teasing their older brother Hugh.

Everyone understood the match had come to an immediate end. Everyone except Isabel, who remained locked in position, waiting for Percy to serve. She threw an impatient glare over her shoulder. "Well?"

"I believe that's the match, *wife*." He couldn't help that last word, meant as a tease, but somehow it didn't feel like one.

Isabel threw her racket to the ground in disgust. Percy wanted nothing more than to throw her over his shoulder and march her to bed. The woman had become a drug in his veins. Only more of her would do.

"What did I miss?" Lucy stood at the edge of the court, looking very much like she would enjoy nothing more than to join in and contribute to the chaos that had broken out. How much Percy liked his daughter. If only he could convince her to like him, too.

Mrs. Gardiner came to her feet and dusted herself off. "Miss Bretagne, Miss Radclyffe, come and walk with me." She waved the girls over. "We must discuss how you would like your dresses remade for the dance. We only have a few days, and we must look our best for such a lively occasion. What are your favorite colors? Miss Radclyffe, please tell me that yours is plum."

"I believe purple is a mourning color, Mrs. Gardiner," replied Miss Radclyffe.

The girl was practical and forthright. Percy approved of her as the dearest friend of his daughter. Not that he had the right, as Lucy had made clear.

"Oh, dratted social convention," said Mrs. Gardiner. "But right you are. Perhaps we can sneak a pale shade of lavender into the trim without anyone noticing. Come, let's take your measurements."

The trio tossed distracted farewell waves over their shoulders as they strolled toward the manor house, already deep in sartorial conversation.

Hugh looked on like a forlorn pup as he watched them recede into the distance. A tennis ball thrown by one of his more daring brothers bonked him on the side of the head with a loud *pop!* The lad snapped to. "Who did that?"

The boys giggled and blew raspberries at their oh-so-serious brother. Hugh stood alone, on the brink of decision. Mind made up, he raised his arms above his head, hands clenched into claws, face contorted in ferocity, and bellowed a loud roar. "Don't let me catch you!" His brothers scurried away, screaming in delight as Hugh tore after them, snatching up the littlest of the group and tucking him under one arm, as he continued his charge down the hill toward the pond.

That left Percy alone with Isabel.

Her cheeks flushed bright, he couldn't resist reaching out and tucking an errant tendril behind her ear. Any excuse to touch her, to take a hit of her intoxication.

Awareness stole into the air.

"I should return to the cottage," she said in a voice not very sure of itself. That voice implied she might be convinced to stay. "I may be needed to help with the babe."

Percy's fingers itched to take her hand. He resisted. "Isabel, about last night—"

"And don't you have matters to attend in the stable?" A smile that wanted out quirked about her mouth. "Your natural habitat."

All this evasion was getting them nowhere. He needed more facts. He decided to start at the simplest place. "We need more honesty between us."

All remnants of her smile faded entirely.

There was so much he must tell her. That he knew she was a woman in need. That he understood the powers of circumstance and bad luck, of their ability to bend one to their will and strip one of choice. That he understood this because he'd been through that particular gauntlet. That he didn't want to see her life ruined because Montfort had caught her between his teeth.

That he didn't only want to tup her and himself into sweet oblivion, that he wanted to protect her, too.

"If it isn't Lord and Lady Percival," Percy heard at his back. Isabel's eyes widened on a point over his shoulder.

Percy pivoted, and his hands clenched into fists at his sides. "Montfort."

Slightly out of breath, the man stopped before them. "By the by, Bretagne, I neglected to commend you on your return to good health. You were looking rather dead to the world when last I saw you."

"Appearances can be deceiving," Percy said, seething with rage and futility. "I would think you know that better than most."

Percy glanced at Isabel and took in her guarded gaze. His hackles rose.

Deathly fear shone from her eyes. What had the man done to her?

It was all Percy could do not to grab Montfort by the neck and squeeze until all the life had drained out of him. He should have done it years ago. How many more lives had the man destroyed since then?

"I believe..." Isabel swallowed. "I believe I shall join the other ladies."

She fled as if the devil was at her back. He was.

Alone with Montfort, Percy cut right to it. "What's your game?"

"*Game?*" Montfort had the audacity to chuckle. "Haven't you heard? I'm out of the game, have been for almost two years. Don't you think the life of a country gentleman suits me?"

Percy snorted. "What's your business with Isabel?"

Montfort gave his familiar smile, the one of an adult indulging a child, secure in the knowledge the child would eventually wear himself out. "Speaking of business, there is a bit I must discuss with you. Tiny Tim's? Pizzy's Pleasure Palace? Tsk, tsk."

"Aye." Percy wouldn't deny it.

"You reached a hair too far with Number 9. It won't stand."

"I never thought it would."

All the false jollity faded from Montfort's visage. Left in its place was the cool, dead stare of a spider.

Montfort was coming for him. *Good.* Let him. This was exactly what Percy had been aiming for these last few months, to draw Montfort out. To make him strike.

But revenge was no longer his only goal.

Percy squared up to Montfort, who didn't flinch. The man's connections within the halls of power had made him untouchable for so long that he believed himself permanently so. "Listen to me and listen closely. Isabel is someone I—"

"*Love*, is it?"

"—Someone under my protection," Percy finished, not a little shaken by what he'd almost said. "You will not use her the way you used me."

"Now, Percy, your situation was altogether different. And, if you're honest with yourself, you know that our time together was the making of you into a man."

A swell of rage surged inside Percy. He curled it into a tight ball in his gut, even as it clamored for release. "If any harm comes to her, I shall find you, and I shall end you."

"Such dramatics. All I want for Isabel is the safety of her and her dear, beloved family."

Lies.

Montfort's mouth curved up into the patronizing smile that never managed to reach his eyes. "I've always valued that about you, Bretagne. Your tenacity."

"I have no value to you. I'm no longer your asset."

Percy followed his instinct and added, "And neither is Isabel."

Montfort's mouth pursed with displeasure and released the next instant. "What silly notions you youth get in your heads these days."

"Your day is coming, Montfort."

"Oh, it will be interesting to see whose day comes first." With that, Montfort took himself off, his step measured and confident, back to the manor house.

Or back to Hades where he belonged, for all Percy knew.

A reckoning was coming. The man hadn't bothered to deny he was coercing Isabel. Montfort was the sort of man who gave no thought to the destruction of a life, if that end was the means to his goal. A dozen years ago, he'd used Percy in his weakest moment without an ounce of compassion or compunction.

As one who knew Montfort's ruthlessness firsthand, Percy was the one person uniquely positioned to help Isabel.

But he needed her trust first.

How to convince her to join him to ensure Montfort's downfall? Percy needed to know what debt Montfort was dangling over her head. It involved her family, that was obvious. But what were its details?

Further, how had she gone from the Spanish court to a London gaming hell? What was Montfort's involvement? She would give Percy none of that information if she didn't trust him.

Blast. He'd likely already mucked up his chance. How could he gain her trust if all she saw in his eyes was desire?

He was trapped inside a devil's paradox. On the one side, he needed to get closer to her. On the other, he needed to keep his distance from her.

Neither outcome seemed likely, nor even possible.

18

Percy settled against the stall's slatted wall and watched the newborn foal, all gangly legs and wide black eyes, nuzzle up to his dam and begin to suckle.

He'd volunteered to keep an eye on Princess Polly through the night. The first twenty-four hours following a red sac birth were the most dangerous for the dam as infection could set in. Before him was the future of the stable, and he would see them through this night.

"You missed this, didn't you?"

Percy glanced up to find his father at the stall gate. "Like the blazes," he admitted.

The duke entered the stall and settled beside Percy onto dense hay. In parallel, they took in the view. "My bones might be getting too old for this. This is young man's work, to be sure."

It sat wrong inside Percy to hear his father speak thusly. He'd missed so many years. Why? Protecting his country, he might have said in the past, which was but one small part of the full truth. The whole was much more complex and didn't reflect well on him as a son.

In the here and now, he knew that look on his father's face. Father wanted to talk and not simply about the surface matters they'd kept to since Percy's return to England. This conversation would go deeper. He supposed it was about well time.

"The papers have been drawn up," began the duke. "They arrive from London in the next few days. All that is required are our signatures, and Gardencourt will be yours."

"It's too generous of you, Father." Percy hesitated. "I don't deserve it."

The duke waved his words away. "Nonsense. It's been waiting for you to return and make something of it." He jutted his chin toward suckling and dam. "You're off to a good start. Besides, Isabel seems to adore the place."

Percy remained silent. He didn't want to contribute another word toward the lie of his marriage.

"In truth, you seem to have a great girl in her. With her beauty, she doesn't have to be much more, but she has a brain in her head that she's willing to use. And she possesses the sort of compassionate demeanor that would be a boon to you in the running of the estate."

Percy nodded, silently agreeing with his father on each point. "You make her sound like a veritable paragon."

"She might be, but one thing I know she isn't."

"And what is that?"

"Your wife."

If Percy hadn't already been sitting on the ground, his legs would have given out from under him. But, really, what should he have expected? One didn't pull the wool over the duke's eyes easily. "How did you know?"

"Because you're not the young man you once were. You wouldn't tether yourself to a woman you hardly know without thought to consequence." The duke tapped out a beat on his bent knee. "Can I ask you why?"

"You could, but you might not like the answer."

The duke nodded. "I thought as much."

Percy swallowed back nausea. Would he never stop being a disappointment to his father?

"Do you remember when you saved the kitten from the carriage wheel?" the duke asked.

"I might have a vague recollection of such an event."

"Well, you couldn't have had more than six years on you. From what I was able to gather from Frau Gerta, she was walking you and Michael to the park when you spied a kitten in the gutter and snatched it up just before it was crushed beneath a carriage wheel. What a row you caused when you brought the creature into the house. Mrs. Landry threatened to quit on the spot. Do you not remember?"

"There was an injury, correct?"

A faraway smile entered the duke's eyes. "The carriage clipped your shoulder and nearly dislocated it. So, there you were, one arm hanging useless from injury, the other clutching a frantic kitten, not about to let go."

Percy, too, smiled at the memory. "I seem to remember her clawing my face to get away. She won that battle. Was she ever seen again?"

"Became the best mouser the kitchens ever saw, according to Mrs. Landry. Do you recall what Michael said?"

Percy put on his best impersonation of his brother. "*What an ungrateful creature.*"

"And your response?"

Percy shrugged. "Some childish piffle, to be sure."

"You told Michael that she was a wild creature and she was just being herself and you wouldn't have her any other way. You went on quite passionately, but I'll never forget what you said next. *Not every creature needs to be tamed.*"

That sounded exactly like the sort of thing Percy had said on more than one occasion, and at ages embarrassingly older than six years. He'd been incredibly idealistic, even into manhood.

"When you were running wild all over London," the duke continued, "I knew exactly who you were, and the man you would grow into."

"How disappointed you must have been when I didn't turn out that way."

"Percy, look at me." With great reluctance, Percy did as his father bid. Piercing blue eyes bored into his. "You are exactly that man. You always have been."

"Which is why you helped Olivia divorce me?" Percy found himself saying with no small amount of bitterness. In all the months since he'd returned, the subject hadn't been broached between them. The time had arrived to have this out in the open, for Percy harbored a grievance.

"It took you by surprise, didn't it?" the duke asked.

"Yes."

"Do you think I could have prevented it?"

"I know you could have." Such was the power the Duke of Arundel wielded in Parliament.

"Did you desire to come home and resume your unhappy marriage? Continue leading a life separate from your wife's? For that was the existence both behind and ahead of you and Olivia."

"I never thought I'd survive to come home. Still... *why* did you help Olivia secure it?"

"I saw an opportunity to deal with an untenable situation." The duke lifted one hand. "There was Olivia, who I'd come to love as my own blood. I wanted her to have a chance at happiness." He lifted his other hand.

"And there was you, my son. I wanted to give you the chance to begin anew when you returned to England."

"But Lucy," Percy began. Here it was, his grievance. "She's my bastard because the marriage was set aside. I don't think she'll ever forgive me."

"You think Lucy is upset by that? Stop keeping yourself to yourself and let the chit know you. She will come around."

Percy wasn't sure it was in his daughter's best interest to be associated with a man like him. That was nearer the truth of the matter. But he couldn't admit such a thing to his father, not with the way he was looking at him, his golden boy. It was too much. Percy hadn't been that boy since the Battle of Maya.

"But, Percy, I must say something to you, and I'm not sure how."

Percy's pulse doubled. "Yes?"

"Whatever it is that you're caught up in now, be careful. I can't lose you again. Those years you were unaccounted for were the worst of my life."

"You have my word, Father." A promise Percy hoped he could keep. Yet if matters went sideways with Montfort...

Well, they wouldn't.

The duke held Percy's eye until, at last, he nodded. As he rose to his feet by slow stages, it was all Percy could do not to assist, but he knew better than to offer.

"Son, you're in need of a proper shave. I shall send Drummond to the cottage in the morning."

"Drummond?" Percy asked, astonished. "He's still alive?"

"Too mean for the devil to take, I suspect."

"He must be eighty."

"Eighty and three on his last name day."

"And this is the man you'd like to apply a straightedge to my neck? I thought you wanted me to remain amongst the living."

The duke snorted. "That man has the sharpest eye and steadiest hand in England. He will be there by eleven of the clock."

With the duke gone, Percy was left alone with Princess Polly, her foal, and his thoughts for company. He slumped against the boards and closed his eyes. The mare was making it through without infection. If only other matters would sort themselves out so easily.

These last few days, it seemed that every decision he'd made in his life, both wrong and right, had converged on him. In all honesty, he was mightily tempted to collapse beneath its weight and let it pull him under.

To do so, however, would be unworthy of the man his father believed him to be. Even if Percy understood at a fundamental level that he wasn't and would never be that man, his father thought him so.

Those years you were unaccounted for were the worst of my life.

As if Percy needed more motivation to pursue Montfort to the ground, he had it. The year Montfort had held Percy under his influence had hurt the duke, a hurt that still resonated within his father's eyes.

Montfort must be stopped. It wasn't a matter of *if*, but *when*.

19

I sabel took the stairs one careful step at a time, precious cargo in her arms. "*Pequeño* lion, why won't you sleep?"

Wide black eyes steady upon her, Ariel blew bubbles by way of slobbery reply, and Isabel had no choice but to smile and nuzzle the top of his fuzzy head. "You win."

Her feet found the ground floor, and she began pacing about the drawing room—plumping goose-down pillows, arranging fresh-clipped roses in their vases—any little activity that kept her moving and Ariel content and quiet. Anytime she stopped for longer than ten seconds, his chubby face scrunched in the disquiet presaging a very loud squawk. If only he would nap.

Since yesterday's encounter with Montfort, she hadn't left Rosebud Cottage, pleading a return of the megrims. Predictably, the duchess's tonics had appeared both morning and night. Blessedly, Isabel didn't have to drink them as they'd arrived by servant.

However, by remaining ensconced in the cottage, Isabel had no choice but to assist in Eva's rather ambitious sewing project. Not only were they reworking dresses for the Misses Bretagne and Radclyffe, but for

Tilly and Nell, too, since they would be partaking in Gardencourt's breakfast and dance as it was a day to be enjoyed by all.

An hour ago, they, along with Eva, had ventured to the village to pick out a few pieces of trim, which was how Isabel ended up with the baby. Not that she minded. The little mite made her smile down to her toes.

Her ear picked up the not-too-distant drone of male voices. The sound was coming from the servants' corridor. One of the voices she knew. *Percy.*

Curiosity piqued, she found herself creeping toward his room, her heart doubling its beats with each step. Although confined to the cottage, she had stayed decidedly away from this part of it, which hadn't been necessary. Percy hadn't been here.

She'd have felt his presence.

Like now.

She reached the open doorway and blinked at the sight before her. In the corner nearest the room's lone window stood a shirtless Percy and a man who looked as old as the earth.

"Drummond," Percy began, weary, as if he'd already spoken his next words a dozen times over, "I am perfectly capable of shaving myself."

"You're saying you didn't have a valet all those years?"

"That is precisely what I am saying."

Drummond shook his head, mournfully. "'Tisn't proper that a son of the Duke of Arundel shaves his own beard. 'Tis right shameful."

The *son of the Duke of Arundel.* There were times when Isabel forgot that fact about Percy.

The men went quiet of a sudden, and her gaze met Percy's in the mirror. It held for a fluttery heartbeat.

"I reckon this'll be the newest Lady Percival?" Drummond asked.

Percy cleared his throat. "Isabel, may I introduce the Duke of Arundel's oldest…"

"Watch yourself, boy," Drummond warned.

"…and most loyal…"

"That's better," Drummond cut in, mollified.

"…valet…"

"And all-around man," supplied the valet.

"…Drummond, to you?"

"Most pleased to meet you," Isabel replied.

Drummond eyed her up and down. She straightened her spine and hoped she met his exacting standards.

Seemingly satisfied with his findings, he began packing his straightedge and other shaving accoutrements into a small black case. "You will have your hands full keeping this one"—he jerked a thumb toward Percy—"on the straight and narrow. That's a fact worth knowing." He cut Percy a sharp glance. "I shall be informing the duke of your behavior today, make no mistake."

Isabel stood aside as Drummond shuffled past, mumbling about the young folk these days not knowing what was right and proper. It was only when the front door clicked shut that Isabel's gaze returned to Percy. Amusement crinkled the corners of his eyes, and a chirrup of laughter squeezed through the firm press of her lips.

"What shall be your punishment, Lord Percival? No pudding for dessert?"

Percy picked up his straightedge, steel glinting in the sun. "A day's banishment from the stable was always effective."

Ariel thrust a tiny baby fist into the air and became squirmy in Isabel's arms. She began to sway from side to side, giving him the movement he wanted as she helped him find his thumb. The babe settled.

When she returned her attention to Percy, she found him watching her in the mirror, the straightedge frozen midway along his jaw. The hilarity of the previous moment faded beneath the look in his eyes. *Hunger.* He blinked and resumed his shave.

Isabel's gaze skittered away only to land on his shirtless chest. As the full midday sun streamed through the window at his side, the light caught every ripple of muscle beneath tan skin, illuminating the beauty of him. *Lean. Muscled. Strong. Scarred.* Again, she wondered about those scars. Each had a story to tell, but they combined, too, to tell the story of the man.

It was only when he finished his shave, and slipped his shirt over his head, denying Isabel her view of him, that it occurred to her she hadn't had to stay.

Yet she had.

"You have my sincerest gratitude for saving my life," Percy said as he turned to face her.

"For saving your life? How so?"

"Drummond was as like to slit my throat as to shave it." His chin jutted toward Ariel. "How has he settled in?"

"He's a very sweet young man," she said down to the wide-eyed babe. "But aren't you quite a handful today?" She looked up. "Literally."

"Oh?"

An idea struck Isabel. "Do you have any matters of pressing business to attend to?"

"Am I going to regret saying no?"

Isabel made up her mind that instant. "I think you'll do."

"I'll do?" Percy asked, wary.

"Eva, Tilly, and Nell have gone to the village for a spot of shopping, and it's down to me to look after

Ariel during his nap. But as you can see, the little mite has no interest in napping." Wide eyes stared over at Percy as if to illustrate his aunt's point.

"I'm not sure what this has to do with me." Percy looked poised to bolt.

"Well, you'll hold him, of course. Unless you can sew?"

"Nothing beyond a rudimentary stitch here and there."

"Then it's settled."

"*What* precisely is settled?"

"You shall hold Ariel and walk him around to his heart's content while I rework the bodice of a dress with new frilling." As she closed the distance between them, a possibility occurred to her. "Have you never held a babe?"

Percy flinched, a subtle movement, but she caught it. "No."

Unspoken was that he'd never held Lucy as a baby, his own flesh and blood, and it hurt him.

"Well," Isabel began on a light note, "there is nothing to it. Simply hold your arms out and—" She began to transfer Ariel. The babe gave a warning squawk.

"This might not be a good idea."

"Oh, pish. He will be quite contented once he discovers you have such a very nice chest to snuggle into."

"Is that so?" There was no mistaking the humor in Percy's voice, which had lowered by a suggestive octave.

It was only after he asked the question that Isabel heard her own words. A slow flush crept through her. As if he knew it, the side of his mouth tipped into a devilish smile. *Dios mío.*

"Now, let's try again," she instructed in a tone that she hoped was matter-of-fact. This time the transfer happened smoothly. "There you are. Only ensure his head is elevated properly."

Percy scooched Ariel up a few inches. "Like so?"

Isabel nodded. Her insides went warm. It was the sight of Percy holding Ariel with such gentle care. For his part, Ariel seemed quite content to peer at the world from his newly elevated height.

"Follow me, good sirs." Isabel pivoted on one heel. Behind her, Percy murmured to Ariel, "What say you, little man?"

Isabel's heart performed one of those tidy flips that Percy tended to provoke as she found her favorite place on the sofa before the room's great bow window and picked up her sewing. Tucked into a comfortable corner, from the periphery of her vision, she observed Percy perambulating the room with Ariel, pointing out this portrait of a long-deceased ancestor or that bronze statuette of a proud-chested stallion. The latter, Percy let Ariel grab.

"Careful," Isabel advised, "he wants to snatch up everything and put it into his mouth."

Percy lifted a playful eyebrow at the babe. "Is the world your apple tart?" He pulled away just before the babe swiped over a crystal vase of fresh-cut roses in full summer bloom. "All the flowers about the place, are they your handiwork?"

Isabel nodded. She'd taken to filling the vases in the cottage, small to large, with every variety of blossom she encountered on Gardencourt's grounds.

"I thought so."

She rather liked that he thought this about her. "Fresh flowers make a house a home."

"Do you have a favorite flower?"

Isabel lifted a shoulder. "The rose. Expected, I concede, but I can't help it. I like the idea of the rose."

"What idea?"

"A rose can protect herself."

He nodded, his serious eyes taking her in. "And a rose is beautiful."

Of a sudden, Isabel didn't think they were talking about roses anymore. What he could be saying, well, it quite stole her breath away and made her heart race. She gave a nervous, little laugh.

His gaze tightened intensely on her. "Isabel, you are a rose."

Again, her nervous, little laugh sounded. "I'm hardly an English rose." Quite simply, she was too dark, too foreign, and too Jewish. Facts she was certain Percy understood.

"Not the standard English sort. You're of the wild rose variety. All the more precious for her rarity."

What a thing to say. Isabel wasn't sure she could ever draw breath again. Her gaze broke from his and stared unseeing at the needle and cloth in her hands. She had no response for such words. Even if she did, she wasn't sure she could speak it around the lump that had formed in her throat.

"I imagine the flowers are difficult to come by in London," he said.

He'd changed the subject, for which she was grateful, truly, even as another part of her, a part that must be given no leeway, craved the other talk. "I happen upon them sometimes."

"In Cheapside?" He was fishing for information about her.

She nodded. No harm in giving him this.

"I take it you live above *Galante: Dressmakers Extraordinaire?*"

A sheepish laugh escaped Isabel, and she nodded. Eva had been so excited by the name that Isabel hadn't a choice but to agree to it. It was quite grandiose.

"That is fine work," he said, jerking his chin toward her lap.

Isabel stared down at the bodice she was reconstructing with velvet edging as if concentrated deeply on her work. In truth, she was hiding the gratification that surged through her at his praise, fearing he would see it in her eyes. "Are you an expert on ladies' attire?"

Percy snorted. "Hardly." He began to sway from side to side as Ariel had become fractious at standing still for too long. "I'm simply pointing to the fact that if this is an indication of the quality of your wares, then you must run a successful shop."

"We do." Her brow crinkled. "Or we *did*. We met with a few challenges this year."

He grew utterly serious. Once again, he was the devastating man she had first encountered. She couldn't help feeling he'd purposely maneuvered their conversation to this point. "Isabel, what were you doing in Number 9?"

"I think that's been fairly established." Oh, that she didn't feel a hot blush pinking her cheeks.

The intensity within his gaze didn't let up. "But how were you obliged to be there?"

Isabel broke from his gaze. She had to. He was hitting too close to the matter. She glanced at Ariel snugged safely in Percy's arms. "He's fallen asleep."

Percy gazed down at the babe. The look in his eye softened, and Isabel's heart contracted. The vision of a strong man holding a small babe with tenderness and care, well, it was too much. She set aside her sewing and came to her feet. "Here," she began, crossing the room. "I'll take him to his bassinet."

She held out her arms for the transfer. Unlike earlier, when Ariel was awake, they had to move more carefully so as not to wake the babe.

First, it was Percy's scent that reached her, his body

heat infusing sandalwood with *him*, a scent she'd so very recently come to know, intimately. Then it was the feel of him, for she couldn't *not* touch him—the tensile length of his forearms, the brush of fingertips across the back of his hand—as she shifted Ariel from his to her arms.

"You have him secure?"

His face lowered as he spoke. He was close, so close she could lift onto the tips of her toes, lean in ever so slightly, and press her lips to his.

It would be so simple. And *right*.

It would make matters infinitely more complicated. And *wrong*.

She stepped back, breaking away from a moment that couldn't—*shouldn't*—be. Over her shoulder, she said, "I shall be a few minutes, will you—?"

"I'll be here."

She should feel mortified about her unasked question and that he'd intuited it so easily. But she couldn't quite summon the feeling. A lightness had filled her at the reassurance. She wanted him here when she returned downstairs.

What a dreadful, awful, wonderful feeling that he knew her so well. It could lead nowhere good, of that she was certain, but, mayhap, inside Rosebud Cottage they could let its magic spell protect them from the harsh realities of the world outside its walls and not worry about where matters would lead.

Rather, they could just *be*.

And leave the future for later.

20

P ercy watched Isabel disappear up the stairs with the babe. He had finally worked the conversation around to where it needed to be, then he'd—entirely too predictably—become distracted.

Pay a mind to your priorities, man.

He couldn't protect Isabel if he couldn't win her trust.

And how could he win her trust if he rhapsodized like a smitten swain? Really, what was that rose talk all about?

He wasn't certain, except it was the truth. A truth he didn't think she trusted in herself. She was beautiful, *and* she could protect herself. Two rare qualities to find within one woman.

A voice echoed in his head that sounded suspiciously like his old self. Not his old, wicked self, but a self even older, the one who held a capacity for joy.

It was true that she'd become a need in his veins. No use denying it. But…

It didn't feel so very wrong or terrible.

It felt strangely *right.*

He couldn't shake the feeling that she was an addiction that was *good* for him. The wickedness she provoked, well, was it so very wicked?

Her light step tapped down the staircase, and he busied himself with an arrangement of purple foxgloves so as not to look the besotted fool he felt. Still, he was unable not to observe her from the corner of his eye as she resumed her place beside the bow window. She was in every way as the duke had described her—beautiful, intelligent, compassionate—but more.

She was *fresh.*

The way the sunlight caressed her, catching streaks of rich, light brown in her sable hair, lingering on cherry red lips parted in concentration on her work. Even Nature couldn't resist her.

He was but a mere man. What chance had he?

"Do you enjoy arranging flowers?"

His hands froze, clutching a small bunch of pink Sweet Williams, and his gaze lifted. Amused eyes shone out at him. "'Tis"—he labored for a word, any word—"soothing."

Her eyebrow lifted. She was enjoying this. "*Soothing?* You've never struck me as the sort of man who particularly needs soothing."

Percy picked up the vase. "This would look lovely on the console table at your back."

"Is that so?"

In truth, he didn't know, or care.

In truth, he was seeking an excuse to cross the room and be near her, which he did in quick fashion. He placed the Sweet Williams in the center of the console and, as if it had only now occurred to him, settled on the opposite end of the sofa. Her attention remained decidedly fixed on her sewing. 'Twas time to stop acting like a lovesick swain and start getting some answers. "I've found myself curious."

Isabel didn't lift her gaze. "Curious?" She pulled the needle through cotton.

"About your connection to the Spanish royal court."

Her fingers froze mid-sew. "Yes?"

"And your father is no longer tailor to Ferdinand?" Something—a question, a foreboding—hung just out of reach here.

"The King no longer requires my father's services."

The same look he'd noted in her eyes when she'd encountered Montfort shone there now.

Fear.

And, of a sudden, he understood. "Lord Bertrand Montfort has connections to every court in Europe. In fact, it would come as no great surprise if he were acquainted with King Ferdinand's tailor."

Isabel's sewing fell to her lap, a fact he doubted she had any awareness of. The fear in her eyes expanded. He doubted she could draw breath in this moment."This debt owed Montfort," he continued, softly, soothingly, as if wooing a wild animal to come closer, "is it your father's?"

Her brow crinkled, frozen in a state of bewilderment. Then it released. Gone was the fear, replaced by a spark of fire. "Is it so easy for you?"

"Is what so easy for me?" he asked, wary. The ground beneath his feet felt like it was beginning to shift.

"To separate yourself from your family."

The statement hit Percy like a solid blow to the solar plexus. He hadn't only been observing her. She had been observing him, too.

"It is our family's problem," she continued. "What affects one, affects *all.*"

The implication of her words landed like a follow-up uppercut to the jaw. *Family.* Percy had neglected his; she would never abandon hers. He deserved her scorn.

But, now, the flare of anger faded from her eyes, and she looked upon him with a sort of contrition. "A dozen seamstresses and tailors sewed for Papa at the royal court," she began, gently moving the conversation in a less combative direction. "He oversaw the purchase of materials and the construction of all the servants' uniforms. But only his hand sewed the king's clothes. There isn't a stitch he is unequal to."

But Percy couldn't let the matter go, even if she heaped an avalanche of scorn upon his head. "Why isn't your father in England with his daughters?"

Her gaze slid away. "Matters became complicated, so Eva and I left first. He will be following soon. We've been given assurances."

"By Montfort?" Percy needed a yes, or even a nod, anything that would convey trust.

Instead, Isabel concentrated on her stitching. "Every little stitch is vital to the integrity of both the garment and its maker. Papa taught us that."

She wasn't ready for that depth of trust yet, and Percy knew better than to push. Besides, the light was returning to her eyes. He liked it. He felt himself drawn into her like a magnet meeting its polar opposite. She had the power to illuminate and chase away his darkness.

How cold it had been in the shadows all these years.

How warm was her light.

"When a woman wears a well-constructed gar-ment," she continued, fervent, "and she feels those stitches perfectly aligned with the curves of body, it gives her confidence. No one else in the world can wear this garment like she, because it was fashioned solely for her. More than fine fabrics, this is the luxury that has been the sole preserve of the rich."

"And you would like to change that?" He wanted her

to keep talking and telling him of her hopes, dreams, and goals. It was damned attractive.

"Oh, yes, very much. An entire segment of the middling classes crave bespoke fashion they can afford. Our idea is to keep costs down with carefully chosen materials, using the latest creations by Eva. She is a genius of design."

"And you run the business side?"

Isabel laughed. "Eva cannot be trusted on her own in a fabric shop. It would be all shantung silks and jamdani muslin and debtors' prison."

Percy felt himself smiling along with her.

Of a sudden, she shot upright on a pained, "Oh!" She held up her forefinger. On its tip beaded a drop of blood.

Before she could bring it to her mouth, Percy crossed the short stretch of sofa between them and caught her wrist. "May I?" he found himself asking.

Another, "Oh," fell from her lips, this one soft and very possibly inviting. Eyes wide, she nodded.

It was all Percy needed.

Gaze refusing to release hers, he brought her finger to his mouth, and she drank in a quick sip of air that caught in her chest. His tongue stroked across the tip, and he tasted her. *Metallic. Bitter. Sweet.* With a guttural growl, he took her finger inside his mouth and sucked.

She gasped.

It felt perverse, this pulling of blood from her, but there was no part of her he didn't want to taste.

His mouth moved to her palm slightly sticky with a thin sheen of perspiration, to her wrist, thin blue veins beating a fast pulse beneath his lips. The only sound in the room was the shallow in-and-out scrape of her breath against her throat. A flush the hue of a dusky pink rose crept up her décolletage, up the length of her neck, brightening her cheeks. Desire was writ across her face, in the sway of her body forward. She enjoyed it, this being tasted.

He retreated an inch, and distress crinkled her brow. He rather enjoyed holding her in the palm of his hand. "Here is the thing about me that you should know, Isabel," he said in a raspy voice that he hardly recognized as his own.

He reached down and lifted her feet to his lap. Her brow crinkled further, this time in curiosity. He began unlacing her boots.

"Once I start to indulge, I can't stop."

One, then the other, boot clattered to the floor. He feathered light fingertips along the instep of her foot, tickled toes curling, to her ankle, to the hem of her dress primly in place just above.

"You were correct in one regard the other night."

He didn't need to clarify which night. They both knew.

"Oh?"

"The deprivation. I *had* become addicted to it, if only for its safe haven against my true nature." His hand roved higher, pushing her dress above her knees where her white cotton stockings were held up by light blue satin garters. He started to untie them and stopped. They could stay. The blood quickened in his veins and rushed straight to his cock, which was already at half-mast.

"But now I've tasted *you*." He pushed her dress higher, bare thigh revealed to the light of day.

"What are you—" she began, breathless. "What are you doing?"

He ignored the question. "Like so many wretches bound to an addiction, once I have a taste, I'm lost." He tore his gaze from her exposed flesh and met her eyes. Once he caught sight of her sweet quim, there would be no stopping him. "I've never gotten the knack of satiety."

He met a question in her eyes. She truly had no idea what he was about. Yet he met permission to carry her into the unknown.

His cock swelled into hard readiness, and he tried to tamp down its expectations. This was about a different sort of pleasure.

He nudged her dress a few inches higher until, at last, her cunny was revealed, the mound of curly hair dark against her skin, bathed in the full wash of midday sun that poured through the window. Primitive ache welled inside him. *Mine.* "Spread your legs for me, Isabel."

Her body went rigid with sudden tension. "*Spread my legs?*" she whispered, shocked, yes, but also...*intrigued.*

She wanted to see what he would do next.

She bent her knees and blossomed for him like the wild rose she was, revealing her pink and glistening quim by slow increments. Lust streaked through him as he bent forward, his hands reaching beneath her sweet bottom, sliding her toward him, even as he positioned himself between her legs, resting one of her feet onto his shoulder.

"What are you—?" began a protest he knew propriety would demand.

With great reluctance, he lifted his head. "Do you trust me?"

She took her plump lower lip between her teeth, indecision writ across her face. A trio of rapid heartbeats galloped past. At last, her lip released, and she spoke the only word in a language of a hundred thousand that he wanted to hear. "Yes."

Unable to hold himself in check an instant longer, he bent his head, inhaled the scent of her, sunshine and honeysuckle and *woman*, and touched his tongue to *her*.

"Lord Percival!"

He almost corrected that prim, breathless *Lord Percival!*, but decided he rather liked it. He stroked his tongue along the wet length of her slit.

A breathy, "Oh," slid from Isabel's throat. She threw one arm over her head as her hips tilted up and legs fell open wider. She had to have more of what his tongue offered. He smiled against her and flicked.

The fingers of her other hand wove through his hair and clenched. "Oh, that is nice." She wasn't shy about her desire. Yet one more thing he liked about her.

"Only *nice?*"

He'd stopped, and her hips squirmed at the loss. She bit her bottom lip. "It just feels so...*so...good.*"

His tongue laved across her sensitive skin as a reward. She gave a great groan of relief as she pressed his head.

She wanted, *needed...more.*

And he would give it to her.

His tongue found the sensitive place just below the hood of her sex. Her hips bucked as she gave a sharp cry of pleasure. There it was, the place that would make her come apart beneath him. His cock had begun throbbing. The tip of his tongue stiffened and focused on this tiny patch of nerve endings, stroking in tight circles, flickering in sharp taps. With each touch of his tongue, her body opened to him, even as it tensed. Her gasps grew sharper, more plaintive. She was close, so close, and wet, so wet. "Come apart for me, Isabel."

The fingers of both her hands tangled in his hair, her eyes squeezed shut, face tensed in sweet distress, lips parted as she strained oh-so-eagerly for exquisite release, her entire being reduced to the patch of skin where his tongue touched her. She was a wanton, dependent on him for the one thing she craved in this world.

A few more flicks of his tongue, and there she went, breaking beneath him, crying out her pleasure as her sex shattered, her quim pulsing its release in quick flutters. His cocked *begged* him to take her now. She was willing and ready, and he was certainly willing and ready. But…

If he took her now, he wouldn't be able to shake his craving for her…

Ever.

"That was…*oh*," she breathed.

Her chest heaving beneath the confining corset that remained in place, and her cheeks bright with sated desire, she was a glory in the sunshine. Her eyes slid open, and her mouth curled into a smile no man in the history of time had ever resisted.

Yet he must.

He inched back and pulled her dress down until it reached the middle of her thigh. Her head canted to the side in question as he settled back to his side of the sofa.

"Is that—" she began on a confused sputter. "Is that all?"

Percy willed his cock into submission as his eyes shifted away from her too-direct gaze. "That was for you."

In a sudden sequence of efficient motion, she pushed forward, and, before he could blink, she sat atop him, legs straddled to either side of his thighs, her hands angling his face up, forcing him to meet her in the eye.

"I am *desperate*"—her contralto voice cracked on the word—"to feel you inside me." One hand reached down, between their bodies, and stroked the hard length of his cock through strained wool. "Would you deny me the pleasure of you?"

"Isabel," he began, his voice reduced to gravel in his throat, "I would deny you *nothing*."

They were the truest words he'd ever spoken.

She leaned into him, her head angling, her breath whispering across his neck, lifting goose bumps along his skin, before lush lips found his neck and nimble fingers the closure of his trousers, the next instant freeing his cock. Her slender hand wrapped around him and squeezed as she positioned herself above, her sweet cunny hovering tantalizingly out of reach.

He caught one hand behind her neck and brought her mouth to his, breath mingling, tongues tangling, as she lowered herself onto him, her quim hot and slick. Against every instinct, he grabbed her hips, preventing her from going too fast. Instead, he entered her one deliberate inch at a time. She was so deliciously *tight*.

She groaned into his mouth, and a wildness began to build inside him. Trembly hands clutched his shoulders, and she gave her hips a mindless swivel. Now it was *him* groaning into *her* mouth.

"Oh, the feel of you," she moaned into his ear. "I need it—*oh*—I need it—*oh*—"

She'd lost the ability to finish a sentence. No matter. He knew how it ended. "*Deeper?*" He gave a hard thrust of his hips as he brought her onto him, and his inhibitions fell away.

"Oh, yes, and—*oh*—and—"

"*Harder?*"

She threw her head back in abandon. There was only him and her and this *need* that held them in its grip.

"And—*oh*—" she continued, "and—*oh*—"

"*Faster?*" he growled into her ear.

"Oh, yes."

His mouth found her neck, her décolletage, hands pulling her bodice down to reveal a sweet rosy nipple. He took it inside his mouth as he brought her down on him, one relentless thrust after another. His release built with each stroke, but he wouldn't reach it, not without her.

He made his strokes shallow, and she moaned in frustration. *Good.* The tease had her straining toward all the pleasure his cock could offer, *if only he would just...*

"I need more," she dragged out between quick breaths. She was *desperate* for more of him. "*Please,*" she begged.

That *please* did things to his insides. He impaled her —*deeper, harder, faster*—just as she wanted.

"Yes," she breathed in repeated litany, a plea, a prayer, her nails digging crescent moons into his shoulders, only heightening his lust, as she became wild in his arms.

She inhaled a deep gasp and held, the balance of the world suspended on the tip of a needle, as she hung at the edge of release. Then she tipped over into mindless oblivion, her quim clenching around his cock. He had no choice but to follow her as he broke, his climax crashing on him with relentless abandon, pleasure cascading through his veins with every pump of his heart, until soon—*too soon*—it was over, and he was left gasping for air, sweat trickling down the hollow of his spine.

From a distance, a thought came to him: He'd spilled his seed inside her. *Twice.*

Stupid. But the aspersion lacked any substance behind it. What was the worst that could happen? She could be with child? He would have to marry her in truth?

The consideration didn't disturb him as much as it should.

She slid to the side and off him entirely. It was all he could do not to grab her and place her back on top of him, *where she belonged.* She stood and let her dress fall to her ankles, and he tucked his manhood back into his trousers.

She stared down at him, her breath still shallow, bewilderment shining in her eyes. She was wondering what had come over her. *Raging lust,* he could tell her.

"That was—"

"Unexpected?" he finished for her. He couldn't entirely agree, if he was being dead honest.

The exterior door swung open on sudden hinges. In trooped Mrs. Gardiner, Tilly, and a young servant whose name had entered and exited Percy's brain the instant he'd learned it. As one, their chatter died away and their feet came to an abrupt stop.

Although their expressions couldn't differ more radically from one another, it was clear as the blue sky that each understood what had just transpired between him and Isabel on the sofa from which he was now rising. Eyes wide as saucers, the young servant's mouth had formed a silent "O." A saucy smile smirked about Tilly's mouth and twinkled in her eyes.

And Mrs. Gardiner, well, her eyes had narrowed into razor thin slits and she looked fit to run him through with a curved saber. "Is all as it should be, *querida?*" she asked, low and hard. It was clear she didn't trust him. Or any other man, he suspected.

"Quite, Eva," Isabel said quickly. Too quickly. "Quite as it, umm, should be."

While the words might lack conviction, the meaning behind them didn't. She was assuring her sister that what had just transpired had done so with her consent.

Solemnly, Eva nodded her acceptance.

All eyes swung toward Percy. He took this as his cue. "It was my pleasure," he began and instantly realized his mistake. It was that word, *pleasure.* Tilly snorted, and Isabel's eyebrows met in consternation. He began again. "It was enjoyable"—another snort from Tilly—"to tend your nephew while you sewed." He gave a slight bow. "Good day."

Without a backward glance, he strode out the open door, Tilly's mocking laughter at his heels. Once he'd been a spy and consummate liar, able to pull the wool over any eyes on the spot. Well, he was rusting up. Either that, or Isabel had jumbled his brain beyond all recognition. Neither possibility offered peace of mind.

As Percy made his way across the estate toward the stable, his step slowed beneath the weight of his thoughts. *Do you trust me?* he'd asked. *Yes,* she'd replied.

To have her trust felt like he'd been given everything he'd ever desired. Not to use and steer her, as he'd done with others' trust in the past, but to protect her. It was with her complete trust that he could shield her from Montfort.

His heart soared at the trust he'd been granted, only deepening the addiction to her that no longer felt like wickedness. It felt honest and true and…

Blast.

He was besotted.

That was the truth of the matter. And it didn't feel so very wrong or wicked. In fact, it held not a trace of vice. He could upbraid himself. Try to talk himself out of it. But *why?*

For her own good, chimed a small voice that had him crashing down to earth. She might be pure and good for him, but was *he* good for *her?*

In the darkest corner of his heart, he knew the answer to that question.

Right.

The light that had been, the shadows of the past—of *reality*—stamped out. They understood the truth, even if the rest of him didn't. He changed the direction of his feet. He didn't need to go to the stable. He needed to contact Hortense and check on her progress.

The clock was ticking.

For Isabel.

For his heart.

21

Isabel stepped from beneath the avenue of lime trees that lined the lane leading into the village's market square. The full stream of mid-morning sun poured its suffusive warmth into the air and her.

"'Tis nothing short of a glorious day," Miss Bretagne exclaimed to everyone and no one in particular. The girl felt so much and so deeply that Isabel experienced a niggle of worry for her. Eva had once been such a girl.

Isabel dismissed the thought. The fact was Miss Bretagne held too much wealth and privilege to ever suffer such a fate.

Besides, it was too splendid a day for futile worry. All that was required of one was to bask in the combined glory of yellow sunshine, verdant trees, bright flowers, and a thoroughly sated body.

Isabel's pace lagged behind Eva and the Misses Bretagne and Radclyffe, and she allowed herself a secret smile at that last bit. It was possible she was becoming a wanton woman for there was no denying that devastating man had wreaked pleasure upon her body in ways she'd never conceived. That a tongue could be put to such a use...

To think of it now, amongst the upright and proper

denizens of the village's market square, felt slightly sinful. Because, oh, how she wanted Percy to unleash his wicked tongue upon her again.

Eva shot a glance over her shoulder. "*Querida*, are you feeling quite well? You look flushed."

Isabel willed her gaze to remain steadily neutral in the face of what Eva left unsaid and the look in her eye implied.

"Would you mind very much if we pop into the circulating library?" Miss Bretagne asked, oblivious to the staring match between Isabel and Eva. "I must return, oh, it's quite a lengthy title." She dug a book out of her carry-all bag and read out, "*The Private Memoirs and Confessions of a Justified Sinner* by Mr. James Hogg. In truth, I'm shocked they carry such a book. They must have believed it a religious text." She gave an unladylike snort. "I can assure you it most definitely is *not* godly. Anyhow, I'd like to inquire if they happen to have—Oh, Mina, what's the title of that book by the American chap?"

"*The Last of the Mohicans?*"

"That's the one! I'm in the mood for an adventure."

"And when aren't you?" Miss Radclyffe asked. "I would posit that your thirst for adventure is one of the primary qualities that makes up the composition of you." It was clear from her tone she enjoyed this about her friend.

Impatience radiated off Eva. "Meet me in the mercantile when you are finished." Her sharp eye turned on Isabel. "Would you care to help me pick out a few pieces of trim?"

"I believe I'll explore the library's offerings." Isabel had successfully avoided being alone with Eva since yesterday. She wasn't about to break her streak now.

No choice but to concede defeat, Eva gave the group a tight nod and proceeded down the sidewalk, alone.

Isabel followed the Misses Bretagne and Radclyffe inside the dimly lit circulating library. It had the comforting musty scent of settled dust, aged leather, and yellowing paper of all libraries. While the girls quizzed the steward about any new novels, Isabel ambled deeper into the space. Quite unexpectedly, she happened upon a familiar figure bent over a thick tome. "Miss Fox?"

The lady straightened and removed her reading spectacles. "Lady Percival, what a surprise."

Isabel couldn't quite return the sentiment. This was precisely the sort of establishment where she would expect to find Miss Fox. "A little light reading?"

Miss Fox chuckled. "Oh, enjoying the local history. Did you know that the yews in the churchyard were planted to provide the local militia with wood for their longbows? And that the rectory is haunted by a woman who lost her way to Dent five hundred years ago and perished on the church steps during a snow storm? Shivering from cold, she lurks in corners, knitting and murmuring, *'Tis so cold, so cold, so cold,*" she finished on a dramatic tremble.

Miss Radclyffe's head appeared around the corner of a bookcase. "Lucy and I are moving along to the mercantile." Her eye caught on Miss Fox. "Oh, hello, Miss Fox. Would you care to join our shopping expedition?"

To Isabel's great surprise, Miss Fox rose. "I should find that most pleasing. I've been sitting too long and could use a spot of exercise."

Outside, the Misses Bretagne and Radclyffe strode ahead, and Miss Fox laced her arm through Isabel's, so that they strolled arm in arm.

"My sister," Isabel began, searching for light conversation, "has the idea that the ladies should have hair garlands for tonight's musicale. Perhaps you would like one?"

"Oh, I wouldn't want to trouble you," Miss Fox demurred, an air of surprise and bewilderment hanging about her.

It only now occurred to Isabel that Miss Fox might lead a full life, but mayhap a lonely one. Very possibly she didn't have friends who offered her small kindnesses on a whim. Given her father's predilection for gaming, Miss Fox had seen the unsavory side of human nature, Isabel was certain of it. In this, Isabel felt a sympathy with her. She understood how layers could accumulate on a person until one's real self was buried, safely, deep beneath. Miss Fox was one such person.

Their group had traversed no more than half a block when they reached the village's lone mercantile. Through the window, Isabel could see Eva examining several lengths of trim laid out by the proprietor. The Misses Bretagne and Radclyffe pushed inside, the bell that hung above the door jingling in their wake. When Isabel made to follow, Miss Fox's grip on her arm tightened, preventing her from entering. Isabel tossed the woman an inquiring glance.

"Lady Percival, would you take a turn about the market square with me while the others do their shopping?"

Surprised, Isabel nodded her agreement and soon found herself perambulating the square with a confoundingly silent Miss Fox. Absent were her usual slew of questions, pokings, and proddings. "You are quite meditative today, Miss Fox."

Miss Fox cut Isabel a quick, penetrating glance. The woman appeared to be in the midst of an internal debate. Strangely, Isabel found herself waiting on pins and needles. At last, Miss Fox seemed to have reached a decision. "Do you know the Savior of St. Giles?"

Isabel shrugged, somewhat puzzled by this turn of conversation. "I must confess that I haven't been as breathless about the story as others I know." Namely, Tilly.

"Over the last few months, he has won a few gaming hells off the hands of their owner."

A feeling prickled to life inside Isabel, one that made her stomach defy gravity.

"And," Miss Fox continued, "in liberating London from the grip of its palaces of vice and perversion, he has caught the attention of some very powerful men."

Isabel's mouth went dry.

"And angered them."

"Oh?"

"One powerful man in particular."

"Do not call me by that silly name."

Those had been the exact words Percy had snarled at the conclusion of their card game at Number 9. Now she understood what he'd meant by them. *That silly name...*

The Savior of St. Giles.

"Many rumors abound about the identity of the Savior of St. Giles," continued Miss Fox. "Some believe him an Italian prince. Others an East India Company nabob. One theory, however, I'm inclined to believe. Would you like to hear it?"

Isabel nodded, wondering how she could move at all given the rigidity of her muscles.

"'Tis whispered the Savior of St. Giles is none other than the younger son of a powerful duke in England." Wide, disingenuous eyes rounded on Isabel. "Shocking, no?"

Isabel cleared her throat and attempted to rally. "Is that the worst possibility? Such heroics would burnish the reputation of any young man."

Miss Fox shrugged, as if indifferent to her tale. The

woman was anything but, Isabel knew it. "If there wasn't more to the story."

"More?" Isabel's gut churned.

"Quite. It seems the Savior of St. Giles is a façade for a truly reprehensible villain."

Isabel willed calm breath in and out of her lungs. "A *villain*?"

Miss Fox leaned in and reduced her voice to a whisper. "A *seducer* of virgins."

It was only after she'd shut her mouth with a snap that Isabel realized it had gaped open.

"Word has it he used all his powers of persuasion," continued Miss Fox. "You know the sort of powers—noble family, considerable wealth, dashing good looks—to ravish a destitute, young virgin with promises of marriage and security. It's said he's even duped the poor chit into thinking herself already married to him. Who knows how many innocent virgins he has deceived, debauched, and discarded in like manner." Miss Fox paused, and every nerve in Isabel's body frazzled on end. "At least, that's how the story will run."

Isabel's stomach dropped to her feet. "*Story?*"

"Do you, by chance, read the *London Diary*?"

Isabel gave her head a slow shake.

"No, you don't seem the type. Well, it's a scandal sheet that my father owns, although few in Society know it."

"Is this one of the publications he won in a bet?" Isabel had the presence of mind to ask.

Miss Fox nodded. "Would you like to know why Cheswick and I are here?"

"You're friends of the duke and duchess?" One had to ask the question, even if one already knew the answer.

Miss Fox hesitated. "A rather powerful man has given the *London Diary* exclusive rights to the story.

Splashed across the front page the headline will read, *Savior or SEDUCER of St. Giles?* Rather salacious and attention-grabbing, wouldn't you agree?"

The words emerging from Miss Fox's mouth kept getting worse and worse. Would there be no end to them?

"When?" Isabel croaked.

"In a few days' time, I should imagine. The story is quickly developing."

"Why are you telling me?"

Miss Fox's sharp eye held Isabel's for a charged moment. "I like you."

Isabel wasn't sure she could return the sentiment. "Why have you agreed to run the story?"

"One should always be cautious to whom one becomes indebted. My father exercises no such caution."

Isabel only now noticed they'd circled around to the mercantile when a door jangled open and out poured Eva with the Misses Bretagne and Radclyffe, tidy parcels in hand.

A happy flush brightened Eva's cheeks. She did love a successful shopping excursion. "Isabel, I hope you're ready to sew this afternoon." She addressed her next words to Miss Fox. "Would you happen to be handy with a needle? We'll be needing all hands on deck."

"I fear not," Miss Fox demurred. "I'm sorely vexed that I shall miss tonight's entertainment. I do enjoy a village musicale. So many ranges and varieties of talents."

As their party moved along, Isabel remained linked arm in arm with Miss Fox.

"Lady Percival," Miss Fox began, "I do hope I haven't shocked you too deeply with my tale." A leaden beat of time passed. "It was related with the sincerest of intentions. Now, if you will pardon me, I must fetch my reading spectacles from the library."

Although she did believe the intention behind Miss Fox's revelations to be meant for good, Isabel's overriding feeling as she watched the woman stride away, her feet a determined *click-clack* against gray cobblestone, was *good riddance*. For it was clear: Miss Fox knew her marriage to Percy was a falsehood. It was no coincidence that she'd arrived with Montfort. He'd brought her and Cheswick to Gardencourt Manor for the express purpose of exposing the 'Seducer' of St. Giles.

"Do not call me by that silly name."

Percy was the Savior of St. Giles.

It was a shock, to be sure, and yet...

It wasn't.

She should have seen it before now. But she'd been blinded, initially by her failure that first night, then by the flurry of events thereafter. In truth, she hadn't given the Savior of St. Giles a passing thought. The phantom hero of harlots was nothing to her.

Except, now, she knew he was no mere phantom.

Now, she knew he was very much a man.

The revelation, and its implications, stole her breath away. Percy hadn't been in that gaming hell to dive into the sea of iniquity. He'd been there to drain it.

A powerful man—Miss Fox's words—was looking to expose Percy. Isabel knew of one such powerful man.

Lord Bertrand Montfort.

He would take issue with the Savior of St. Giles's interference with his operations.

And the Savior of St. Giles was *Percy*?

The knowledge only compounded the feelings that had been accumulating for him, and complicated them, too. For here was the terrible truth of the matter...

Montfort intended her to be the instrument of the Savior of St. Giles's ruin—of *Percy's* ruin.

A thought clawed to the surface. *What if...what if* she

warned Percy what was about to befall him and, by extension, his family?

Family…

What about *her* family? What would befall Papa and Eva and Ariel if she issued such a warning?

Montfort would take no such betrayal lightly. The repercussions would be swift, fierce, and final.

Yet how could she betray Percy, the man who had claimed not only her body, but likely, too, her heart?

She must push aside her heart. It had no say in the matter, not when she held her family's future in her hands. Yet another layer accumulated by life. This one would be thicker and heavier and harder than all the others combined.

So thick, heavy, and hard it might crush the heart it protected.

22

What made the assembly shine?
Robin Adair.
What made the ball so fine?
Robin was there...

Although a girl of no more than twelve years sang "Robin Adair" before the assembly, Percy felt the song's sentiment down to his soul, which replaced Robin with *Isabel*.

Wearing her Sunday finest, the girl soldiered on through the popular, melancholic tune with a sweet soprano voice that filled the assembly room up to its high coffered ceiling and couldn't help but pull emotion from the most hardened of hearts, even as a telling shake trembled through it, a tremor that understood she sang for a duke. In fact, the entire village was keenly aware of the Duke of Arundel and his family sitting prominently in the front row.

Intermission couldn't arrive soon enough for Percy. It wasn't the performances, both vocal and instrumental and of varying quality, that had him tapping his fingers impatiently on his knee. He'd rather enjoyed them, truth be told. Rather, it was the seating order.

Somehow, he'd come to sit at one end of the row and Isabel at the other, the entire family between them. Further, every time he tried to catch Isabel's eye, the duchess was making a *sotto voce* observation into her ear.

At last, the girl ended the song on a note that only slightly cracked, and the gathered broke into bright applause. The girl beamed with a shy smile that held no small amount of relief as she bobbed a quick curtsy and scurried off the small raised platform. The mayor, one Squire Noble, hastened into her place. "Shall we adjourn for refreshment and reconvene at the half of the hour?"

Permission granted, the room split into fifty various conversations as bodies stood to stretch stiff legs. The duke ambled toward the dais and congratulated Squire Noble on his granddaughter's exceptional performance. Lucy and Miss Radclyffe took the mayor's words to heart as they strolled arm-in-arm down the center aisle to inspect the multitude of savory and sweet tidbits arrayed for the gathering's consumption, Hugh at their heels.

The path mostly clear to Isabel—the duchess proved a tenacious conversational partner—Percy approached, drawn to her light like a moth to the flame. Isabel's eye met his and skittered away. It was like the sun peeking out from behind a black cloud long enough to fill the air with a warm glow, only to slip behind it, plunging the world back into the cold dark.

It was possible the analogy contained no small dollop of mawkish melodrama. Still, he couldn't help feeling exactly so. She'd needled her way into his blood and down deep into the marrow of his bones.

All his earlier vows and self-castigations had fallen away the moment he'd caught his first glimpse of her tonight, wearing flowers in her hair and a newly re-made dove gray dress trimmed with a short verdigris fringe that brought out the emeralds in her eyes.

There was no denying it: he was a man besotted. The race of his heart as he'd handed her up into the carriage. The intake of his breath as he'd sat beside her, filling his lungs with her sunshine and honeysuckle. He knew all the signs.

After how any days? Four? Or was it five? The number hardly signified. It was long enough to know her and want her. Really, this fall into mad, deep infatuation had been inevitable.

Yet it didn't change what his mind knew and what his heart forgot with every moment spent with her: he could have these feelings, but never act on them.

Isabel deserved a better man.

Still, as her "husband," wouldn't it appear odd if he didn't go to his "wife" and twine her arm through his and lean in to inhale deeply of her?

So, he did, producing a gratifying dusting of goose bumps along the elegant length of her neck.

The stream of the duchess's latest observation halted mid-flow, and one busy hand stopped spinning the oxidized silver ring set with a large cabochon emerald on her other. Wide, unsurprised eyes flashed back and forth between him and Isabel. "Well, I see it now."

What *it* she spoke of was clear. He and Isabel positively vibrated with *it*.

Isabel tensed at his side. He wondered about that stiffness. A subtle shift in her attitude toward him had occurred since they broke their fast together this morning.

Then, her eyes had been unable *not* to cast shy glances his way. Her mouth had been unable not to tip up at the corners when his hand had brushed hers. He hadn't bothered pretending the contact accidental. Instead, he'd thrown her a rakish smile, the one he'd tossed about so indiscriminately in his misspent youth, the one that never failed to draw a breathy exhalation from the opposite sex. That smile hadn't failed him this morning when Isabel sighed and her eyes glazed over with desire.

Now, the duchess with her busy, keen eye noticed Isabel's sudden rigidity. "My dear, is one of your megrims attempting an encore? Shall we send for my special tonic? It could be here within the half hour."

At the duchess's offer, Isabel blanched as if she'd already swallowed a tumbler full of the noxious substance. "Your offer is most generous, ma'am, but my head is quite well."

"Sweeting," Percy cut in, "I believe all you need is a turn about the room. Perhaps a peek at the stars?"

Grateful eyes met his. The sun had returned.

Before Percy could act on the words, a familiar form caught the edge of his vision.

Hortense.

Hair pulled back in a tight chignon and covered by a lace mob cap that managed to age her by a few decades, she was attired in the sort of respectable, drab brown that wasn't likely to draw the curious, stray eye. She flashed him a quick cut of her gaze before disappearing through the exterior door that was open to let in cooling night air.

Her meaning was clear. He was to follow.

Which meant tearing himself away from Isabel, for if he was going to succeed in protecting her from Montfort, he must hear what Hortense had to say. The woman wouldn't be here if she hadn't uncovered vital information.

To protect Isabel, first, he would have to betray her.

"On further consideration, the duchess's tonic could serve as a preventative, my love."

My love. The endearment rolled off his tongue with disconcerting ease.

Isabel's eyebrows drew together in distress, and her eyes flashed hot at his treachery. Her mouth opened to deliver what was sure to be a vociferous rebuttal, but before she could counter him, the duchess took her by the hand. "Come with me, Isabel. We shall have you fixed up presently. You know what that Benjamin Franklin had to say. *An ounce of prevention is worth a pound of cure.*"

As the duchess led her away, Isabel cut Percy one last glance over her shoulder that was one part betrayal and two parts pleading, with a dash of pique thrown in. She wouldn't be forgiving him anytime soon.

Later, he could make it up to her in a way she quite deliciously enjoyed.

He shook off the idea. Hadn't he vowed to avoid any such future encounters?

Yet, when he was with her, he had trouble remembering precisely why.

Outside, he spotted Hortense some distance away near the path that led to the riverbank. The instant she saw him, she disappeared down the trail. He didn't see her again until he reached the village's five-hundred-year-old stone bridge.

She stepped into the moonlight, and turquoise eyes shone up at him from beneath her ridiculous mob cap. It simply wasn't a Hortense item to wear. "Well, Bretagne, you wanted Montfort's attention. Now you most certainly have it," she said by way of greeting.

"What have you learned?" he countered, ready as she to get this conversation underway.

"Answer me a question first. Are you a Whig or a Tory?"

"Neither. Can't tolerate politicians. To the one, they suffer from an overinflated sense of their value in the world."

Hortense nodded. Most involved in espionage echoed this view. Once politicians got involved in an operation, a spy's work increased tenfold, if it wasn't blown entirely to bits.

"You've heard the Tories recently secured their position in the general election?" she asked.

"No surprise there. The Whigs are a right mess."

"Well, one powerful Tory got it into his head that one couldn't be too sure."

"And?"

"*And* started running an operation in various hells and brothels about London."

"What sort of operation?" A lightning quick rush of anticipation preceding a revelation flashed through Percy's veins. How many years had he lived for this feeling?

"Of creating *situations* where lords might feel compelled to vote a certain way, if said *situations* were kept quiet. You know the sort. Ones involving gaming debts. Pious lords with young girls, *virgins* even. The sort of situation the Savior of St. Giles recently stumbled into."

Of course. "A political blackmail scheme."

"And I suppose you know who's behind it?"

"Montfort."

Even in the near dark, Hortense's jaw gave a reflexive clench and release. "You know his line, the one that justifies all his actions."

"*For the good of England.*"

"He's stopped influencing governments on the Continent and now has started in at home."

"Using old spy games to destroy the opposition."

"But now Montfort has a new game afoot. A bigger fish on the hook."

"A bigger fish than a future marquess?" Even as Percy asked the question, dread curled in his gut. Montfort had all but explicitly told Percy that he was coming after him. This wasn't new. Yet he couldn't shake the feeling that Hortense was about to tell him something new, and ugly.

"In a way." She paused a beat. "To him." Another beat. "Of late, an upstart folk hero has been interfering with Montfort's operation."

"He knows I'm the Savior of St. Giles."

"It seems you were effective in gaining his attention, except for one problem. You weren't hitting him in his bank account. The first cheap hell you shut down, he shrugged off as no big loss, but put him on the alert. The second had him planning how to handle the situation. But Number 9 took him by surprise. It was the step too far. Neither he nor his conspirators at Whitehall could tolerate further interference after their scheme to secure the vote of the future Marquess of Clare was frustrated."

"What does he plan on doing about it?"

"Funny you should ask. You see, the son of a powerful English duke is a rather big fish, particularly when that son has already garnered a significant amount of notoriety. However, Montfort has assured his inner circle in Whitehall that he is very close to getting the situation under control."

The dread in Percy's stomach curdled into a hard knot. The new and ugly had arrived. "How?"

"He has an agent placed very close. *Intimately* was the word used. It's only a matter of a day or two."

There it was. *Isabel.* He'd lost track of her during this conversation. He'd known from the beginning she was under Montfort's control.

Blast.

He'd offered to help her, even vowed his protection,

and she'd rejected him. Now, he understood why. She'd been playing the game on a different plane from his all along.

Percy had known Montfort was coming for him, and he knew Isabel to be beholden to Montfort in some way. But he hadn't considered Isabel would be Montfort's weapon against him. A pretty face had played him for a fool, the oldest story in the espionage book, a fact Montfort understood well.

"What do you know about Isabel Galante?" Hortense asked. She understood precisely who Montfort's *intimately* placed agent was. And she didn't have time for Percy's self-recrimination.

"A bit," he ground out. *Too much...*

Not near enough.

"But not that you were her mark," Hortense stated.

"No."

Hortense had known Percy for years. She would see he was affected. "We have options."

"Options?" The moment he asked the question, Percy felt like a nodcock. Hortense was the one thinking like a spy, not him. He was thinking like a jilted lover.

"First, we need to find the missing piece of this puzzle."

"Which is?"

"What is her motive? It would be folly to assume it aligns with Montfort's."

It didn't. Even as Percy experienced the betrayal he had no right to, he understood.

"It is our family's problem. What affects one, affects all."

Isabel hadn't betrayed him, because her allegiance had never been to him. It was to her sister, her nephew, and her father. They were everything to her. She would do anything to protect them. Even align with Montfort.

Oblivious to his inner turmoil—or unsympathetic

to it, more like—Hortense stayed on task. "Let it play out a little longer. Perhaps we can—"

"Use her," Percy finished. Hortense's business-like tone had begun to grate on his nerves. "I won't allow it."

Incredulity spread across Hortense's face. "*You won't allow it?*"

She did rather have a point. Those years on the Continent, she and he had been foot soldiers in Lord Nicholas Asquith's little spy army, equals. It would appear that, lately, he'd grown damned comfortable in his status as the son of a duke. Hortense happened to be one of the few people in the world who didn't give a good goddamn about that.

"We can't trust her."

"Bretagne, it defies belief that she would have an ounce of loyalty to Montfort. She is a pawn. Bring her in."

"Her reasons have naught to do with loyalty to Montfort."

It was only the truth. It became clear to Percy that Isabel was as much his enemy as Montfort. The woman was on a mission to save her family. Nothing and no one was going to stand in her way. Alongside the anger and frustration sheered the pang of loss, another emotion he had no right to.

For his sanity, Percy needed to redirect this conversation away from Isabel. He needed to think like a spy, not like a heart-sick lover. "Hortense, dig deeper into who Montfort's conspirators at Whitehall are. We can bring them all down."

Hortense shook her head. "I don't care about those men. You and I know Montfort is the head of the snake. If we don't cut it off now, with one decisive blow, he will slither through unscathed."

"Have you considered what Nick would do?"

"*Nick?*" Hortense scoffed. "You'll get nowhere by

throwing Nick at me. He's a family man now. Completely out of the game. But between you and me? He would pursue this. *Here. Now.* We have the opportunity to deliver to Montfort everything he has coming to him."

Percy nodded. She was right. Absolutely, unequivocally right. "Are you returning to London?"

She shook her head. "I'm staying just up the road at the Queen's Arms." She held his gaze, not yet finished. "I've been hired on at Gardencourt Manor as extra help for the village breakfast tomorrow."

"So quickly? I would think the housekeeper would have required references."

"Oh, I have an excellent set of references from our dear friend Lord Nicholas Asquith. He sends his regards."

Of course. Hortense was thorough.

"I have a feeling about tomorrow, so be ready, Bretagne. You're going to need me." She turned to leave and stopped, asking over her shoulder. "And the Savior of St. Giles? Where does he stand in all this?"

"Haven't you heard? The Savior of St. Giles is retiring."

Hortense gave a curt nod and disappeared into the night. Not three seconds later, a rustling sounded in a dark clump of shrubbery some ten feet away. Percy's head whipped around, and he scanned the gray night for the source. This wasn't the indifferent shuffling of animal, but the measured movement of human. "Who's there?"

Out from the hedge clambered none other than Lucy.

Shock traced through him at the sight of his daughter and the curious expression on her face. Of course, she always wore that expression, so it could be nothing. But he knew in his gut that wasn't the case in this instance.

What had she heard?

Eyes narrowed, she approached, her step slow and deliberate. No denying his daughter had a distinct feel for the dramatic. "The *Savior of St. Giles?*"

23

Knowledge shining in her eyes, Lucy stared at Percy as if this was the first time she'd ever laid eyes on him. "*You* are the Savior of St. Giles?"

He could pretend he'd been discussing gossip with Hortense. But Lucy would see straight through the lie and trust him even less than she did already. It wasn't an option. "Yes."

"Who was that woman you were speaking with?" Her head canted quizzically to the side. "One of your freed harlots?"

Percy shook his head. "Someone from a former life."

Lucy's eyebrows, which had drawn together, released. "So the whispers I've heard about you are true."

"What whispers?"

"That you are a spy."

He wouldn't deny it. Only the truth would do for his daughter. She was old enough and intelligent enough to handle it. "I am no longer a spy."

"You *were* a spy. And, now, you're the Savior of St. Giles." She moved closer. It wasn't lost on Percy that this was the most conversation they'd ever exchanged. "When are you *not* pretending to be someone else?"

"I'm your father. That's genuine and—" He hesitated. She was going to scoff him out of England when he spoke the next part. "And important."

"*Important?* To whom?"

"To *me.*"

"You've had a funny way of showing it all these years."

This was the conversation they needed to have, the one he'd been waiting for, and somehow it had caught him flat-footed. "Lucy, I—"

"Tell me about the gaming hells," she interrupted. "Are they truly the bastions of debauchery, vice, and sin described in novels?"

The girl wanted to change the subject. He would let her. "Worse, I imagine. The endings at those places aren't happy for the people who work there."

Her eyes widened. "And you own *two,* according to the scandal sheets."

"Two that I've shuttered. I've sold most everything off. They now stand empty."

"*Empty?* What about those people with the unhappy endings? Where did they go? You can't very well sell them off."

"Pardon?" This conversation had just hooked a left turn.

"The harlots you *rescued.* Where are they?"

"They're in a house in Seven Dials where they can sort themselves out." He wouldn't mention that most of the women had refused his offer of shelter.

"Sort themselves out? I can't imagine that a woman who has been reduced to whoring—"

"Lucy," he cut across her. He might not be much of a father, but even he knew aristocratic young ladies didn't speak such words. That she'd done so with such ease…Well, he suspected he had much to learn about his daughter.

For her part, Lucy plowed on. "Such a woman

wouldn't have many options for *sorting herself out*. In fact, I would think she had just the one. And you've taken it away from her."

For all her high-spiritedness, Lucy was one pragmatic girl. Who had rendered him stumped. Was she getting at what he thought she might be getting at?

She spoke his suspicion aloud. "You must provide them with an alternate occupation."

Percy raised empty hands. "I haven't any occupation to give them. I've secured their freedom and a roof over their heads."

"And?"

"And *what*?"

Lucy released a blustery sigh. "Every occurrence has three phases." She ticked them off with her fingers. "Before, during, and after. Have you stayed for the *after* in your entire life?"

"Pardon me?" He was fairly certain he'd just been insulted by this daughter who might see him too clearly.

"It's the same with this Savior of St. Giles business. You obtained freedom for the harlots, but now what? Every good act can have a negative effect if it's not seen through. Really, how much evil have *good* acts wrought in the world?"

"You've acquired a bit of wisdom in your short number of years."

Lucy shrugged a shoulder. "I read a considerable amount. More intelligent people than I have said as much." Her direct gaze skittered away, and her expression went suddenly shy. "The same is true for how things worked out with you and Mama. And with you and me."

How vulnerable and young she appeared now. Percy called upon the heavens for the correct words. "I would like to change that."

Lucy's gaze found his. "St. Alban offered to adopt me."

Gutted, that was the word for this feeling inside Percy. "I wasn't aware."

"This was before you returned to London."

"Did you agree to it?" He had to know.

"I told him thank you, but no. I am content with being a bastard."

A groan emerged from the deepest reaches of Percy's gut. There was no stopping it. He wanted to howl and rage. A *bastard*. His daughter was a *bastard*.

Because of him. Because of his impetuousness and his inability to see matters through to the end. All those years ago, he hadn't stopped long enough to consider that Olivia might be with child when he'd sped off to the Continent for war and vainglory. Truly, he'd thought it would be a lark. What a useless man he'd been.

"If we were a different family," Lucy continued, "there would be consequences for me, but we're one of the most powerful families in England. My bastardy doesn't impact my life in the least." She shrugged. "The *ton* is run amok with high-born bastards."

Lucy's cheeriness only increased Percy's feeling of wretchedness. This awful fact that she had accepted for herself, he hadn't accepted for her. "I would like nothing more than to be a father to you."

"It might be too late for that. But—" She hesitated, and Percy felt his life hanging by a frayed thread. "It might not be too late for *us*. I've come to admire how you never fail to arrive for our weekly appointments to watch me read. It demonstrates a care for the *after*."

It was only when his breath released that Percy realized he'd been holding it. A hope he'd long suppressed, for it would have been too painful to give it room to breathe, surged. Whatever form she wanted their relationship to take, he would accept. "I've noted your affinity for novels in particular." He tried for light.

She laughed. "They do open one up to new worlds and other sorts of lives. For instance, about those harlots of yours."

"They're not really mine, Lucy."

"You're responsible for them."

"I'm not sure that I am."

"You are, and here's what I think. Loads of heroines in the novels I read have occupations of some sort. So, if you can't employ these women, then we can help them learn a skill."

"I'm not qualified—"

"Apprenticeships, that sort of thing."

The *we* she spoke warmed Percy through his bones. "Nothing stops you when you when you set your mind, does it?"

"Not especially."

"It seems I've met my match in you." If this mad venture she was proposing was how they could reach a more permanent *we* status, then it was how they would proceed. They would attain suitable occupations for the harlots who had agreed to stay at the Seven Dials house. He would find a way to explain it to her mother. "Shall we return to the musicale?"

Lucy pulled a face. "Must we?"

"We must." What was that tone in his voice? Was it…*fatherly*? "Someday, Gardencourt Manor will be yours."

"*Mine*?" Lucy's eyes went wide as saucers. "Won't it go to the son you will father with my new step-mama?"

Percy searched and detected no hint of bitterness in the question, only curiosity. "Gardencourt is unentailed. It will be yours. Part of embracing it is to take an interest in *all* of it, including village musicales—*especially* village musicales."

Lucy nodded solemnly. "You're saying I must see it through."

"All the way to the *after*."

As they returned to the assembly room, Percy posed another question to Lucy. "Did you follow me tonight?" He had to know if she'd possibly heard more than the Savior of St. Giles business.

"I, um, yes and no," she stammered. "While Mina, Hugh, and I partook of refreshments, I noticed you slip out the exterior door. Not long later, Mina decided it would be best if she left during intermission, because she is rising early in the morning. Something about Mars and Venus before sunrise. You know how she gets."

Percy didn't, but he let Lucy continue. "Anyway, Hugh volunteered to see her safely to Gardencourt, which got the duchess all het up—you know, propriety and all."

"I have a vague memory of the concept, yes," Percy remarked drily.

"Well, after it was all sorted, I found myself quite alone. Then I remembered you, so I decided to investigate and discovered you to be none other than the Savior of St. Giles."

From there, Lucy began chattering happily at his side about all manner of subjects, ranging from her favorite novelist—*Miss Jane Austen, of course*—to the stern headmistress of her school who had single-handedly eradicated the school's rat problem with her withering glare—*It's what I admire most about Mrs. Bloomquist, God's truth.*

Percy wanted to bask in this new beginning with his daughter, an outcome he had been striving toward these last nine months, but the revelations from Hortense kept pushing to the forefront of his mind. Well, one revelation in particular. Isabel was Montfort's *intimately* placed agent.

The pain of loss hadn't subsided. By increments, he understood what had begun to bud inside him for her. That feeling but one step past infatuation, a feeling he'd denied himself for so many years.

Bitterness swelled. This was Montfort's special talent, the poison touch. Nothing thrived beneath Montfort's hand.

His strike was imminent, tomorrow likely, with the village providing distraction and cover at Gardencourt. Until then, Percy would play his cards close. Montfort —and Isabel—would have to come to him.

He would be ready.

24

Simmering with equal parts pique and puzzlement, Isabel shot one last withering glare at Percy's back before allowing herself to be led away by the duchess. The man had abandoned her to a fate worse than death —a duchess intent on dispensing her special megrim cure to the afflicted.

Thankfully, the duchess became distracted from her mission by various gentlemen and their wives who were angling to further their acquaintance and meet the newest Lady Percival. Isabel couldn't isolate the exact moment it had happened, but she'd begun responding to the title without hesitation.

In one of the lulls between greetings and introductions, the duchess leaned over conspiratorially. "It would behoove you to use this little trick I've picked up over the years."

"Oh?" Isabel asked. It rather warmed her how the duchess had taken her under her wing. She hadn't been the recipient of such generosity in a very long time.

"You learn one specific fact about each person and remember it like your life depends on it." A woman of elder years approached. "Observe," the duchess commanded and stepped forward. "My dear Mrs. Cleaver, how do you do? Was your spaniel bitch delivered safely of her pups?"

The other woman's face broke wide into a gratified smile. "We have puppies coming out of our ears. Eight of them! Such silly little moppets." Mrs. Cleaver hesitated as if screwing up her courage. "I would be most pleased to make a gift of one to your grace."

"Oh, that I could, but you wouldn't believe the sneezing fits when I come within ten feet of the little lovelies. 'Tis one of the tragedies of my life, to be sure."

Mrs. Cleaver appeared wholly crestfallen, but only for a moment. Until her eye settled on Isabel. "Or mayhap the future lady of Gardencourt would enjoy her very own lap spaniel?"

The question quite took Isabel by surprise. "Mrs. Cleaver, your offer is most generous, but—"

The duchess shot Isabel a barely perceptible nod, its meaning clear.

She was to accept the pup.

"Do dogs give you sneezing fits, too, my lady?"

"I wouldn't wish to deprive anyone of the pup they've been promised." Isabel hoped against hope that would settle the matter.

The beaming smile returned to Mrs. Cleaver's face. "I have just the girl for you, my lady. Shall I bring her to the breakfast tomorrow?"

"The following day, if you don't mind very much, Mrs. Cleaver," the duchess cut in. "Lady Percival will be quite occupied with our guests on the morrow."

As Mrs. Cleaver took her happy leave and the duchess led Isabel through more rounds of introductions, the reality of Isabel's position landed on her, hard.

She wasn't Lady Percival. She was, in fact, an imposter, and it was Mrs. Cleaver's generosity that made the fact too obvious. Lies and deceit didn't sit still. Instead, they dropped onto a placid surface and rippled outward, affecting all they touched.

Speaking of lies and deceit, Percy...

Percy was the Savior of St. Giles.

Miss Fox's revelation from this afternoon still shook her.

Yet it fit together. He'd been a spy for a dozen years. He was intelligent, serious, and capable. And, in truth, when she'd seen him tonight in his evening blacks, looking utterly, devilishly handsome with his dark curly locks tousled to perfection, she saw that he could be none other.

Lord Percival Bretagne was absolutely the dashing Savior of St. Giles.

And when he'd taken her hand in his and assisted her into the carriage, she'd experienced a fleeting joy that had become reflexive at his touch.

A knot of anxiety twisted in her gut.

She would betray him. What feelings she'd developed for the man must be stamped out and denied oxygen. They were pure fantasy.

But the way he'd been gazing upon her tonight...

As if she were the sun and he a planet caught in her orbit, well, it made her insides flip over. It made her want to succumb to the fantasy and pretend all other cares away.

A quick movement caught the periphery of her vision, and she knew the form the instant before she gazed upon it directly.

Montfort.

His chin jerked toward a quiet corridor, instantly quelling Isabel's pull toward delusion. Reality in the form of one loathsome man beckoned.

"Ma'am," she spoke *sotto voce* to the duchess, "if you could point the way to the Ladies' Retiring Room?"

The duchess waggled a finger in the direction of the

very corridor Montfort had indicated. Isabel nodded her thanks and bade reluctant legs to move. At the hall's end, Montfort waved her into an empty room.

Once inside, the door clicked shut behind her. She kept her back to Montfort as long as she could, but the man was patient. He wouldn't speak until she faced him, his silence told her. She pivoted, a sudden sheen of perspiration slicking her palms.

"You play your role so well, Isabel Galante," he began. "Even from across the room, one could believe you utterly and completely besotted with your husband."

Isabel felt a blush rise, but she held her tongue. Montfort would like nothing more than for her to deny it.

"Is it all an act? I do wonder." He pretended to consider the possibility.

Isabel's hands clenched into fists at her sides. Oh, that she could slap the smug smile off his face.

He pulled a thin square of paper from his breast pocket. "That said, I've detected a deficit of concentration on your part, which is understandable given the luxuries at your disposal. How fortunate *this* arrived in the post."

He held out a missive, its seal already broken. Isabel closed the distance between them barely enough to snatch the letter out of his hand. She flipped it over, instantly recognizing the handwriting. *Papa.* Her head jerked up. "How long have you had this?"

"Oh, you know how letters can get shuffled and misplaced." The man lied in his teeth, Isabel was sure of it. "I knew it would be just the thing to help you remember your purpose."

Isabel gave him her shoulder and absorbed the letter in a quick scan. Its contents were mostly impersonal—Papa would have known Montfort would read it first. Only Papa's parting lines mattered:

Remember what I told you when we last spoke, cariña. I continue to feel the same.

—Papa

With deliberate care, she refolded the letter and placed it in Montfort's extended hand. "Can you perhaps enlighten me as to what your dear Papa meant by the last part?"

Isabel thought fast. "That he loves Eva and me more than anything in the world."

A lie.

Papa had spoken much more pragmatic words upon their final meeting.

Montfort's eyes narrowed on her, skeptical. "What a loving family you are." He tucked the letter inside his overcoat. "Tomorrow is the day."

Isabel controlled her breath, even as her lungs wanted leave to catch it. *Tomorrow.*

After her talk with Miss Fox today, she should have expected as much, yet the timing caught her by surprise. And now she must tell Montfort a truth, one that had become quite precious, only to be mocked the instant she spoke it. But hadn't she vowed to do *anything* to save her family?

Here was the test.

She screwed up her courage to speak the words she must. "There is something I must tell you—"

"Is it about the little matter of your maidenhead?"

Isabel nodded, mute. Was there nothing too terrible or personal for this man to speak aloud?

"I planned that you might anticipate matters with the ever-so-dashing Lord Percival Bretagne. You do make a damned attractive couple, I'll give you that. No matter. Sheets are no longer necessary."

Isabel's stomach lurched. It was all so repulsive. Were there no depths to which this man wouldn't sink?

"When I give you the signal, you lead Percy to me. I

do want to see his face when he comes to understand the fate of those who betray me."

A shiver went up Isabel's spine. She detected a message in there for her.

It was happening. It was really, truly happening.

And it was really, truly wrong.

"Remember, Isabel," Montfort continued, "your dear Papa's life. Eva and her sweet, little Ariel's lives, depend on your actions tomorrow. Do not fail them now."

Montfort exited the room first. Isabel stood still, her feet mired in quicksand. It wasn't only the weight of what she would do tomorrow that had her legs refusing to budge, but, more, the reminder of Papa's parting words to her, his true ones.

Do not let Montfort use me as a weapon to manipulate you into doing his bidding. Promise me, cariña.

She'd nodded her promise through tears, but she hadn't obeyed. How could she? How could she abandon Papa to rot in a prison in Madrid? How could she abandon the future she and Eva were building with their shop in London? And Ariel? What of his future if she failed?

She must see this one, awful thing through.

Tomorrow. So soon. *Too soon.*

At last, she picked up her feet and made her numb way to the main assembly room. Once there, she felt *it*, a frisson of specific energy pulsating through the air, of the sort but one man held the power to spark.

Percy had returned.

It was as if the man had the power to alter the very chemistry of oxygen into an element more vibrant.

Across the room, he stood, the long, lean line of his body suggesting ease, a looseness, as he made light conversation with the duchess, the mayor, and the mayor's wife. But one would be wrong to accept that surface appraisal. His dark eyes were scanning the room. He was searching for her, Isabel knew it. A shudder of excitement raced through her. Then his gaze found her and slowly raked up her body until, at last, he locked onto her eyes, and her heart gave the fluttery *pitter-pat* of a girl experiencing love for the first time.

Oh.

Another flutter.

Was she, in fact, that girl, *now*?

He broke the contact to answer a question, and Isabel noticed his daughter at his side, her arm linked through his, her bright gaze taking him in without a hint of her customary resentment. A shift had occurred between father and daughter, possibly a reconciliation. Isabel's heart found this one flicker of light through the darkness.

"Ah, Lady Percival," the duchess called out, her thoroughly bejeweled hand—Isabel counted no fewer than ten diamonds of varying shapes and sizes twinkling in the light—waving Isabel over. "Do join our discussion of the benefits of a morning ice bath upon one's constitution." The woman's singular focus returned to the mayor and his wife who appeared as-yet unconvinced. "I haven't been feeling quite the thing of late as it's middle of summer, and there is no ice to be had in this charming hamlet of yours." One could see she wasn't charmed in the least.

Unable to resist, Isabel cut Percy a quick glance, certain they would share in a private amusement. The duchess could be too much at times. Even so, one couldn't help but delight in her. That was what they would exchange with a single look.

What she found in his eyes, however, sent her blood running cold.

Flinty and hard was the way he stared down at her. Quite the opposite of the man who, as recently as half an hour ago, had been sending her looks that could light a furnace and keep it ablaze through winter. His expression now was the stuff of a January snow storm.

A chilling shard stabbed through her. What had changed in the last half hour?

A jolly chuckle erupted from the mayor. "A jump into icy water? That sounds exactly the sort of business a young Lord Percival Bretagne would get up to. Seem to remember a tale about a January dip in the sea on a dare. The boy was the scourge of the county in his day."

A sheepish smile played about Percy's mouth, even as the duchess remained undeterred. "I've no interest in saltwater and seaweed, I can assure you, Squire Noble."

A determined Miss Bretagne cut in, "What's this *scourge* business?"

The mayor barked another merry laugh. "The boy was—if you don't mind me saying all these years later—the sort of young buck who had a bit of wildness to him." The mayor's wife nodded her emphatic agreement. Miss Bretagne's smile broadened. "Much in the habit of riding breakneck across the countryside and flying down the lanes at speeds too precipitate for our environs, which tend toward the dozy and content. Discomposed more than one of our venerable citizens."

Eyes wide and serious, Mrs. Noble inserted. "Old Charlie Martin claimed it drove him to drink."

The squire waved the notion away with a dismissive flick of the wrist. "Eh, twaddle. Charlie Martin was draining ten cups a day to the dregs before Lord Percival was in leading strings."

Miss Bretagne shot her father an admiring glance. Percy returned it with an indulgent smile, one that said she was getting no more from him on the matter of his uncivilized youth. Their reconciliation would have warmed Isabel were it not for Percy's altered manner toward herself. The freeze of his cold shoulder hurt.

"Speaking of horses," Squire Noble began, "it has

been a long while since we've seen Gardencourt's stable run. Word has it you still have the stock?"

"I'm thinking of trying it on at Newmarket in about two years' time. Princess Polly just foaled a contender, I believe."

"Princess Polly?" the mayor asked. "The Barb from Paragon's line?"

"The very one."

The mayor clapped Percy on the back. "That's the stuff."

Even as Isabel pasted a smile onto her face—one that said, of course, she'd known her husband's plans for the future—this plan for his future was one Percy hadn't shared with her. Of course, she chided herself, she wasn't truly his wife. What right to his future plans had she?

And the future of two years from now?

It was too far to fathom.

The very awful near future would destroy any chance that might have been for them.

Something Percy said just pricked her ear. "What was that, dear husband?"

His cold stare landed upon her. "I was explaining to Squire Noble that I shall be sleeping in the stable for the foreseeable future. With Princess Polly just foaled, I'll be keeping an eye on her during the night."

Squire Noble's well-tended belly shook with a sly chuckle. "And you newly wed? That's dedication, old man."

"Gentlemen," the duchess cut in, sharp, "a young lady is present. Mind your tongues."

Percy pulled his watch from his pocket. "In fact, I should be returning now." He bowed to the small group. "Lucy, are you staying?"

"I believe I shall to the end."

Percy nodded approvingly, and a private look

passed between father and daughter. He turned to leave and stopped. "Lady Percival, I believe you will wish to enjoy the remaining evening's entertainments and ride back with the family." He wasn't stating a belief so much as telling her what to do.

While part of Isabel wanted to defy him, the coldness in his eye had her shrinking away from rebellion. "Of course, husband."

Percy met her eye mid-bow. For the flicker of a moment, another emotion replaced the coldness, one she hadn't time to read for in a blink, it was gone, the ice returned. He finished his farewells to the group and strode away.

He was lost to her.

Except, in truth, he had never truly been hers.

"Lady Percival?" Miss Bretagne asked. "Would you care to take a walk about the room before the second half of the musicale begins?"

Even through the numb shell that had begun to harden around Isabel's emotions, she experienced a trace of shock. "I would find that most agreeable."

As they began their stroll, arm in arm, Isabel sensed an uncharacteristic hesitation hanging about Miss Bretagne. At last, the girl's tongue untangled itself. "I must extend my apologies for having been a dreadful beast to you when we met. Shall we be friends?"

A lump solidified in Isabel's throat. "I should like that, Miss Bretagne."

Wretched guilt twisted through Isabel. Such a future friendship wasn't possible.

The girl's face scrunched up. "Since you're my step-mama, perhaps you can call me Lucy. And may I call you Isabel?"

Isabel nodded. "That would be most welcome."

As they continued to wend their way through the crowded assembly rooms, Lucy happily greeted anyone who happened into their path. Isabel remained silent in her thoughts, false smile pasted onto her lips. A sequence of thought kept whipping through her mind in terrible refrain.

To save one father and daughter, she would have to destroy another father and daughter.

Yet what alternative had she?

Over and over it went, and she couldn't find a way out of it, for every word was true. She had no choice but to do everything in her power to save Papa, even if he thought otherwise. If their roles were reversed, he would act no differently.

But it was the scandal that would ensue for the Bretagne family that had her tied up in knots. Horrible lies would be spread through London and England about Lucy's father once the *London Diary* published its story. Reputations would be ruined. Whatever fragile bond Percy had formed with his daughter, destroyed.

Just as the musicale was set to resume, Isabel took a seat between Lucy and the duchess, who whispered a concerned, "My dear, are you quite the thing?"

Before Isabel could concoct one of the lies she'd become so proficient at telling, Montfort leaned forward, eyebrows waggling. She hadn't noticed him on the other side of the duchess. "Shall we hear the pitter-patter of little feet in nine months' time?"

Bile rose in Isabel's throat.

"Lord Bertrand Montfort," said the duchess, bristling. "We do *not* speak of such matters in public—or at all, I dare say."

Still, when the room fell silent for the second half of the musicale, the duchess gave Isabel's hand a light squeeze. Delight glittered in the other woman's eye. The possibility of babies tended to spark such twinkles.

And Isabel thought she couldn't sink any lower.

SHE CREPT into the dark butler's room, chilled and damp with the night, and found the narrow bed, empty of *him*.

Isabel slipped beneath the meager blanket and curled onto her side. All that was left of him was his scent, already grown faint.

She pushed tomorrow away, closed her eyes, and tried to conjure yesterday. Of him, her, and Ariel, playing house.

Then, of him and her joined as one for a fleeting moment.

She would live in that moment forever, if she could.

How was it possible she'd known him for a week? How was it possible for one heart to become so inextricably twined with another in so short a time?

Tomorrow, she would be strong.

Tomorrow, she would do what was required of her.

Tonight, she would be weak.

Tonight, she would dream of yesterday.

25

A breakfast that began at four of the clock. Whether in Spain or England, it was the aristocratic way. And, in all honesty, Isabel couldn't help thinking it a delightful concept.

To break one's fast this late in the day was an indulgence known only to those of the highest tiers of society. But today, at Gardencourt, all were welcome to enjoy a taste of aristocratic life.

In the conservatory, surrounded by orange, lemon, and lime trees recently denuded of their fruit for all manner of treats—lemon tarts, lemon cakes with strawberries and cream, lime punch, orange pudding—Isabel stood beside the duchess, greeting villagers, exchanging pleasantries about the beauty of the weather—a cooling breeze holding off the summer heat—and encouraging all to enjoy themselves, which the large quantity of rum in the lime punch rather encouraged. Cook had even sung a rhyme while she stirred:

One of sour
Two of sweet
Three of strong
Four of weak

Truly, Gardencourt was at its finest. The townsfolk dressed in their Sunday best on a Saturday. Children racing across the verdant field on the other side of the ha-ha, Lord Exeter's wild gaggle of boys leading the fray in a merry chase, big brother Hugh in tow. The town elders, along with the duke and Lord Exeter, enjoying a light tea at tables set beneath the oaks beyond the terrace. Just a few steps from the conservatory splayed the large white tent where the dance would take place later along with an informal supper.

Earlier, Isabel had spotted Lucy and Miss Radclyffe overseeing those preparations and consulting with the string quartet brought in from London about the music list. Lively fiddle tunes were an absolute must, as the villagers, and the duchess in particular, expected informal country dances. Lucy, however, had other dances in mind. Well, one dance—the waltz—which the musicians agreed to insert into the rotation every fourth song, Lucy had happily informed Isabel, who suspected a bit of additional coin was involved.

It was a jubilant day with every member of the Bretagne family doing his or her part. Even Lady Exeter was greeting visitors who couldn't help being awestruck by a lady of her elevation stooping so low as to offer them a *good day*, for she couldn't help making one feel so.

All the Bretagnes save one.

Percy.

"Now, Isabel," said the duchess once a large group of women had moved along, *ooo*-ing and *aah*-ing over the exotic plants of the conservatory, "if you have half a brain in that pretty head of yours—and I believe you do —you will call this gathering the First Annual Citrus Day Breakfast and Dance and establish it as a yearly event for the village."

"That is a splendid idea," Isabel replied, voice carefully neutral. A splendid idea for a different future mistress of Gardencourt Manor. A true one.

The duchess gave Isabel a magnanimous nod. "I am pleased to have given you the idea. Now, pray tell, where is that husband of yours?"

Isabel attempted a light laugh that soared with all the lift of a deflated air balloon. "Oh, you know Percy. He is at the stable, showing the men the future of Gardencourt's racing stock." How naturally the lies flowed from her mouth these days. Her view of herself as an honest person might have to change.

"That boy is horse mad, always has been." The duchess released the length of pearls she'd been twining round her fingers. "I suggest you go and find your husband. Then explain to him that it is his God-given duty as a scandalous and dashing man to give our female villagers a thrill by showing his handsome face." It was clear the duchess's suggestion was, in fact, a command.

Isabel took her leave of the ladies and entered the happy tide of the festivities, a gaiety to which she was immune. Since last night, a numbing shell had hardened around her, allowing no emotions to penetrate. For if she let herself feel, it wouldn't be joy she experienced. Quite the opposite, in fact.

'Twas better to feel nothing.

In the distance, she spotted Tilly and Nell, dressed in their remade finery, garlands in their hair, strolling arm in arm across the close-cropped lawn, four would-be swains at their heels, each vying for a pretty smile and an encouraging word. While Nell appeared overwhelmed by the attention, the same couldn't be said for Tilly, who understood the power of a saucy smile and a bold rejoinder over a young man. Or five young men, as the case now was.

Isabel continued her scan of the grounds and discovered no trace of Eva. The old Eva wouldn't have missed these festivities for the world, but the new Eva was different, more measured in her choices. The new Eva worried Isabel, for she couldn't feel that Eva was truly being herself, save one glimmer of hope: Eva was with her son. Eva had, at last, formed a bond with Ariel, and Isabel's heart, which felt achy, bruised, and sore, experienced a swell of happiness for this one bit of good.

The feeling lasted but a moment, for her feet continued moving toward the stable, toward *him*.

Although she was doing the duchess's bidding now, there would be a time today—in five minutes or five hours—when she would be serving Montfort. She'd seen him, sitting beneath a sprawling oak with the other men, looking like the most English Englishman who ever walked the earth, red-faced with jollity, secure in the position of wealth and privilege the accident of birth had afforded him in life.

Montfort, however, hadn't yet given her the scantest bit of his attention. She was nothing to him until it was time to move her pawn on the board.

Isabel's gaze caught on the thin form of a serving girl, weaving through the festivities, bent on one task or another. Dressed in the same garb as every other servant, there was no reason for Isabel's eye to follow the girl, except that she felt the compulsion. There was something familiar...

It struck her.

The servant was the woman from that first night, from the carriage.

Hortense, Percy's friend.

Well, *friend* might be stretching the matter. Associate seemed more appropriate. Hortense knew Percy was the Savior of St. Giles and had assisted him.

The fact that she was *here—today—*meant she could have been here...

Last night.

It could explain Percy's coldness. Perhaps Hortense had uncovered information in London—information about Isabel.

An echo of last night's chill traced through her. The fact that Hortense was here today meant more.

She and Percy were anticipating action.

Isabel should run to Montfort and tell him, but she wouldn't. With Hortense here, Percy might have a fighting chance against Montfort. Although it went against her interests, her spirits experienced a slight lift.

She stepped inside the grand stable and stopped, inhaling deeply of horse, sweat, hay, and earth. For all the raucous festivity outside, this place was its opposite. Dim and cool and quiet, except for the odd rustle and whicker of a horse. The stable lads must have been enjoying the day with everyone else. But Percy was here, she knew it.

She ventured down the wide center aisle, on the alert for any sign of him. At last, she heard it: from the gable end of the stable came a murmurous susurration of *shoosh, sloosh...shoosh, sloosh...*

Isabel lifted her gaze and found the hay loft.

Up the ladder, she followed the sound. Her head poked above the loft floor, and all the breath whooshed from her lungs at the sight greeting her eyes. Some twenty feet away, Percy was sorting through horse provender with a pitchfork. But it wasn't his task that held her transfixed, rather the lean, muscled length of his body in motion.

Her eyes roved across his form from knee-high boots, to thighs bunched beneath well-fitted trousers, to shirt undone and open nearly to navel, revealing chest muscles that flexed and released with his labor. Sweat sheened every inch of visible skin. *Dios mío*, the man was a damned devastating sight.

He rested his pitchfork against the wall and swiped his hand across his brow. Isabel cleared her throat. His gaze swung to meet hers and held. Time did that funny thing it always did when she looked into his eyes. It fell away.

Nothing relevant existed outside what existed between them.

His mouth twisted with irony, and he spoke the one word that could bring her back to reality. "*Wife.*"

She blinked. She swallowed. She wished it was true.

She gave herself a mental shake.

It was too late for wishes.

"*Husband.*" She finished her climb and stood facing him, her stance a mirror of his. "Your presence is requested in the conservatory."

The man, whose eyes burned and continued to hold hers, shrugged.

"By the duchess." Isabel spoke the title like it was a trump card.

He shrugged again, the gesture telling her in no uncertain terms that she would have to do better.

She glanced about the loft flooded by afternoon light from windows at either end and populated by all the usual animal provisions and implements. Except in the corner stood a narrow, tidily made bed, a lantern atop a short, three-legged stool beside it. "Is this where you're sleeping?"

He shrugged. *Again.* "I'm accustomed to it."

Pique that Isabel had no right to, rose. "Back to *that*, are you?"

ISABEL'S TART question hit Percy like a sharp blow to the sternum.

She wasn't speaking of the bed, or even of his new sleeping quarters. With a few well-aimed words, she'd summoned into the room his self-denial, the place he returned within himself when the world presented him with uncertainty and chaos. Within privation lay control.

His jaw clenched and released. He wouldn't be baited into a conversation about it, not with this woman who had arrived here, cheeks delicately flushed, eyes bright, looking like the freshest pastry on the rack. So unspoiled and sweet, he could hardly look at her and keep to his side of the loft.

He'd been waiting for Montfort to reveal his hand, and Isabel, here, now, could be it.

So, yes, keeping an unrelenting hold on himself in the face of his strongest addiction was his only hope. Just look what happened when he let up? He went and fell head-over-heels in—

He stopped himself there.

"You're not even dressed for the fête," she continued.

"I'm dressed about the same as many of the local men, who are dressed in their best."

She flinched. His barb had stung.

Percy gathered his wits and began thinking like the spy he once was. "Of course, you spent your childhood in close proximity to the Spanish royal court, you would have a keen appreciation for how to dress appropriately for one's station."

Isabel's eyes narrowed, and her head canted to the side in question, but she gave no other response.

Percy considered his options. He could tell her to leave. He could cut her completely from his life. But neither of those actions would give him what he really wanted from her, what he *needed.* "Why?" he found himself asking.

"*Why?*" she repeated. She was trying to buy time, and he had none to sell.

"Why are you doing Montfort's bidding?"

She shifted on her feet, and indecision flickered across her features. Another fraught moment passed, during which she seemed to arrive at a decision. She settled a hip onto the window frame at her back, her form limned in golden light, like a medieval Madonna.

"One day a powerful Englishman—" she began.

"Montfort?" Percy cut in. He would have her speak the man's name and have it entirely out in the open.

She nodded. He detected nerves in the way her hands clutched together tightly in her lap. "Montfort approached Papa about passing along any court information or intrigue that might catch his ear. Oftentimes, the presence of servants are forgotten. My father refused. Then"—a hesitation—"he was convinced."

"How?"

"Montfort had worked out the origin of our surname."

"How is that significant?"

"Galante is a name that fell out of use by our people a few hundred years ago. My grandfather thought it would be safe for our family to start using it again."

Our people. Safe. She was referring to her Jewish ancestry. "Judaism is no longer banned in Spain," Percy observed.

"But you must know it is difficult to live openly as a Jew there, and impossible for a Jew to be tailor to the king." Her hands tightened into fists, and a tremble reached her voice. "We are seen as untrustworthy devils, even as child snatchers."

Percy nodded. It was the harsh truth.

"Montfort impressed this fact upon Papa most persuasively. It was understood exposure would follow, if Papa didn't agree to Montfort's demands." Her eyes lifted to meet Percy's. Gone was her light. In its place, darkness. "You'll have noticed that Eva and I have Spanish given names. We attended Catholic Mass, but..."

"But?"

"There were certain traditions of our true faith that we practiced at home. Traditions the king wouldn't have tolerated in his tailor."

"I've noticed you wear the hand of Fatima."

Isabel pulled the necklace from her bodice. "Muslims call it by that name. For the Jews, it is the hand of Miriam. It was Mama's hamsa, and, yes, another remainder of our heritage."

Percy had vowed to keep his emotional distance from Isabel—she was his enemy's pawn—but he couldn't, not with the unresolved pain he saw in her eyes. "How long before he was caught passing information to the English?"

"Three years."

Three years was an eternity to have one's neck bared to the blade of potential exposure. "And your father was imprisoned?"

Eyes brimming with unshed tears, she nodded.

"Then how did you and your sister come to be in England?" Before she could open her mouth, Percy answered the question. "*Montfort.*"

"Montfort transported us and offered us a place to stay," she said, voice cleared of emotion as she recounted the facts. "Fortunately, Papa had planned for an emergency. Eva and I refused any more help from Montfort and used the monies to find a suitable shop and start our dressmaking trade. A few months later, Montfort arrived at our door to give us the chance to both serve our new country and free Papa. The debt that Eva and I had acquired by accepting his help to leave Spain obliged us. Eva volunteered to go with him without any idea of what he had planned for her."

"Which was?"

"To use her beauty and body for his own ends."

Anger surged hot through Percy. "He turned her into a prostitute."

"He used the word courtesan, but, yes. When she finally came home, she was addicted to laudanum and several months gone with child. Ariel was born sickly."

"But that wasn't the end of it," Percy stated. Isabel still hadn't explained her involvement.

"A few months after Eva returned, Montfort came back and explained that our debt wasn't paid. I needed to take my sister's place at Number 9."

Percy's anger grew spikes and tapped into a vein of pure rage. This was how Montfort bent others to his will. "Now it wasn't simply about freeing your father, but about you, Eva, and Ariel staying in England."

"You know the story from there."

"And you believed Montfort?"

"On each and every point."

"Why?"

"Because he seems all powerful." With a sudden surge of agitation, she pushed off the window ledge. "The lives of my family are at risk," she said, a plea in her voice.

She wanted him to understand. And he did. All too well. "You have no choice."

"He's coming after you now."

"And using you to do it."

She nodded, abashed. "But why? Why is he coming after you?"

"I did treat his beloved niece, Olivia, rather poorly when we were married," Percy said, trying for flippancy.

Grave eyes stared out at him, unconvinced by his forced lightness. "That isn't why, though, is it? And it isn't simply about this Savior of St. Giles business."

A frisson of surprise traced through Percy. "You know about that?"

"I have my sources, too."

He exhaled a humorless laugh. "Touché."

Isabel remained dead serious. "Montfort wants to *destroy* you. *Why?*"

26

Of a sudden, the pitched ceiling of the hayloft seemed to compress and squeeze in, making it difficult for Percy to draw breath.

For such a small word, Isabel's *why* asked much of him, and in direct opposition to how he should be handling her.

He should treat her like an enemy agent, like all the words that flowed from her mouth were lies spun to wrap him in her web, leaving him vulnerable to Montfort's strike.

But he couldn't. For here was the thing:

She had bared her soul to him.

And he would do the same for her. Not because he wanted to, but because he *needed* to. He needed this woman to know him, thoroughly.

And once she did, no longer would she gaze upon him as she did now, with openness and a care resembling affection.

Once she saw him for who he truly was, she would find it easy to walk away from him.

And that was precisely what she needed to do: not walk, but *run* as fast and as far from Lord Percival Bretagne as she could.

"It has been fairly established," he began, "that I was a vainglorious young man in search of valor on the battlefield."

She nodded and moved toward the stack of hay, plucking out a stem of straw. She began to worry it between her fingers, her silence encouraging him to continue.

"I was seasick the entire voyage to Spain. Byron failed to mention that possibility in his poetry. But my enthusiasm and thirst for war wasn't dampened one bit."

Why did she continue to look upon him with those intent eyes of hers? Why wasn't she put off already?

"Then came the Battle of Maya, my first battle. My only battle. It was a right slaughter from beginning to ignoble end. I believe Wellington calls it his lasting shame."

"How did it end for *you*?" The sympathy contained within that *you* was almost too much.

"After I picked up *this*"—he indicated the slash running along his right cheekbone—"a cannon ball cratered the earth a few yards away, and the world went black. My countrymen took me for dead and retreated through the mountain pass without me."

Isabel's hand flew to her mouth. "No," she whispered. "How did you survive?"

"Days later—or weeks. Those early memories are hazy—I awoke in a modest farmhouse, being cared for by a Spanish family that consisted of a very old woman and her very young great-granddaughter. The rest of the family were either dead or fighting, which was as good as dead. The cannon shot had wiped my memory clean. I couldn't have told you my name, but my body was whole, if battered. As my strength returned, I began helping around the farm. They were in need of a man about the place. Picked up the language by bits and pieces, too. After a few months, an Englishman darkened the door."

"Montfort."

"He was passing through the territory when he picked up a rumor about an Englishman in the area. When he found me, he said I was an English soldier."

"But"—Isabel's eyebrows drew together in bewilderment—"you were thought dead for over a decade."

"Another bit of intelligence from your source, I presume?"

She shrugged, unabashed.

"Montfort didn't tell me the full story of my true identity. He left out that I was Captain Lord Percival Bretagne. He gave me the opportunity to continue serving my country."

"This is when you became a spy."

"My newly acquired Spanish was useful, along with the French I'd retained. There are any number of ways a man can be an asset to his country. Some operate in the light, like soldiers and diplomats. And others do their work in the shadows."

"And you became one of the latter men?"

He wanted to draw closer to Isabel. Instead, he used that energy to retreat to the window on his side of the loft. Here, he could speak the words he needed to make her understand. "I did."

"But what of your memory?"

"It came to me at night, in my sleep, but nothing I could hold onto in the light of day."

"Then how—?"

"Do you know of Lord Nicholas Asquith?"

"I've heard the other ladies speak of him."

"I had been doing Montfort's dirty work for about a year when I traveled to Vienna during the Congress. I was there to keep an ear out for what was being negotiated in the shadows. It was only by chance that our paths crossed. Nick knew me in an instant, as we were brothers by law. Our wives were sisters."

"Is there no one in England who isn't related?" Isabel asked, exasperation in her tone. It was charming.

"Not in the *ton*."

Her seriousness returned, and she plucked out another stem of straw. "Lord Nicholas Asquith helped you recover your memory?"

Percy nodded. "Montfort had been keeping me secluded from anyone who would know me."

"Oh, what a cruel thing."

"Nick concocted a plan to stage my death for Montfort's benefit."

Isabel's brow lifted to the ceiling. "How…how bold."

"Aye, that it was. In truth, I didn't think it stood a chance of success." Percy shook his head, still in wonder at the luck of it all. "But it did."

"And it freed you from Montfort. Yet—" A tense beat skipped past. "Yet you didn't return home immediately?"

At last, they had reached the moment, the one where Percy would reveal his true self to Isabel and sweep that soft look from her eye. "Before I hied off to Spain, I was a terrible husband. Did your source tell you that?"

"I believe it was implied."

"I caroused every night. I placed reckless wagers on anything that moved or breathed. I had a mistress."

"Oh."

Had she flinched? He should warn her to brace herself, for there was more.

"By the time I left England, I had a wife who couldn't stand the sight of me. And when Nick told me I had a daughter, I knew I'd make a terrible father. Olivia certainly didn't need me, so I stayed on the Continent and embedded myself in the small network Nick had formed, which operated without Montfort's knowledge. I could protect England and my family, and not trouble them with my continued existence."

"I can see a nobility in that reasoning."

"There is but one problem." Still, she didn't understand. Well, she would. "It was a lie."

"A *lie?*"

"I stayed in that life for one person. Myself. *Not* for England. *Not* for my family. I'd formed an addiction to the life of espionage."

Isabel opened her mouth to speak and hesitated. "I'm not sure I understand."

"It seduces you in. Gets your brain moving and your pulse jumping. I'd become a necessary man. For the first time in my life, I was useful. I didn't know the first thing about mattering in England, but on the Continent, with my memory fully returned and as part of Nick's network, I did."

At last, he'd arrived at the essential truth of the choice he'd made. The truth he'd never spoken aloud to anyone. The truth that filled him with shame every time he saw his daughter. "I stayed away because it was the easier path."

Isabel's eyebrows crinkled together. "*Easier?* I would think the life of a spy a sight more difficult than the life of an entitled lord in England."

"Oh, that's where you're wrong. Staying on the Continent was much easier than returning to England and attempting to forge a useful life here. And it was much easier to stay away than to return and right the wrongs I'd done to my father, my wife, and my daughter when I'd abandoned them for the glories of war."

Isabel's direct, green eyes locked onto his, searching him, seeing into him, down to his shameful, rotten core, he was sure of it.

"And yet"—she took one step, then another, and another—"here you are. In England. At your father's estate. Sharing the same air as your daughter."

As she closed the distance between them, Percy felt the change in his body, its reaction to her. The rush of his blood. The coil of his muscles. The race of his heart.

"You are *here*, doing the hard work."

Percy wanted to break from her gaze, at the grace she offered, but he couldn't. By increments, she continued moving toward him, slowly as one would with a feral animal, and, with each step she took, her power over him increased.

"Last night," she said, "I noticed that you and Lucy were different with one another."

"Aye, we—" He was having a difficult time getting the word out. "We've reconciled, or have started, at least."

Closer, Isabel stepped, now not five feet from him. "And how does it make you feel?"

He understood what she wanted him to say. That he felt *right*. That it was the first time in over a decade that he'd felt so. He turned away from the thought, not ready to accept her absolution. "How I feel about it is of no consequence. Only Lucy has that right."

"Sometimes," Isabel began, "we must make a choice in the space between one moment and the next. Just a tiny lick of time that will decide all the moments to follow."

She was speaking of him, but also of herself. This woman had experience with such moments. Still, a hard truth must be spoken. "The consequences don't have much care for the cause. Not a dozen years later."

"Here's what I know about the consequences of your time on the Continent. You became more than a useful man, you became a *good* man. I don't think many people know that about you."

Percy scoffed. "When I returned to England, I still couldn't face it. I saw Montfort embraced by Society, even by my family, and I burned for revenge. That is what brought me to Number 9 and all those other hells. The Savior of St. Giles wasn't there to save society from its sins of the flesh and gaming. It was to expose Montfort for the fraud he is, which made it all the easier for me to ignore the fraud I am."

"You are not a fraud," Isabel insisted. "You are a good man."

"Shall I give you a detailed account of the acts I committed for Crown and Country? Of my *useful* work? Of my sins? Will you be my confessor?"

Only a few feet of dusty floorboards lay between him and her. Her face tilted up so she could hold his gaze. It was all he could do not to stroke his finger along the line of her jaw.

"You don't need a confessor," she said, her soft, intimate contralto pouring into him. "You need something else."

"What?" The question emerged raw and vulnerable, unable to mask the feeling that stirred inside him.

"You need to be touched *here*"—her finger traced the scar along his right cheekbone—"and *here*." She pushed the fabric of his shirt wide and touched, one by one, the scars scattered across his skin.

She inched her body closer, so close her breath pulsed against his neck in short, warm bursts. Percy's own breath caught in his chest, and his hands remained empty and still at his sides. All he wanted was to fill them with this woman, her sweet, lush curves, her dark, silky hair, *her*. To do so, to slip into the stream of this desire was both dangerous and utter folly, but when had those considerations ever stopped him?

She rose to her toes and touched her mouth to the

cup of his ear. "What you're in need of Lord Percival Bretagne, is tenderness."

"Isabel," Percy began, because he must, "is this wise?"

He heard the breath catch in her throat. His heart banged out three hard thuds. She pulled back far enough to meet his eye. "No."

If a no was ever a yes, hers was.

That instant, Percy was lost, come what may.

"*You* are my addiction, Isabel."

OH, the way his words transformed feeling into physical sensation, from her fingertips to her toes to her sex to the very center of her heart.

She pressed her palm against his chest, and he moved with her when she pushed. She met him step for step, until the back of his legs reached the bed in the corner. She tugged his shirt from his trousers and lifted.

Here, he stood before her, muscular and gorgeous in the muted light. A fine dusting of hair spread across his bare chest, narrowing at the segmented muscles of his stomach, disappearing below the waistband of his trousers, his hard manhood straining against the cloth. Heat flushed through her at the sight, at her power over this man.

The light of day revealed yet more about him. She had noticed the scars on his body before, but now she better understood them, that they were healed only on the surface of his skin. This man carried hurt with him every moment of every day.

When she touched him again, it was to feather fingertips gently across his marked skin. Without thinking, she pressed her mouth to one particularly nasty scar, puckered and red, less than a year old, she would wager.

Oh, the velvety growl that tore from him.

As she bussed kisses from one scar to another, his hands wove through her hair, tugging it loose from the chignon at the nape of her neck. Lower, she explored until she reached the waistband of his trousers. His manhood but a few wicked inches from her mouth, she dropped to her knees.

Her fingers had just slipped one button free of its loop when his hand closed over hers. "Isabel, I'm not sure you know what you're doing."

She sat back on her heels, piqued at the interruption, at the *nerve*. "Did you know what you were about when you took me with your mouth?"

A shocked beat of time ticked past. Then his lips curled into a smile that could only be characterized as wicked. "You know the answer to that question."

The memory shot a pulse of lust through her. "I want to feel you in my mouth. I want to taste you." Oh, the wanton words that flowed from her lips.

His hand released hers. "Far be it from me to deny a lady what she wants."

Isabel made quick work of the buttons. The cloth flapped open, revealing his hot, hard manhood, thick and ready. Her eyes lifted. His gaze burned into her as trembly fingers trailed across the long length. Instinctually, they wrapped around him, and his breath went shallow.

She squeezed. He moaned. If she kissed him now, she would find that his mouth had gone dry, she knew it.

She leaned forward and touched her tongue to him. So very hard. So velvety soft. He groaned and wove the fingers of one hand through her hair. Slowly, she stroked him with her tongue, from base to tip, her gaze never wavering from his.

What she saw in his eyes was a rawly sexual, naked intimacy, stripped bare. Here was only him and her and this desire.

Deliberately, she opened her mouth and took him in. His eyes drifted shut, and an exhale poured from him in long release, his fingers clutching her hair.

The scent of him. *Male.* The taste of him. *Salt.* The feel of him. *Man.*

In unison, her hand and mouth moved on his thick, hard length, as she took him in and out, too big for her, but so too perfect. Her thighs pressed together as her sex ached and throbbed with desire. Unexpected how this giving of pleasure only increased hers.

His hand began guiding her head, and she doubted he was aware of the motion. Deeper he pushed inside, and she groaned. His slitted eyes blazed into her. "Can you take it?"

In response, she sucked him in deeper. What a strange role. How shocking that she enjoyed it, this playing servant to his cock. She held none of the power, and all of it.

More fully, she took him in, but not all of him. He was too big. Her fingers closed around him, following the rhythm he was setting. Her other hand reached around and grabbed his tight arse, muscles bunched beneath her grasp. Still harder went his manhood, and an agonized, "Oh," burst from him.

His fingers released her hair, then caressed her cheek. "Isabel."

Her eyes met his, and her tongue swirled around the thick head of his shaft.

Conflict shone in his eyes. "Not like this."

She pulled back, and the slick length of him slipped

from her mouth. She licked her lips, the taste of him lingering.

Dark yearning glittered in his eyes. "Rise."

She obeyed, the shifting sands of power intriguing her, increasing the stakes and her desire.

They each held all the power.

They each held none of it.

Both masters and slaves to this implacable lust.

"Turn around."

Again, she obeyed, her body trembling and liquid, her breath shaking through her, as back to him, she waited for—skin alive to it—his touch.

At last, his fingers found the ridge of her spine, making quick work of the fastening of her dress, the knot of her corsetry, pushing dress, corset, and chemise off her shoulders, every article of clothing above her thighs falling to a pool at her feet.

She pivoted to face him, gratification streaking through her as he took her in, the curves of her thighs, her waist, her breasts, upturned nipples hard as cherries, her sex beneath its dark mound of curls, hot and liquid and wanton.

"I want…"

If possible, his eyes went darker. "What do you want, Isabel?"

"I want your touch."

"Want it? Or do you *need* it?" He closed all distance between them. "Do you *crave* it? Do you *hunger* for it?"

The breath caught in her chest on a sharp inhalation. "Yes," she exhaled.

He reached out and grabbed her hips, pressing their bodies together, his shaft thick and hard against her belly. He slanted his head, and his mouth whispered against her ear. "Will you *die* without it?"

"I shall perish into dust," she returned, certain of its

truth. She liked the way he spoke her past words back to her. He wanted, needed, craved, hungered for *her*.

His mouth never left her, his breath sending goose bumps racing across her skin, as he kissed her from ear, across jaw, until, *oh*, at last, his lips found hers, their hard press imbued with the longing, desire, and ache of all they'd experienced together, of all they knew of each other, and of all they had yet to learn.

Her tongue tangled with his, and like the breaking of a dam, of a sudden, time went fast. Her hands found his shoulders, and his clutched her waist as he swiveled them around and fell onto the bed. His boots clattered to the floor. He grabbed both her wrists with one hand, stretching them above her head, and propped onto his elbow with the other, his body poised beside her, his cock hard, ready.

They drank each other in, the moment carnal, yet vulnerable, *exposed*.

Urgently, she wanted him, but slowly, too. She recognized the same feeling in his eyes. They had to take what they could of each other now, for this moment was fleeting. They would never have another like it. This was what their eyes told each other.

The moment could tip into the purely carnal—oh, how it wanted to—for so strong was the bond between them. But so, too, did another bond connect them, one of an emotion neither dared speak. It deepened, *heightened*, the carnality. It transformed the physical into the soulful.

Still, the physical...

Her body wanted more of it.

Her back arched, impatient, the motion thrusting her breasts up, taking the moment where she needed it. The intensity within his eyes cut through to some deep, dark part of her. He rolled onto her with quick efficiency, his face inches from hers, his manhood pressing against her quim.

His knee nudged her thigh. "Spread for me."

Her legs went wide, hips tilted, eager to take him in. With a long, slow thrust, he entered her. A breathless, "Oh," escaped her parted lips before his head bent and his lips took hers in a kiss that stole all the rest of her breath away. Deeper, he pushed inside her, taking her groan into his mouth.

His hand was tempered steel around her wrists, holding them fast above her head, as he thrust in and out of her, slowly, deliberately, exquisitely in control. Her hips gave a wild, impatient buck—why wouldn't the man just…just…give her *more*—and humor shone in his eyes.

"Do you trust me?"

"Yes," she said, without hesitation, with an absoluteness that she wouldn't think about now.

He must have seen it in her eyes, for serious intent replaced amusement. His face angled into her neck, his thrusts became more intentional, more focused, his control, exacting. His hips rearing back, her body opening wider to him. His hips thrusting forward, her head arcing as he filled her. His ridged stomach tensed, a trickle of sweat running down his neck, down his chest, his body fully concentrated on the task of delivering pleasure to hers, stroke by measured stroke.

How it taunted and teased, just out of reach. "Let me touch you," she begged. "I need to feel you."

He released her wrists, and her hands went not to his glorious body delivering relentless pleasure with every thrust, but to his face, cupping either side. In his eyes, she found not only lust, but also that emotion neither of them dared name.

"Use up all your wickedness on me," she whispered into the space between their mouths.

He increased the rhythm of his hips, and she met him stroke for stroke, as her body joined his in the headlong tumble toward release. As one, their bodies tensed and stilled for an exquisite beat of time that held them suspended outside its narrow confines. Out here, the two of them, stretched infinity. Release broke upon them and carried them to this place only they knew. The blaze of their skin, the rasp of their breath, the slam of their hearts, one.

Oh, that she could be one with him until time had no more use for either of them.

But time had no care for her wants. It beat on. And the heat of their bodies cooled. And the pounding of their hearts slowed. And he rolled off her, to the side so that still he touched her, but the solid weight of him was gone.

She ached for the loss, not for his body—although that was part of it, undeniably—but for *him*. Although, they still touched, he was lost to her.

"There will be a story," she heard herself say. "It will be published in the *London Diary*."

Percy touched two fingertips to her lips to stop her from saying more. "Whatever you must do today," he began, his voice low and gentle, his eyes fast on the side of her face.

She kept her gaze trained on the exposed ceiling rafters. "Yes?"

"Do not hesitate. It's in hesitation that plans go wrong."

Isabel understood in an instant. Percy was giving up his quest for revenge against Montfort so she could save her family.

Heartbreak was a physical hurt, she'd never understood that until now. The poets didn't exaggerate. People perished from this feeling.

"Family is everything," he continued. "Do what you must to protect yours."

No longer could she avoid his gaze. "And what of your family?"

"The Bretagnes shall survive it."

Even as he spoke the words, she detected uncertainty in his eyes. The Bretagnes would survive, yes, but their relationships might not, particularly the one with his daughter. It was too new, too fragile to withstand the burden of scandal that the headline, 'Savior or *SEDUCER* of St. Giles?' would unleash. Lucy would likely hate her father. That Percy would make such a sacrifice…

He was a worthy man.

Noble—not just by birthright, but by his actions.

The emotion Isabel had refused to name surged inside her. So, too, did the anger which had been encased in her shell of unfeeling. No longer could she contain it. None of them deserved this. Not her. Not Percy. Not their families.

Montfort deserved it, though.

How did he keep succeeding in destroying life after life? Where were his consequences? Why didn't he suffer them?

Do not let Montfort use me as a weapon to manipulate you into doing his bidding. Promise me, cariña.

That instant two truths tumbled down onto Isabel.

First, Montfort wouldn't keep his word.

Second, she couldn't destroy the innocent based on a false promise.

The path before her cleared, and she understood what she must do. And *how*. She had held the key since her conversation with Miss Fox yesterday. She simply hadn't realized it.

She scrambled off the bed and snatched her clothes off the floor before shooting to her feet.

Percy bolted upright, concern shining in his eyes. "What is it?"

"I..." Oh, how did she say this without sounding the fool? "I've arrived at a solution."

"You're going to betray Montfort," Percy stated. "You're not the first to make that choice."

By his tone, she intuited others hadn't been successful. "But I intend to be the last. He will not have this power over anyone else. *Never* again. You must trust me."

"It's not you I don't trust."

Isabel kept moving, pulling her chemise over her head, then her corset around her ribcage. She wouldn't waver from her course. She glanced over her shoulder. "Can you cinch my corset?"

Behind her, she heard Percy rustle to a stand. She felt his presence, his warmth and strength, before his touch. His fingers took up the corset strings, and an unsteady heartbeat loped past as she sensed hesitation. Anticipation flared. It was all she could do not to arch her lower back into his hand.

The next instant, he tugged the strings and had them knotted, business-like. She pulled on her dress and allowed him to fasten that, too.

Dressed and set to leave, at last, she faced him, one final time to drink him in. He'd donned his trousers, but his lean, muscular torso was bare and nearly stole her resolve. Couldn't they stay in this loft forever, the world beyond be damned?

He cocked his hip against the wall, and a tousled lock of hair flopped across his forehead. *Dios mío*, the man didn't know how *not* to be devastating.

"Know this," he began, the intensity of his gaze hadn't abated one bit. "You are not alone."

How seductive his words. How easily she could slip inside them. Resolve stiffened her spine. "In this, I am."

Only she could make matters right.

Without another word, Isabel crossed the room and stepped onto the loft ladder before she could think better of it. Before she could flee in the other direction, into Percy's arms, and let the world fall down around their heads, as long as they held each other.

But it couldn't be. Montfort wouldn't let it. The man must be dealt with.

Just before her head dipped below the floor, she remembered one final wifely duty. "Don't forget. The duchess expects you to make yourself available in the tent for the dance. I believe a good number of matrons expect to be swept around the dancing floor by the dashing Lord Percival Bretagne."

"Of course." His dark eyes held hers. "*Wife.*"

A sob choked in Isabel's chest as she broke from his gaze and continued her descent. She would never be a wife to him.

This idea, sparked by Papa's words, would guide her. It would either succeed or make matters worse. There was no in-between. But no longer could she pursue the path she'd started, or remain Montfort's pawn. It wasn't the way Papa would wish to obtain his freedom. He was an honorable man. It was time she acted like his daughter.

Still, worry nagged at her. It was possible she was about to make the worst mistake of her life.

No. She was a rose. It was time she used her thorns to protect those she loved. She was going to save a man worth saving. Even if he didn't understand his worth, she did.

What she was about to do was *right.* Montfort must be stopped. She wouldn't do the bidding of an evil man any longer. She wouldn't allow Montfort to destroy the man she loved.

And what of her family?

Her feet clicked across the herringbone brick stable floor. Their savings were stowed in her travel bag back in Rosebud Cottage. It wasn't much, but enough to start, again. She, Eva, and Ariel would find their way. Through thousands of years of persecution and flight, her people always did. It was their strength.

But her heart…

Would it find its way, too?

It was a question she would face another day.

Today—*now*—she had Miss Fox to find. Yesterday, she'd sensed doubt in the woman, doubt which had led her to reveal Montfort's plan to Isabel, who now had every intention of exploiting the woman's ambivalence and using it to her advantage.

Failure wasn't an option.

27

Beneath the tent, the shadows of candlelit globes dancing happily across its white ceiling and illuminating the assembled below, Percy offered a smiling bow to his third partner in as many country reels, escorted the matron to a group of women giggling like the young lasses they once were, and stepped off the dancing floor, no intention of partaking of the waltz. His role as future master of Gardencourt had its limits.

His face a mask of civility, he scanned the premises for Isabel. No sign of her. He'd made a mistake by letting her go. But he'd only been half dressed when she'd hurried away, and he hadn't seen her since. *Blast.*

He spotted Lucy, approaching. The false curve of his mouth transformed into a genuine smile before faltering with misgiving.

Earlier, he'd lied to Isabel. He wasn't at all certain he and Lucy's nascent relationship was durable enough to weather the scandal Montfort planned for publication in the *London Diary.*

Whatever last joyful moments Percy could get with his daughter, he would take. They might have to last a lifetime.

But what choice had he? His quest for revenge was

petty compared to Isabel's needs, those of life and death.

"Lucy," he began when she stopped beside him, "I must exact a promise from you."

Her eyes narrowed with wary curiosity. "Yes?" she asked on a slow syllable.

"You must pledge not to break more than five hearts tonight."

Her eyes rolled toward the tent ceiling. "Any young man foolish enough to get his heart broken by me after one dance isn't worth worrying over."

"Why is that?"

"Because, Father, any man for me would need to be made of tougher stuff."

Father. The word, the casualness with which it was spoken, knocked the breath from Percy. It was the first time she'd called him by that name. "You're not wrong, daughter."

She gave a careless shrug, her gaze occupied on a point at the opposite side of the dancing floor. "If you will excuse me, I must save Mina from an annoyingly persistent young man who won't stop trying to convince her to dance the waltz with him." Lucy had taken no more than two steps when she stopped abruptly. "Oh, there's Hugh." Her head canted subtly to the side as if she was seeing something she'd never noticed before. "The way Hugh is looking at Mina...Is he—?"

"Yes," Percy supplied. It had only been a matter of time before Hugh made himself obvious to all. Poor lovestruck lad.

Lucy snorted. "Well, that won't work."

"Why is that?"

"For starters, she is too good for him. And, second, he wouldn't be the sort of fellow to catch her interest."

"No?" Percy asked. He enjoyed his daughter's certainty. "Hugh is handsome, wealthy, and will be a duke someday." Based on those qualities, Hugh was exactly the sort of fellow that ninety-nine percent of the female population would snap up in an instant.

Lucy shot Percy an exasperated look. "If we could find a Doctor Frankenstein to reanimate Sir Isaac Newton, that would be Mina's type."

"Who? Sir Isaac Newton? Or Doctor Frankenstein?"

Lucy tapped a pensive finger to her chin. "In truth? Both, methinks. She does love a man of science."Lucy began to move away. "Now, I must save her from Hugh."

With that, his daughter was gone, and a country squire and his good lady stepped into her place. They quite carried the conversation without Percy's help. All he needed to do was nod and offer an aristocratic smile at the appropriate moment as he scanned the tent for…

At last, his patience paid off.

Isabel—on the periphery of the tent, speaking to Miss Fox.

Before he knew what he was doing, he was taking hurried leave of the squire and his lady and crossing the dancing floor, unheedful of the couples swirling around him. It was the shortest distance to Isabel, that was all. "The newly wed," he heard at his back on an indulgent laugh.

Before Percy could reach Isabel, or even snare her attention, she was on the move, threatening to disappear into the falling night.

Blast.

He'd been a fool to let her out of his sight these last few hours. Even if she had a plan—*especially* if she had a plan—he wasn't about to repeat the same mistake.

The raucous cacophony of the festivities fell behind him as he strode across the terrace. Squinting into the darkness, he caught only fleeting glimpses of Miss Fox's white muslin dress ahead as Isabel and Miss Fox entered the trail that led into a dense copse of oak trees. Dogged, Percy followed, his feet guided by instinct and the murmurous susurration of low, feminine voices. He stepped off the path and slowed his step, ears attuned, but the voices had quieted. Then a third voice sounded. *Montfort.*

Ahead, the trees thinned, and he spotted two figures in the clearing. Isabel and Montfort, facing each other like combatants. Where was Miss Fox—?

"Shh," he heard. Not fifteen feet to his left, she stood, palm extended, silently exhorting him to stop.

Percy gave his head a snappish shake, his feet continuing forward. He cared not for the exasperated glare she shot his way. He wasn't about to leave Isabel alone with Montfort. A snippet of their conversation carried on the light breeze.

"'Twas I who was to summon you." *Montfort.* "What is it you want?"

Noisily, Percy began crashing through the underbrush, giving Isabel and Montfort fair warning that a third was joining their party. Isabel's gaze rounded on him. "Percy, you shouldn't be here."

For his part, Montfort's mouth curved into the semblance of a smile, his cold eyes untouched and unsurprised. Percy saw in those eyes what he'd known all along.

This situation was about him and Montfort.

Any damage to Isabel would be collateral, in Montfort's distorted mind.

"Couldn't keep away from your new bride? And you, my dear"—Montfort turned to Isabel—"you had me worried. I thought you'd gone and fallen in love with your *husband.* But here you've done your duty and led the lamb to the slaughter." His spidery smile landed on Percy. "Well, lamb might be a stretch. More of a wolf, I suppose." He shrugged. "Women, perfidious creatures."

Percy stopped at Isabel's side. Nerves radiated off her in visceral waves as she retorted, "I don't think we women have the market cornered on perfidy."

Montfort took the verbal blow in stride. "Cheswick?"

Baron Cheswick emerged from the copse behind Montfort, looking not at all his usual hale and hearty self, but rather sheepish and contrite.

"What does he have to do with any of this?" Percy asked, the answer occurring to him before he'd finished the question. Rumor had it that Cheswick's gambling had procured him a small press. Percy would wager his last farthing a scandal sheet was one of its publications. The *London Diary*, in fact.

"Here is the thing, Bretagne," Montfort began. "Your activities as the Savior of St. Giles can no longer be tolerated. I know you're bored, my boy, but I cannot allow you to carry on. Whitehall could have found a use for you. But you've gotten in the way of business important to the Crown one too many times."

"I hardly think our government condones setting up peers in a blackmail scheme for votes."

Montfort waved Percy's words away like so many flies. "Our government hardly knows what's good for it. That's where men like you and I come in, whether you like to admit it or not. We have the stomach to do what is necessary to keep it running."

"You always did have a high opinion of your methods."

"Sometimes Members of Parliament need assistance in understanding the subtleties of government and their role in it. Call it a well-aimed nudge."

"And how do you propose to nudge *me*?"

"So impatient to reach the heart of the matter?" Montfort shook his head as if he was indulging a fractious child. "If you can't wait to read it in tomorrow's issue, I shall tell you. The *London Diary* is set to run an exposé on the Savior of St. Giles, who has been using his fame to seduce a young virgin. He has even entered into a false marriage with this vulnerable young woman so he could deflower, ravish, and debauch her. And here is the truly scandalous detail that will set tongues wagging for the next decade." He paused to savor his victory. "The Savior of St. Giles is none other than the younger son of the Duke of Arundel, one Lord Percival Bretagne. Every moving part is in place, including your pretend wife, Isabel, who through tears of abject shame and remorse will attest to these facts."

Isabel cleared her throat. "About me." A slight tremor wove through her words. "Am I just one more *moving part* to be placed?"

Montfort's head canted to the side. "Isn't that all our role in the larger scheme?"

Isabel gave a scornful laugh. "You see, Montfort, therein lies your problem. You regard people as nothing more than moveable objects." Fists clenched at her sides. "It leads you to underestimate them."

Montfort held out his hands placatingly. "I hardly think—"

"Miss Fox?" Isabel called over her shoulder. Her gaze remained steady on Montfort.

Admiration for this brave woman swelled inside Percy. Another emotion, too: *Love.*

He loved this brave, admirable, capable woman with his whole heart.

He didn't know precisely what she had planned for Montfort, but the man had better be ready.

Isabel was here to win.

ISABEL INHALED DEEPLY and attempted to quiet the anxiety panicking through her veins and slicking her palms with sweat. This was the moment.

"All this time," she began, "you've been presenting the situation as if there were only two options. Do your bidding and save my family, or fail and lose everything."

Miss Fox stepped forward. "Those are the exact two options Montfort presented my father and me five days ago in London."

"But in truth," Isabel continued, "there is a third option which only occurred to me today." Her eye met Miss Fox's. "Shall I tell him? Or would you like the honor?"

Miss Fox's mouth curled into a shrewd smile. "An exposé will run in tomorrow's *London Diary*, but not the one you think. This one will expose a blackmail for votes scheme, spearheaded by none other than the Earl of Surrey's younger brother, Lord Bertrand Montfort. How many of our most trusted politicians have been compromised? 'Tis a scandal that could rock our government to its very foundation."

Montfort's patronizing smile faltered, and his face turned an unattractive shade of aubergine. "This is thoroughly unpatriotic, traitorous even," he sputtered. He swung on Cheswick. "Has your viper of a daughter been made aware of your debts?"

Before her father could reply, Miss Fox spoke. "Payment of Cheswick's debt is in the process of being delivered to your solicitors at this very moment."

"What is this, Anne? There are no monies for—" Cheswick blanched. "Don't tell me you touched the dowry your mama left you."

"We can discuss it later." Miss Fox gave a shrug and a laugh. Both seemed forced. "You and I both know I shall never use it."

Isabel's gaze crept right to find Percy's fast upon her. What she saw there stole her breath away. *Admiration.* And something more, that unnamable emotion she'd shied away from time and again.

Possibly, the time had arrived to give it a name and a say.

She allowed the note of hope that had been clamoring to sing through her veins its head. Her plan...

It was succeeding.

Further, after this night was through, there might be hope for a future with this man.

Then she heard it—clear, mechanical, unmistakable —the cock of a pistol behind her. Isabel's blood ran cold as she—and everyone—swung toward the source. Unhurried, Eva entered the clearing, gun pointed straight at Montfort's heart. Cold-blooded calm shone in her eyes.

"And what of Montfort's debt? It is not paid that easily."

"Lower the gun, *querida,*" Isabel said, more frightened than she'd ever been in her life. Not for Montfort, but for Eva. "Violence will solve nothing."

Eva gave a shake of her head. "Oh, Isabel, you can be incredibly naïve. This is a unique instance where violence will solve *everything*. It will end a man who uses people as pawns. A man who doesn't care about the outcome for anyone but himself."

"You're wrong there," Montfort cut in. "It is all for England. And you, my dear, are nothing more than a deranged woman."

Eva laughed in a dry manner, which served to undercut Montfort's words. This was no deranged woman. This was a woman all too aware of her actions.

This was a woman who had planned for this very moment.

"Let's not confuse your actions with patriotism,"

Eva continued. "Power is your guiding principle. Not the public power of pomp and circumstance, but what lies behind the curtain. The true power. You see yourself as the puppet master, and we're all dangling from your strings, aren't we? How superior to us lesser creatures you must feel. You don't blink an eye at turning virgins into whores, children into bastards, good men into prisoners left to rot once they're no longer useful to you. What a legacy you'll leave behind, you wretched, evil man. You will never destroy another life for your own twisted ends, not while I draw breath."

"Eva, you cannot do this," Isabel cried out, wracking her brain for words, for any words, that would stop her sister. "Think of Ariel."

Eva's eyes flashed to meet Isabel's for an instant. Pain shone through the calm. "Ariel is exactly who I'm thinking of. Neither my son nor anyone else's son or daughter will find their life at the whim of this man."

Behind Eva appeared a figure, stalking forward, soft footsteps drowned out by the lively fiddle tune playing on the breeze. It was Hortense, still dressed in servant's garb.

"Think of your life," Isabel said, understanding that the longer she kept Eva talking, the longer she delayed Eva pulling the trigger.

"My life is a ruin. I'm nothing more than a used-up whore who thinks about the poppy most of her waking hours and dreams of it at night."

"But we have him. He won't risk shattering his reputation and good name." Isabel held out her hand. "It is settled, *querida*. Let us go home."

Oh, how she wanted to believe her own words.

Eva scoffed. "There you go again, Isabel, persisting in your naiveté. He will *never* stop bribing and blackmailing others to do his bidding. Only a well-earned death will stop Bertrand Montfort."

As Eva finished speaking, Isabel had the sickening feeling Hortense, who continued creeping up slowly behind Eva, would be too late. Then time condensed into a single second as, pistol shaking, Eva squeezed the trigger just as Hortense grabbed Eva's arm from behind, jerking the gun down. But not before a shot fired, leaving behind a ringing in Isabel's ear and the acrid dust of gunpowder in the air.

For an instant, Montfort appeared to have come through unscathed. Then *it* appeared on his lily white shirt: a small ring of scarlet, blooming wider with every beat of his heart. Shock twisting his features, his hands clutched his gut, and he crumpled, first to his knees, then to the ground as a low, animal groan poured from his parted mouth.

The next instant, time sped into a blur as everyone burst into motion and scattered. Cheswick grabbed Miss Fox and rushed into the woods. Hortense snatched the gun out of a shockingly docile Eva's hand before spiriting her away. Percy rushed to Montfort and bent over him, first pressing his ear to the injured man's mouth, then to his chest.

Isabel felt like the only still cog in a well-oiled piece of machinery. It was as if these events were happening in someone else's dream.

Percy was now pushing his hand onto Montfort's abdomen. "Isabel." He jerked his chin for her to come closer.

She willed her leaden feet to move. "Is he—?" She couldn't finish the question around the bile that had risen in her throat.

"He's alive," Percy finished for her.

She registered a wondrous calm within Percy's eyes. The man was made for this moment.

"You're in shock, Isabel," he continued. "So, I'll tell you what to do. And you must listen. Agreed?"

She nodded.

"You must leave. *Now.*"

Again, she nodded, but her feet refused to budge. "I'm so sorry."

"Montfort brought this on his own head. I'm surprised he made it this long without a shot to the gut. Listen to me. Hortense will have taken Eva to Rosebud Cottage. Follow them and collect your belongings. Then go to the stable and tell Stanhope you need the coach and four to transport you to London. *Now.*"

Still, Isabel's feet remained rooted to their patch of earth. "Percy, I—"

"*Go*, Isabel. Before it's too late."

She had yet so much to say to him. "But I—"

"*Now!*"

At last, his command broke through the fog clouding her brain. One foot, then the other, stumbled into motion, leading her through Gardencourt's expansive grounds, toward Rosebud Cottage. Over her shoulder, she stole one last glimpse of Percy, leaning over Montfort, trying to save the man. Trying to save them all.

For that was who Percy was. Those beneath his care were safe. Had she only trusted it sooner.

His words swirled through her mind. *Before it's too late.* But she knew: it was already too late. Their game of pretend was over.

The brief hope that was, evaporated into a hollow void.

28

LONDON

Buried on the third page of the *Times*, tucked below a story about the explorer Alexander Gordon Laing reaching Timbuktu, Isabel located the news item she'd been hunting in the broadsheets these last few months.

Stalwart friend of Crown and Country and younger brother of the Earl of Surrey, Lord Bertrand Montfort, was tragically injured in a shooting accident at a country estate. The grievous event has left him with a shard of shrapnel in his spine. Speculation holds he will never walk again. No further details are forthcoming.

Isabel allowed the newspaper to fall to the table with a papery slap.

A shooting *accident*.

She reread the words to confirm their existence. There they lay in black and white. A relief both calming and upsetting sang through her.

"It is being handled."

Those had been Hortense's exact words that night as they'd rattled toward London inside the Duke of

Arundel's coach and four, packed to the gills with five women and a baby.

Later, after they'd arrived at the shop and it was only the two of them, Hortense had elaborated. "It will be a hunting accident."

"During a country dance? At dusk?" It stretched credulity.

Hortense gave Isabel a hard stare. "Aristocrats do as they like, when they like."

Isabel had no argument for that particular truth.

Hortense then explained it was a preferred manner of explaining away this sort of situation. Isabel shuddered at how many *situations* Hortense and Percy had *handled* for Hortense to be so cavalier.

No matter. The woman's meaning had been clear: the law wouldn't be coming for Eva. It was an assurance Isabel had a difficult time trusting in the light of day, and all the days since.

Today, at last, she could let the matter recede into the distant nightmare from a night that might or might not have happened.

If only.

One person from that night—although she'd neither seen nor heard from him since—refused to leave her thoughts be.

Where was Percy? What was he doing this very moment?

Oh, to have her mind as her own again.

"Miss?" Isabel heard at her back. She pivoted to face Nell, who was smoothing several yards of gray wool across a large rectangular table, one of three taking up much of the room. "Yes?"

"Do I cut it like this?" Nell indicated the vertical length of the cloth. "Or like this?" She waved across horizontally.

Isabel folded the newspaper and tucked it into the

waistband of her apron. "Along the grain, here." She grabbed a pair of scissors. "Like this." She began to make the cut and quickly determined the scissors were dull and would fray the fabric. "I shall fetch a sharper pair."

As Isabel made her way to the back of the shop, her step felt a hair lighter. In truth, a part of her—her heart, namely—would never recover from the events of that strange week or the night that had ended it. That she hadn't succeeded in freeing Papa...

It was a pain that never wholly receded, sticking in her heart with its flat ache. But it hadn't truly been an option, she understood that now.

Bertrand Montfort never intended to keep his word.

But she, Eva, and Ariel were *safe*.

At least, for now.

She wasn't sure she would ever feel safe again or fully trust in the idea of security. She had lived how quickly a life could be turned on its head.

Life had certainly taught her one lesson. No outcome was perfect, and no happiness came without a cost. Life would exact its toll.

She was returning with the scissors when she encountered Eva, carrying three bolts of shantung silk, the finest fabric they owned. In fact, they hadn't yet served a client who could afford a garment constructed of it. They'd been laying these bolts by on the hope that someday they would.

"What is that in your apron?" Eva asked.

Isabel considered lying and telling her sister it was nothing of importance. But it was important, and Eva needed to know.

Wordlessly, Isabel held out the paper and pointed out the article. Eva's face transformed from cheery and open to tense and pinched as she scanned the words.

Once finished, she met Isabel's eye. "Then it's done."

"*Sí*," Isabel replied. She crumpled the paper and tossed it into the rubbish bin.

Eva's face softened in relief. "Good."

"Why do you have such fine fabrics out?" Isabel asked, ushering in a new subject.

The sparkle returned to Eva's eyes. "We shall need them today."

"Do we have clients arriving?"

The bell above the front door jingled, and Eva's face lit up. "That will be them."

"*Them?*" Isabel asked Eva's back.

Eva rushed the silk into the show room she'd dubbed the Serendipity Room before doubling back and streaking past Isabel to the front of the shop.

Isabel's gut churned. She'd come to dread the unexpected. At last, she heard the voices.

Familiar voices.

Her heart kicked up a notch.

Those voices came from a life she'd thought to forget. A life she *needed* to forget, because if she didn't forget that life, she wouldn't be able to forget *him*.

And, oh, how she needed to forget him.

But those voices, *here*, made it an impossibility.

Steps the consistency of molasses in winter, Isabel trudged into the front room to find Lucy, Miss Radclyffe, and a third woman conversing with Eva. If there were ever two birds of a feather for liveliness, it was Lucy and Eva.

Eva caught Isabel's eye and waved her over. "Isabel, come and greet my muses." Mischief shimmered about her. "And their mother, Lady St. Alban."

All sets of eyes landed on Isabel. *Lady St. Alban?* Lucy's mother. The woman who had been Percy's wife, his *real* wife. Isabel went a trifle nauseous.

"If it isn't my step-mama." Lucy rushed over and

gave Isabel a sweet buss on the cheek. "Do you know the date of my father's return? For some reason I had it in my head that it was this week."

Isabel almost answered that she hadn't the faintest idea. Instead, she gave her head a tight shake.

Where had Percy gone? Back to his old life as a spy? And why would Lucy be asking *her*, of all people?

Minutes ago, life had, at last, gone right-side up. Now it was topsy-turvy again.

Lady St. Alban crossed the short distance separating them and took Isabel's hand. "Lady Percival, I've heard so much about you. Although, I fear you look a trifle peaked. Is it possible you're suffering from one of your famous megrims? Should we send for the duchess's special cure?"

"*No*," burst from Isabel's mouth, graceless and abrupt.

A playful smile crinkled the corners of Lady St. Alban's eyes. "If you change your mind, I'm certain the duchess would happily spare a dram for you." Lady St. Alban glanced around the shop, her observant gaze taking in the implements of the dressmaking trade: spools of thread, bolts of fabric, a dress in the final stages of construction. "When Percy returned Lucy and Mina to London, he mentioned that you were quite devoted to your shop and unwilling to leave it while he was away. I find that admirable in a woman."

"What is that?" Isabel barely had the presence of mind to ask. Percy had been discussing her?

"A desire to have a life outside a man."

Isabel blinked. Besides the natural reserve Isabel observed in the other woman's eyes, she detected something more. *Knowledge*. What precisely had Percy told this woman?

Isabel's stomach did its usual flip-flop at the thought of him.

Lady St. Alban's eyes fixed on a point over Isabel's shoulder and lit up. "Oh, how lovely."

Isabel didn't need to turn to take Lady St. Alban's meaning.

The roses.

The shop was up to its ears in roses.

Isabel couldn't think about the roses at present. This day was proving too much.

"Lady St. Alban," Eva said, "it would be such a pleasure to make a dress for you." Her gaze turned appraising. "And perhaps a pose for our advertisement?"

"Advertisement?" Isabel asked, relieved to be pulled from other thoughts. This was the first she was hearing of an advertisement. Eva could be bold. It was a fact.

Lady St. Alban gave a breathy laugh. "You flatter me, Mrs. Gardiner, but I shall leave it to the girls. And I have your assurance their names will not be used?"

"*Absolutamente.* Now let me show you the fabrics and mock-up sketches I've done."

As the group of four made their way to the Serendipity Room, Miss Radclyffe gave Isabel a nod and a smile. "Lady Percival, how very nice to see you."

Isabel responded in kind. Ahead, she heard Lady St. Alban ask, "Do you mind if I pull out my sketchbook as well?"

"Is art an interest of yours, my lady?"

"A bit," Lady St. Alban replied.

Again, Isabel was alone, her nerves ajangle with a swirl of emotion. What a morning. She looked down and realized she still held a pair of sharp scissors. *Right.*

She'd taken no more than two steps, when Tilly's voice rang out, "Milady!"

Isabel exhaled a tiny huff of irritation before turning to face the girl. How many times had she told Tilly that she wasn't a lady and not to call her one?

Countless. To no effect.

Tilly held up a dress of ivory muslin. It was one of Isabel's best. "Will this suffice for dinner tonight?"

Isabel inhaled a groan. "Yes, thank you."

The girl gave Isabel a satisfied smile. "And yer rose? Has it arrived today?"

"No."

Oh, the roses.

They couldn't be avoided.

A perfect, different-colored rose had arrived by messenger boy every day since...

Well, since the day after *that* night.

No note.

No sign of who sent it.

In her heart, Isabel knew *who*.

What she didn't know was *why*? To what end?

"It's late," Tilly persisted.

"Or it isn't coming at all," Isabel replied with forced indifference.

"Nah, that ain't it," Tilly said, dismissive. "No man sends a woman a perfect rose every day for fifty-eight days runnin' and stops all sudden like."

"A man might."

Tilly's eyes narrowed on Isabel. "Ye truly don't know nuthin' about men, do ye?"

Isabel wanted to take umbrage, but she couldn't. "I, um, no, not especially."

She knew something—a few somethings—about one man. Or thought she did. Really, she knew nothing.

"Well, I best get to pressin' this dress." With that, Tilly skipped up the stairs, a reedy whistle trailing in her wake.

While Nell had decided to apprentice as a dressmaker, a skill Isabel and Eva could quite proficiently teach her, Tilly had got it into her head that she wanted to be a lady's maid. As Isabel saw it, this presented a pair of problems. One, Isabel didn't need a lady's maid.

Two, she couldn't afford one. She'd offered to inquire about placement or training for the girl, but—and herein lay a third problem—Tilly had no inclination to leave Isabel. In fact, the girl was decidedly set against it.

And the truth was, Isabel had grown fond of her. So, she dressed two, sometimes three, times a day and submitted to Tilly's morning and evening ministrations. She wouldn't let the girl go for anything.

What a rag-tag family they'd formed.

Isabel returned to Nell and began explaining the hows and whys of cutting fabric. Some cloths were destined to become beautiful creations, others, like the medium-grade wool beneath their hands, were of the useful, durable variety. This sort of dress was the bread and butter of their shop.

Eva, however, had other ambitions for the shop, ones that involved the aristocracy. Her sister craved the freedom of the beautiful rather than the workaday.

This activity usually settled Isabel's mind with the rhythm of routine. Today, her mind wandered.

She'd just met the aristocratic lady who had scandalized all London Society by having her marriage set aside by Parliament. Lady St. Alban wasn't anything like Isabel had expected, which was an adult version of Lucy. Instead, the woman was measured and steady, more similar to her step-daughter Mina in temperament. Isabel thought Lady St. Alban the sort of woman she could like.

Again, the bell above the front door jingled. Isabel left Nell with a few parting instructions and rounded the corner to assist whomever had entered the shop. A figure stood just inside the shadow of the door. A man. He was likely lost. They didn't serve male clientele. "Are you in need of a direction?" she called out.

"I believe I have found my way," the man said in Spanish.

Isabel stopped in her tracks and blinked. Her heart became a racehorse in her chest. *Could it be?* She blinked again. *It couldn't.* How could it possibly? "Papa?" she whispered, tears springing to her eyes.

Papa threw his arms wide. "*Cariña, venaquí.*"

With a small cry, Isabel rushed to her father, as if he were an apparition that would vanish the next instant. As he took her in an embrace that perhaps wasn't as strong as the last time they'd held each other, Isabel inhaled. It was truly him. Ghosts carried no scent.

She angled back and took him in, searching for the familiar beneath the tributaries that creased his skin in all directions on his newly gaunt face. A sob equal parts joy, relief, and, yes, grief, escaped her. "How are you *here*, Papa? In London?"

"May I sit while I tell the tale?" he asked, his voice rasped and winded. "My strength isn't what it once was."

"*Sí*, Papa, this way." She hooked her arm through his as much to be closer to him as to provide support. She led him to the cutting room. There, she settled him into the chair with the most cushions. Nell met them with wide, silent eyes. "Will you fetch my father a pot of tea?"

Nell nodded once and flew down the corridor.

Papa glanced around, his keen eye sharp as ever. "You've arranged your shop very sensibly."

Isabel perched on the edge of the chair opposite him and leaned forward, taking his hands in hers. They were dry and warm and *home*. She inhaled another sob. "How are you here, Papa?"

He shook his head, as if in disbelief himself. "By a miracle."

"Papa, please tell me."

He released a heavy sigh and nodded. "It was night, after the prison had gone quiet and settled into sleep.

My cell gate swung open and in slipped a wisp of a woman. She beckoned me to follow her."

A possibility occurred to Isabel. "A woman? English?"

"French, possibly. She wasn't one for talk."

Isabel knew—she *knew*—the woman's identity. *Hortense.*

"She led me through a maze of tunnels until we reached a small gate. Two horses were waiting. We headed north to Bilbao."

"That's a long journey."

"Traveling mostly by night, it took us several days to reach the port. She deposited me on the dock and wished me safe travels. A man took charge from there."

The breath hitched in Isabel's chest. "A man? What sort of man?"

"An Englishman."

"Tall and lean? Dark hair that flops around?"

A humorous light entered Papa's eyes. "*Sí.*"

"Wolfish?" She wouldn't say *devastating.*

"The man mentioned you."

Isabel's heart sprang into a full gallop. "Oh?"

"He knew you."

"Did he bring you here?"

"*Sí.*" Papa reached into his breast pocket. His hand emerged holding a...*rose.* "This is for you."

"How did you..." Isabel wasn't able to complete a thought, much less a sentence. This rose had quite stolen the ability away. "Who...?"

"It is my understanding you know *who.*"

"Oh, *erm,*" she began, taking the pale pink rose with fingers that had gone trembly. She had risen to a stand without realizing it. "Nell!" she called.

The next instant, the girl clanked around the corner, bearing tea service. "Miss, I was just—"

"No matter," Isabel said, impatient. "Please take my

father to Eva. I must..." The sentence remained unfinished, her feet already on the run.

Through the front door, she flew, her blood singing through her veins with the certainty that *he* was waiting on the other side. But...

No *him*.

Not that there was a shortage of men as she scanned the lane. Men bustling about their business, coming and going, some tall and dark, even handsome, but none of them, *him*.

Isabel slumped her shoulder against a conveyance that could only be Lady St. Alban's carriage, viscountly crest emblazoned on the side, and her heart sank. Percy had journeyed all the way to Spain to free her father and hurry him to London only to leave without saying good-bye?

Tilly was correct.

She truly knew naught all about men.

A dark head bobbed above the back of the team of four's lead horse for an instant before ducking back down. Isabel's heart lurched. If only she could see the man's face...

"Percy?" she squeaked.

A face popped up.

Isabel blinked.

Before she gave her heart leave to soar in her chest, she needed to be certain her mind wasn't playing tricks on her.

She blinked again.

It was him, unshaven and unkempt as if he'd taken not a lick of rest in all the weeks since she'd last seen him. But *him*, devastating as ever.

It was all the permission her heart needed to take wing.

"What...what are you doing?"

"Checking this horse's hoof. He was holding it aloft."

"*Oh.*" A horrible possibility occurred to her. "Were you about to leave without…without…"

His head cocked. "Calling on you?"

His gaze burned into her, and all she could do was nod.

"I wasn't going anywhere, Isabel."

She believed him.

"I thought to give you and your father a chance to reunite in private."

He stepped around the team and onto the sidewalk, stopping before her not a yard away. An invisible string stretched between them that begged to be tugged.

Isabel grew a bit shy of him, the enormity of what he'd accomplished settling into her. "*How* did you free him?" she asked. "I was so certain Montfort was the only way."

Percy shrugged. The man *shrugged.* "He isn't the only man with connections."

In that instant, the meaning of Isabel's life came into focus. Her life could tick along with her moving through it for any number of days, weeks, months, or years, but it would lack all meaning without this man.

So, she needed to ask another question, one whose answer held her future happiness in its hand.

She held up the rose. "Why did you send them?"

29

P ercy hesitated.

Not because he didn't know the answer to Isabel's question, rather because he didn't want to scare her away with it.

Yet he couldn't *not* speak it.

"To remind you every day who you are. That you are not alone," he said. "That you are *safe*."

"Oh."

"And to thank you."

Her eyebrows knitted together, confounded. "Thank me? For what?"

"For acting selflessly that night. For standing up to Montfort and refusing to do his bidding at great potential cost to you and your family. For not subjecting Lucy to another round of scandal. You are the heroine of this story."

"I only did what was right. I should have done it sooner." She indicated the carriage beside them. "I suppose you know its owner?"

Percy nodded. "Lady St. Alban is inside your shop with the girls?"

"Eva has found her dream muses." A hesitant beat passed. "She's rather nice."

Percy didn't need to ask which *she*. "She is."

"I can see why you would have fallen for her."

Even as Percy grew impatient with this line of conversation, he knew he must offer an explanation. "We were young." It was only the truth, and hopefully it would be enough, for he didn't want to talk about that woman. He had other words to say to *this* woman. "About our marriage."

"I don't particularly care to hear the details of your marriage to her," Isabel said quickly.

"Not of my marriage to *her*. My marriage to *you*."

"If you will recall, there was no marriage to *me*."

Percy jerked his thumb toward the shop. "That's not what that lot in there believe."

"And why is that? I had a rather strange conversation with your daughter."

"What with managing Montfort and his official story, then hieing off to Spain, I never found the time."

It was *a* reason, but not the truest one. Why was he avoiding what he'd come here to say and...*ask?*

Because she had every reason to reject him, that was why.

"Thank you."

"What are *you* thanking *me* for?" Percy asked, exasperated. A feeling of indebtedness wasn't how he wanted to approach what he'd come here to say.

"For protecting Eva."

"The bullet that finally found Montfort had been on its trajectory for decades. Your sister only pulled the trigger."

"Will he—?" Isabel began and stopped, unable to ask the terrible question aloud.

"Report it to a magistrate?" he finished for her.

She nodded.

Percy shook his head. "He doesn't want his good name blackened by the revelations that would follow."

"What an ugly situation."

She was correct, but Percy didn't want to talk about ugly situations, but, rather, potentially beautiful ones. He tried again. "About *our* marriage."

"I won't hold you to it, of course. It wasn't real." An uncertain beat of time passed. "None of it was."

"None of it?" he asked. "Some of it felt very, very real."

Subtle pink brightened Isabel's cheeks. "You take my meaning, Percy."

"What if—" He held her gaze steady. "What if I enjoyed being falsely married to you?"

"*Enjoyed* it?"

Her breath hitched in her chest on a swift intake, and his heart raced like a green youth's. "What if—?" he began again.

"Yes?"

"What if I want you to hold me to it?" He reached out and tucked an errant wisp of hair behind her ear. No longer could he not touch her. "What if I would like to stop pretending and make it the truth?"

"Impossible," she uttered on a whisper.

Impossible was such a definite word, but the way she spoke it left an opening. He intended to slip inside it. "What impossibilities stand in our way? In case you don't remember, I'm the son of a duke, there isn't much in this world that isn't possible for me."

Gone was her breathlessness. In its stead had settled her familiar quiet resolve. "I won't marry you simply because you don't want to admit to your family that we aren't truly wed."

"The thought never crossed my mind."

"We knew each other for such a short time. Was it long enough to know if it isn't only desire? If it is truly—"

"*Love?*" he finished for her.

A sudden spark of fear flared through him. Was it possible he'd come all this way only to lose her?

It wouldn't happen. He wouldn't allow it.

She would believe in their love.

"Here is what I know about Isabel Galante. You have nerve, tenacity, and intelligence. When you enter a competition, you play to win. Family is first, even other people's family, and you will defend it until your last breath." He stepped closer. "I love your unflinching green eyes. I love your lush, red lips, particularly when they wrap around my—"

Her eyes went round with shock. "Lord Percival!"

Her chastisement only emboldened him. "And your face, Isabel, it's the loveliest I've ever beheld. The way it transforms when you cry out in rapture."

"You really shouldn't speak such words on the street."

"I don't simply love these things about you. I love that they combine to form *you*, my addiction."

"Your *addiction*," she repeated. He could see the word didn't sit well with her.

"Before you, I thought an addiction was all wickedness, and I did everything in my power to stifle it. But you helped me see it is how I use my nature that matters. Let me love you. Let me keep you *safe*, for the rest of our lives. Since you entered my life, I'm a better man. But if you feel what was between us was purely physical and no love can exist, then I shall walk away from you, a better man."

She closed the distance until they were separated by only a thin sliver of air, its molecules pulsing with the energy specific to them. "I would die."

There it was, conjured up by three small words. All their desire. All their love. The two mixed together, inextricable.

"Lord Percival Bretagne, I shall love you to my dying breath."

The earth could have stopped spinning on its axis for all Percy knew, for all he cared, for all he saw in her direct green gaze. Nothing else mattered.

Percy reached one hand around to the small of her back and the other to the downy nape of her neck. He angled his face, and his lips met hers in a tentative touch, a light press of his skin upon hers, her sweet scent of sunshine and honeysuckle wrapping him in her warmth. It was a moment he could live inside for all eternity.

Then her arms wrapped around his neck, and her kiss demanded more. A kiss that ravished and devoured and elicited a few randy whistles from the odd passerby.

Percy didn't give a fig. Isabel was his.

He wanted everyone to know.

Reluctantly, he broke the kiss, both of them breathless. "Now, go and pack a bag. Five minutes before I follow."

A shocked, breathless laugh escaped her. "You wish to elope?"

"I've always thought the phrase, *married by anvil priest*, held a certain panache."

Her smile faltered. "What about my family?"

"On the journey over, your father and I had time to talk about pasts and futures."

That nervy light entered her eye, the one he loved. "You asked him for my hand. Presumptuous."

"I wasn't taking any chances."

Her head canted to the side, flirtatious. "Is this the Lord Percival Bretagne I've heard so many whispers about?"

He tucked another errant tendril of hair behind her ear. Really, she had the most perfect ears. "What Lord

Percival Bretagne?" he asked, distracted, yes, by her perfect ears.

"The wild one."

Now, he was distracted by the low, sultry note in her voice. "I could tell you," he began, desire threading through his words, "but wouldn't you rather see for yourself?"

"Very much." She wove her arm through his. "I don't need a bag. I only need you."

Oh, this woman had daring to spare. He couldn't wait to spend the rest of his life with her.

"Us against the world?"

"The world doesn't stand a chance."

"I love you, Isabel Galante."

"I love you, Lord Percival Bretagne."

He took her hand in his, and they walked into their future.

She was his addiction.

She was his cure.

She was *his*.

And he was hers.

EPILOGUE

LONDON, 24 MARCH 1827

The quartet struck bows across strings into the opening notes of a Diabelli composition, and electricity lit the air alive.

A scandalous waltz was on its way.

And not just any waltz, but the first official waltz of the newly wed couple these elevated members of the *ton* were gathered to celebrate beneath the sparkling chandeliers of the Duke of Arundel's resplendent ballroom in the first ball of the Season.

As Lord Percival Bretagne led Lady Percival to the center of the floor, a rapt silence descended. They were the sort of couple who evoked such a response. He, tall and lean and possessed of the specific dark eyes and curly locks that set female hearts aflutter no matter their age, for which the world had Lord Byron—God rest his soul—to thank.

And she, well, she was the sort one wanted to hate on sight with her lovely face and assured green gaze and skin that only glowed to greater advantage the longer it soaked in the sun, unlike her English counterparts whose skin only grew pink.

Yes, it was agreed by all they were an enviable

345

couple who quite belonged to one another. That Fate could have it any other way was inconceivable.

The dual forces of momentum and effervescence carried them along as their feet found the buoyant rhythm of *one-two-three...one-two-three...*

She smiled up into his eyes, and he down into hers. "*Husband,*" crossed her lips.

"*Wife,*" responded his.

They weren't a couple given much to words. It had been remarked upon.

The hot glances they laid upon one another...

Well, those had been remarked upon, too.

"Oh, dearest dear," murmured Lady Bertrand Montfort, who had been forced to attend the ball without her husband, who had been tragically injured some months past and therefore unable to accompany his wife.

The Duchess of Arundel paid no mind, by now accustomed to her friend's prim exclamations. Even so, she couldn't help but silently agree. It might be indecent the way Percy was holding Isabel, hand pressed into the lowest point at the small of her back, the full length of his body tight against hers as they moved in perfect unison. They appeared to be but one *one-two-three* away from taking each other, here, in the center of the dancing floor.

Oh, dearest dear, indeed.

Young ladies were present.

She nearly said as much to the duke at her side, but the expression on his face was so happy and contented as he tapped out the rhythm with his feet that she let the matter pass, unremarked.

Besides, those young ladies, the Misses Bretagne and Radclyffe, hadn't noticed. They had long since grown accustomed to notorious displays of affection from the adults in their lives. Miss Bretagne was simply counting the number of beats until she could finagle her cousin Hugh, the young Earl of Avendon, into taking her for a spin atop mahogany. Miss Radclyffe was counting the number of beats before she could slip away and avoid that exact same occurrence.

Across the ballroom floor buffed to high mirror shine stood the family of the bride. Don Ariel Galante, the bride's father, struck a rather dashing and elegant form for a man of advancing years, and his Spanish accent could send a susceptible lady into a swoon, if one wasn't properly prepared. The look of love in his gaze as he watched his daughter swirl around the dancing floor in the arms of her beloved, well, it rendered him all the more attractive. The duchess had half a mind to set her dear spinster friend, Miss Dunfrey, upon him.

As for the bride's sister, Mrs. Eva Gardiner, she kept one eye upon the happy couple—one might even detect a wistful sheen in that eye—and the other upon shy Nell, who sat unobtrusively against a back wall and thought she would die if anyone addressed her, and saucy Tilly, who cast her roving gaze across the proceedings and drank deeply from her champagne glass. Champagne was the sole luxury she missed from her past life at Number 9.

It was an unusual arrangement—hosting servants as guests at a duke's ball—but the bride had requested their presence and one didn't nay-say a bride. Mrs. Gardiner felt glad of it. Becoming part of the English aristocracy hadn't, and wouldn't, change Isabel. Though life would lead them in different directions, they would ever be sisters.

Only a few measures of the waltz remained, and the bride and groom had been left to their own devices far too long. Lord Percival gazed upon his wife with an affection that most of the assembled silently agreed was too private, too *intimate*, to observe directly.

Most, that was, save one: his bride, whose ardor mirrored her groom's. The hand that had rested chastely upon his shoulder stole up to caress the nape of his neck. An aghast *ton*—well, an aghast Lady Bertrand—watched on, equal parts shocked and transfixed by the heat that sparked off them. They were combustible. Lady Percival chafed that her hand was gloved, and therefore unable to touch her skin directly to his.

Later.

In truth, she'd already had so much of this man—*so very much*—yet she was always left wanting more. The newly wed, a guest might mutter with an indulgent shake of the head, but Isabel knew in her heart that her wanting was different. It would forever hunger…

For *him*.

The music crescendoed into an exhilarating finish, but not the buzzing in Isabel's body, soul, and heart. The man in her arms gazing upon her with the world in his eyes would continue to devastate her all the days of her life, she knew it. Every set of eyes gazing upon them in hushed silence shone with the same knowledge.

Isabel rose to the tips of her toes and pressed her lips to the cup of his ear. "Why is everyone so quiet?"

A knowing smile curled at one corner of Percy's mouth, and a dark, sinuous shiver glittered through Isabel. "They are waiting," he murmured, low and velvet.

"*Waiting?* For what?"

"For *this*."

He angled his face and drew her into a kiss that might have started chaste but deepened into a ravishment quite suddenly and unexpectedly. A few shocked titters may have raced through the crowd, but so, too, did a few hearty claps and a girlish groan of shame that very possibly emerged from Miss Bretagne.

For her part, Isabel paid them no mind.

Here, in her arms, was love and safety and…

Forever.

The End

ALSO BY SOFIE DARLING

All's Fair in Love and Racing
Odds on the Rake
The Duchess Gamble
Wager With a Siren

Shadows and Silk
Three Lessons in Seduction
Tempted by the Viscount
Her Midnight Sin
To Win a Wicked Lord
At the Pleasure of the Marquess
One Night His Lady
Nell and the Runaway Duke

ABOUT THE AUTHOR

Bestselling and award-winning author Sofie Darling's passion for historical romance began in middle school the moment she cracked open *Wuthering Heights* by Emily Bronte. An instant and enduring love affair was born.

Sofie spent much of her twenties raising two boys and reading every romance she could get her hands on. Once she realized she simply must write the books she loved, she finished her English degree and set pencil to paper. (Ticonderoga #2 is her quill of choice.)

When she's not writing heroes who make her swoon, Sofie enjoys a nice weekend hike, a visit to a crumbling medieval castle whenever she gets the chance, and a slightly codependent relationship with her beagle, Bosco. Visit her website.